Author Serena Chase refers to the Eyes of E'veria books as "a series within a series."

Why? Because each two-book set within the greater Eyes of E'veria series features different lead characters and a freshly re-imagined fairy tale. The first two books, *The Ryn,* and its sequel, *The Remedy,* feature lead characters Rynnaia E'veri and Julien de Gladiel in an epic reinvention of the classic Grimm fairy tale, *Snow White & Rose Red.* Books three (*The Seahorse Legacy*) and four (*The Sunken Realm,* coming in 2015) treat another Grimm tale, *The Twelve Dancing Princesses,* with an equally fresh and epic scope and feature lead characters who both served minor roles in the first two Eyes of E'veria novels.

Welcome back to E'veria

D1446688

To The Waverly Public Library

THE REMEDY

EYES OF E'VERIA

BOOK TWO

Find yourself in the fairy tale!

Serena Chase

SERENA CHASE

THE REMEDY
Eyes of E'veria Book Two
Serena Chase

The Remedy (Eyes of E'veria, book two) The heir to the throne of E'veria must fulfill a two-hundred-year-old prophecy to save her Kingdom from being overtaken by an ancient evil.

This is a work of fiction. Names, characters, places, and incidents are the product of the author's imagination. Any resemblance to actual people or entities, living or dead, or to businesses, locales, or events is entirely coincidental. That being said, if a reader should happen to discover a secret passage to E'veria or meet a Veetrish Storyteller out there in the wide world, please let us know . . . because that would be awesome.

Image credits as follows:
(character photo) copyright 2012 Lincoln Noah Baxter / (edited iris copyright 2013 Jodie Gerling)
Abstract flames Image 63166120 Copyright Fenton, 2013 Used under license from Shutterstock.com

Cover design by JG Designs www.jodiegerlingdesigns.com, Manhattan, KS

ISBN: 1499704453
ISBN 13: 9781499704457
Library of Congress Control Number: 2014910130
CreateSpace Independent Publishing Platform
North Charleston, South Carolina

DEDICATION

For Dave, Delaney & Ellerie
...the brightest stars in my universe

& Rachel Rigdon
... because your enthusiasm for these stories nearly
matches my own.

PART I:
THE SCROLLS

ONE

By the time the Cobeld retrieved his brother's body from the Great Wood of Mynissbyr, there was little left but bones, hair, and the dagger that had done the job. Too frightened to linger in the wood, he shoved the small, rotting corpse into his pack and ran the first leg of the long journey home.

As soon as he arrived at the ancient camp in the northern foothills of Mount Shireya, he surrendered the remains and made his way up the slope to the well. After he had refilled his flask, he found a spot to await the Seers' verdict.

Even now, the Seers circled the dead Cobeld's bones, attempting to divine whether or not the fabled Bear-men of Mynissbyr had risen from their two-century hibernation to once again haunt the Great Wood, seeking Cobelds to kill.

A flash of cold light came from within the beard of the Cobeld to his left, signaling that another curse had completed its work. He turned a question toward the Cobeld, one of nearly three hundred who had gathered tonight.

"Killed him." The old fellow's lips parted, showing yellow teeth worn down nearly as short as his own. "Hit by an arrow."

"A good idea, that," he said.

"It was, indeed." The satisfied fellow cackled, but then scowled. "Although spending my evenings wrapping Dwonsil arrows with curses from my beard is nearly as tiresome as the company of the warriors themselves. Fools, every last one of them."

Since the clansmen of Dwons had allied with the Cobelds against E'veria, the range of the Cobelds' curses had increased exponentially.

"Fools, yes," he replied. "But useful fools. If progress continues at this rate, the Kingdom of E'veria will be ours within two years. Perhaps less."

The other Cobeld nodded and turned his face back toward the bones. The fellow spoke without turning his gaze, "You brought the bones back from the Great Wood, yes?"

He nodded.

"Any trace of the Bear-men?"

"Not that I saw, but . . . ?" He shrugged and let the thought hang.

Between the strands of his long, gray beard, the fellow's lips pursed. He lifted his chin toward the bones. "What do you think killed our brother?"

"A dagger," he said with a shrug of his narrow shoulders. "There were no fang marks. No sword, either. I doubt it was a Bear-man."

His statement was most likely true, but his flesh crawled with dread at the thought of the fabled beasts he had somehow evaded during this recent trip. Like the ancient Cobeld beside him, like all his "brothers" gathered here, he remembered the battle in which the Bear-men of Mynissbyr had come at them roaring, swords aloft, as the prophecy had fore-told they would. Two centuries had passed since that day, but he would not forget the terror of seeing the beasts pour out of the Great Wood, led by, of all things, a black-haired girl.

Along with the rest of the Cobelds that survived the day, he had fled the Mynissbyr border and had stayed with his fellows in the shadow of the cursed mountain, Shireya.

Only in recent years, since one of their brethren had succeeded in killing the prophesied Ryn, had they ventured forth, finally exacting payment for their humiliation. But it was to this place they were forced to return all too often.

"Have you visited the well since you returned?"

"I did." He nodded. "As soon as I turned the remains over to the Seers. Good thing, too. My flask was near emptied."

In ancient times, the underground spring that now fed their well—and their power—had flowed into a tiny pool at the base of the mountain. That pool was once known as a place of healing. Of miracles. In those days, they had been ordinary men—no, *extraordinary* men—who had sworn fealty to Sir Cobeld of Shireya and had called themselves by his name. The name of the one who *should* have been King. Cobeld understood power and how to wield it. It was he who had drained the pool by rerouting its feeding stream to his own property. It was he who discovered how to use Shireya's water to curse their enemies after—

After The Great Battle was lost.

They had been created here, due to that defeat, and turned from mighty warriors into small, wrinkled old men who, though not impossible to kill—as evidenced by the bones the Seers now examined—never grew quite old enough to die. But without a woman among them they did not reproduce. In the centuries since that ancient battle, their number had only decreased.

Ah, but not so their infamy. He consoled himself with that thought. Though they were few—less than six hundred Cobelds remained—all E'veria feared them.

The five Seers hummed a series of unintelligible words and then turned as one. The entire camp of gray-bearded Cobelds grew instantly silent.

"We have seen!"

With their old eyes closed, the Seers began to sway. Left. Right. Left. Finally they spoke, again as one. *"With eyes the hue of jeweled sky and head ablaze with fire,"* they chanted, *"the Ryn Lady E'veria will Cobeld's curse exile."*

His eyes narrowed. What bearing could that old prophecy have on them now? E'veria's current King had neither Queen nor heir. There was no Ryn.

The Seers swayed again. Right. Left. Right. Suddenly, their eyes popped open. "The Ryn Naia lives!"

No, he thought, shaking his head. *It's not possible.*

The baby was killed within her mother, nineteen years ago. The Queen had ingested Cobeld-tainted tea and consumed a deadly curse. She died before the child exited her womb. How could it be that the baby—the Ryn—had survived?

"We have been deceived!" the Seers cried. "The bones confirm it! She lives!"

His gaze fell again to the skeletal remains at the Seers' feet. He did not understand how the Seers' incantations over the bones produced information, but they had rarely been wrong. Whoever that rotted mass had been, he must have come in contact with the royal child for her to leave such a clear mark of life—and the possibility of their kind's death—upon him.

All these years, they had thought her dead. But if the prophesied Ryn, the red-haired, blue-eyed, female heir to the throne lived . . .

The prophecy thrummed its threat against his skull. Death's maw seemed to open within his mind, ready to suck him into darkness.

It was said she would find the hidden Remedy that would heal the damage his kind had wrought. That she would make the water from their well, and thus, their beards . . . useless. Curseless.

No!

Without the power of those curses he was nothing but a shriveled old man. Perhaps less than even that. Yes, he might seem to be little more than a corpse courier now, but he had once been a warrior! He had commanded a legion of warriors! And now he and his kind would be defeated by a flame-haired girl?

The indignity of his brother's failure to kill the Ryn Naia at birth, and the possible future it could bring down on them all, rose within him. His scream ripped open the silence that had fallen and was immediately echoed by the primal cry of every Cobeld present.

"Find her!" the Seers shrieked. "Kill her!"

Two

The small boat didn't even wobble as I turned and lifted my hand to wave to the Andoven people gathered on shore. A part of me hated to leave this isle and my new friends, but if I stayed I would fail not only them, but my Kingdom.

My throat tightened and I waved with a little more vigor. I had spent only a few weeks sequestered among them, but in that short time many friendships had been forged.

"*Tura hathami Ryn Naia!*" On the beach the cheer rose again and my mind, now attuned to translating the words of the language known as the Ancient Voice, accepted their blessing, "*Long live the Reigning Lady. Long live Princess Rynnaia!*"

"May it be so." Nestled on the narrow seat beside me, Sir Julien de Gladiel affirmed the people's hope, but when my Andoven tutor echoed the sentiment from his place behind us near the front of the boat, his tone implied he did not share Julien's optimism.

For one who had not yet reached his thirtieth year, Edru possessed a rather developed bent toward pessimism. I was determined to help him overcome it, but so far I'd made little progress.

I glanced over my shoulder to where Edru sat with Dyfnel, whose expression seemed to agree with Edru's tone.

"Ah, now. You needn't sound so dark about it," I said, giving the two Andoven men the larger half of a smile. "I am part Andoven, you know. And since your people have such exceptionally long life spans, at least a bit of that longevity must have rubbed off on my blood, don't you think?"

"Our lifespans may be long," Edru said, "but perhaps it is because we so seldom leave the safety of our isle. I apologize if my tone offended you, Princess Rynnaia, but I have read Lady Anya's scrolls. Therefore, I am cautious."

"Indeed." Dyfnel's agreement was intoned with a hope so dim it seemed a portent of my early death. "A successful end to your quest depends upon the successful navigation of the dangers on your way there," the old Andoven physician added. "You would do well to be cautious, rather than to act under the illusion that the Remedy will be easily found."

Easily found? Did my miniscule attempt to lighten the mood make these men think I took this task lightly? The entire Kingdom depended on our success!

As I turned to face the shore, I tried to snuff out my irritation with Edru and Dyfnel by concentrating on the brighter colors of hope emanating from the thoughts of those gathered on shore.

I sighed. As someone brought up in the merry province of Veetri, it never ceased to amaze me how the Andoven, who so prized their intuitive wisdom, could misinterpret the slightest bit of merriment and manage to sour a moment. I suffered no illusions as to the dangers of the coming quest. I had memorized every line of Lady Anya's prophetic scrolls. But Lady Anya had also prophesied that I would find the Remedy and that our people would finally achieve victory over the Cobelds. I refused to allow fear—or even caution—to poison my hope just yet.

Rynnaia. The precious voice of my mother called out to my mind from her sickroom, deep within the castle. Reaching out and latching on to my thoughts, she held them as if in an embrace, chasing Edru and Dyfnel's pessimism away.

Mother, I answered, closing my eyes to fully concentrate my thoughts on her.

Until the day I arrived on Tirandov Isle, I had believed, along with the rest of E'veria, that Queen Daithia had been killed by the Cobeld curse she injested during childbirth. But the well-circulated tale of her death—and mine—was an elaborate deception undertaken by my father, who had hidden us both away to keep us beyond the Cobelds' reach.

Even after I learned the truth of my identity and was finally able to access the inborn Andoven gifts I had not even known I possessed, I believed her dead. How glad I was to be wrong—and how thankful I was for our shared Andoven lineage. Our gifts would allow us to speak through our thoughts even when I was leagues away from this isle, while she stayed here, awaiting the healing benefits of the Remedy I was tasked to find.

Be safe, my sweet daughter. You carry my very heart with you.

That last statement was truer than either one of us wanted to admit. Every day, the curse she had received combined a little more dangerously with the unusual blessing she had imparted to me at birth. True, the curse had not killed her immediately, as the Cobelds had designed it to, but it had been working toward that goal for the past nineteen years. Even now, I sensed the weakening of her heart, as well as the rest of her body—and I could not help but feel a little guilty for the distress she so valiantly tried to hide. Her blessing strengthened my Andoven abilities beyond what they should have been by heredity alone, but the cost to her health was dear. The more my gifts developed, the more her essence seemed to drain away, making even the simplest conversation an exhausting event.

Be strong, Mother. I will find the Remedy for you. I will.

Not just for me, Rynnaia. For all E'veria, she reminded me. *You are the Ryn.*

Her voice and colors faded from my mind as sleep claimed her consciousness once again. But with those last few words, she reminded me that as the Ryn, the heir to the E'verian throne, I had to put my personal concerns aside for the good of my people. Even if it meant my mother would die.

A tiny shudder shook my head. *No.* I refused to accept that possibility. I wasn't ready to lose my mother. I had just *found* her.

Sudden warmth covered my hand, pulling me from my gloom. *Ah, Julien.* I closed my eyes and soaked in the peace offered by the slight pressure of his hand on mine and then stole a look at the knight himself.

Sunshine caught upon Julien's dark blond hair and sparkled amid the short strands of the triangular knight's beard that circled his lips and covered his chin. As if he felt my eyes upon him, he turned. When he smiled, light danced in his emerald-green eyes, sparking a flash in my midsection that once again melted the tender spot in my heart that bore his name.

I turned my hand over and wrapped my fingers around his. How would I have coped with the tumultuous emotions of these past weeks, and the frightening implications of my newly discovered heritage, without him? First my protector, Julien quickly became my friend. But something new had taken root between us over the last few weeks, something that

let him know when I needed to borrow a bit of his strength.
Like now.

"Has it been only three months since you suffered to
nurse a mangy bear back to health?" he asked.

Mangy bear, indeed! I laughed. "Considering all we've
been through, it seems I've known you much longer."

Although I had spent the majority of my life with a duke's
family in Veetri, I had passed the last two years with my
aunt and cousin in a secluded old lodge in the Great Wood
of Mynissbyr. It was there I met Julien, a true Bear-man of
Mynissbyr.

The first storm of winter had arrived that night, bringing Julien with it. He was lost, or so he thought, and out of
his head with fever. Wearing a bear-skin cloak that made him
appear as a beast of legend, I had thought him a threat to our
safety. Therefore, I introduced myself by sending a dagger
into his arm.

Good thing he was the forgiving sort.

"I am rather glad the Bear-men of Mynissbyr turned out
to be less frightening than the Veetrish Storytellers led me to
believe," I said, but my soft laugh was followed by a sigh as
I looked off over the calm waters of this strange sea. "That
night is like a scene from another lifetime."

And it was, in a way. Once Julien had regained his health,
everything I knew was upended, and the painful questions
that had plagued my childhood were answered. The missive Julien delivered from the King revealed me as Princess
Rynnaia E'veri. *The Ryn.* With that truth in hand, my Andoven
gifts—and the maternal blessing that accompanied them—
had been released.

At first, those new abilities frightened and perplexed
me, which was likely why my father had ordered me to come
to Tirandov Isle to be tutored. But now that I had received

instruction from those who shared my gifts I was much less afraid. Now, not only could I distinguish the thoughts of others, but I could construct barriers to hide my own. I could silently speak to both man and matter without the slightest regard to proximity or distance, and I had even managed to locate my uncle and Julien's father, who were being held captive by our enemies.

But an even more significant dimension was added to my identity during my time on Tirandov Isle, one that illumined a tragic emptiness within my soul and filled it with light. And it was Julien de Gladiel, my beautiful, patient knight, who had helped to lead me to the place where I was open to that illumination—and to receiving a love I had never even known existed.

"I'm so glad you're here," I whispered to him now. "Thank you."

"There is nowhere I would rather be." Julien's voice was quiet, but intense. "Well, that's not entirely true." He paused and a slow smile infected his words. "I would much rather be at the end of our quest, with the Cobelds' curse exiled and you safely installed at Castle Rynwyk."

"I must say I agree with your sentiment. But I will admit that I am curious to meet my father. I should see to that before taking off for the Remedy, don't you think?"

A thrill of anticipation sent a shiver across my shoulders. In a short time I had gained not only the knowledge of my name and the use of my gifts, but the mother I had believed dead and the father who, though I had doubted his love for most of my life, I could now hardly wait to meet in person.

Was he as anxious to meet me? And when he did, would he be . . . disappointed?

I shook my head, unwilling to let my old insecurities gain a foothold, and hoping I was beyond such crippling fears.

I took a deep breath. *I am the Ryn.*

The pinkish fog that surrounded Tirandov thickened, completely enveloping us within it, and I could see the isle no more. But when I turned my gaze back to Julien, I wondered at his suddenly warrior-like expression.

"Why such a fierce countenance, Sir Julien? One would think you did not relish returning to the mainland."

"Tirandov Isle is safe, Princess." Julien's scowl deepened. "We have no such assurance about the sea beyond this fog or even the mainland once we reach it."

"Cazien would let us know if we were in any imminent danger, don't you think?"

"I think our captain's definition of danger might be a little less conservative than mine." Julien's tone was dry as one of his eyebrows angled down toward the bridge of his nose.

I couldn't help but laugh, even with Julien's frown so pronounced. "Well, he is a pirate."

Dyfnel chuckled. "Captain Cazien knows Her Highness is with us. If any mischief was afoot, I'm sure he would not only know of it, but endeavor to keep her from it."

Julien's scowl deepened. A metallic flash colored his thoughts when he spoke. "I'm sure Cazien is quite capable," he said, giving me a long look, "when his eye is on the sea."

"The Seahorse Pirates are allies of King Jarryn," Edru said. "The Ryn will be safe."

Julien gave a quick nod, but his scowl lingered, letting me know that it wasn't the unknown enemies of the seas he feared so much as the flirtations of our handsome young captain.

"He's my cousin, you know," I reminded him, even though it gave me a little thrill to know Julien objected to other men flirting with me.

"Your *distant* cousin." His jaw clenched, sending the short golden hairs at the tip of his triangular beard jutting outward.

15

I looked away to hide my smile.

A kiss of sweetness scented the air, a fragrance I had not noticed when coming through Tirandov's fog the first time.

"It is the lilykelp," Edru explained. "It has just begun to bloom." He gasped. "Forgive me. I've grown so attuned to listening to your thoughts during our lessons that I infringed upon your privacy. My deepest apologies, Your Highness."

"Accepted." I smiled at my tutor's suddenly pale face. "In truth, Edru, had you not brought it to my attention, I would not have even noticed."

I had become fairly adept at camouflaging my thoughts while on Tirandov Isle. I drew upon that skill now, closing my eyes and reaching for strands of gray within my mind, the technique by which I could mask the colors of my emotions in a formless cloud. In this way, I could retain some privacy, at least, and prevent those with similar abilities from peeking into my mind. It took very little effort to guard myself thus, but as new as my abilities were to me, I often forgot to maintain the boundary. Considering the company we were about to join, I was glad to be reminded.

Captain Cazien de Pollis had a bit of Andoven ancestry himself, and he had proven himself rather intuitive the last time I had sailed aboard *Meredith*. There were some things I'd just as soon keep to myself, and although it was considered extremely bad manners for an Andoven to listen in on another's thoughts without permission, Cazien was, after all, a pirate. I wasn't sure he recognized the rules of Andoven etiquette.

Or *any* sort of rules, for that matter.

It wasn't long before the fog began to thin and I could just make out the shape of the pirate vessel awaiting us. Moments later, the current gently bumped us against Cazien's ship and ropes slapped down toward us with a loud *thwump* against the sides of the larger ship.

Julien and Dyfnel secured the ropes to the rode hooks and Julien hollered up, "Solid!" before moving to the seat plank directly across from mine and offering his hands. "Hold on."

I gripped his forearms as he did mine, but the first heave still jarred me. And the second. With each tug of the rope my stomach jumped into my throat and then fell to my feet just as swiftly before finding its rightful place again.

When I finally looked up—for I'd found that looking down was a mistake—it was only to find Cazien's grin trained on me.

"You're looking a little green, Rynnaia." He laughed. "And you haven't even gotten to the fun part yet!"

I didn't like the sound of that.

Like me, Cazien had been born to his position, and though only a matter of months older than my nineteen years, he'd captained his own ship for several years already. Just as Julien worried about my cousin's definition of danger, I couldn't help but flinch a bit at the thought of what he might consider "fun."

As soon as the bottom of our boat was level with the railing, Cazien jumped up so that his feet were on the ledge of the side of the ship and his shins pressed against the rail.

"Here we go, Princess. Now stand up, turn toward me, and put both of your arms out in front of you."

I let go of Julien's arms and did as the captain commanded.

"Steady her if you would, Sir Julien."

Julien shifted to sit behind me. He lightly rested his hands at my waist.

Cazien peered around me. "I can trust you to let go of her at the proper time, yes?"

"Of course." Julien's voice was tight.

"Good. Now lean toward my sweet *Meredith*, Rynnaia, and . . . trust me."

At that, I had a moment's pause. But that brief moment was all I had time for because three pairs of sun-bronzed hands gave the side of our boat a giant outward push that introduced my stomach to my spine. We swung out so far I could see the water below and then back toward the rail. As soon as my arms were level with Cazien's he slipped his hands in their crooks and pulled.

As the deckhands pushed the longboat for another outward swing, my feet flew out from under me. Cazien lifted me up over the rail and swiftly down onto the deck with the same grace that might have been affected had we been dancing in the Grand Hall at Holiday Palace instead of boarding a ship in the middle of the sea.

"I have to hand it to you, Rynnaia." Cazien winked at me. "Most of the lasses scream the first time."

"I'm not like most of the lasses then, I guess," I said, lifting my chin in defiance of the scream that still begged to be released.

"No." Cazien's eyes shone. "You most certainly are not."

Julien's feet hit the deck beside us. My eyes widened. "You jumped?"

He nodded. "I've done it before."

The sailors gave the boat another swing and we moved to make way for Dyfnel and Edru.

"Do you know the state of things on the mainland?" Julien asked our young captain.

"Port Dyn is still secure, but Luce has not fared as well." Cazien's expression darkened. "When last we were in port, Luce was nearly overrun by Dwonsil warriors, the blasted traitors. They might've taken the city by now."

"And Cobelds, too?"

"Not that I heard, but it is possible since they've allied with the clans from Dwons. I aim to return as soon as I've delivered Rynnaia to her father." He paused. "It's rumored the men of Dwons are now wrapping their arrows with hairs from Cobelds' beards."

"*What?*" Julien's eyes widened.

"It's said the Cobelds speak the curse, pluck out the hair, and wrap it around an arrow. The Dwonsil warriors wear gloves to avoid contact with the cursed hair. But when they fire their bows, even a flesh wound becomes deadly."

"'Divided beard will grow its purse,'" I whispered. When Cazien arched an eyebrow in my direction I repeated the phrase. "It's a line translated from the scrolls we took to Tirandov." I turned to Dyfnel, who had been deposited on the deck by one of Cazien's burly sailors just in time to hear Cazien's report. "Do you think Lady Anya foresaw that the Cobelds would give hairs from their beards to the Dwonsil warriors and be able to cause more damage?"

His brow furrowed. "It does seem to match meaning to that verse of the prophecy."

I nodded. "Perhaps the 'purse' is whatever the curse gives them. Its payout, so to speak. When a hair of the beard is given to a Dwonsil warrior, it goes farther than it would if used only by a Cobeld."

"Indeed." Cazien said. "But even after all these years, I still can't understand why the men from Dwons would want to secede from E'veria. Ah, but that is why I stay out of politics." He shrugged and the darkness in his eyes brightened. "At least Port Dyn is still secure. And now that Rynnaia is equipped for her quest, all will soon be put back to rights and the Queen will take back her throne."

I nodded, grinning. "I can hardly wait to— *What* did you say?" My mouth fell open. I closed it. "How do you know about my mother?" I had thought the Queen's survival had been known only to my father and the Andoven at Tirandov. "Did the Andoven tell you?"

Cazien smirked. "Who but the Seahorse Heir would your father entrust with the secret transport of his queen?"

"But you would have been a baby!"

Cazien laughed. "I'm not the first Seahorse Heir, Rynnaia."

I was about to question Cazien further, but the stronger colors of a familiar regret came from the Andoven physician, stealing my attention. "Dyfnel? You were there." My statement entailed a command that he tell the story.

Dyfnel nodded. "We kept your mother hidden—"

"We?"

"Your father and I. We kept Queen Daithia hidden at Holiday Palace until she had recovered enough from your birth to be moved. Your parents feared that even if the Cobelds believed you had died, if it was known the Queen had survived the curse, even as ill as she was, they would worry she and the King would eventually produce the Ryn Naia."

"But couldn't she have been kept hidden at the palace?"

Julien put a hand on my shoulder. "The Cobelds infiltrated one of the most secure fortresses in the world that night, Your Highness. If they'd done it once, they could do it again."

"At the time it seemed a better course to perpetuate the illusion of their success," Dyfnel said. "The Cobelds would have no reason to seek the death of a Queen and Ryn who were already dead." He sighed. "Perhaps our logic was foolhardy, but we had little time to formulate a plan to guarantee your safety. It was all rather quickly decided. Captain Pollis left with you the night you were born, delivered you into the care of Lady Drinius, and then returned to Port Dyn for the Queen."

"Captain Pollis." I turned back to Cazien. "So it was your father who helped us?"

"My mother."

I gaped. "Your mother was a pirate?"

"Aye," he nodded. "And the fiercest Seahorse Captain ever upon the seas."

"And your father—?"

"My father is not affiliated with the Seahorse fleet." He looked away. "If you'll excuse me, Princess Rynnaia, I have duties that need my attention."

Without waiting for a reply, Cazien stalked to the bridge, and after a few barked commands from our Captain, *Meredith* was out of the strangely still Andoven waters and sailing on the choppier waves of the Southern Sea.

$\mathcal{T}$ H R E E

$\mathcal{J}$ulien followed me to the railing where I joined Edru in watching the antics of dolphins swimming alongside the ship. Suddenly, a few small sparkles of light within the waves caught my eye. I grabbed Julien's arm.

"Look!" I pointed to the glittering wave. "Enikkas!"

Had it been only days ago that I'd learned of these beautiful creatures' existence? I had spent weeks studying the history of E'veria and the many names of the First King, Loeftryn de Rynloeft, but it wasn't until I swam with the enikkas, the tiny creatures of comfort and light, that I understood why the First King, long dead but undeniably present, should be interested in me.

So much had changed within me following that swim with the enikkas in the Bay of Tirandov. That night, The First had claimed me as his own.

As I had claimed him.

Somehow my grip on Julien's arm had moved downward and my hand now rested within his.

Julien squeezed my fingers. "I will never forget that
night."

"Neither will I," I whispered. "I'm so glad they stayed so
you could swim with them, too."

"Swimming with them was remarkable," he said. "But
the radiance on your face was even more beautiful, more
unforgettable."

When I looked back at the water, the enikkas were gone.

We were both quiet for a while, staring into the water, seeing what only memory could recall. Finally, he spoke. "Would
you like to sit down?"

I thought about it. "No. I think I'd like to walk a bit."

Walking was my plan, and other than navigating around
the occasional barrel and pile of neatly coiled rope, there was
little to keep me from it.

I was surprised to find Cazien not at the helm, but sitting on the upper deck. A board on his lap held a book, a
ledger of some sort, and in his hand, a quill moved at a
quick pace.

I stared at Cazien's hand as ink flowed onto the page in
neat, rhythmic strokes. Something about the sound of his
quill against the page sparked a memory. I paused to close my
eyes and recapture it.

I had found an old book of poetry in my guest bedchamber at Fyrlean Manor, Julien's family home. The book bore no
title, nor did it name an author, but as I read the poem a part
of me was transported across time to a separate place where I
was allowed to meet Lady Anya, its author.

Also known as the Oracle Scribe, Lady Anya was Julien's
ancestor, his many-greats-grandmother. Still, that day she
appeared to me as a young woman with coal black hair. I
recognized her by her bright green eyes, so like Julien's and
his father's, and even though I knew—I *knew* she had died

centuries before my birth, for those few moments I knew her as a friend. Likewise, she knew who I was.

When we met on that ethereal plane, Lady Anya was in the midst of writing the very poem I had been reading; a poem which spoke—prophetically—of me. We spoke, however briefly, and it was from her that I first learned of the quest on which I would soon embark, of the scrolls which would serve as our map, and of the Remedy we would—hopefully—find and use to defeat the Cobelds.

Cazien's quill ceased its scratching, bringing me back to the present moment. I opened my eyes to find he had paused only to dip into the inkwell.

I shook my head, forced my mind back to the scrolls, and resumed my stroll about the decks, but with every step the rhymes of the scrolls pressed more heavily upon my mind.

Nine marks stand guard to guide the way.
Three tasks upon the Ryn will prey.
Death stalks the path with fierce desire,
and a counsel of four will strike the pyre.

The scrolls went on, of course, to describe the nine marks and three tasks in riddles worthy of a Veetrish Storyteller, painting frightening pictures that, while not quite clear enough to understand, held such imagery of danger that it could nearly still the blood. I only hoped that when we came upon the landmarks they would be easily recognized.

But I had my doubts.

"You're going to wear a hole through my deck if you insist on pacing like that, Rynnaia."

Cazien's voice was so near I assumed it was in my head. I paused and looked up to the deck, expecting to see him at the wheel of the ship. Instead he was immediately to my right, perched on a barrel. He gazed at me with a strange intensity that belied the smirk on his face.

The pirate's head was uncovered today, his black hair tied back with a leather strip at the nape of his neck. The cloudy sky gave an almost blue tinge to his black curls and brought out more of the white flecks in his ice-blue eyes, so startling against the bronze glow the sun had wrought on his complexion.

My eyes took the path from Cazien to the bridge and back. To move from the bridge to the deck he would have had to practically brush right by me. How had I not noticed him?

"I thought you were—"

"Devilishly handsome?" He waggled his thick black eyebrows. "I know."

"Well, you're half-right," I mumbled, rolling my eyes.

Julien snorted.

Cazien just laughed. "You seem rather deep in thought, cousin. Might I ask the direction of your worry?"

"I was thinking about the scrolls."

"Ahh." Cazien nodded, and setting one arm across his waist, he rested his right elbow in his left hand and flicked the little patch of hair beneath his lip back and forth. *Flick, flick. Flick, flick.* "They're tricky little rhymes, aren't they?"

"Yes." I nodded. "The scrolls speak in riddles, with imagery that will likely be impossible to decipher until we actually see it." My shoulders dropped as I exhaled a heavy breath. "And there is a bit at the end that is rather odd. It's written by the same hand and ink as the rest, but in our modern language. The rest of the poetry had to be translated from the Ancient Voice."

"True." Cazien nodded. "But that bit at the end confirms Lady Anya was an oracle as well as a poet, yes? And it explains your visitation from her at Fyrlean Manor."

"Exactly." I had told Cazien of my time-bending experience the last time I'd sailed with him. "But still, it was so . . . peculiar. And . . . lovely." Almost three months later, that experience still left me awestruck whenever I pondered it.

"How do you know about the postscript?" Julien's voice was strangely cold and layered with suspicion. "Did the Andoven tell you?"

Cazien shifted and looked away. "Not . . . exactly."

Julien crossed his arms at his chest. His expression, while seemingly neutral, seemed to carry the mildest hint of a threat. "Care to elaborate?"

Rather than answer Julien's question, Cazien looked at me. "Rynnaia, did you know Lady Anya sailed on this very ship?"

"She did?" I looked about. Cazien's ship hardly seemed old enough to have been around two hundred years ago. "Surely you jest." I laughed. "A ship can't survive two hundred years!"

"Ah, but a Seahorse vessel can. Especially one as unique as *Meredith*."

"Don't change the subject, Captain." The threat in Julien's voice was a bit more pronounced this time. "Tell us how you know the contents of the scrolls."

"Patience, knight. I'll get to that." Cazien shot an irritated glance toward Julien and then turned back to me. "One of Lady Anya's dearest friends happened to be the wife of a Seahorse captain," he said. "She made several seaward ventures with them. On one of those voyages, they entered into a mutually beneficial," he paused and I sensed a certain amount of unease in the phrase, "agreement. Together, they devised a plan by which the scrolls would be protected."

"What sort of agreement?" I asked.

"The captain swore a Legacy Oath to ensure the scrolls' survival. The oath bound not only him, but every future

Seahorse heir, to complete a specific errand until the prophesied Ryn had come of age."

"An ... *errand?*"

"Each successive generation was charged with finding, collecting, preserving, and re-hiding the scrolls to ensure they would survive until the appointed time of their discovery." He took a breath. "And, always, the heir was sworn to refrain from revealing that knowledge to anyone, even the next generation, but for three clues the Seahorse heir was to be given prior to beginning his or her errand."

I blinked. "How ... elaborate."

"You have no idea." One dark chuckle bounced off the pirate's chest. "But it would appear Rynloeft blessed the Oath, because the scrolls were preserved until the prophesied Ryn was ready to complete her quest," he said with a wink in my direction.

"You knew?" Julien stood. "You knew where they were *all along?*" Julien clenched his fists until his knuckles turned almost white with the strain. "All these years my family has searched for the scrolls, hoping they might lead us to the Remedy, and the entire time, *you knew where they were?*"

Julien's hand moved to his sword. In the same instant, Cazien slid off the barrel, his hand on his cutlass. But neither man drew his blade.

I took a step back. Suddenly, every sailor aboard the ship had his hand resting near some sort of weapon.

"Answer me!" Julien roared.

Cazien's eyes flashed, but his words betrayed no emotion other than marginal boredom. "You would do well to consider to whom you bellow, knight, and to whose mercy you may someday need to appeal."

"And *you* should consider that I represent the interests of the King of E'veria and the Ryn," Julien spat his reply.

"Did your people not realize the scrolls you went to such pains to keep hidden were a map to the Remedy? If I find that you've withheld information that could have saved our Kingdom from the horrors of the Cobelds, I won't care what little boat you sail on. I will lead you to the gallows myself."

Sparks of silver and red flashed in the periphery of my thoughts, seeming to come from every direction at once. Julien's derogatory comment toward *Meredith* had launched anger into the thoughts of every sailor within earshot, though they didn't show it outwardly. They all mirrored the bored, even slightly amused, countenance of their captain.

"The gallows you say? On what . . ." Cazien's voice paused and then dimmed as the vowels elongated his final word, ". . . chaaarge?"

The young pirate's back was to me, but— Oh, he did *not* just yawn, did he?

One look at Julien's livid face confirmed it.

My knight's eyes narrowed. "You, Cazien de Pollis, are a traitor."

"A traitor?" Cazien laughed. "How can I be a traitor to a King who is not my sovereign?"

I reached a hand out to Cazien's arm, but he rotated his shoulder as if to shrug me off. "Stay out of this, Rynnaia."

Julien's voice lowered, becoming even more dangerous. "You will not speak to E'veria's Ryn with such disrespect."

"Captain," Dyfnel said as he came alongside me, "perhaps further conflict could be avoided if you explained the Seahorse Legacy a bit."

Dyfnel took my hand from the pirate's arm and led me a few paces away.

Stay back, he spoke to my mind. *Just in case they come to blows.*

"Fine." Cazien took a deep breath. "Much like Her Highness here, I was born into my position," he began. "I inherited it from my mother, who inherited it from her father, and back a long way through history until you get all the way to Brennon de Andov, who married Meredith E'veri, for whom this ship was named."

"That far back?" I blinked. I had studied my genealogy in the library on Tirandov Isle and learned that Meredith E'veri was the youngest daughter of King Stoenryn, a Knight of The First and the man who succeeded Loeftryn de Rynloeft himself as King of E'veria. Brennon, however, would also be a distant ancestor of mine. He was the second son of Andov, another Knight of The First and the first Regent of Tirandov Isle.

"Yes, *cousin*. That far back," Cazien said. "From the first child born to the union between Brennon and Meredith until this present day, the Seahorse Heir has been assigned a task, an errand, if you will, to be completed before he or she is able to officially take over as Admiral of the Seahorse Fleet and Monarch of Eachan Isle." He arched an eyebrow and tilted his head at Julien, a reminder that, at least politically, as Monarch of Eachan Isle, Cazien de Pollis was on equal footing with my father. "Part of my errand, as with several generations before me, was to find where the Lost Scrolls of Anya had last been hidden and to then move them to a new location, as revealed to me by," he paused, "the other part of my errand. In addition, I was sworn to never reveal what I knew of them until—"

Cazien's monotone recitation abruptly cut off. He shrugged, but the momentary clenching of his jaw argued with his nonchalance. "Until now, I suppose you could say," he said finally. "In any case, I completed my errand. When my mother sailed to Rynloeft, I took my place as Admiral and Monarch and stayed true to my Legacy."

I tilted my head. "Your mother sailed to ... Rynloeft?"

Rynloeft was a word most often heard in association with the First King of E'veria, Loeftryn de Rynloeft. Yet it also referred to a place. The place he had come from. A place I had been taught was unreachable while yet alive.

Cazien's nod was accompanied by a gentling of expression. "That's how we sailors refer to death, Princess."

"Oh. I'm sorry."

He waved a hand.

"When, might I ask," Julien's voice was low and his eyes had darkened to a deadly shade of green, "did you complete this 'errand' of yours?"

Cazien shrugged. "About four years ago."

"But you knew the Ryn lived."

"Yes."

"And Captain Pollis knew as well."

"Of course."

"In other words, when last I sailed upon this ship, along with King Jarryn and my father, you two pirates held life and death in sway over the Queen—nay, the entire Kingdom?"

"It's not as simple as that, mate." A muscle twitched in Cazien's neck and his fingers once again rested on the grip of his cutlass, "And I would suggest you not speak of the Seahorse Legacy in that tone again. It is as dear to me, if not dearer, than the oath of the Bear-men of Mynissbyr."

Julien's sword was out in an instant. "Our oath is to find the Remedy and to see the Cobelds defeated. Your legacy is the exact opposite! It could cost our Queen her life! She's dying from the Cobeld curse, Cazien. She needs the Remedy!"

I had not marked when Cazien lifted the cutlass from its place at his side, but the tip of his blade now touched Julien's.

"And that is a difficult truth to accept," Cazien said. "But even Daithia's death would not remove my responsibility to serve my Legacy."

"But if you'd given the scrolls to the King, the Remedy might have already been found!"

"You have *read* the translations, haven't you de Gladiel?"

Julien gave a stiff nod. He and I had passed many hours studying them, committing them to memory while on the isle.

"Then you know at least a few of the dangers your Princess will face when she seeks the Remedy. I think even Queen Daithia—perhaps *especially* Queen Daithia—would agree that Rynnaia was not yet ready to begin her quest at the time I completed my errand. Indeed," Cazien scoffed, "even a Bear-man of Mynissbyr would not have sent a fifteen-year-old girl—nay, would not have presumed to send *anyone* who had not yet sworn fealty to The First—to defeat the Cobelds."

I sucked in a breath. "How do you know about that?" It was only three nights past that I'd swam with the enikkas and sworn my fealty to The First!

Cazien spoke into my thoughts. *Even the sea, as mysterious as she is, could not keep such news to herself, Rynnaia.*

I blinked several times, attempting to understand how water could transport a memory—especially one so recently made—to him. Was he able to speak to . . . the sea? Or had he somehow communicated with the enikkas themselves? I would have asked, but Julien's anger arrested my attention.

"A knight would not have hidden something so important, so vital to the Kingdom's survival, from her King!"

"And yet your King hid the Ryn from his entire Kingdom!" Cazien shot back. "Blast it, man! Are all knights so vain as to believe they are the only ones whose decisions are dictated by duty?"

"*You* accuse *me* of vanity?"

"I am bound to my Legacy in ways you cannot imagine," Cazien hissed. With each word the pirate pressed forward until the two blades crossed just inches between his neck and Julien's chest, not that Cazien seemed bothered by the difference of height. "I'm as bound to it as Rynnaia is bound as the Ryn. To have gone against what my Legacy demanded would have meant rebelling against The First himself."

With a twist of his sword meant to disarm the knight, Cazien stepped back, but Julien turned at the same time, spinning a full circle until his blade rested at Cazien's neck.

It was then I noticed a second blade in Cazien's left hand. And the flat of it pressed under Julien's chin. For all Julien's superior size, it appeared he was equally matched in skill. This could not end well.

"Stop it!" I stepped forward. "Drop your weapons. Now!"

With a scowl that ground his teeth almost audibly, Julien complied. I was a bit surprised at that until I remembered who I was.

"Cazien . . ." I warned.

"I'm afraid I don't take orders from you, Rynnaia." His words were lit with a lighthearted smile that I assumed was meant to needle Julien, who by nature of his oath, was required to obey my command. "But I *do* like you," he acquiesced. "And it pinches my heart a bit to see you so upset over our little squabble. I will, of my own free will, of course," he added, "decline the opportunity to injure your loyal knight." In a flash his weapons were stowed.

"Thank you. Now clasp hands and part as friends."

Julien shot me a look of disbelief, as did Cazien.

"Clasp. Hands." I repeated, crossing my arms. "We are friends. Allies, at the very least. And we will remain so, regardless of whether or not we understand the other's motivation or deeds."

Julien closed his eyes and took a deep breath. When he opened them he took a step back and held out his hand.

Cazien!

The pirate jumped ever-so-slightly when I shouted into his mind.

"Oh, fine." He clasped Julien's hand and gave it one solid shake. Both immediately retracted.

By Rynloeft, it was like dealing with my brothers, fighting over the last bit of pudding!

"Again," I said. "And mean it this time."

Cazien was the first to offer his hand this time. "Friends?"

Julien clasped it. He gritted his teeth and nodded. "Friends."

"Good," Cazien said after they repeated the oh-so-manly shake again. "You know, I achieved my part of this particular Lady Anya business to the letter. If anyone is at fault," he said, tossing a wink my way, "it's whoever took so long to find the scrolls."

"*I* didn't find them." I wrinkled my nose.

"I know that," he said, making a comical face. "It couldn't be you."

I opened my mouth and a little sound of offense escaped. "And why not?"

"Because you're the Ryn!" He laughed and waggled his head while crossing his eyes and said, "Future Queen of E'veria, and all that rot, that's why!"

Julien sheathed his sword, "So you would place the blame for this on my sister?"

Cazien stilled. "Your . . . sister?"

"Yes," I offered, "Julien's sister is the one who found the scrolls."

Cazien blinked several times, almost as if he was having trouble focusing on my face. His own paled beneath the color the sun had wrought upon it. "Erielle?"

I tilted my head. "You know her?"

Cazien nodded. "It was . . . years ago."

"My family accompanied the King on a voyage once," Julien said. "On this ship."

"Truly?" Cazien rubbed a hand against the back of his neck. "Your sister found the scrolls?"

"Yes. In a cave in Mynissbyr. Behind Brune Falls," Julien said. His lips pressed hard together in the instant before he added, "But you knew that already, didn't you?"

"I didn't know . . ." Cazien's gaze rested in a space where no one stood, as if he was dazed. "I knew where the scrolls were, of course. I put them there. But I didn't know who would find them. I thought . . ."

He looked over at me and blinked, but I still had the sense he wasn't really focusing on my face.

"I thought the prophecy was wrong," he whispered.

"Wrong about what?" I asked. He didn't answer. "Cazien?"

"He speaks of a different prophecy, perhaps?" Dyfnel mused when it seemed the young pirate was all but lost to the conversation.

Cazien shook his head—a brief, violent shake as if a fly were on his nose. He pressed his hands to his temples. In that unguarded moment I caught a rare swirl of color and emotion, but only one stray thread I could define amidst his normally indiscernible thoughts.

It is decided, then.

And whatever it was, he was none too happy about it.

"What's decided, Cazien?"

"The rest of my life." His tone was droll, yet held a vague sense of futility. He blinked, and not even a swirl of gray was left in his thoughts for me to see.

$\mathcal{F}$OUR

$\mathcal{T}$he mood aboard *Meredith* was tense for most of an hour before I tripped on a pile of rope and a nearby sailor began to sing about a clumsy girl who stumbled upon a treasure chest of jewels. At first I was embarrassed to have inspired the man to sing, but there was something refreshing about being around people who weren't my subjects. As the other sailors joined in, the humor of the lyrics soon had me laughing along with everyone else. I sensed no disrespect from their teasing, only the good-natured fun of camaraderie and an acceptance without regard to my rank. The song, though sung at the expense of my pride, served to relax the tension that had crept into my shoulders during Julien and Cazien's disagreement. I was almost sad when it was over.

I stood at the rail with Edru, but followed Julien out of the corner of my eye as he made his way to the bridge and spoke to Cazien. When Cazien slapped him on the back and I noted the smile on Julien's face, I breathed a little easier. He joined Edru and me a few moments later.

"I still have a hard time justifying the pirates' omission," he said after a long silence. "When I think of your mother, of how she's suffered all these years . . ." he trailed off. "But I handled it badly. And for that, I apologize. I have also apologized," he said carefully, "to our captain."

"Thank you," I said. "But I must admit I thought your arguments valid. I don't understand Cazien's legacy. Perhaps I'm not meant to," I sighed. "But he's right in at least one thing. I wouldn't have been ready for this quest four years ago." A humorless laugh escaped my lips. "I'm hardly ready for it now."

"I'm not sure anyone could truly be 'ready' for something like this, but The First is faithful to insert his strength into the places we are most weak. If he has set you on this quest, he will see it through."

We were quiet for a long while, gazing at the sea. But every now and then, I found my eyes had wandered to the knight at my side. The mist and breeze from the sea had made Julien's dark blond hair curl a bit tighter than usual. He stood at the railing, his back to me and his feet set as wide as his shoulders, as his gaze traversed the sea, seeking a possible threat to my safety. He looked very much the part of the fearsome warrior, as, I supposed, befitted his position as a knight of the King and the future Regent of Mynissbyr.

"Switch out the colors, lads!" Cazien called from the bridge. Moments later, the sailors' cloaks had been turned inside out, placing the blue fabric, embroidered with a serpentine seahorse design, inward. Now facing outward, the "lining" of their tunics was a dull tan color, reminiscent of the tunics and surcoats worn by crews of merchant ships. Likewise, the blue Seahorse banners, which had waved proudly from all three masts, had disappeared, replaced with the innocuous red-and-white stripes of a merchant ship. As I gazed toward the bow, even the masthead looked different.

The smiling feminine form, roughhewn and worn, was suddenly unfamiliar.

Trying to keep Julien's tension from seeping into my mind, I moved to the railing near the ship's bow. As I stood there, I recognized that something was different about *Meredith*'s figurehead, but I couldn't put my finger on exactly what.

"Another part of the Seahorse Legacy, I think." Edru came up beside me. "I have studied it as well and I cannot seem to recall what has changed, though I know it is not the same figure it was before. Ah, well." He turned and walked away.

I closed my eyes and tried to picture the figure that had graced the bow of the ship this morning, but I couldn't.

Open your eyes, Rynnaia. Cazien whispered into my mind. I did and found him right beside me.

Watch.

He climbed over the rail, causing my heart to lurch, and leaned out to touch the base of the figurehead. At his touch, a dull film seemed to fall away and the flawless craftsmanship of *Meredith*'s true figurehead was suddenly revealed.

"This is the image of Meredith E'veri," he said, "with whom we both share a common ancestor."

"King Stoenryn," I said, nodding. "Her father."

Cazien had descended from King Stoenryn's youngest daughter. I, from his eldest son.

If this ship's figurehead was accurate, Meredith E'veri had been a fiercely beautiful woman. Her expression was an intriguing mix of determination and joy, and her hair, carved of wood, but so expertly that it looked caught by the wind, flowed out behind her as she leaned over the neck of a—

"What is that thing she's riding?"

"A seahorse of the Gilled Cavalry."

"I thought seahorses were small," I said. "Like the one on your chain."

Cazien fingered the silver charm at his neck. "They may have the same name, but they aren't the same animal."

"Oh." The animal beneath Meredith E'veri was bigger than Salvador, Julien's gigantic horse. It did look a bit like a horse, but its face was bonier, its neck gilled, and its mane appeared more like kelp than hair. "Are they real?"

"Aye. They're real."

"Still?"

He nodded.

"Have you ever seen one? Up close?"

"I have." Cazien nodded and I sensed a respectful affection in his voice.

"It's beautiful. She's beautiful."

"Aye." He smiled. "But I don't think it's wise for either *Meredith* or her steed to be seen in Port Dyn. Mine is a rather famous ship, you see, and once rumors of pirates being in port begin, it's all 'Hide the women!' and 'Alert the guard!' and all that nuisance."

I laughed. "I suppose you're right."

Cazien placed his hand back on the wood. It blurred for an instant before the rough-hewn carving was all I could see.

"You're not Veetrish, are you?" I asked, thinking his gift similar to that of the Storytellers.

"No," he chuckled. "Not even a bit."

"Thanks for showing me whatever it was you just did."

"My pleasure." He leapt back over the railing and onto the upper deck beside me. His next words caught me by surprise. "I have something to tell you, Rynnaia. Might I be bold?"

"Except for when you're being cryptic, I daresay you have no other way of speaking." I laughed.

"You love Julien." He didn't give me time to respond. "I'd have to be the weakest of the Andoven not to see it. When you're near him your very colors intensify. Ah! That color in your cheeks confirms it."

When I tried to swallow, my mouth was dry. "It's that obvious?"

He grinned. "As are his feelings for you."

"Then why do you vex him so by flirting with me?"

"I'm a pirate." He shrugged. "It's our way. But you needn't worry that I have designs on E'veria's Ryn. Even though I believe you would make a fine pirate," he said with a wink, "nothing could ever come of a romance between E'veria's Ryn and a Seahorse heir."

I frowned. "Not that I think of you that way of course, but . . . why not?"

"I belong to the sea. You belong to the land. And we're both sole heirs of realms that can never be successfully combined," he continued. "Even if you had not already given your heart away, it would be foolish for me to seek it for myself. Our positions alone make us incompatible. Besides," his tone darkened and his gaze became somehow separated from the moment, "my future has already been deter—"

"Land, ho!" The cry came from somewhere in the rigging far above us. "Port Dyn, dead ahead!"

"Rynnaia," he said slowly, "might I ask you an odd question?"

I couldn't imagine an odder conversation than that in which we'd just engaged. "I can't promise to have the answer, but you're welcome to ask."

"Julien said it was his sister who found the scrolls."

I nodded. "Yes. She did."

"Erielle was just a little girl when I last saw her." He leaned against the railing and flicked the patch of hair beneath his lip. "I wasn't much more than a boy myself. Wasn't even captain yet." A smile teased the corner of his mouth. "Still, she managed to knock me down and put a dagger to my throat."

I laughed. "That sounds like Erielle."

"What about Erielle?" Julien asked as he came up behind Cazien.

Cazien's smile fell for a moment, but when he turned toward Julien his expression was welcoming. "I was just telling Rynnaia about the time your family sailed with us and your sister tried to kill me."

A slow smile spread across Julien's face and a chuckle rose from somewhere deep within his chest. The sound warmed me and seemed to ease the tension still occasionally sparking between the two men.

"I'd nearly forgotten about that," Julien said and laughed again. "She's always been a discerning one, Erielle. If I remember right, she called you a 'worthless sea dog', too."

"That she did." Cazien smiled, but his wasn't as wide as Julien's.

"Why?" I aimed my question at Julien.

My knight's brow furrowed. "I don't actually recall." He shrugged. "But I do know my father nearly thrashed her for it."

I turned to Cazien. "Do you remember what happened?"

He nodded. "It was over a picture I drew. It came out badly and I wouldn't let her see it."

"That's right," Julien said, squinting as if trying to recall what was so wrong with the portrait. "You drew her to look older than she was, didn't you? Or was it something about the eyes?"

"It was both." Cazien's jaw worked a minute, almost as if he didn't want to admit the problem with his art.

HE REMEDY

"Captain?" A dark-skinned youth approached. "Do you have orders?"

"Aye." He nodded at Julien and then me. "Excuse me."

He turned to walk away. "Cazien? Wasn't there something you wanted to ask me?"

He shook his head no, but even as he walked away the question found my mind.

What color are Erielle's eyes?

I blinked. Well, he'd said the question was odd.

I know it seems odd. Even though his back was turned he saw my thought. *But it's important. What color are her eyes?*

I thought about it. *Blue.*

They're not green yet? Like Julien's? He sounded surprised. Shocked, even. And perhaps even a little . . . relieved?

No. Maybe a greenish sort of blue, but they're nothing like Julien's.

And what did he mean by *yet?*

I asked, but he was already engaged in shouting orders as we breached the port. All I received back from him were a few brief waves of confusion and then . . . nothing. Not even a swirl of gray.

$\mathcal{F}$ I V E

$\mathcal{I}$ t was early evening when we finally docked. The scene at Port Dyn was the exact opposite from the foggy, sleepy stillness of the morning we'd left for Tirandov Isle. Movement marked every inch of space on the docks and on the ships moored there. *Meredith* sailed in unnoticed amongst the other red-and-white striped merchant flags, no one on shore the wiser that pirates were in their midst.

A gruff sort of order reigned beneath the outward chaos of bickering sailors and merchants on the docks and the creaks and groans that accompanied the loading and unloading of barrels, crates, and casks.

The southernmost port in E'veria, Port Dyn was on the cusp of spring. The day was warm enough that I could have gone without my cloak, but even though the sun would soon set, my appearance might cause a stir.

"You've been quiet this afternoon," Julien said softly. "What's on your mind?"

"The scrolls." The poetry that would decide the future of E'veria was never far from my mind.

"Oh, is that all?"

"Is that *all*?"

When I turned, the quirk of his lips and the sparkle in his bright green eyes told me that he was teasing.

"Well, no, actually," I admitted. "I'm also thinking about what it will be like to finally meet my father, while wondering if I'll be any good at being a princess, and questioning how we'll be able to figure out the scrolls' mind-bending riddles enough to find the Remedy." I sighed. "Everything is all jumbled up inside me. All twisted like that rope." I pointed to the coil near our feet, braided around a belaying pin. "Except not nearly so neat."

Julien nodded and rubbed his beard. "I've tried to imagine what it would be like to meet my father for the first time and I find that I can't. He's been a constant presence since I was born. Even when he was away, as he often was, he was a known factor." He shook his head. "The thought of us being strangers is beyond the reach of my imagination." He paused. "Are you nervous?"

"Yes," I said. "And . . . no," I contradicted myself and laughed. "It's odd. I'm not really that worried about what he will think of me anymore. I know who I am and I accept who he is. But to meet a King in person, and to think of being introduced to his subjects as one requesting their fealty after having been part of an elaborate deception? That, my friend, is a bit intimidating." I let out a heavy breath. "I hope the Kingdom will give me a little . . . leeway," I stole a term I'd heard aboard ship, "in figuring out how to be a princess."

"They will. If the people share even a fraction of the excitement I felt in discovering who you are, you will have all the time you need."

Julien's confidence buoyed my spirit. "Thank you."

"Rynnaia." Cazien stepped up beside me and spoke in a low voice. "It would probably be best if you wait below until the escort arrives from your father."

I had my hood up, but the breeze was strong. One displaced breath of wind could reveal me. I nodded. "I suppose you're right."

"I sent your trunk on to the palace. I also spoke to your father." He tapped his head and grinned. "I imagine your escort will arrive before your things even make it up the hill."

I followed his gaze up toward the cliffs where the white stone palace glistened in the light of the lowering sun. Something caught my attention that was different from the last time I had taken in this view. "What is that flag? The big one?"

"That is the King's flag," Julien said. "It is raised only when he is in residence."

The King.

My father.

Closing my eyes, I took a deep breath to still the fluttering fairies in my stomach. When I succeeded, I found they'd left a question in their wake. "Do I have my own flag, too?"

"Uh, no," Julien said. His lip twitched. "Not that I'm aware of."

"Ah, don't be too disappointed, Princess," Cazien laughed. "Look there," he said, pointing to the winding road that led from Holiday Palace to Port Dyn. "He's practically sent an army for you!"

Indeed, it was a large guard. At least twenty-five horses surrounded a carriage as it made its slow descent.

"Is that an unusual way for him to transport a guest to the palace?"

Cazien tilted his head. "Do you consider yourself his guest?"

"Uhhh . . ."

The pirate laughed again. "To answer your question, *yes.*
It is unusual. And I probably should be offended, considering how famous and royal I am myself. Indeed! I do hope you
impress some manners upon the King for receiving foreign
dignitaries. All I usually get when I come into port is a message to the effect of 'Have a nice walk up the hill, Caz. See you
at table.' Or something like that."

My eyes widened. "Truly?"

"No." He shook his head and slapped me on the back,
but not too hard. "I'm jesting. Now, weren't you about to go
below?"

"Why bother?" I looked toward the carriage and horses
snaking down the cliff. "They'll be here soon."

"Ah, but there you're wrong. It's market day in Port Dyn.
The hawkers will make your escort's passage slow. It could be
two hours or more until they arrive. And since I am currently
in charge of your safety," Cazien said, eliciting an annoyed
frown from Julien, "I must insist you remain out of sight."

The sun had almost disappeared by the time Cazien came
to tell me my escort had arrived. I pulled my hood back up
over my hair and followed him up the steep stairs to the deck.

I paused at the gangplank. "Will I see you again, Cazien?"

"Oh, yes. Most definitely. Perhaps sooner than you think."
He angled a thumb toward Julien, whose hand rested at my
elbow. "Certainly sooner than *he* wishes you would."

Julien moved his hand from my elbow to the small of my
back. "Do what you wish, pirate. I've a difficult time perceiv-
ing you as a threat of import."

The hand on my back was softly laid, but proprietarily so.
Heat rushed to my face.

Cazien laughed at my discomfort with a tone that said, "I
told you so!" But when he addressed Julien, his expression

lacked gaiety. "I'm glad you've chosen to postpone your dislike of me for a later date, de Gladiel," he said, his countenance darkening. "I've no doubt it will serve you well in days yet to come."

"What is *that* supposed to mean?" I asked.

Cazien turned a suddenly wistful gaze my way. "I do wish I could tell you," he said. "But since I can't, it might save a lot of time if your knight just killed me now."

"Julien is not going to kill you."

"Not at the moment, anyway," Julien inserted. His tone was dark, but his eyes danced with humor. "But I am intrigued that you might allow me to consider it in the future."

A thought from our earlier, interrupted conversation occurred to me. "Cazien, does this have anything to do with—"

"Perhaps."

I was about to say "Erielle" but he heard the direction of my thought before I spoke it. "Would you care to elaborate?"

"Not today," he said. *But soon,* he added silently. *And I hope our friendship does not suffer when that day arrives.*

I stared at him long and hard, but he didn't flinch.

"You are an incorrigible menace, pirate," I said finally. "Will you ever cease tormenting me with cryptic, leading statements that you have no intention of decoding?"

"Hmm." He angled his eyes toward the mainmast and flicked his patch of beard. "It's highly doubtful."

When Cazien returned his gaze to me, his grin once again sparkled with mischief and I couldn't help but return it.

Cazien leaned over to kiss my cheek, and as he did, he whispered in my ear. "Take heart, Rynnaia. Trust that you are exactly where you are supposed to be and that all will be made known to you when the time is right."

"You're not speaking of Erielle anymore. This is about the scrolls, isn't it?" I whispered back.

"Yes." His nod brushed the whiskery scruff of his cheek against the smooth skin of mine, but his next words sent an even bigger chill down my spine than did the tickle of his breath in my ear.

"Your success will help secure the future of my Legacy, as well as your own. Take heart, cousin. I believe you are up to the task."

I swallowed and tamped down the anxiety his remark spawned in my chest. "But if I fail, the Kingdom will fall to the Cobelds."

His whisper was like a shrug, assuming and nonchalant, "Then don't fail."

Cazien gave my shoulder a quick squeeze, and when he straightened, his voice boomed. "Now get off my ship, the lot of you. I've work to do and I can't stand around mollycoddling a bunch of Andoven all day." He winked, and with a swish of his cloak that gave me just a glimpse of its blue lining, strode away.

Julien offered his arm and a grin. "Are you ready to go meet your father?" He chuckled. "I imagine he's more than ready to meet you."

S I X

$\mathcal{T}$ he closed-carriage ride through Port Dyn and up the winding path to Holiday Palace seemed to take forever, but it wasn't my father who greeted me when I arrived.

"Eri-*ullgh*?"

Her name came out as more of a grunt than a greeting when Erielle careened into me and nearly crushed my bones in a hug. The force of it knocked the hood from my head. I panicked for a minute, worried about being recognized, until I remembered where I was.

"You're taking me with you!" Erielle cried. "Thank you, thank you, thank you!" With each enthusiastic expression of gratitude her arms squeezed more tightly around me. "I'd contemplated returning to Mynissbyr, but when King Jarryn told me of your request, oh! I'm so glad I didn't go!" She squealed. "Thank you! Thank you!"

"Erielle, the Princess won't be able to take you anywhere," Julien said drily, "if she can't breathe."

"Oh!" She let go. "Indeed. I'm sorry."

A furious red stained Erielle's cheeks, which was quite unusual considering how difficult it was to embarrass Julien's little sister. We had become friends when she accompanied Julien and me from Mynissbyr but she had stayed in Port Dyn while I traveled on to Tirandov Isle. Erielle was already quite experienced in traveling the countryside disguised as a boy, but I was not. I had desperately needed her help on that journey to the coast and she had most willingly given it.

"I'm so glad the King agreed to my request," I said, but curiosity begged me to check the color of her eyes.

They were a greenish sort of blue, as I'd told Cazien earlier, but compared to Julien's emerald eyes? Definitely blue.

Erielle frowned. "Is something . . . wrong?"

"No." I smiled and shook my head, idly wondering if my piratical cousin wasn't slightly daft. But I didn't have time to linger on the thought because as soon as Erielle took another step back, I noticed the knights.

A few paces away, two men knelt with their heads bowed and their swords offered across open palms. Just beyond them, at a landing on the stair, a large portrait of my mother, painted when she must not have been much older than I was now, smiled down on us.

I wasn't sure who to approach first, but at least I knew what to say. The words were somehow engrained in my heart—one of the gifts I had discovered since learning I was the Ryn. I decided to approach them as I would words on a page: left to right.

I carefully placed my open palms under the flat of the first knight's sword and lifted it into the air. "I accept your sword, your fealty, and your service on behalf of my father, King Jarryn, my mother, the Queen, and myself in the hope that I will honor your faith in me."

Hmm. That came out differently than the last time I was in this situation. But it felt no less right.

The knight arose and after I placed his sword back into his hands I looked up . . . up . . . into a face that was entirely familiar to me, and yet . . . not.

"Gerrias de Gladiel?"

His eyes widened. "Yes, Your Highness."

Other than his height, he looked very little like his brother and nothing at all like his sister. Gerrias was very tall and had the same green—yes *green*—eyes as Julien. But there the similarity ended. Whereas Julien had the same golden blonde hair as his mother and sister, Gerrias's hair was black like Sir Gladiel's. The resemblance to Gladiel was so marked that, were it not for his relative youth, I might have mistaken Gerrias for his father.

"It is my great pleasure to meet the final member of the Regent's family. Thank you for your service to me and to the Kingdom of E'veria."

He bowed, took a step back, and sheathed his sword. I turned to the second knight, took his sword, and repeated the acceptance of fealty I'd given Gerrias.

When the second knight took his sword back and met my eyes I found it even more difficult to retain the formality of the moment than I had with Julien's brother.

"Kinley?" I squealed. My hand flew to my mouth, reminding me to finish the little ceremony. "Thankyouforyourservi cetomeandtotheKingdomofE'veria!" I gushed in a most un-princess-like fashion.

I waited just long enough for him to sheath his sword and then I threw my arms around his neck.

"Kinley!" I buried my face in the shoulder of the eldest of my three Veetrish "brothers." After a moment of hesitation, his arms went around me and his posture relaxed. I lifted my head, not at all ashamed of the moisture in my eyes. "I've missed you so much."

"I've missed you, too." Kinley's voice was thick with emotion, but his Veetrish brogue rang like a song in my heart. His lips quirked. "So would you break my neck instead of bruise my arm, now that you're a princess?"

I loosened my hold. "If I did, it would be only because you deserved it!" I planted a quick kiss on his cheek.

He gave me a slight squeeze. "Ah, Rose. You've no idea how I've worried about you these past few years."

"Rose?" I wrinkled my nose. "Who is this 'Rose' of whom you speak?"

"My deepest apologies, Princess Rynnaia. I once had a sister named Rose and your face quite reminds me of her." He let go of me and took the tiniest step back. Warmth lit his smile as he fingered a lock of my now-copper-colored hair. "My sister was a right little scamp, she was, with hair the color of a raven's wing."

"A right little scamp? Continue your flattery, knight, and I may yet bruise your arm." I lifted my fist and drew it back in a mocking threat.

"You've an odd definition of flattery, Princess," he said with a chuckle. "But I'm glad to see the raven has flown and brought us a flame in her place. I must admit I struggled a bit to try and imagine you thus after I learned the truth. But," he paused, "I find it rather suits you, Princess."

"Thank you, Kinley." I leaned over and placed another quick kiss on his cheek.

"The King could have entrusted your care to no better knight." Kinley looked up. "Julien de Gladiel! I've missed you, friend." My brother stepped forward and clapped Julien on the shoulder. "Thank you for watching over Ro—Rynnaia, I mean—these past months. She tends to invite risk, that one."

He shot me a lopsided grin before turning back to Julien. "It was a comfort to know my sister was safe in your care."

"It's good to see you, too, Kinley." The nature of Julien's grin was so genuine that the Veetrish part of my heart, the corner that prized family, hearth, and home above all else, warmed to know that my brother already considered Julien a friend.

Julien turned to me. "Perhaps you would like to be shown to your chambers to ready for your meeting with your father?"

"I'll take you," Erielle spoke up.

When I glanced her way, her eyes sparkled as if she'd just played an immense prank on someone. Or that she was *about* to. I hesitated.

"Come on, Princess." She grabbed my hand. "This way."

"You'll still be here, Kinley?" I asked, unable to hide the quiver in my voice. Until that moment I hadn't admitted to myself how intimidated I had felt on the road up to Holiday Palace. Having my brother near made it a little less so. "You'll still be here after I've met my father?"

He nodded. "I am ever at your service, Princess Rynnaia." He winked. "And your father's, of course."

"Good." With a last grin in his direction, I let Erielle pull me toward the wide marble staircase.

After passing through a seemingly endless stream of wide corridors which were lined in the green-veined marble that was the hallmark of Holiday Palace, Erielle finally stopped at a set of guarded double doors. She introduced me to the knight at guard and I went through the whole sword-taking ceremony again. Finally, he opened the door.

A series of tall but narrow arching windows graced the far wall, and rich beige curtains with a golden sheen hung at intervals between them. The walls were a deep pinkish color and the upholstery matched the curtains. The room contained a large white-stone fireplace and enough seating for several guests. I wandered past several interior doors, only one of which held a bed. But it was a massive, canopied structure the likes of which I had never imagined.

When I turned to Erielle, the wonder of it must have shown on my face. I had expected to be led to a bedchamber. But Erielle had taken me to an entire suite of rooms.

"This is all . . . mine?"

"All yours," she confirmed with a nod, but then her shoulders shuddered. A little laugh escaped her and she brought her hand to her mouth.

"What's so funny?" I asked. "Other than the shock that must be written all over my face?"

"That's not it at all," she said. And then a real laugh broke through. "Not at all."

She walked over to an enormous upholstered chair and plopped ungracefully into it, throwing her legs over one of the chair's arms.

"Well?" I moved toward her, abandoning one curiosity for another. "What's so funny, then?"

"First, I have to ask you something. Woman-to-woman."

Woman-to-woman? I was nineteen, but Erielle was more than two years younger. Even though the rest of the world would likely call us such, I wasn't sure either of us qualified for that sort of label. I waved my hand. "Well? Get on with it, then!"

"Have you and Julien come to an understanding?" She interrupted herself with a laugh. "Oh, Rynnaia. In all my life, I've never seen Julien so—" She had to stop speaking because a laugh built from her abdomen and slowly took over her body. Her shoulders shook with it. Finally she took a breath. "So raptly attentive to," she gasped out a giggle, "a young lady."

Her laughter was the sort that was infectious, and even though I didn't know why I was joining her in it, I couldn't help myself.

"What do you mean?" I asked between breaths.

In a flash of movement she righted herself in the chair. "Oh, it was glorious! He could barely take his eyes off you!" Erielle paused and cocked her head. "But may I be so bold as to ask . . . how do you feel about my brother, Princess?"

I let out a heavy breath and fell into a neighboring chair in much the same fashion as Erielle had moments earlier. Heaving a sigh, I leaned my head back and looked up at the ceiling. Could I say the words aloud?

"I love him."

With a squeal, Erielle jumped from her chair and proceeded to pull me from mine. "I knew it! I knew you were meant for each other! Are you to be my sister, then?"

"Whoa, now, Squire de Bruin." I called her by the male alias she had assumed on our ride from Mynissbyr to Port Dyn. "Julien hasn't even spoken to my father yet! We haven't even courted!"

"Oh!" Erielle's hand flew to her mouth. "Your father! He's waiting for you, remember?"

"Did my clothes arrive? I'd like to freshen up a bit."

"Yes. They've been pressed and are already hanging in your dressing room. It's just through here. Come on."

I followed Erielle through the beautiful bedchamber, past the giant bed, and into a dressing room that was as big as the bedchamber I had occupied on Tirandov Isle.

I had given quite a bit of thought to what gown I wanted to wear when I first met my father, and although I had many beautiful choices, when I ran a hand through them, it still seemed the best. I pulled it down.

"Oooh. That's lovely," Erielle breathed as she reached out to touch the luxurious folds of bronze. "I've never seen such fabric!"

"It's from Tirandov. Would you help me with the buttons?"

With Erielle's help I quickly changed and decided, upon her request, to let my hair flow freely down my back. A familiar box sat on the vanity table. Inside was a silver circlet, fashioned to resemble vining roses. I gingerly lifted out the crown that had once been my mother's and placed it on my head. The flowering vines met on my forehead at a gleaming piece of tirandite stone, which was carved in the diamond-in-a-circle design known as the Emblem of the First. When it touched my forehead, the tirandite stone glowed orange for a moment before settling back down to a slighter glow.

"You really are the princess."

"Yes." I winked at her. "But I'm sure Rozen will have to visit every now and then just to keep things interesting." She laughed at the mention of the name I had taken when posing as Julien's young Veetrish squire on our journey to Port Dyn.

I checked my reflection one last time. "How do I look?"

"Perfect. Come along, Your Highness. We've kept the King waiting long enough, and I need to stay in his good graces—at least until we leave to find the Remedy!"

"Do you often fall out of them? His good graces, I mean?"

"Not that he's mentioned, but . . ." Erielle thought about it. "My father and brothers often chide me for being too free with my speech around the King. And with my actions as well, to be honest. But your father doesn't seem to mind. He's always been rather indulgent of me." She tilted her head. "Perhaps because he missed you so much?"

I swallowed the sour taste of jealousy that formed at the mention of their closeness. "Perhaps."

"But he won't have to miss you anymore. Come along then, Princess! We can't keep His Majesty waiting!"

I followed Erielle back out into the corridor. Once outside my new suite of rooms, she led me only a bit farther down the hall to another guarded door. We repeated the fealty ceremony, and even though I was indeed grateful for the sacrifice and service each of these men made for the Kingdom, I couldn't help but wonder if there was some way I could gather them all together and get all the formalities out of the way at once.

Once I had given the knight back his sword, the guard bowed to me and knocked lightly on the door. A second later the word "Enter" came from within.

The guard pushed the door open and stood just inside.

Erielle smiled and patted my arm. "Don't worry," she whispered. "King Jarryn is my father's best friend. I've known him my whole life. You will like him. I know it." She gave me a small curtsey and then turned and walked back down the long corridor.

"Your Majesty," the guard spoke in a formal tone. "Princess Rynnaia is here to see you."

As he stepped aside, my breath caught. This was it.

S E V E N

$\mathcal{T}$he King rose the moment I crossed the threshold and the guard slipped back into the hall.

My father's dark brown hair took on a russet glow where the light hit it, especially near the gold circlet that rested across his forehead, and a few silver hairs peeked out at his temples and dusted the triangular beard that surrounded his mouth.

He wore a long moss-green tunic over a linen shirt and fawn breeches. Brown boots reached to just below his knees. His attire was of simple design, but richly tailored, and he stood straight. Tall. His tunic was belted with a scabbard the same brown as his boots and his right hand rested on the golden hilt of his sword, not out of threat, but from habit. Comfort. Despite everything about his authoritative presence, the warm expression in his eyes—almost as deep a blue as mine—bade me approach.

We stood like that for an elongated moment. But just as I stepped toward him, he moved out from behind the desk and closed the space between us. His arms encircled me.

"Rynnaia."

His tone was caught somewhere between a whisper and a groan. It overflowed with emotion that now poured out of his mind and into my heart.

"My daughter," he whispered. "My daughter!" He crushed me against his chest and I opened my mind wide to allow him to see what I could not put into words.

A rush of color hit me with a force so strong it felt as if my feet had left the floor. He must have felt it, too, because he released me and looked down into my face.

"I love you." His voice was tender, but fierce, slamming the words into my heart, and his cheeks were as wet as mine. "I love you, Rynnaia. Never doubt my love. Never."

For years I had thought of myself as abandoned and betrayed by a man whose name I wasn't even allowed to know. But his love cradled me now. Surrounding and carrying me, my father's love gave me the strength to stand before him, confident that it had always been this strong, this full, and that it always would be.

"I love you, too, Father." The words were simple, but they held a deep truth I had only recently uncovered. My heart had made room for him, expanding to hold what he so freely offered. Indeed, what he had always given, but unknown to me and from a distance.

"So often I feared you would hate me for sending you away. And when I found out what that woman in Veetri had done to you, what she had led you to believe . . ." He took a shuddering breath. "I was often tempted to reach past the protections we put on your abilities and check in on you. But the guards on your mind were stronger than my abilities could conquer."

"You tried?"

His smile was a tad sheepish. "More than once, I'm afraid. It never worked. Dyfnel and your mother worked with me to create that protection, you see, and their abilities far surpass my own. My efforts only produced frustration and exhaustion." He smiled. "But it is just as well. Had I accidentally revealed myself to you that way, it might have put you in greater danger than even that woman could conjure."

"Mrs. Scyles was cruel, but she was ignorant and prejudiced by her own misfortune." Lord Whittier's housekeeper had never liked me. When she discovered I colored my hair black with ebonswarth root powder, an illegal substance, she used that knowledge to threaten me. "Over the past several weeks I've come to believe that even her betrayal was for my good. Had she not betrayed me to the Cobelds, I might very well still be in Veetri, completely unaware of who I am. And the Remedy would be even farther from our grasp."

"Your mother told me you had been changed. I see that she is right."

"How often do you speak to her?"

"As often as possible." His smile warmed my heart. "Until recently, we spoke every day." He didn't have to tell me that my mother's deteriorating health made that impossible now. "But I haven't been to Tirandov Isle in three years."

"Why not?"

"It was roughly four years ago that the Dwonsil clans allied with the Cobelds. Since then, the Kingdom has required my presence here on the mainland."

"I'm sorry the blessing she gave me was so costly." And truly I was. Even the mention of my mother brought a light to my father's eyes.

"Her sacrifice was willingly made, as was mine." He smiled. "It's not the way I would have chosen to spend the last nineteen years of our marriage, but it's enough to know that she is still with me and that we still have hope."

He motioned me to a seat. When I had finished adjusting my skirts, I raised my eyes to the King sitting across from me.

"You remind me so much of your mother," he said with a sigh. "But you are a remarkable young woman in your own right. You've even impressed your great-grandfather. And believe me, that is not an easy task." He chuckled. "Lindsor has spoken with me daily since he arrived at Tirandov. You've made quite a favorable impression on him."

I smiled at the thought of my great-grandfather. "I'm quite fond of him, as well. It was at his urging that I finally overcame my fear and contacted you."

My father's smile dimmed. "You were . . . afraid of me?"

I hesitated, wanting to choose my words carefully. "I didn't grow up in a palace. Away from royalty, a common person gets something of an idea of a . . . a stern perfection of sorts when you think of the King. I wasn't afraid of my father—well . . . maybe a little," I admitted with a smile. "But I was most certainly afraid of being a disappointment to the King."

His eyes filled with compassion. "And now?"

"The first time we spoke, while I was on Tirandov Isle, something shifted. I felt . . . connected to you. Were we not Andoven, the truth of your feelings, of why you sent me away, would be harder to reconcile with what we've been through. But being able to see into your mind, into your motives, and into your heart . . . ?" I shrugged. "I saw love. And I knew it was real. Now I don't care that you're the King. I'm simply glad to know my father."

A bit of Veetri stirred inside me, aching to be set free. "Besides," I added with the cheekiest grin I could muster, "by the look of my rooms it would appear that there are some benefits to being a princess, even if I am getting a rather late start at it."

The King's chuckle began like a deep rumble, but it glimmered somehow as it made its way to the surface. The sound was like fresh, dark honey drizzled in a warm cup of wine.

"I regret every moment we've been apart, Rynnaia." His voice grew suddenly wistful. "And never have I felt it as poignantly as now. I must admit, it is difficult to know how to be a father to a grown woman without having seen to your upbringing myself." A smile broke through. "I am glad you look so much like your mother," he said. "Otherwise the people might not as easily accept that their Ryn speaks with a Veetrish brogue when her parents do not."

I bit my lip. "I'm sorry. I'll try harder to sound . . . correct."

"No, no. That's not what I meant at all. Your accent is charming. And it comes as no surprise to me. I placed you in that particular home, Rynnaia. Even though they didn't know it at the time, and even though I used Drinius as an intermediary, Lord Whittier's family was chosen for you specifically by me."

"Thank you." I didn't know what else to say. Lord and Lady Whittier, Kinley, Lewys, and Rowlen were so very dear to me. I couldn't imagine a childhood apart from their influence.

"Drinius and Gladiel stored up information to feed their anxious King, piecemeal, when the years grew long. Their tales of you were a great comfort. Sir Gladiel especially seemed to delight in your accent. He told me once that it was stronger or weaker depending upon your mood."

A flush crept into my cheeks. "He wouldn't be the only person who's said so."

He nodded. "But regardless of how many years passed, Drinius and Gladiel spoke of you in the terms of a little girl. A child. When Kinley came, I was forced to admit that you were growing up. Kinley didn't see you as a little girl. He described a lovely and spirited young woman who could definitely hold her own. Everyone who knew you as 'Rose' has loved you." He sighed. "I will admit that I was jealous of their affection. And, if your mother is to be believed, another man may soon rile a different sort of that emotion in me."

"Julien." His name was out before I had the sense to seal my lips. A hot flush crept up my neck and my eyes found a particularly interesting spot in the upholstery on which to dwell.

"Ah, so it is true," my father said, smiling. "Not that I doubted. Your mother is most perceptive of such things."

There was a moment of pure silence and then that dark-honey laugh erupted from my father's lips. I looked up.

"Julien de Gladiel." My father's tone held a pleased sort of amusement with which his smile did not argue.

He leaned back in his chair, tented his fingers, and then pressed them flat and rubbed his palms back and forth. His smile grew pensive. "Rynnaia, it appears as if I may soon be called upon to perform a father's worst duty." He sighed. "I can't say that your mother didn't warn me, because she was very clear it would be forthcoming. I just didn't expect it so soon."

"Didn't expect *what* so soon?" I stopped short of comparing his cryptic leanings to Cazien's. "What is a father's worst duty?"

"Oh, Rynnaia, surely you know. A father's worst duty is allowing some young man to court his daughter."

Heat burned my ears. I was glad my hair kept them hidden lest they light the chamber with the force of my embarrassment.

"I've no objection to Julien," my father said, but then tilted his head. "But what of your feelings, Rynnaia? Would you welcome his suit?"

I swallowed, but found no moisture in my mouth with which to form a reply, so I just nodded my head in the affirmative.

"Courtship is not necessarily the same thing as betrothal," he said, "but the sealing of that bond is its general aim." His voice grew solemn. "The E'veri family always marries for love."

His statement held an unspoken question. A question for which he expected an answer.

I squirmed in my seat and bit my lip. Moments ago I had admitted the same to Erielle, but it was a bit more difficult to say those words to the King. Finally, I nodded. "I love him."

His smile bloomed. "I could not have chosen better for you if I had arranged the match myself. Which, of course," he added with a wink, "I wouldn't. Julien has been a balm to my soul. He's like a son who has grown into a friend. He's an exceptionally gifted knight. And wise beyond his years."

I nodded. "His council and friendship have been invaluable to me."

"Julien would make a fine King someday, should your courtship progress to that point. He would be an excellent choice to rule alongside you."

Were we really talking about this? Already? How had the issue of my father's jealousy toward those who had known my childhood turned into a discussion of marriage and ruling and—

A moment of uncertainty fluttered through my chest.

"What's wrong, Rynnaia?"

"I'm not sure if it is still his intention to ask your permission to court me," I said. "We haven't spoken of it for a while. It's possible he's changed his mind. Or perhaps," I paused to chuckle, but the sound was drier than I intended, "he prefers to wait to declare his intentions until we see if I make it out of Mount Shireya alive."

"Do not even jest about that. Please."

"I wasn't jesting." I said honestly. "Maybe he fears getting too close and then . . . you know."

"That doesn't sound like Julien."

"Still." I met his eyes. "He may have changed his mind. Perhaps you won't be called upon to perform that duty after all."

The King leaned back into his chair. "Perhaps," he said slowly. "Just the same, I'm glad to have ascertained your feelings. It will make it easier for me, should the question arise."

Of all the subjects that could have come up in my first face-to-face meeting with my father, romance and courtship—and marriage!—had not even entered my imaginings as a possibility. I trawled my mind for a way to change the subject to more neutral ground.

"Have you been told the contents of the scrolls?"

"Not entirely. The Andoven gave me a rough outline of sorts, but now that the scrolls are here, I intend to study them at length."

"Have you decided who will accompany me?"

"Are you so anxious to be away from your poor father?"

"No!" It was then I noticed the amusement in his eyes. "It's not that. But . . . mother is depending on me."

"As are many other loyal E'verians." He leaned forward, and in that instant, transformed from father to King. "Our situation is precarious. We have a plan in place to try to draw the Cobelds and Dwonsil warriors away from Shireya, but it isn't without its risks. If even a rumor that I've sent you—or anyone, for that matter—to Mount Shireya were to surface, the Cobelds would abandon whatever course they may be on elsewhere and retreat to defend their home. I've found that rumors are all too common these days and difficult to put down, even when false. I think the plan is coming together, but without my top advisors . . . ?" The faces of Sir Gladiel and Uncle Drinius flitted across his mind. "I fear I'll miss an important detail."

My heart tugged at the affection and worry he held for the two knights, now imprisoned among enemies in Dwons. Gladiel and Drinius were not only the King's top advisors, but his closest friends. He had entrusted them with my safety for most of my life. They were dear to me, as well.

Married to my mother's adopted sister, Uncle Drinius had, in many ways, served as a father figure to me when I did not know the identity of my own. Gladiel also held a special place in my heart. Not only for the friendship and service he had provided me and my family, but because he was Julien's father. I was nearly as anxious as my father for their safe return.

"Have you sent anyone to recover Gladiel and Drinius yet?"

"As of yet, I have not." He sighed. "But plans are being made. With the Dwonsil warriors' new way of using the Cobelds' beards, everything is more complex. Even if we should take the fortress, it is unlikely we would be able to unlock the cells since they are cursed."

I had accidentally discovered the missing knights' location while learning to use my Andoven gifts. I had also detected a cursed hair from a Cobeld's beard that night. It was woven into the lock of the cell where Drinius and Gladiel were held. The knights themselves had confirmed its presence—its threat. To touch it, to touch even the metal it was wound about, could mean instantaneous death.

"Could an Andoven do it?"

"The Andoven are just as susceptible to the Cobeld curse as anyone else," he said. "Not to mention there are few Andoven who would be willing to travel the difficult road to where the knights are held."

I nodded. "But what if they were able to open the lock without touching it?" An idea began to form in my mind. "What if they could open it with their minds?"

"I've never heard of that being an Andoven ability, Rynnaia."

"It is. My great-grandfather can do it," I said. "And so can I."

He blinked. "You can?"

I nodded.

"Another benefit of your mother's blessing, I presume?"

Again, I nodded. When I was born, before the guard had been put on my abilities that rendered me unable to access them until I was told my real name, my mother had spoken a powerful blessing over me. She had petitioned Rynloeft on my behalf and said, "Rynnaia, I give you all that I am." What she didn't know at the time was that her blessing would encompass not only all of her abilities, but the Andoven gifts of many generations before her. As most Andoven, like my mother, are without natural siblings, mine was a vastly undivided inheritance. Thus, the explanation for my unusual combination of abilities, as well as the increased strength of those I'd directly inherited from her. Unfortunately, the moment I learned my identity and the blessing had been delivered, it began to drain her very life.

My father pursed his lips, considering that new bit of information, and then shook his head. "It's bad enough that I must send you after the Remedy. I will not let you try to rescue my knights as well. We will find another way."

"But what if I could do it without going there?" A thrill of hope shot through my chest. "I think I could do it, even from here. Lindsor taught me." I paused. "Well, sort of."

The King arched an eyebrow. "Sort of?"

"It's a long story." A story that involved a near-kiss and a misunderstanding with Julien. I sighed. If I told him, I feared it would bring us back to the embarrassing subject of romance and I preferred to steer away from that. "What matters," I said instead, "is that unlocking a door is a very easy thing for me to do."

"No. You've enough to face. I'll find someone else."

"But they were caught on the way back to the Bear's Rest! They are imprisoned because of me!"

"They are imprisoned because they have sworn an oath of loyalty to me." He didn't raise his voice, but his tone said, "*I am the King. Do not argue with me.*"

I lifted my chin. "I have a duty to them as well, don't forget. Not only as repayment for their service, but as the Ryn."

A muscle moved in his jaw. Clearly, he was unaccustomed to having his judgment questioned.

"*They* have vowed to protect *you*, Rynnaia, not the other way around. Both would gladly die in that cell if it ensured your safety. Your duty is to E'veria. And to me. As King."

He still had not raised his voice, but the range of color in his emotion showed I was treading on dangerous ground.

But I was right. I *knew* I could do it.

I arose from my seat and paced a few steps before turning back to face him. "Would you rather lose a hundred knights trying to open a cursed door than allow me the chance to do what I can to save our friends?"

"*Yes!*"

I jumped a bit as he came out of his chair and finally gave in to the desire for volume, but I didn't back down. I kept my eyes locked with his, using my mind to convey what my tongue was too angry not to trip over.

You are being unreasonable!

I am being your father! He stood inches from me. A wiser person might have been intimidated, but I refused to flinch.

They need me!

E'VERIA—NEEDS—HER—RYN!

My mind vibrated with the power of his message, but I did not give in. We continued to argue, shouting silently until a knock on the door interrupted us.

Our voices were laced with hostility as we both shouted, "ENTER!"

The double doors swung open with such ferocity that they slammed into the walls behind them and sent several framed pieces of art to the floor.

My father's arm shot out and pushed me behind him at the same moment his sword left its scabbard.

"Julien?" The King's voice was breathless, angry, and . . . puzzled. "What in the name of all the—"

"Sorry," I mumbled and let out a hot breath. I had not meant to open the door so viciously, but my emotion had taken the command from my mind and had given it a few extra— well several extra—measures of force.

My father turned. *"You* did that?"

I nodded, unable to meet his eyes. Shame flushed through my center over letting my anger take so much control, but part of me still seethed from our argument.

"My apologies for interrupting," Julien began. "I could come back later if it would be more convenient."

"Don't bother," I snapped. "It would seem you have impeccable timing."

The left side of Julien's mouth quirked upward. He arched an eyebrow.

Oh! He hadn't been speaking to me. I sucked in a little breath. Without thinking, my temper had led me to usurp the authority of the King.

"Father, I'm sorry."

He gave a little nod, followed by a sad sort of smile that humbled me to my core.

"Your Majesty," Julien's voice had the smallest hint of laughter beneath its respectful tone. "My apologies. If you'd like me to come back later . . . ?"

"Come in, Julien," the King sighed. "My daughter and I were just, ah, discussing different strategies for retrieving your father and Drinius."

"I see." Julien shut the doors behind him. "No doubt Princess Rynnaia would like to go and rescue them herself."

A tiny sound caught somewhere between betrayal and surprise escaped my lips. I crossed my arms and glared at him.

My father resumed his seat, looking tired. "It appears you know my daughter much better than I."

Shame at my outburst—no, my *repeated* outbursts—rushed through my blood. My arms fell to my sides and I looked at the floor.

"Let's just say this isn't the first time she has slammed a door that I had hoped to use in a bit gentler fashion."

There was an amused sparkle in Julien's tone and I lifted my eyes, but he wasn't looking at me.

"But," he continued, "at least she slammed it open this time instead of locking it shut." He turned, and when he had the audacity to wink at me I re-crossed my arms and resumed my glare.

Julien chuckled and then proceeded to ignore me. Striding across the room as if he owned it, he took the chair I had occupied just moments ago.

The nerve! Everything about his demeanor made it clear he was completely at ease in the King's presence.

A stab of jealously surprised me. *That is how I would behave if I'd known my father all my life.* The shame returned.

Instead of affecting a confident ease with the King, I had acted like a spoiled child, determined to have her way.

I took a deep breath. "I'm sorry, Father. I was disrespect-
ful and stubborn. Please forgive me."

He pushed back his chair. In another instant he was beside me. My father lifted my chin with his fingers. His eyes
were almost as moist as mine. "I will always forgive you,
Rynnaia. Can you forgive me for being a King unused to others questioning him?"

"Yes, of course." I blinked my tears away. My heart was
heavy, but not in a bad way. It was simply full. And, just as I
had so often recovered from a spat with one of my brothers
in Veetri, a sudden rush of merriment forced its way from my
mouth. "Besides, I like my rooms too much to give them up!"

My father's eyes widened just long enough to realize I
was joking, and then he tipped back his head and laughed.
Encircling my shoulders with his arm, he led me to a settee
and sat down beside me.

I relished the feeling of his arm around me. As Julien gave
the King his report about all that had transpired since he had
been sent to the Bear's Rest to find me, I leaned into my father's side and closed my eyes. The rich colors of love and
forgiveness surrounded me and I relaxed into their warmth,
ignoring the conversation and simply reveling in the wonder
of knowing my father's affection at last.

$\mathcal{E}$ IGHT

"$\mathcal{W}$ould you be willing to try that, Rynnaia?"
My father's voice grabbed me out of a half-doze. I straightened, hoping I hadn't drooled on the King's tunic. "I-I'm sorry. I wasn't paying attention."

"I was just telling your father about some of the more unusual abilities you discovered while we were on Tirandov Isle."

"Oh." If Julien had gone into any detail about when I had locked him in the library, I was glad I'd missed it.

"You mentioned that you might be able to unlock Gladiel and Drinius's cell without touching it," my father said. "Could you do it from a distance?"

"I think so. Lindsor said my desire to communicate with a person or object was more important than distance." I nodded. "Let me show you."

I closed my eyes and sent my thoughts toward my father's door. In a breath, my mind traveled inside the keyhole and tripped the locking mechanism.

I opened my eyes. "Julien, would you mind trying the door?"

He walked over and tried to open it. He shook his head and grinned. "It's locked."

I closed my eyes for a moment. "And again?"

He turned the knob and it opened. He closed it again and returned to his seat.

"You know as well as I that distance won't restrict Andoven communication. Do you believe I can do it?"

"It would certainly seem so," he said, but I could tell from the colors swirling about my father's thoughts that, while he was pleased with what I could do, he was not entirely convinced it was without risk.

"We know too little of the Cobelds," he continued. "It's possible they will know if their curse has been tampered with. The timing of such a venture would be crucial to its success."

"We'll need to distract them," Julien said. "And lead them away from the fortress."

My father nodded. "I will meet with the Knights' Council. Once a strategy is in place I will dispatch a few regiments to Dwons. Perhaps if they engage the enemy it will give the prisoners time to escape after Rynnaia unlocks the cells."

"But it will take a long time for the regiments to reach the fortress," I said. "Won't I be leaving for the Remedy before then?"

"Yes. It will be tricky. We will have to find a way to alert you when they are in position."

"Why can't *you* tell me?"

"I'll be on the road to Salderyn. The fortress where the knights are being held is over two hundred leagues in the opposite direction."

"Why should that matter? You're Andoven. Won't you be contacting the knights along the way?"

"I am *part* Andoven, Rynnaia, but I'm not like you and your mother," he said with a tender smile. "And while distance does not hinder my ability to communicate with those of Andoven lineage, it is beyond my gifting to find the mind of anyone who is not."

My abilities were so new to me that I often forgot that gifts differed among the Andoven themselves and even faded, generationally, when a line was "diluted," as the Elders phrased it, by marriage to someone of non-Andoven lineage.

"I can contact anyone, if I know who I am looking for," I said. "But how will I know when?"

"You will be rather consumed with your own responsibilities," my father said. "It would be easier if they contacted you. But who among them could?"

"Are there no Andoven knights enlisted in the regiments, then?" Even as the question left my lips I recalled how most of the people of Tirandov Isle opposed their people being involved in military matters. My father shook his head. "Of course. I forgot. But even if a member of one of the regiments was only *partly* Andoven it could be accomplished. Is there a knight who can fulfill that position?"

"Not a knight," my father said, absently rubbing his beard. "But there is someone, I believe, who might be willing to serve in that capacity."

Considering we were discussing the rescue of his father, Julien's grin caught my attention as strange. I tilted my head. "What are you smiling so smugly about?"

"This," he said, his grin widening. "This is good."

"What is?"

"This." He made an outward circle with his palm that I assumed was supposed to encompass my father and me. "The King and the Ryn, discussing war strategy." He laughed. "It's so . . . *right*."

I shared a grin with my father. It *did* feel right. I turned back to Julien. As I met his gaze, a familiar flash of bright emerald and burnished gold caressed my mind. The warmth of his smile filled me to the tips of my toes.

My father cleared his throat.

Hmm. I was going to have to work a bit harder at blocking my thoughts from the King.

"Rynnaia, I believe Sir Julien and I have a matter of some import to discuss," he said, sounding strangely formal all of a sudden. "Would you excuse us? I don't imagine we'll be long."

I stood and Julien did as well. My father remained seated, which, I supposed, was his right as King.

"Dinner will be served shortly in the dining hall," he said, just as I reached the door. "I'll come to collect you when we're finished here."

"Of course." I gave him a curtsey, and not sure whether I should or not, favored Julien with one as well. My father returned the gesture with a simple nod of his head, but Julien, who had stood up when I did, dipped into a full bow. As he arose, his slow wink caused my cheeks to flush in a way that confirmed the topic they would be discussing.

It appeared as if King Jarryn was about to perform a father's worst duty.

$\mathcal{N}$ I N E

$\mathcal{T}$rying to affect the air of a princess, I asked a guard to summon Erielle to my chambers. A few minutes later, she arrived.

I stood at the fire, using every bit of self-control I possessed to avoid sneaking into Julien's thoughts as he and my father spoke.

"Did you want to change into something else for dinner?" Erielle sounded confused.

"No. I need to ask you something," I paused. "Woman-to-woman."

A smile pulled the left side of her mouth upward. "Of course, Your Highness. Ask away."

I paced back and forth a few times, not sure how to begin. Finally, I moved to a chair. She took the opposite one.

"I need to know about courting," I said. "At court. What's it like?"

"And you're asking because . . . ?"

"Because I think my father and Julien might be discussing it right now!" I bit my lip to stop the little squeal that threatened to escape.

Erielle's eyes danced. "My brother has never been one to waste time." She laughed. "What do you want to know?"

"Everything. You've spent time at court. What's expected of me?"

"Ahh. That's easy," she said with a sly smile. "Any young woman being courted should expect to be treated like a princess." She laughed at the irony and so did I. "Of course, what I mean is, when a knight courts a young lady she should expect extreme felicitousness."

"But Julien is courteous by nature."

"Oh, but courtesy is different in courtship. It's much more involved. But . . . how to explain? Hmm." Erielle leaned forward and rested her chin on the balls of her hands. She thrummed her fingers against her cheekbones. "Most courting begins after a knight and a young lady have only just met," she said. "Since you've already known Julien for some time it will be different for you, I suppose. But I imagine many things will be the same."

"Such as?"

"Oh, I don't know. Strolls in gardens. Partnering at balls. The recitation of poetry in public . . ." She doubled over dramatically and made a retching sound. "And may Rynloeft help you," she said, straightening and putting a hand to her chest, "should Julien deign to sing a ballad. No one should have to suffer that."

I laughed. "But what of the young lady being courted? What is expected of her?"

Erielle shrugged. "From what I've seen, the young lady generally does a lot of needlework and fanning. A few have been known to compose their own bit of verse, but those are generally kept private between her and the knight, thank Rynloeft. And if, after a good bit of that nonsense, the lady and knight still seem disposed to one another, the negotiations begin."

"Negotiations?"

"Betrothal issues. Political posturing, land changing hands, dowries, that sort of thing."

Suddenly, courtship didn't sound all that appealing. But being the Crown Princess should exert at least some influence, shouldn't it? "Does anyone ever, you know, skip over the nonsense bits?"

"I suppose. But I doubt you'll be allowed that, in the public eye as you are. Or as you soon will be, rather. Courtship can be entertaining to watch from the outside. But a royal courtship?" She let out a long whistle. "After a while, I can only imagine that it would become ridiculously tiresome for the two people involved. I don't envy you your courtship, even though I know my brother will do his best to keep it a dignified affair. In fact, I hope to avoid it for myself altogether."

I tilted my head. "You don't wish to fall in love someday?"

"Of course I do! But not until I've had my fill of adventure. And certainly not by such absurd means as *courtship*." Erielle stopped, her eyes widening. "There I go again, being too free of speech with the royals. I meant no offense."

"None taken."

I sensed my father's approach before he knocked on my door. Now that we had finally met in person, our Andoven connection was undeniable, as was something else, something entirely . . . *E'veri*. I could only assume it was something linked to me being the Ryn, a title he had once possessed, but its strength was greater than any connection I'd yet experienced, even with my mother.

Other than a greeting and a smile, we didn't speak as I took his arm and allowed him to lead me through unfamiliar corridors. Before today, I had only visited Holiday Palace once, as Julien's guest at a ball given here by the Regent of Dynwatre. I had worn a black hairpiece and a set of gray-tinted spectacles that night and had been introduced as "Rose de Whittier." Tonight, however, I would be entering the dining hall as the Ryn.

We paused at the door for the herald to announce our presence.

"I rarely feel the need to engage this particular service of my heralds," my father whispered, leaning down to my ear. "Your mother broke me of the habit years ago. Although I'd grown up having my every move within the palace announced and gave it little thought, she considered it quite pretentious and let me know in no uncertain terms that she would not stand for it." He chuckled. "But I felt that today warranted at least a little formality."

As the herald opened the doors, my father let go of my arm and took my hand instead, positioning my arm so that my elbow was bent and my hand was level with but slightly ahead of my shoulder, resting atop his. It was an odd posture that I couldn't imagine keeping up for long, but it felt unaccountably elegant and regal, just the same. When I closed my eyes and pictured what we might look like to an observer, I was sure it was.

The young herald tapped an ornate wooden staff against the marble floor just inside the dining hall.

"His Majesty, King Jarryn E'veri," the herald called out in a voice loud enough to make the flames in the fireplaces flicker.

I couldn't see into the room, but the sound of chairs scraping against the floor allowed me to assume that everyone—and it sounded like a *lot* of everyones—stood up at the mention of the King.

"And Her Royal Highness," the herald paused, "Princess Rynnaia E'veri."

My father gave my hand a light squeeze and moved into the dining hall where the mysterious "everyone's" eyes were on me.

The room was shaped like a severely elongated oval, just wide enough at the narrow ends to comfortably accommodate the long wooden table at its center and at least twenty-five chairs on either side. The widest points of the room each sported a marble fireplace that kept occupants comfortably warm. Murals, cracked with age, covered the walls and high ceilings with scenes of blossoming flowers and trees, seeming to pay homage to an eternal season of spring. It was quite beautiful, but not so much that it made one afraid to breathe.

My father led me to the far side of the room where two ornate chairs waited at the head of the table, and then to their right, where a smaller but similarly fashioned chair remained empty. Somehow I knew that two of these chairs, one at the head and mine to the side, had sat empty for a long time.

Nineteen years.

Seeing my thought, my father spoke into my mind. *Too long.*

I was glad that I knew enough to wait for the King to sit first. Once seated, he looked up at me and arched an eyebrow toward my chair.

Immediately, I sat. When I looked across the table, I met a familiar pair of emerald eyes. *Julien.* Having him near made me breathe a little easier.

As soon as everyone else had taken their seats, my father rose. In a slight panic, I looked to Julien, not knowing whether I should rise or stay in my seat.

As if he knew the answer I sought, he gave a slight shake of his head. I remained in my chair and looked toward my father to see what would happen next.

With his elbows at his waist, he reached his hands out in either direction, palms upward. When Julien gave a slight nod, I laid my hand upon my father's right. Julien did the same at his left. Everyone joined hands.

"Giver and Sustainer," my father's deep voice forced my attention back to his face, "our Mighty First King." With eyes closed and face tilted upward, he beseeched a blessing upon those gathered at the table. Taking a deep breath in through his nose, he exhaled, and with his breath, spoke one of the First King's names for which I had a particular fondness.

"*Embral e' Veria.*"

It was a combination of words in the Ancient Voice that, depending upon the translator, might paint a slightly different picture. But always, in essence, it was a name meaning *Unlimited Power governed by Unquenchable Love.*

The sound of that name, spoken by my father's voice, reminded me of a memory he had hidden inside my soul long ago, a memory of a visit I'd received from him when I was eight years old, but that I'd only recently been allowed to access.

My eyes burned with emotion, so I closed them, and as I tilted my face upward, I gave my father's hand a light squeeze, thankful for the tender memory and for the newly acquired knowledge that gave it such greater meaning.

"Our One True Hope." He finished the litany of names, though they all spoke of one divine person, The First. "You have blessed this King, your servant, by bringing my daughter home. You have provided for Rynnaia's safety these many years and you have seen fit to woo and welcome her under the banner of Rynloeft at long last. Thank you for these gifts that you shower upon your servants and our Kingdom in these desperate times. We thank you for your gracious provision at this table, both the food and the friends that partake of its bounty, and ask that you comfort those of our people who are not so blessed as we are tonight. May we honor you above all else as we seek to restore truth and peace in E'veria."

May it be so. The passion of my thought echoed around the table, but no one spoke it aloud. My father squeezed my hand.

I opened my eyes to find his upon me. My throat was tight with emotion, but I took a breath and finished his request for blessing with my agreement.

"May it be so." I was surprised by the confidence in my voice with my throat constricted so. I smiled as the words echoed around the table. My father let go of my hand, placed his on his heart for a moment, and then took his seat once more.

No sooner had he leaned back in his chair than the doors at both ends of the dining hall opened and a parade of servants came through carrying covered platters and pitchers. Beginning with the King, a pair of servants delivered a portion to each person's plate while another pair worked together to fill our goblets with a beverage scented with the essence of peaches. But it wasn't until the King had taken his first bite and declared it, "most excellent," and I, in turn, had sampled a bit of the roast duck, that the others at the table began to eat.

"Your Highness, it is indeed a great pleasure to finally meet you," the knight to my right spoke after a few minutes. "My name is Risson de Sair, and were we not at table, I would welcome the opportunity to pledge my sword and fealty to your service."

"Thank you, Sir Risson," I replied. He said we hadn't met, but he looked strangely familiar. "From which province do you hail?"

"Dynwatre, Your Highness. Born and raised in a little village just north of here. Canyn, by name, though it's little more than a wayside inn and a sword smith."

"Do you still have family there?"

"Indeed. A wife, three daughters nearly grown, and three sons, though only two are yet living. My eldest met up with a Cobeld when he was just a lad."

My breath caught. "I'm so sorry."

"Thank you." Risson's smile was sad. "He was a good lad. A helpful sort. He just offered help to the wrong old man."

A chill crept up my spine. How well I knew the ease at which a Cobeld could coerce aid with intent to kill. If not for Julien, my life would have ended alongside a stream in the Great Wood of Mynissbyr.

"My other boys grew up a bit more cautious," Risson continued. "One is squired to a knight in Nyrland and the other just completed his apprenticeship with the local sword smith, who as it so happens, is my very elderly father."

I sensed he would rather talk of the living. I couldn't blame him. "You didn't wish to follow your father's profession, then?"

"I'm the youngest of five sons by quite a lot." He chuckled. "With four brothers ahead of me and each of them married with sons of their own, my father's small forge grew much too crowded for my restless soul. I found wielding swords preferable to forging them."

"Risson makes Canyn sound of little account, but it really is a tidy little village," my father interjected. "And you'll never find a sword of better quality than one that's been forged by Sair House."

"I'll be sure to pass your compliments on to my father when next I see him, Your Majesty."

"Do." My father nodded and took a sip from his goblet.

The formality of our entrance seemed to wear off as discussion continued around the table. As I engaged others in conversation, I found that Risson's loss was not unusual. Nearly everyone had lost a family member or close friend to either the Cobelds or their allies, the Dwonsil warriors, at some point over the last few years.

Some still had loved ones suffering from curses that hadn't killed, but rather had maimed or inflicted illness. When they spoke of the future, it was with the assumption that I would find the Remedy. That their loved ones would heal. That they would live.

My chest tightened with each new loss—and even more with the responsibility of each fresh hope that had been kindled by the simple fact that I yet lived. The burden of the prophecy that bore my name, a burden that had been tempered for so long by excitement and optimism, grew heavier as the meal progressed.

My father spoke mainly to Julien, inviting Risson and the other knights nearest our end of the table to join in as he updated Julien on military matters.

"Father," I asked when there was a break in the conversation, "did I hear you mention Sir Kiggon?" I was acquainted with few souls outside the families by whom I'd been raised, but that name was familiar.

"Yes. Do you know him?"

"Indeed." I nodded. "He visited us at Mirthan Hall once. Do you know if Lewys de Whittier still serves with him?"

"I'm afraid I don't know. But I expect Kiggon to arrive in the next day or two, along with two companies from the Regent of Nyrland. Perhaps de Whittier will be among them."

Small talk continued around us for quite a while after the remnants of our meal had been removed and a small serving of stout pudding, dotted with dried fruit, delivered. Finally, even the pudding was cleared away and my father stood.

"Knights." With one word he grabbed the attention of everyone at the table. "Please attend me in the war room in one hour. We have much to discuss this night."

The knights at the table gave silent nods, but no one seemed in a hurry to leave the hall.

"Princess Rynnaia."

I hadn't even realized that Julien had risen from his chair until he stood beside mine. "Might I have the pleasure of your company for a stroll in the gardens?"

I swallowed. "A stroll, Sir Julien?"

Was he asking what I thought he was asking?

"The paths are well lit," he explained. "And the moon is full. But if you're too tired, I understand."

"No, I'm not tired, but—" I bit my lip and looked at my father.

A ghost of a smile played at the corners of his mouth and he appeared as if he were trying to look stern as he gave a nearly imperceptible nod.

I slipped my hand into Julien's and rose from my chair. "It would be my pleasure, Sir Julien."

He tucked my hand in the crook of his arm, gave a short bow to my father, and led me from the dining hall. As we crossed to the opposite doors by which I had entered, I was conscious of many eyes boring into my back and not a few sharply colored pings of male jealousy directed toward Julien—and a few more vivid, of the feminine variety, toward me. But amidst the varying spectrum swirling about, I was able to isolate one that was particularly sweet with laughter.

"Erielle . . ." I whispered, turning slightly back toward the room. I turned and the little imp gave me a slow, knowing wink.

"I'd rather hoped we could have the gardens to ourselves," Julien spoke in a low voice that none but I would hear. "But if you'd prefer to have my little sister accompany us, I will, of course, oblige."

"No, I just—" When I saw the sparkle in his eyes I knew he was joking.

A tingle traveled from the crook of my arm, where it entwined with his, and through the rest of me, settling with a jumpy sort of rhythm in my belly. We exited the dining hall, walked through another unfamiliar set of corridors, and finally ended up at the landing of a stairwell. When I looked to my right, I noted that it spilled out near the entrance by which I had arrived at Holiday Palace. To my left, it descended toward another wide corridor. It was in that direction we turned and kept walking for some time.

"Are the palace gardens in Salderyn, Julien?" I teased. "For I believe we shall be in the capital city shortly."

He chuckled. "We're almost there."

And indeed, as soon as we turned another corner we met a wall of glass doors and windows that sparkled with the glow of countless high-hung lamps beyond.

A man stepped out of the shadows as if he had been waiting there for the express purpose of opening the doors for us. Perhaps he had. A sea-born breeze touched my face with a tender chill that didn't linger as we crossed the marble terrace and continued down the wide-carved steps to the gardens below.

$\mathcal{T}$ E N

$\mathcal{A}$ low green hedge bordered the garden path, carrying the scent of lavender, but a sweeter variety than that with which I was familiar. In the way of statuary, there was very little, unlike the gardens on Tirandov Isle, where glowing Tirandite stone was used as both light and art, but some of the plants themselves were carved into shapes of animals, people, and creatures caught somewhere in between. The light of the moon gave an extra measure of visibility, but in truth, the plentiful lamps were more than enough to ease our way. We turned a gentle corner and a mixture of deeply sweet and slightly spicy rose perfumes caressed my nose.

"Ohhh."

Julien paused. "This is your mother's rose garden."

We had stopped directly in front of an arching arbor which was covered in tiny blooms. It was too dark to discern their exact color, but I imagined them to be somewhere between white and pink.

I inhaled the delicate perfume. "I could close my eyes and it would still be just as beautiful."

"To me, it appears as little more than bracken and thorn, when compared to you."

So this was courtship. I ducked my head. "You flatter me."

"Not a bit." With one finger he lifted my chin. "I assume you know that I asked your father's permission to court you."

I shook my head. "I didn't know for sure, but when he asked to speak to you privately, I wondered if it would come up."

"It was the oddest conversation," Julien smiled. "One moment we were discussing the weather. The weather of all things!" He laughed. "And the next he was asking what my intentions were toward his daughter. I'd not seen that side of him before."

"He's had no need to show it."

He nodded. "I suppose you're right. Princess Rynnaia?" The tiniest hint of doubt colored his words. I wrinkled my nose at the formal address. "Would you be agreeable to accepting my courtship?"

"Yes."

"Are you certain? I don't want you to feel obligated to accept my suit because of the time we've already spent together."

"I don't."

"You've not had the opportunities other young ladies have had to pick among suitors." He went on as if he hadn't heard me. "I saw many of the knights at table glancing your way. Pedar, Owen, Kile . . . they're all worthy knights, all men of whom your father would approve. Men who would be—"

"Julien, stop." I placed a finger on his lips. "I'm sure there are hundreds of good men in E'veria, but there is only one who could hold my heart the way you do. You have my heart, Julien. There's no one else for me."

If possible, the color of his eyes seemed to deepen to a green in which I could nearly drown.

I took a step back, crossed my arms at my chest, and gave him the smile few outside of Veetri had seen. "In fact, you've held my heart for quite some time, you thickheaded Bearman. So you'd best accept it and commence with the courting, lest my dagger find a new mark upon your arm."

"I never thought I'd court a Veetrish girl," he said. "Especially one with such violent leanings."

"And I never dreamed I'd desire the attention of a legendary brute," I parried. "Especially one with such detestable taste in horses."

I winced, wondering if Salvador could hear me from the stables, and if so, I hoped the giant gray horse would know I spoke in jest.

Julien, however he may have wondered about my desire to accept his courtship, had no doubts concerning my affection for his horse. A smile spread across his face and my own soon mirrored it. Any residual doubt melted away. The deeper our gazes connected, the tighter the coil with which our hearts wound round each other, and something familiar, yet not entirely discovered, simmered beneath the surface of my skin. It lingered just beyond my reach but was full of promise.

Julien reached for my hand and brought it to his lips.

Color exploded from my mind, down my arm, and through my fingers to his lips, a spinning whorl of green and gold and orange and blue. Julien's colors and mine, dancing to the tune of his touch.

"Oh, there you are, Julien." Kinley's voice stilled the orchestra in my mind. "I wondered where you'd—oh."

I froze, but didn't turn around.

"My apologies, Sir Julien," Kinley said. "It would seem I've come upon you at a most inopportune time, my friend."

I waited, expecting to hear his retreating footsteps. When no sound came, I turned around, feeling a little like a child caught with my finger in the pudding before it made it to table.

"*Rose?*" Kinley's smile fell. I didn't correct him. "Are you . . . ?" he began, but then thought better of it. "Does the King . . . ?"

"Yes," I nodded. "And yes."

His eyebrows lifted, and as they lowered the grin that took over his face was one I knew well.

I narrowed my eyes. Oh, yes, I knew that look and of what it was a portent. And I wasn't about to let my big brother spoil my introduction to the art of courtship. I turned the rest of the way around and put my hands on my hips. "I believe you were about to go, weren't you, Kinley?"

"*Was* I?"

He stood only a few feet away, grinning as if he hadn't anything better to do with his time than to make my skin catch on fire from embarrassment. Resting the elbow of his right arm in his left hand, he rubbed his thumb and forefinger over the beard encircling his mouth.

"Yes," Julien said. "You were."

"And yet," Kinley countered, "I can't quite bring myself to leave. I could have sworn I saw my best friend kissing my sister's hand! But I suppose I could've been mistaken."

Julien's voice was dry. "Your timing is rather rotten, de Whittier."

"My apologies."

"And yet," my suitor copied my brother's tone, "you don't really seem all that apologetic."

Kinley just grinned, and when I looked at Julien, he was grinning back at his friend.

"This has been fun, but I suppose we really should be going to the council soon," Kinley said finally. "While you two have been meandering the gardens, the hour has nearly passed."

A moment of panic seized me. "I don't know if I can find my chamber by myself."

"I'll escort you back there after the council," Julien said. "Or perhaps your father will. Don't worry."

"Where should I go until then?"

"You're the Ryn," Julien explained. "You'll be expected at the council."

Ah. Of course.

I am the Ryn.

ELEVEN

Too busy trying to identify landmarks that might help me navigate the immense palace on my own, I spoke little on the long walk to the war room. If they noticed my preoccupation, neither Julien nor Kinley mentioned it.

A sudden feeling of suffocation pressed down upon my chest and I paused mid-step. Apart from the hours spent in sleep, was a princess ever allowed to be alone?

Julien rested his free hand upon mine, which was in the crook of his arm. "Is something wrong?"

"No," I said. He nodded, but even though the look in his eyes was not convinced, he didn't press.

Eventually we came to the correct door. Made of dark wood, it bore a carving of two swords, crossed, and above them, as if nestled into the point at which the blades met, was the diamond-in-a-circle design known as the Emblem of the First. Above the Emblem appeared a series of words that, to one who couldn't translate the Ancient Voice, appeared to be nonsense.

"Wait."

Both Kinley and Julien paused. I stared at the words and they seemed to take on motion, though I knew the knights would see no change. Accessing another one of my Andoven gifts, the letters and symbols rearranged themselves until they became readable script.

"Every choice a battle," I read aloud. "Every battle a choice."

Julien nodded. "That is the creed of the King's Army. It reminds us to be wise, purposed, honest, and discerning."

"Indeed," I said. Kinley's hand was already on the door-knob. I nodded and he opened the door.

I recognized the War Room. Though I had never been here in person, the first time I'd successfully contacted my father from Tirandov Isle my mind had found him here.

The room was long with an extended oval table at its center. At the far end, where I would have expected a window, open wooden compartments were built into the wall, each housing collections of scrolls.

My father was the only person in the War Room when we entered. He stood at the end of the long table, bending over a scroll that was unrolled and weighted at each corner by a round black stone the size of my palm.

"Rynnaia." He looked up and smiled. "Did you enjoy the gardens?"

"Very much. I can hardly wait to see them in the daylight."

"Ah, I see you've brought a pair of my knights with you. The rest of the council should be arriving shortly. If you'd like, I can brief you on the strategy of which they're already aware."

I moved to join him. "I'm curious to know who you've picked to send with me to Mount Shireya."

He nodded, but looked troubled. "I wish it were all of them. But stealth will not allow it. I've asked Kinley to join you."

I shot a relieved glance at my "brother."

"Besides Kinley and Julien, I'm sending two additional knights. Gerrias de Gladiel and Risson de Sair."

Ah. Sir Risson, who had been seated next to me at dinner. He had a good ten to fifteen years on the other knights and I sensed a thoughtful patience about him that would likely temper the relative youth of the rest of us.

"Although Erielle is to serve as your companion, she is not without skill and will also provide a reasonable defense should the need arise." His sigh suggested he was still not convinced of the wisdom behind my request to include Julien's sixteen-year-old sister on our quest, but he did not voice his concerns. "And with Dyfnel and Edru rounding out your number, I expect you still might gain a little more notice than I'm comfortable with on your travels."

"We could split up for the first part of the journey," Kinley said. "Send half the team ahead into Shireya."

My father pursed his lips and nodded. "It would help. But I'm still concerned that Rynnaia should be guarded well enough. Especially since she will have been made known."

I tilted my head. "But that won't really be a danger beyond Port Dyn for a while, will it? Even the fastest horses couldn't spread the news through all nine provinces in the time it will take us to reach the mountain."

"Under normal circumstances, no. But I did not wish to seem to favor the southern provinces with the news and cause even more unrest. Therefore, before I left Castle Rynwyk I dispatched teams of messengers to all the Regents with instructions to decode and deliver their missives on the fifteenth day of this month," he said. "My letter charges the Regents with spreading the news throughout their individual provinces that the Ryn and the Queen live."

My heart beat a little faster. In only three days I would be known not only here and on Tirandov Isle, but throughout all

E'veria. To friend and foe alike. What would that mean? What would the people expect from me? How would they respond to finding out their King had lied to them for nearly twenty years?

I gave a slight shake of my head to ward off my fear that I might better attune to my father's voice.

"At the same time I dispatched those messengers, I invited various nobles from all nine provinces to a ball at Holiday Palace."

Did he say a *ball*? Surely not. Not *now*. I must have misheard him. "You invited the lower nobles to come here, but not the Regents?"

"In these dark days, I believe it unwise for the Regents to stray too far from their homes. For most of our provinces," he paused, and a sad smile rested on Julien, "the people need the sense of order a Regent's presence can bring."

"Ah." I nodded. Mynissbyr's Regent, Sir Gladiel, could not bring that to his people. But then again, Mynissbyr was sparsely populated and protected as much by its legends as by the Regent's men.

"In any case," my father continued, "the nobles were given express instructions to arrive at the palace no earlier than the morning of the sixteenth and told the ball would be held the following evening. It would appear those messages, at least, made it through. Many are already in Port Dyn."

I thought I had misunderstood him earlier, but there it was again. "A ball?" I made a face and almost laughed. "You would throw a ball . . . now?"

"Yes." He nodded. "Absolutely, yes. The Ryn is alive. The Queen is alive. A celebration of some kind is both politically and emotionally necessary for the health and well-being of the Kingdom." He paused. "Also, we need witnesses from noble families, people who have actually seen you, to take the truth of your survival back to their home provinces."

"I see." A ball made sense, I supposed, when he put it that way.

He wrapped an arm around my waist and pulled me to his side. "This ball will be a trifling event compared to what shall come, my dear girl. After you've returned from retrieving the Remedy and your mother's health has been restored, we will celebrate your official installment at Castle Rynwyk, a feast from which my personal coffers will not soon recover, so vast will the celebration be!"

"At the Academy they taught us that, traditionally, the Ryn is officially installed on the first day of a new season," Kinley said, his brow creasing as he traced a path from Holiday Palace to Mount Shireya and to Castle Rynwyk in the capital city of Salderyn.

"Traditionally," Julien said drily, "the Ryn is installed as an infant."

"True." Kinley nodded. "But the first day of summer is an ambitious timeline. Unless you are looking toward autumn, of course, Your Majesty."

"I am not."

I blinked, my eyes following the path Kinley's finger had just taken with disbelief. "So that means I have just two months and seven days to find the Remedy, ship it to Mother, defeat the Cobeld curse, and travel to Salderyn for my installation."

"If the installation has to be postponed, that is the least of my worries," he said. "But I've never yet set an ambitious timeline that has not been met. The important thing is that the enemy believes you are traveling with me to Salderyn rather than seeking the Remedy. If we can convince them of that, it might afford you the time necessary to make it to Mount Shireya undetected."

And then the real danger begins, I thought.

My father's head jerked. I winced. I closed my eyes and mentally reached for the strands of gray that would protect my father from seeing my darker thoughts.

"Would that it was anyone else going but you," he whispered fiercely.

The door opened then, but my father only tightened his tender grip on me.

I was intensely curious to observe my father leading his knights. But if I was totally honest with myself, I had to admit that I was curious to watch my father do anything at all. For so many years I had wondered about him. What he looked like, the sound of his voice, his name . . . now I knew all those things, but I'd only scratched the surface of who he really was. King, knight, husband, father—I wanted to see him move through every bit of his identity and know him better for it.

The knights filed in around the table but remained at ease. For some reason, the informality pleased me and I was able to add another name to my father's list: friend.

"Knights."

Sudden quiet fell as my father spoke.

"Once the news of Rynnaia's survival hits the port, there is no doubt it will travel with speed. This will work to our advantage. If all goes as planned between now and then, I expect to leave Holiday Palace on the second day of next week. We'll leave under full guard and fanfare, as fits the news of Rynnaia's survival, but it will be a guise only until we meet up with the army near the village of Yeld." He pointed to a spot on the map. "The princess and her squad will then depart for Shireya."

My father took a deep breath. "Once the army joins us, the added arms should confirm the presence of the Ryn to the Cobelds. We must be vigilant in protecting the closed carriage so that no one will see it is empty."

There were nods and mild vocal expressions that were more grunts than words.

What if it wasn't empty? As soon as the thought occurred I sent the question to my father. *What if someone was inside, posing as the princess?*

My father turned to me. *You may speak aloud here, Rynnaia. You are the Ryn. The knights will respect what you have to say.* He had to turn his attention from me when Julien spoke.

"If we could find someone to ride in the carriage on the princess's behalf," Julien said, thoughtfully rubbing his beard, "and if the imposter was believable and occasionally seen with you, Your Majesty," he added, "the Cobelds would be more likely to converge in that direction and free the path to Shireya."

You and Julien think along the same lines, my father spoke to my mind. *That is good. A Ryn must always seek a reigning partner with whom he or she can reason and agree.*

I tried to deny the flush that crept up my neck at his allusion, but my ears burned with it.

"It's a good addition to the plan," an older knight said as he gazed toward me. "But it would be difficult to find a believable double for the princess, even if a lady could be found who would be willing to face such certain peril."

Kinley spoke up. "But what if the princess is recognized elsewhere in the meantime?"

Every eye in the room rested on me with a sudden intensity that made me squirm.

"Princess Rynnaia bears a rather noteworthy resemblance to the Queen," Kinley continued, frowning. "What if someone sees her on the way to Shireya?"

Kinley had never met my mother, but her portrait hung in the entryway of Holiday Palace. No one who had seen the Queen or her portrait would deny our relation.

"I don't think we have to worry about that," Julien said, chuckling. "The princess quite excels in the art of disguise."

"But that was when everyone thought she was dead," Kinley argued. "No one expected to see her, so they didn't. Now that protection is gone."

"Hmm." Julien glanced down the table. "Risson? You attended the Regent's Ball here last month, did you not?"

"I did," Risson agreed. "Several of us were here that night."

"And did you make note of the princess at that time?"

"As you well know, the princess was not at Holiday Palace at that time." The older knight laughed. "Indeed, a lady with such a strong resemblance to the Queen would have caused quite a stir."

"Sir Risson," I spoke up, "if I remember correctly, we were partnered briefly during the Chauminard," I said. "I stood next to your wife, I believe, and when we circled the round, we spoke, however briefly."

The knight's eyes widened. "Begging your pardon, Your Highness, but as much as I have eyes only for my wife, I believe I would have remembered dancing with you."

"Then you will be relieved to know that I was not quite myself that night." I gave him a kind smile. "I came to the ball wearing a black hair piece and was introduced as Rose de Whittier. And although the Duke of Glenhume does not deny me use of his association, Sir Kinley is not my brother by blood."

The knight's crinkled eyes widened. "Forgive me, Your Highness. I did not recognize you."

"Exactly!" Julien exclaimed. "But Rose de Whittier is not the only alias Her Highness has at her disposal. I doubt that even her Veetrish brother," he tipped his head in acknowledgment of Kinley, "will recognize the princess for who she is when we leave from here."

"May it be so." The King's solid approval turned our minds back to the business at hand and it was past midnight when the meeting finally adjourned.

"We will meet again tomorrow evening," my father said, "after the additional regiments from Nyrland and Sengarra arrive." He removed the stones from the corners of the map and rolled it tightly. "Until then, knights, rest well and train with victory in mind."

The knights filed out and a herald came in and presented my father with a note. As he read it, he frowned. "Alert the infirmary," he said and excused the herald.

With that, the King offered me his arm and escorted me to my chambers.

"Rynnaia." When he paused at my door, a wave of grief flowed from his shoulders and stole my breath.

"Father? What is it?"

He reached for my hand and pressed it between both of his. "I've received word that both Sir Kiggon's and Sir Ahlvir's regiments were attacked. I've ordered the palace infirmary prepared to host the injured who survived."

The air trembled as I pulled it into my lungs. My free hand covered my mouth.

Lewys.

My father's eyes were moist, but I suspected the emotion was more mine than his. Still, that he empathized so touched me.

"I was not able to ascertain whether or not Lord Whittier's son was among those traveling with Kiggon," he said. "I'm sorry. I know your bond with that family runs deep. I will let you know as soon as I learn more."

I nodded. "Thank you."

"If you need anything, anything at all," he said, squeezing my hand, "no matter what the hour, come for me. Or call out to me with your mind, and I will come to you."

The surety of his love surrounded me. On impulse, I stepped up on my tiptoes and kissed his cheek. "Good night, Father," I said. "Sleep well."

When the door closed behind me, however, I wondered if sleep would come for me at all. Knowing that Lewys could be injured, or worse, weighted my heart. Yet fear for my brother contrasted sharply against the lightness that shimmered from thoughts of Julien and the courtship that had now officially begun.

As my eyes began to droop, I rested my fingers upon the spot on my hand that his lips had touched.

TWELVE

A bugle call awakened me the next morning. Its tune tickled my memory, pulling me from troubled dreams in which my three brothers, in turn, stepped up to defend me from a Cobeld's attack.

I sprang from my bed. Or tried to, rather. Somehow I had ended up sprawled in the middle of it, tangled in the linens like a fish in a net. Once I finally freed myself from my bonds, I had to crawl the length of my body and then some before I reached the edge of the massive bed.

A dressing gown had been laid out for me and I shoved my arms into it as I made my way to the window. The bugle called again, and the standard preceding the bugler appeared, familiar to me. It was Sir Kiggon's flag, battered, but flying proudly ahead of the beleaguered band of knights. They had just come through the gates.

I flew to the dressing room and pulled out an Andoven-made gown that was especially easy to get into by myself. Once I'd pulled the laces as tight as I could around my mid-section, I turned to the looking glass.

My hair was in worse shape than my tangled sheets. In fact, it more resembled yarn that had been turned out of its basket and given over to the delight of a kitten than hair. With a grunt of annoyance I pulled open the drawers of the dressing table until I found a wide-toothed ivory comb. With a grimace, I forced it through my mess of copper waves. Over and over I pulled, working each knot until it either untangled or tugged free of my scalp.

"Whatever its crimes, Princess, I hardly think your hair deserves that harsh of a sentence."

I jumped. "Erielle!"

"Give it over. Let me help with the back."

I gladly relinquished the comb.

"Your father asked me to serve as your lady's maid until you have time to interview others for the position," she said. "If I'd known you were awake I would have come sooner." She shrugged. "But other than your poor head, it looks like you survived without me."

"Do you have maids?"

"When I'm forced to dress like this I do," she said with a scowl toward the looking glass.

Her gown was the color of fresh raspberries with yellow ribbons for its laces. Erielle was a feminine vision of spring, and I told her so.

"Ach," she complained, looking down at her dress. "All these ribbons and ties. Give me trousers and a soft leather tunic any day over these fripperies. Besides being entirely impractical—where on earth am I supposed to put my broadsword, I ask you?—I prefer to dress myself. Not that I mind helping you, of course," she added.

"Of course," I responded. "Not that I believe you are unarmed, broadsword or not."

Her sly grin was all the confirmation I needed.

"There. I believe you are tangle-free," Erielle said after a bit. "How would you like it styled?"

"I think up. Something simple. I'll be visiting the infirmary today."

Rynnaia. My father's voice broke into my thoughts. *Lewys de Whittier is here. He is wounded, but it is not severe.*

I heaved a sigh of relief and thanked him for the information. As soon as Erielle finished my hair she escorted me to the infirmary.

The large chamber was near capacity and I found Lewys easily because Kinley was already at his side.

"Lewys!"

He was sitting up on the edge of a cot, a fresh bandage on his shoulder. He turned his head as I approached. His mouth gaped open and then his head swiveled to look at something to the left. I followed his gaze and found a portrait of my mother.

"Oh, by the way," Kinley said with a grin. "I forgot to mention that our little sister, you know, Rose? Well, she's the Ryn."

"Hello, Lewys."

"Rah-oh. Er. Ah!" Lewys sputtered. "Rose?" He blinked. "What happened to your hair?"

"The black dye washed out." I shook my head. "In Veetri it was dyed. This is what's real."

Lewys reached a hand forward as if to tug on one of my copper curls and then swiftly drew it back. "Your name's not Rose."

Again, I shook my head. "It's Rynnaia."

"Rynnaia," he whispered, and then a slow smile spread across his face. "Well, if that's not the best news I've heard in a while, then Veetri's green hills have turned to gold!" He tilted his head back and laughed, but it was cut short by a groan and his hand flew to the bandage on his shoulder. He winced.

"You're hurt!" My words came out as an accusation. "How could you let that happen? I've been worried sick!"

"*You've* been worried?" His eyebrows rose and then immediately narrowed over his topaz eyes. "*You've* been worried? You? It wasn't *your* sister who disappeared without a trace, without a word." He paused. "It's been three years since I laid eyes on you, Rose! Two, since you left Mirthan Hall for who knows where. Worried, ha! Let me tell you about worried, little girl."

It was as if the years fell away. For as many scrapes as he and Rowlen had led me into, Lewys had never trusted that I could get out of a single one on my own. Tears sprang to my eyes, fighting against the need to laugh from the sheer relief of finding my middle brother alive.

"Oh, Lewys." I stepped forward, leaned down, and gently wrapped my arms around him, careful not to bump his wound. The tears in my eyes spilled down my cheeks and onto his neck.

"Ah, Rose. Don't cry. You know I didn't mean it."

"It's not that." I sniffed. "I'm just so glad you're alive. The Dwonsil warriors are poisoning their arrows with cursed hairs from the Cobelds' beards. I was so—" I didn't want to say it and get him going again.

The buzzing sounds of talk and aid had retreated, enveloping us in an eerie silence. I let go of Lewys and wiped my eyes as I straightened.

I turned a full circle. Every eye that was conscious and able was on me.

"Hel-loo," I said, lifting my hand and giving a little wave. "I'm Rynnaia."

Erielle giggled.

"Her Royal Highness," Kinley corrected in a loud voice, "Princess Rynnaia E'veri."

The silence swelled, seeming even thicker and more oppressive after Kinley's boast.

Finally, a small voice broke the stillness. "I thought you was dead!"

I turned, and in the far corner a small boy of about eight stood on a cot, a bloody bandage wrapped about his head.

"Well? Are you?" He called across the room. "Are you dead?"

"Ah, no." I smiled weakly at him. "I'm not dead." What in the world was a child doing with a wound like that? In a soldiers' infirmary, no less!

"That's Rogan," Lewys said. "Sir Kiggon's newest page."

"His page?" I turned, whispering. "But he's just a little boy!"

"Don't tell him that," Lewys laughed. "He'll likely gut you."

"Lewys!" Kinley hissed. "She's the Ryn! And a lady. A little respect."

"My apologies, Your Highness. That was a crude thing to say." He sighed. "Ah, but I'm glad to see there's a little bit of the Veetrish left in you. Under all that royal red hair there may still be a de Whittier hiding, I think."

I nodded. "Indeed."

The Veetrish had strong ideas about the importance of giving a child a sense of home and hearth. Family was the most treasured thing a Veetrish person had. The ability to tell a good story was second. Living among them for nine years of my life, naturally I'd acquired something of their views for myself.

"Come now." Lewys scooted over and patted the cot. "Have a seat. I want to know everything. Start with what happened after your birthday ball up until this very moment. Don't leave a detail by the wayside."

And so I did, beginning with the fateful day Lord Whittier's Head of Housekeeping had been confronted and let go for threatening me with false accusations of witchcraft and for disparaging both my character and that of my uncle, Sir Drinius, and continued through my trip with Sir Gladiel to the Bear's Rest and the frightening night Julien showed up at our door, half-dead, wearing a cloak made from the skin of a bear, and looking like a beast out of a Storyteller's tale. All was going well until I mentioned trying to free an old man who'd gotten his beard stuck in a log. And that it turned out to be a Cobeld.

"You *what*?!"

"Don't worry. Julien killed the nasty old fellow." I patted his arm.

Lewys covered his eyes. Kinley dropped his head into his hands and groaned.

"Might I remind you two," I said, crossing my arms, "that if anyone in Veetri would have bothered to tell me that a real Cobeld looked like someone's grandfather instead of portraying them to be the hideous monsters from the Storytellers' tales, I wouldn't have nearly been killed." I added a *hrrumph* to underscore the validity of my argument.

"Yes, Princess." I hadn't realized Julien had joined us until his voice rumbled from behind me. "But if you would have remained in the house as instructed, you wouldn't have been put at risk at all."

"True." I smiled sweetly up at him. "But at least outside I might have been able to run away from a mortal threat." His lip twitched and I knew he had noted the thickening of my Veetrish accent. My grin widened—as did my brogue—as I pressed on. "But when you barged into my bedchamber at Fyrlean Manor and put a sword to my—"

"Did you threaten my sister?" Lewys stood and swayed a little on his feet.

It was an evil thing, to pit my overprotective brother against my suitor. But I couldn't seem to help myself.

"Sit down, Lewys," Kinley said, grabbing his arm, "before you fall and end up with a bump on your head as well."

Lewys shook off Kinley's hand. "Well?" He glared at Julien. "Did you?"

"Yes. But in my defense," Julien said with a slow grin, "she quite deserved it."

I held back a laugh. He was right, of course. It was my first attempt at disguising myself as a boy—and a quite successful one at that! Julien had entered a chamber in which he expected to find a princess, and found a gangly, bespeckled, black-haired squire, instead. Naturally, he had assumed his flame-haired Ryn had come to harm. When I explained the situation to Lewys, he reluctantly agreed with Julien: I deserved it.

By evening Lewys was released to the barracks and I saw him very little the next day. Not, of course, that I would have had time to chat even had our paths crossed. I quickly learned that being a princess was not at all what the Storytellers made it out to be. My time was not my own to spend as I willed, but belonged, and rightly so, to the workings of the Kingdom. But even as I attended meetings with my father, visited recuperating knights, and wrote letters of condolence to the families of those who had fallen—letters that would not be sent until after I was announced to the Kingdom—there was not a moment my mind was not troubled.

I worried how the Kingdom would react when the King's messengers delivered the shocking missive announcing my survival to the Regents. The knights were happy and hopeful that I was here, but would everyone react so when they found out that an almost twenty-year-old "truth" was a lie?

THIRTEEN

The day before the ball, the Shireya contingent met in the War Room to discuss the scrolls. Each person had their own copy of the translations spread before them while we awaited the King, who had yet to see the scrolls.

My father finally arrived, having been detained with other kingly duties. He took his place at the table, but as his gaze slid over the group, he paused on Erielle. A frown creased his brow, but he didn't comment.

"If you don't mind, Father," I said, "I'd like to ask Erielle to read the translations since she found the original scrolls."

I didn't think it hurt to remind him of the role Julien's sister had already played in the quest for the Remedy. Besides, it seemed only right that she be the one to present them to the King since she was the one who had found them.

Erielle had spent the previous day closeted with Edru, Dyfnel, and the translated scrolls, studying their riddles. She had a sharp mind to match her adventurous spirit and I hoped she had obtained a fresh bit of insight that would convince my father that she was, indeed, an integral part of our success.

My father nodded. "Very well."

From the first time I'd read the scrolls for myself on Tirandov Isle I had been convinced that, though she was never mentioned within them, Erielle's presence within our group was necessary. I could not easily explain the surety by which I had come to this conclusion, but I knew it came from a place beyond me, yet within me. It was almost as if The First himself had whispered the command in my ear and fixed it in my heart. Even though a part of me abhorred the thought of exposing my young friend to the dangers the scrolls promised us, I was sure—deeply, entirely sure—that Erielle's unique value to our group would be revealed at a critical point in the quest.

Erielle smoothed her hands across the shiny page, sealed with a thin coat of wax to protect the ink, and began.

"*Nine marks stand guard to guide the way. Three tasks upon the Ryn will prey. Death stalks the path with fierce desire and a counsel of four will strike the pyre.*" She looked up. "What follows seems to be a mix of information about the Cobelds and their curses, a description of the nine marks and three tasks, and . . ." she paused to scowl at the page before her, "quite a riddled lot of mess." She sighed, lightly cleared her throat, and continued.

"*More than men, but less than same for lust of power and need of fame, Cobeld's minions of one mind must feed their beard from cursed shrine. One dip, one drink, one curse, return. Whisker used and curse is spurned. But put in skins, wine of disease disperses death, and chaos breeds. They carry with them just enough to feed their maledictive tuft. The single limit to their curse, divided beard may grow its purse.*"

Risson gave a resounding *hrrumph* and said, "What the Cobelds did not discover on their own, the Dwonsil warrior's cunning has claimed. Dividing their cursed beards among the weapons of Dwons has increased the revenue of their curses manyfold. And I don't even know where they're finding all these clansmen warriors to do their bidding."

My father's look was grave. "While we were not paying Dwons the attention that might have thwarted the revolt, the clans grew. As did their resentment of our rule."

I sensed that when my father said "we" he spoke of several generations of Ryns.

"The dividing of the beards has widened the breadth of each individual curse," he continued. "But we should be thankful that one Cobeld on its own is incapable of more than one curse at a time." He nodded at Erielle. "Please go on."

"*Hasten Ryn to mountain's base where Scoundrel Ally shows his face. Weary not his strange replies, he'll serve you well when shown the fire. Knows he the path to enter in, though he'll not follow chosen Ryn.*"

"Your Majesty," Risson spoke up again, "do you know anyone who might fit the description of a 'Scoundrel Ally'?"

"Hmm." My father leaned back in his chair and rubbed his beard. Suddenly, he laughed. "Cazien de Pollis would certainly meet that mark."

Erielle's golden head shot up. "Who?"

"The Seahorse pirate," Julien said. "You remember him, don't you?"

"You should." My father chuckled. "I don't think I'll ever forget the look on Cazien's face when you tackled him to *Meredith*'s deck and held his own knife to his throat!"

Erielle's cheeks bloomed, but she didn't look up. "I seem to recall something like that. But I was just a little girl."

"How old were you?" I asked.

Again, she shrugged. "Eleven? Twelve? I don't know."

"So it wasn't all that long ago," Gerrias teased, poking her ribs with his elbow. At that she did lift her face, if only to glare at her brother.

"You disarmed a Seahorse captain?" Risson's voice held an air of both shock and admiration. "And threatened him with his own weapon? Why?"

"He wasn't a captain yet."

Ah, so she *did* remember.

"He drew a picture of her," Julien said, "but he wouldn't let her see it."

My father leaned forward. "Something about the eyes being wrong, wasn't it? He wanted to do them over."

The eyes. He must have drawn her with green eyes.

But if green had been wrong then, why would he think they would have changed now? He'd been as surprised as if it were completely normal for a person's eyes to suddenly change hue.

My father looked at me and I realized he'd heard my thought, or at least enough of it to want to address my confusion. "Her eyes could yet change color, I suppose," he said. "Julien's eyes weren't green until he was knighted."

My mouth dropped open and I looked at Julien. "They weren't?"

He shook his head. I couldn't imagine him with eyes any other color than the brilliant emerald green that sang across my dreams.

"Neither were mine," Gerrias said. "We were both born with eyes about the same color as Erielle's. But with our first official utterance of the Knight's Oath, they turned."

"Gladiel was the same," my father added. "It is a family trait common to all knights of that line, but one I've not seen outside the family of the Regent of Mynissbyr. Since there hasn't been a female born to the family since Lady Anya herself, I suppose it hasn't been tested on a girl."

"That's right." I blinked. "You're the first girl in two hundred years."

"I am." Erielle's still-blue eyes sparkled. "Perhaps we should test it, Your Majesty. Were I to be knighted—"

Three male voices—her brothers' and my father's—spoke as one, "*No.*"

Her brow creased. She closed her eyes, took a deep breath, and opened them. Clearly, she had voiced this request before.

"Well, then." She let out a quick but heavy breath. "Although I'm sure I enjoy being made sport of," she said in dry voice, "I really don't think this conversation is doing anything to help us locate the Remedy. Unless, Your Majesty," she said, turning to my father, "you think Cazien de Pollis is the Scoundrel Ally in the scrolls?"

After thinking about it for a moment he shook his head. "No, I don't imagine that he is. I don't believe Cazien would ever willingly travel as far inland as Mount Shireya."

But he traveled as far inland as Brune Falls. I thought back to his admission to hiding the scrolls. *Is Shireya any farther from the sea?* When I met Julien's eyes, I knew he was wondering the same thing. Neither of us voiced our question. And when my father said, "No, it must be someone else," and urged Erielle to continue reading, I put the question in the back of my mind.

"*Cell doors broken by the light, stairwell down to dark of night. Should the fish skill not be known, do not continue past the throne. Take a breath but don't expel. Brace for descent, ride the swell. Drip with caution cold as fear, beware a danger ever-near.*"

My father held his hand up and Erielle paused. "Do you swim, Rynnaia?"

"Yes, Father. Rowlen taught me."

"And the rest of you?" Everyone affirmed they could swim. "Good." He looked at Erielle. "Go on."

"The Ryn must travel deaf and blind, unsheathe the swords as arrows fly. Through night-drenched caverns of silence dimmed, casting spears from halo's rim, the fire returns from foreign lair to call down defense, unimpaired."

Erielle looked up, but although my father's frown had creased further, he did not motion for her to stop. She took a breath.

"A dive through water strangely warm. A lone voice chorus takes its form and Isle stone no hand has mined illumes the path to long-sought brine."

"I'm no Storyteller," Kinley interrupted, grating his fingers back and forth over his hair, "but is anyone else bothered by the random style of phrasing in this poet's rhyme?"

"I wondered who would first note its irregularity," Dyfnel said with a smile. "I should have known it would be the knight from Veetri." He turned his gaze to the King. "Our best guess is that even its construction, as irregular as it is, was purposefully done and but another riddle to decipher."

"It is bothersome to the ear," said the King. "Well met, Kinley. But as Dyfnel said, as far as we know, even that annoyance could be another clue."

When all eyes turned again to Erielle, she looked back to her scroll.

"A pool which teems illuminate precedes living precipitate. The Remedy rests through shadowed door within the Sacred Mountain's core. Only one may take the rise, with mane of fire and sky-jeweled eyes."

"Only one may take the rise?" my father asked. "It speaks of Rynnaia having to climb something?"

"Perhaps," Edru offered.

My father ran a heavy hand from his forehead down to his chin. I empathized. My reaction had been similarly fatigued the first time I read the scrolls.

When he waved his hand for Erielle to continue, she hesitated. I met her gaze. Having already memorized the scrolls while I was on Tirandov Isle, I knew why she had stopped.

"Go on, Erielle," I said, watching my father as she began to read.

"No sword or dagger at her side, The First alone will serve as guide. Ryn Naia's past on future bears and memory serves to foil the snare. For Ryn alone must foe engage and settle in eternal cage."

"Alone?" My father bolted upright. "You'll face the enemy . . . alone?"

"According to this, yes."

My father's eyes slid shut. I reached for his hand. *The First will be my guide,* I said to his mind. *He promised to be with me.*

He opened his eyes and gave me a single nod as he squeezed my hand.

Erielle's voice was a bit huskier when she moved to the next section. *"Shale of flour from the loaf, in water dropped, a moment soaked. A pinch is all for healing's start, but time alone completes the art. Ingested by Cobeld accursed, a gift of healing from The First."*

"The Remedy, Your Majesty." Dyfnel smiled. "And directions how to administer it."

The King nodded wordlessly, but hope for my mother flashed across the worry that had consumed his thoughts since Erielle had begun to read.

"Lock the foe where lies no floor. A gift released when the way is sure." Erielle paused to scowl at the odd stanza break. *"The best door of the former three, north and out it will you lead. A trusty thief waits for to serve. Withdraw the Healer and the Cur. War rages on Shireya's step, but Ryn must onward with her quest."*

"Stop. Go back to the Healer and the Cur," Gerrias said.

Erielle repeated the lines again.

"Well, the Healer must be you, Dyfnel, since you're a physician," Gerrias mused. "Is the Cur the same person as the 'Trusty Thief' we'll meet in the beginning?"

Risson scowled down at his own copy. "We won't know until we meet him, I suspect."

"Read that last line again, Erielle." My father's command was spoken as if he'd not even noted the discussion going on around him.

"But Ryn must onward with her quest."

"Onward?" His voice rose and his tone revealed his irritation as much as his clenched jaw. "There's *more*? But she's found the Remedy at this point!"

"There is quite a bit more, I'm afraid," Julien, who had refrained from commenting thus far, spoke up. "As we saw in the beginning, it appears the Cobeld curse is dependent upon them drinking from a tainted well. The Andoven at Tirandov are of the opinion that the water comes from an underground spring that originates at the location of the Remedy, within the core of the mountain. But we can't be sure what is metaphor and what is literal."

There was a long pause. Finally, Erielle said, "Should I go on?"

"Yes."

She nodded and lifted the scroll. *"Split the loaf to find the bit to medicate the Cobeld pit. The globe illumes with radiant shine until dropped in poisoned wine."*

Kinley groaned. "This unruly pattern of rhyme will likely do me in before the Cobelds even get a chance."

Though I knew he was exaggerating, I heartily agreed with the sentiment.

Erielle took a breath. *"Oracle's daughter scales the slope, takes the mantel, drops the stone to nullify the Cobeld curse and purge the poison from its work."*

"Sounds like you'll be a busy girl, Princess," Gerrias said.

Erielle glanced at her brother, and then looked down again. "There's something about this line that bothers me," Erielle frowned at me. "I can't figure out why Lady Anya refers to you as the Oracle's daughter. Unless, of course . . ." She looked over at my father. "You wouldn't happen to be an oracle, would you?"

"Hardly. And I doubt the Queen would lay claim to that title, either."

The room was silent for a moment, each person concentrating on their own copy of the scrolls, each of us intent on figuring out what that line could mean.

"What if Lady Anya sees Rynnaia as her symbolic daughter, since she's the one who is fulfilling the legacy of the scrolls?"

The word "legacy" rolled around in my head, attaching itself to a picture of a pirate. I shook my head, as if that would clear Cazien from my thoughts. I suppose I could be considered part of Anya's legacy, the one entrusted with bringing the prophecy to fruition, but . . .

Silence stretched. Finally Dyfnel said, "It seems as good an explanation as any."

Shrugs and nods made their way around the table before Erielle took a breath and read on. *"Emerald bonds to seal the Ryn, a toast expels curse taken in. Souls conjoin, a third concurs. Hope consumes the saboteurs!"* The sudden smile in Erielle's voice was infectious. Her voice took on strength as she finished the poem. *"One Name of Power in purest form removes the stain of Cobeld's thorn. An army parts, in panic, flees. A King of Truth gains victory."*

"Finally!" Kinley raised his fist up in the air, grinning. "Uh, sorry. I just thought it was about time something good happened in our poorly constructed poem. The King gaining victory sounds rightly good to me."

"It does, indeed!" Julien grinned and slapped him on the back.

"Go on, Erielle," my father said.

She looked up. "That's all. Well, except for the postscript."

My father arched an eyebrow. "The postscript?"

"The author left a note after the end," Dyfnel explained. "It seems to have been recorded by the same hand and is itself a poem, but it was not written in the Ancient Voice like the rest of the text."

My father ground his teeth and looked at Erielle, one eyebrow arched as if to say, "Well, get on with it."

"Right." She nodded. *"Awakened I with death-gripped quill, ink before me, memory stilled. Unaware, I'd scribed a chart penned by my hand, not from my heart."*

She took a breath. When she spoke again, her voice was laced with a sense of destiny. *"A restless night brought new a dream of who would find what I had seen and where to hide the Poet's verse: a map to lift Cobeld's dark curse. Before the moon set I began to carry out the First King's plan."* Erielle glanced at me and grinned. *"But suddenly the Ryn of flame, unborn borne on vapored plane, appeared behind the Poet's desk to learn about her coming quest. Advised I she whose time had come, but come not yet by time undone. And when her form removed from sight, these words I wrote till end of night to hide away until the time when read will be prophetic rhyme."*

"Poor girl," Kinley said. "Clearly she understands the use of meter. Can you imagine waking up with a collection of words copied down in your own hand but so crudely composed?"

"These copies are translations, remember?" Erielle sounded a bit defensive. Then again, it was her ancestress who penned it, so perhaps she had the right. "It might have read more lyrically in the original language."

"I wonder which was more shocking," Julien mused. "Waking to this poetry? Or having a beautiful red-haired princess, one who won't be born for over two hundred years, arrive unannounced in your room? It must have been . . . something."

Silence reigned for several minutes. Strangely, I *could* imagine, since I'd been the one transported across the planes of time to speak with Lady Anya.

"That's all, then?" My father let out a long breath.

Erielle nodded.

He scowled at the top of the table. "The geographic landmarks seem vague, at best."

"Yes," Edru answered the King. "But our hope is that, with eight of us familiar with the scrolls, the likelihood of that recognition will increase."

"Commit them to memory, each of you," the King commanded. "If you see to no other task over the next few days, see to this one."

When I found my bed that night I was exhausted, but a cold thread of unease crept into my thoughts even as sleep rushed in to still it. In just a few short hours it would be known across the Kingdom that my mother and I lived. Families who had lost loved ones to the Cobelds' curses might rejoice at the news, but I couldn't help but wonder about those whose red-haired daughters had been killed in the Cobelds' desire to thwart the prophecy.

The harsh reality was that, because I lived, those lives were needlessly forfeited. If it had been my red-haired mother, sister, or friend who'd fallen prey to a curse, I'm not sure I would be so quick to forgive my King.

Regardless of his good intentions, tomorrow my father would be revealed to his people as a liar.

And I, as the lie.

FOURTEEN

A somber assembly of knights surrounded the King's table to break their fast the next morning, and although no one mentioned the coming announcement, I sensed it lingered in everyone's thoughts. My father was unusually quiet as I pushed the food around on my platter, finding nothing there that appealed to the gnawing in my belly. Anxiety, it seemed, would not be appeased by something so menial as food.

The King attended to nameless duties throughout the rest of that day and into the next, but I found it difficult to keep my hands busy enough to distract my mind.

The day following the announcement found me in the company of Julien and Erielle, who had come to my chambers with the intent of studying the scrolls. But by late afternoon the poetry could no longer hold my attention.

Surely by now the Regents had spread word of the news they'd received. Tonight, there would be a ball and I would get a taste of how the rest of the Kingdom felt about my father and me, now that the truth was being spread. What would the reaction be around the Kingdom when the people discovered their King had been deceiving them for so long? How were they, even now, reacting to the news?

The question was ugly in my mind. Knowing the kind, truth-loving man my father was, it felt cruel to even assign such a label as "liar" to him, but what else could I call his scheme but what it was? And I, at the very center of it, was nearly as duplicitous. Would the people be angry about the lies, or would they rejoice, understanding his motives? Would the losses they had suffered these years allow them to agree that hiding me and my mother away was a necessary defense against the Cobelds, or would they see it as an unforgivable breach of trust with the people of E'veria? I'd been protected from knowing about the prophecy to secure my identity, but did enough of the people know of it to see the hope it offered?

A light, early supper was brought for the three of us, but I could barely eat. My stomach twisted tighter with every moment the ball drew nearer. Carriages had begun to arrive late in the afternoon, and even though I had purposefully blocked my mind from ascertaining the mood of our guests, I couldn't help but wonder about it.

I paced off and on, reciting bits of the scrolls' poetry, quizzing and being quizzed by Erielle and Julien, but more often than not, I interrupted my own concentration with more troubling thoughts.

Through night-drenched caverns of silence dimmed, casting spears from halo's rim . . .

Night-drenched caverns. Thoughts of darkness, of traveling through pitch-black caves inside Mount Shireya, shadowed me almost as much as my worry. *What if E'veria loses all faith in her King when they learn the truth?*

I paused at the window and watched another carriage roll through the gates, and then shook my head and tried to move my mind back toward the scrolls. *Silence dimmed.* I ruminated on the phrase. *How do you dim silence?* I resumed my pacing. *Will the people be able to forgive my father?*

"Rynnaia."

I jumped at the sound of my father's voice, for I had neither sensed nor heard his arrival.

I turned. Both Julien and Erielle were gone, but I had not noted their leaving, either.

"What's on your mind, child?" he asked gently. "I can barely hold a thought together with your colors battering my mind as they are."

"Oh!" My hand flew to my mouth. "I'm sorry, Father." I closed my eyes and reached inside my mind for the gray swirls that would protect him from my worry.

"That's not what I meant," he said as he crossed the room. "I want to know what's bothering you so much that you are soon to wear a hole through your rug. Sit down and talk to me, Rynnaia. I am your father and I want to listen to you. And give you comfort, if I may." He took my arm and led me to a chair. He took the one opposite mine and waited while I composed my words.

"The announcement was yesterday. By now the news has traveled nearly everywhere, I imagine."

He nodded. "And?"

"I'm worried the people will think you a liar. That they will feel betrayed by the deception. Or that they will doubt the truth of it and believe the announcement itself is a fabrication."

"Ahh," he said. "I see." He was quiet for some time. "That has always been a possibility at the back of my mind. Any lie, even if told with good intentions, is still a lie. If there is a negative reaction when the truth is revealed, we can only trust in the power of truth itself to use it for good. We must rest in the hope that the truth will be rejoiced over rather than despised."

I nodded, but emotion lodged in my throat, bearing worry heavily upon my spirit. "I would rather remain unknown if the revelation results in the people loving you less."

He rose from his chair and knelt before me. "Rynnaia," he said, his smile gentle, "give the people time and have faith in their resilience. Even if they resent the truth, it cannot be changed. You will be their banner and their hope. In time, their Queen.

"You've moved among the wounded, you've spoken to the knights, the servants. You've heard of their losses, of the travesties and pestilences and deaths doled out to our people by the Cobelds. It's not just the E'veri family who has suffered these years, Rynnaia. Our separation was difficult and your mother's illness has been a constant ache in my soul, but when weighed against the losses so many of our subjects have faced?" He shook his head. "Indeed, our suffering is minimal in comparison."

Tears sprang to my eyes. He was right.

"The Cobelds have hurt people in every corner of our Kingdom. We are at war, Rynnaia, and as King I am under no obligation to validate strategies of war." His tone softened. "But I believe my explanation for the deception was very clear in the messages I sent to the Regents. If they do their duty, the truth will be cause for celebration, not disgrace. E'veria's beloved Queen Daithia yet lives! There is a living Ryn and, not only that, the Ryn Naia from the prophecy! They will find hope enough in that, of that you can be sure."

I leaned forward and my tears released onto his shoulder. His arms came around me and he stroked my hair. "I am so proud of you, Rynnaia. You are more than I ever dreamt of in a daughter . . . and in a princess."

"Th-thank you." I sniffed and pulled back.

My father handed me a handkerchief, his eyes full of compassion. "Just another few hours and you will be dancing at the ball," he said and stood. "You have nothing to fear. You are the princess and the Ryn. And the King could not be happier to have you on his arm."

"I love you, Father."

"I will never tire of hearing that," he said with a smile. "I love you, too, Rynnaia. So very much. Will your mind rest easier now?"

I nodded and gave him a tremulous smile. A golden gleam touched my mind. "Erielle's on her way." I laughed. "I hadn't even noticed she'd left."

"She'll be coming to help you ready for the ball, I assume." He gave me a solid nod. "I'll leave you to that business. As I recall from when your mother was still here, it's a bit more involved for a lady to ready for a ball than it is for a man." I smiled when he chuckled and leaned over to kiss my cheek. "I'll be back around to escort you to the Grand Hall."

I had chosen a moss-green gown to wear, the same color as the Kingdom's banner. After Erielle exclaimed over the shimmery quality of the fabric, she helped me dress. The wide-scooped neckline touched the tips of my shoulders and sheer ribbons in shades of copper and green trailed from the short sleeves, swaying in the breeze made when I walked, but otherwise leaving my arms bare. The bodice of the dress had similar ribbons attached to it, but they were not free-flowing as on the sleeves. Those ribbons were stitched to the fabric of the dress with a glistening golden thread that crisscrossed the ribbons diagonally until they reached a point just below my waist, and from there hung loosely over the gown's skirting, swaying with the movement of the many shimmery layers below.

"Those ribbons remind me of a willow tree I used to climb near the river," Erielle said when I twirled. "But with the copper mixed in with the green and your flaming head of hair," she added with a laugh, "it's a bit like that old willow caught on fire."

Her gown was the palest pink, the bodice embroidered with white flowers that also circled the hem.

"If I'm a willow—"

"A willow *on fire*," she corrected.

"Indeed." I laughed. "Then you must be a flowering cherry."

She grinned. "It suits. Cherry trees are small like me. So, what other adornments can I affix to your branches?"

I had quite a selection of jewels at my disposal, but after sampling several elaborate pieces from the chest, I decided the extravagance of my gown called for something simpler. To that end, my only jewelry would be the pendant given to me by my mother just before I left Tirandov Isle, and the silver circlet of vining roses that had once been hers, but had rested on my head nearly every day since I had received it. It was special to me not only because it had been a gift to my mother from my father long ago, but because it carried her Queenly emblem, the flower whose name I answered to for the first nineteen years of my life.

Erielle pulled my hair back, tucking, rolling, and pinning the sides away from my face, but letting the back hang free. As I lowered the crown into place, the familiar heat of the Emblem of the First greeted me as a brief, bright orange glow in the looking glass. As the light transferred pleasing warmth to my forehead, it brought with it the memory of the voice of The First, the voice that had transformed me in the bay at Tirandov. And with that memory, the assurance that regardless of what would come, he would be with me.

The sky had darkened while I'd readied for the ball. Soon enough, Erielle departed so that she could be announced with her brothers, and I stood near the fire in an attempt to ward off the chill of nervous energy that trickled about my limbs as I awaited the approach of my father. When he knocked I stayed near the fire but opened the door with my mind. He entered.

In the short time I had known my father he had never *not* looked like a King. But tonight, he looked even more so. He wore a moss-green tunic over his ivory shirt with black breeches and boots. Medallions graced the golden sash that crossed his chest from shoulder to waist, and in place of the simple circlet he usually wore, a most definite crown increased his height by the length of my hand from wrist to fingertip.

"Isn't that heavy?" I couldn't help but ask.

He smiled. "It's not as bad as you might think," he said and then laughed. "But I must admit it feels a bit heavier than I remember. It's been a long while since I've had occasion to wear it."

He leaned over and kissed my brow and I flinched, expecting the big crown to fall.

He chuckled. "Don't worry. It's quite secure." He stepped back. "You are a vision, Rynnaia," he said. "Even if you were not the reason for the ball you would be the belle of it. Now, let me tell you how things will proceed."

His tone became slightly more formal, but still retained its warmth as he explained how the evening would progress.

"Protocol dictates you dance with the higher ranking officials first."

I nodded, having expected as much.

"I am pleased to tell you that I rank highly enough to be your first partner." He winked and I laughed. My smile faded, however, as he began to recite a series of partners in a list so long I couldn't possibly hope to remember them in the expected order. But when he mentioned that someone called "The Herald of the Dance," a master of protocol, would apprise each man of his turn, I suddenly found I could breathe again.

He resumed listing the partners protocol dictated I danced with and why, speaking of these rules as if they were common annoyances. I wondered how I would ever learn them all.

"Next will be Kinley. Whittier's other sons will each be given their dance," he said, "and then I imagine you will be surrounded by others who will demand your time."

"Whittier's other sons?" I asked. "But only Lewys is—" I gasped. "Surely you don't mean to say that Rowlen is here?"

My father's eyes widened. "I'm sorry, Rynnaia. I thought you knew. Whittier's youngest son arrived just this morning. I didn't know myself until I received a petition from him offering to provide entertainment."

An undignified little squeal of glee escaped my throat and I gave my father an impulsive hug that was fast and tight enough to illicit a slight grunt.

He laughed. "I had hoped you might find a loving home with Lord and Lady Whittier," he said. "I am thankful your bond with that family is so dear."

"They are very protective of me," I said after my heart steadied. "With all three of Lord Whittier's sons here, I fear they may interrogate any man who asks for a dance before they allow him near me."

"All the better," he said with a frown and a nod. "It is too big a hall and too large a crowd for me to be able to watch you every second." He paused. "There are a few nobles in particular that, while protocol allows each a dance with you, I do not wish you to suffer their company overlong. The herald has been informed. Their time with you shall be brief."

"Anyone in particular?"

"The Earl of Ganeth is the first who comes to mind." He chuckled. "He is a sweet old man, but has caused many a young lady injury while dancing." His smile fell. "Another would be Tarlo de Veir, the youngest son of the Duke of Port Dyn."

"Is E'veria so full of poor dancing partners, then?"

"Not at all." A line formed between my father's brows. "Tarlo is known as a particularly fine dancer, as I understand it. Quite the charmer as well." His tone darkened. "But there are rumors that his loyalty may not be as well established as his charm." He patted my arm. "But you needn't worry. I've assigned knights to shadow anyone whose allegiance I've been given particular cause to doubt. But be wary, just the same."

"Will there be many here tonight who fit that description?"

"A few." He sighed. "Five years ago I would not have imagined the clans of Dwons would secede from their Regent's authority and find league with the Cobelds. Now we are at war with our own people." He paused, shaking his head. "In these circumstances, I believe caution is prudent. The guest list was carefully drawn, but who knows what resentment or greed could cause a weak-willed person to betray his Kingdom? It is times like these that I wish I had your mother's ability to look into the minds of non-Andoven people. I am glad it's a gift you share with her, though I don't envy the noise in your head." He smiled. "Adjusting my own guard to be up to the task of having Dyfnel, Edru, and you in the palace at the same time has been . . . interesting."

"I understand completely."

"I'm sure you do." He nodded, his mood suddenly solemn. "Be on your guard, Rynnaia," he said, tapping a finger at his temple. "And should you feel at all threatened, do not hesitate to forego Andoven etiquette and seek the truth of a possible enemy's thoughts."

"Do you think there will be spies in the crowd?"

"It is possible. Among our nobles there are those who are motivated more by greed than justice. It is an all-too-common result of being brought up in privilege."

Suddenly, a face sprang vividly to life in his mind. The young man was handsome, but the thought of him deepened my father's scowl.

"Tarlo de Veir." My father named the man in his thoughts when he sensed my question. "He will be shadowed closely."

"May I ask by whom?"

"Sir Kile de Poggen."

"Ah." At last, a name I recognized. Sir Kile had visited Mirthan Hall shortly after he and Kinley were knighted. "I didn't know Sir Kile was here."

"It's unlikely that you would have seen him, though he has been quite near you," he said with a smile. "Kile has served as the night guard for your chambers since you arrived. His shift begins at midnight and ends at dawn. He is relieved of duty each day before you rise."

"I will be sure to thank him for his service if I see him in the crowd tonight."

"And speaking of the crowd," he said, "our guests are all accounted for and awaiting only for us to commence the dance."

He stepped back, bowed, and held out his hand. "May I have the honor, Princess Rynnaia?"

$\mathcal{F}$ I F T E E N

$\mathcal{A}$lthough I had made some progress in learning my way around the palace, I had never been up the particular set of stairs, nor down the hallway that led us to the balcony of the Grand Hall. Below us, our guests would have arrived through a much more ornate hallway over which arched a forest-like path of trees carved from marble. This hallway, however, was not only much simpler in design, it was unencumbered by other people, and at its end stood an arched doorway with no door. Instead it was covered by a velvet curtain and flanked by two men wearing the uniform of the palace heralds.

We stopped a few paces before the curtains and the heralds pulled them open. A small, dark vestibule stretched to meet another curtained doorway.

"You'll wait here while I give a short speech," my father said. "When the herald announces you, the curtains will be drawn back and you may join me on the balcony."

I nodded and tried to swallow, but my throat was suddenly dry.

My father squeezed my hand. "You are first and foremost my daughter, Rynnaia. I am so proud of you. Moreover, you are the Ryn and the Crown Princess of E'veria. Be of good courage. You are an E'veri."

He nodded to the heralds. The curtain was pulled back. He stepped through and the curtain closed again. A moment later, the distinctive thrum of the chief herald's staff against the marble balcony floor sounded.

I hadn't even noticed the noise wafting up from the Grand Hall until it suddenly stilled. The silence was so pronounced I could hear the herald's intake of breath before he announced my father.

"His Majesty, King Jarryn E'veri!"

I had expected cheers, or at least a slight smattering of applause, but silence reigned. Was the lack of reaction a sign of respect to the King? Or was it, as I feared, born of a more pointed emotion?

"Good citizens of E'veria." My father's voice was loud enough to carry to the farthest corners of the Grand Hall, but it was as velvet as usual, without any trace of a shout. "Yesterday you learned the greatest, most preciously guarded secret of my reign, a secret which allowed my daughter to grow up without the constant threat of Cobelds thwarting the purpose to which she was born."

He paused. "It may seem an odd thing to allow for celebration while our land suffers under the oppression of our enemy, but the occasion calls for nothing less and much more than I am able to give you. Tonight, we celebrate because the Ryn lives!"

Immediately, the crowd's silence was broken by a raucous cheer, but I couldn't help but note that the cheer seemed limited, even though it was robust, considering the size of the Grand Hall.

Our knights. As my father's words touched my mind I could feel the affection in the smile that accompanied them.

When the cheer died down he continued, "Our Kingdom is experiencing its darkest days since Lady Anya and the Bearmen of Mynissbyr sent the Cobelds into hiding centuries ago. But even though our enemies have removed themselves from exile, we yet have reason to celebrate. And at long last, reason to hope.

"For nineteen years my daughter has been forced to live in secrecy, her identity unknown to all but a very few. Even she did not know of her name, nor," he paused and I felt the cold shrill of his fear for me, "her destiny, until recently. Our enemies were lulled into a false sense of security and I can only imagine how they quake now to learn that all those years ago their evil plot to kill the Ryn and my Queen failed."

Again, the knights cheered.

"It is with great pride and indescribable joy," he said, "that I am finally able to introduce to you my daughter, Rynnaia."

A flash of scorn hit my mind. I closed my eyes, following the crimson-tinged thread of silver to the far west corner of the Grand Hall where, among a small gathering of nobles, a few bore a particularly vivid disbelief among their thoughts.

I pulled my mind back, retreating to protect my emotions within a cloak of gray.

"E'veria," my father's voice rumbled with pride and love, "meet your Ryn."

The herald's staff met the marble again and the vibration of that crack resonated to the roots of my teeth.

The first set of curtains parted. I took a deep breath in through my nose, entirely conscious of the way it caught several times before reaching my lungs, and stepped through the first set of curtains into the vestibule. The curtains fell shut behind me and I was left in darkness while my name rang out over the people below.

"Her Royal Highness, Princess Rynnaia E'veri!"

The second set of curtains opened and I was greeted by my father's smiling face. His hand was outstretched toward me and his eyes shone with tears that he speedily blinked away.

I slipped my hand into his and stepped onto the balcony. In just three more steps, I stood at the white marble rail, at the right hand of the King.

A collective gasp ushered in a silence thicker than any I had heard before, even on Tirandov Isle. I didn't have to look far to know it was due to my resemblance to my mother. But the crowd's surprise couldn't steal the sudden sense of rightness that formed in my belly and moved outward through my blood, stilling the subtle shake in my limbs, and restoring my breath to its proper cadence.

Standing here, beside my father and before our people, I had finally taken the place I was born to inhabit. The warmth of my father's hand on mine and the truth of his love and acceptance, overrode my fears of what anyone else might think of me.

My chin lifted just the tiniest bit, almost as if pulled by a string. Purpose sizzled through my blood.

I am the Ryn.

Suddenly, the silence was rent by the cheers of my father's knights. *Our knights*, he had called them. Even louder than before, the cheer was so celebratory, so optimistic, that one would think I'd already retrieved the Remedy.

"My daughter is beautiful, is she not?" My father's words were laced with the sort of chuckle that warms a room, but his eyes were on me. "And I assure you that her heart is as lovely as her face." When he turned back to the crowd, however, his tone changed. "The Kingdom still suffers under the Cobelds' treachery. The Queen's illness has raged nineteen years due to their curse. And yet," he paused, "we have hope."

With an authority that was as clear as the stony determination in his bright blue eyes, he continued, "Tonight I call upon each of you to serve as witness to this truth. Let there be no doubt that Rynnaia E'veri, the firstborn and only child of King Jarryn and Queen Daithia, is alive and well and has claimed her position as your Ryn!"

The knights cheered again, but this time their voices were joined by more members of the crowd.

"Tomorrow we begin moving toward a true and lasting victory over the Cobelds, but tonight, we celebrate!" A smile spread wide upon his face.

A voice I knew well, Julien's, shouted up from below, "May it be so!"

"May it be so," the King agreed and the affirmation moved through the crowd.

The King nodded to the orchestra master, who turned toward the musicians and lifted his arms. A moment later, to the rousing anthem of E'veria, my father led me down the spiral staircase.

When the anthem ceased, a slower yet merry tune began and the crowd parted for my father to lead me to the center of the Grand Hall. I eased the gray from my thoughts just enough to sample the mood of the room, but the colors swirling about were a little disorienting. I was able to distinguish many thoughts of loyalty and admiration, but also caught a few shards of disbelief and even a few feelings of betrayal.

With my hand still in his, I took a step back, swept my right leg behind my left, and curtsied low. When I arose, the King let go of my hand only to reach for the other and place his left hand at my waist. A count later, his small pressure at my back moved my feet into the dance.

My father swept me across the floor with such fluidity that one would think I had grown up here, with him as my dance tutor. The tune was brief. At its end he leaned down to drop a kiss on my forehead. The next sound I heard was a chorus of ladies' sniffles, but as he leaned back, his eyes met mine and his voice touched my mind.

Be on your guard. As soon as his warning had been "voiced," however, a smile forced a wink from his eye. *But remember to enjoy yourself, as well. It is, after all, a ball.*

The Regent of Dynwatre approached and my hand was thus offered. My father would likely be the only man present given an entire dance with the princess. But he was, after all, the King.

Other dancers filtered onto the floor, and before long, the eldest son of Gladiel de Vonsar, Regent of Mynissbyr, tapped on the Regent of Dynwatre's shoulder.

With a smile and a slight bow, the Regent backed away. Julien bowed and offered his hand. "May I have the honor of a dance, Your Highness?"

"The honor is mine, Sir Julien." The formal words felt silly and rather over-dramatic when spoken to one I knew so well, but there were listening ears about and I was determined to follow the protocol expected of me.

My father's dancing skill was beyond compare, but there was something about being partnered with Julien that infused my own steps with an airy lightness that released anxiety and made me feel as if I was one with the music itself. I connected my thoughts to his. As green and gold filtered into my mind, I didn't have to think about the counts, about the people watching, or whether my feet would get tangled in the ribbons of my gown. Neither of us spoke a word beyond our greeting, but our eyes never disengaged. When Gerrias cut in, even though he was a fine dancer and I enjoyed the ease of his company, I couldn't help but feel a great loss.

A succession of partners followed—no fewer than three per song. For a while I tried to remember their names, but they soon became jumbled in my head.

As my father had predicted, the youngest son of the Duke of Port Dyn was easy to identify, especially with Sir Kile barely a breath away from him all night. When the Herald of the Dance presented him to me, I was impressed by his skill with the lively steps of the Veetrish reel. The equally dashing Sir Kile kept close time with us, much to the exertion of the dowager he had partnered for that particular tune.

Tarlo's long-lashed eyes, the same shade as his cinnamon-brown hair, were set off by a wardrobe that must have cost his father dearly. I doubted Tarlo would be refused a dance by any maiden present, but I did hope the maidens present were a discerning lot, for there was a slickness just under the surface of his smile that seemed to lack the sheen of honor. As my father had suggested, I applied my gift and peered into the edges of Tarlo's thoughts.

"And will you go home to Salderyn soon?" he asked after we'd completed the first turn. His tone was friendly, yet vague. Still, something about the question seemed . . . rehearsed.

"Eventually," was all I said, for in his thoughts I had seen greed and a lust for power that might not hesitate long before considering betrayal.

"It will be a great loss to Dynwatre when you leave us for your northern home," he said with a smile that would likely turn a girl's heart as quickly as it would her head. "And your mother? Will she join you there?"

"When she is able."

"Ah, of course."

He smiled again, but this time his gaze intensified. Even my heart, as well-anchored as it was to Julien's, couldn't help but quiver.

"Your Highness, I find that having you in my arms is doing damage to my heart."

I blinked, caught off guard by the earnestness of his tone. "It . . . is?"

"Indeed." His smile was warm. "A damage that might only be relieved should your father deign to allow me to confess it as the first herald of love."

Well, then! Another quick peek into his thoughts found that I was not the first maiden to receive that particularly poetic bit of flattery. A sour taste filled my mouth and cooled the blush on my cheeks.

"You flatter me, Lord Tarlo! I could not possibly speak to my father's opinion on that subject, of course." I gave him a sweet smile. "But I daresay my suitor would object to your proclamation."

His eyebrows rose like two brown caterpillars, mid-crawl, yet the muscles around his mouth gave away the quick burst of anger at being thwarted.

"You have a suitor, Your Highness? So soon after being returned to your father?" he asked. "And who is this most favored of all men?"

"Sir Julien de Gladiel."

Something unpleasant flashed in his eyes, but it cooled as quickly as it appeared. "Ah," Tarlo said, his smile tinged with what appeared to be sadness.

I was only too glad when the Herald of the Dance interrupted, bringing my next dancing partner. In fact, had my next partner not been Kinley de Whittier, I might have excused myself. After dancing with Lord Tarlo, the desire to wash my hands was fierce. It wasn't that he was unclean in any outward way, but his thoughts seemed to leave a trace upon the skin like that of the garden slugs Rowlen used to tease me with as a child. Few present needed the herald's service so much as I, but I was ever so glad he took his duty—and my father's directive concerning Tarlo de Veir—seriously.

"You look beautiful tonight, Ro—" Kinley chuckled, correcting himself, "Princess Rynnaia."

"Thank you."

"You know," he mused, "I've known you were the Ryn for over three years now, but it's still difficult to reconcile it when I hear your voice. You still carry much of Veetri in your speech."

"As well as in my heart," I said.

"I am glad to hear it." He smiled. "Julien is a good man."

I blinked at the change in subject.

"I say that because, as your brother, I want you to know that I approve of your choice."

The dance required we turn back-to-back then and we couldn't talk for another three measures, but the pause didn't keep Kinley from picking up right where he'd left off.

"Julien and I have trained together, fought together, and," he paused to give me a sly wink, "we've had a fair bit of fun as well." He chuckled. "I've watched him mold mediocre squires into fearsome and honorable knights and I have been witness to him ferreting villains from their hiding places. Julien's a loyal friend and a fine knight. The finest. Not only will he make an honorable husband, he is worthy of serving the Kingdom beside you."

"Kinley, you speak as if I'm already wed, yet we've only begun to court. I can't possibly know if we—"

"Ro—naia." We both laughed at the interesting combination of names that tied his tongue as he interrupted me. "I think your heart knows more than you will admit. Perhaps more than you yet realize." He smiled and surprised me with a twirl that was not necessarily an ordered part of the dance.

I laughed as I spun back into his arms. Kinley's style of dance, so very Veetrish and so lacking the formality of my other partners, relaxed me in familiarity. He led me with an easy grace in which a misstep, if I made one, could be interpreted as a flourish rather than a mistake.

"It is refreshing to dance in the style of Veetri again," I said, as he spun me yet again.

"Not all the ladies I partner would agree. I think they find our freedom disconcerting." Kinley nodded. "But I prefer to believe that what they interpret as whimsy is what makes us more open to knowing our own hearts, more able to see the nuance that defines a person's character, and more willing to reach for an adventure, regardless of the consequences." He gave me a knowing grin, passed my hand into his brother's, bowed, and walked away.

"Princess," Lewys bowed.

"How is your shoulder?" I asked. His eyes had betrayed a moment of pain when he lifted his arm to initiate the twirl this particular dance required.

"Still a bit sore, but I'm one of the lucky ones." His expression grew serious for a moment, but then he smiled. "You know, it's amazing how right you look as yourself." A mischievous glint sparked in his eye. "Now your hair matches your spirit. Wild as fire and just as able to burn those who cross you."

"And you are quite brave to say so, Lewys. Are you, then, feeling so impervious to flame?" We were still bantering when Rowlen appeared, forcing Lewys to present my hand to his youngest brother.

Rowlen bowed in the custom of the Storytellers, low enough to make my own back ache just from watching him. Rising with a familiar twinkle in his eye, he lifted his clasped hands to his chest. Giving me a wink, he pulled his hands apart with a slight flourish and produced a beautiful nosegay of copper-colored roses, tied with a blue ribbon.

"Your Highness," he said, offering the nosegay to me.

I couldn't help myself. Even though I knew better, I reached to take the offered bouquet. But my fingers closed around . . . air.

The vision vanished and Rowlen shook his head. "How quickly she forgets!"

"You do know, I hope, that were there not an audience expecting the perfect behavior of a princess, your upper arm would feel the pain of my exasperation. As it is, however, you will remain unbruised. Unless, perchance, I am able to crush your toe during this lively tune." I held out my hand, which he took with a grin. We danced across the floor, laughing in the delightful exchange of familiar wit.

"Have you yet danced with Erielle?" I asked.

"Erielle, you say?" He furrowed his brow. "Which young lady is she?"

"Don't act as if you don't know, Rowlen. Erielle de Gladiel, of course!"

"Ahh." His smile told me he knew very well to whom I'd referred. "Yes, I've danced with the young lady from Mynissbyr. And I must say I prefer that lovely pink gown to the breeches and tunic in which she was attired when first we met. I prefer it so much, in fact, that I may find another opportunity to compliment her on it during a second dance later this evening."

I grinned. "Beware her brother, Rowlen. Julien is fearsomely protective of her."

"Then I shall do nothing to raise his ire. Although I doubt he would notice who dances with *his* sister while he is so entirely consumed with noting who dances with *mine*."

I ducked my head. "He's asked the King's permission to court me."

"And the King consented?"

"Most readily."

"And are you . . . pleased with the arrangement?"

From anyone else, the question might seem impertinent. But Rowlen de Whittier was not only my foster brother. He had long been my closest friend and most trusted confidant.

"I am. Julien has quite won my heart."

Rowlen's expression softened. He sighed and was about to say something else when, once again, the Herald of the Dance appeared. Rowlen relinquished my hand.

The evening wore on and I was delighted and dismayed in turn by the various men who sought my company on the dance floor. Several hinted at hoping to win my hand—one man even went so far as to list his qualifications as a future King!—but when I was given the opportunity, one mention of Julien's courtship seemed to still the poor fellows' hopes.

For most, however, it was unnecessary for me to verbalize Julien's claim. For throughout the course of the ball, my knight danced with no lady save myself or his sister. And he was always near. More than once, my cheeks warmed when I caught him spearing one of my partners with his gaze.

Proceed with caution, he seemed to warn with that look, *for she shall be mine.*

What he didn't yet fully realize, however, was that I already was.

SIXTEEN

*H*aving been away from Veetri for so long, I was woefully unaccustomed to such vigorous, continuous dancing. My feet cried for mercy for a good hour before the orchestra finally took a break. When they did, I made my way to my father's side, and the gilded chair that awaited me there, to enjoy Rowlen's entertainment.

After my father and I had been served, trays of beverages and hors d'oeuvres were offered to the breathless dancers. When the servants finished their rounds, the Storyteller swept onto the middle of the floor.

"Beyond what I know of him from Kinley," my father said, "I have heard of Rowlen, your Storyteller. He is reputed to have quite an amazing gift."

"That he does." I agreed. "No doubt he will be the Regent of Veetri's Storyteller someday."

"Hmm." His look was pensive. "The Regent's Storyteller, you say?"

I nodded. "It's been his lofty goal to achieve that appointment for as long as I can remember. It's quite an honor," I explained, feeling the need to add, "in Veetri."

Rowlen arose from his deep bow and turned toward the dais where the King and I sat. "For Your Majesty, King Jarryn," he announced. "And in honor of the beautiful flower gracing your side, Princess Rynnaia." He turned in a circle, his arms gesturing to encompass the whole of the assemblage. "And for the people gathered here in celebration of the Ryn's return, I give you a new tale, never before told throughout the realm of E'veria. Though this story is old to me and to our fair Princess, it is one that, until now, I've been unable to share. This night, I give you a True Story," he proclaimed. "I will admit, however," he added with a wink in my direction, "to having taken some liberties with characterization."

Rowlen gave another bow. "People of E'veria," he said, "I give to you the story of The Rose and The Asp."

The Asp.

Of all the tales Rowlen had to draw from, true and otherwise, why would he have chosen this one?

I thought I had put my fear of Aspera Scyles away. That it had died with her to be replaced with forgiveness instead. Gratitude, even. Why then my racing heart and teary eyes just at the mention of the nickname we had given her as children?

I searched my mind, swallowed hard, and checked my emotions. Yes, I had forgiven her. But her actions had scored deep enough questions in my heart that even the memory of them retraced those scars. Perhaps they would always be with me. But they had served a greater purpose, as evidenced by the strong hand of my father, which had reached for my own, unnoticed, while I ruminated over what was to come.

Rowlen bowed again, flourished out his palm, and blew a puff of air toward his open hand. A black shimmer slithered through his fingers, and several ladies shrieked as it formed into a long black snake before it even touched the ground.

The asp coiled and hissed, moving its fanged head in a circular pattern around the room as if to encompass every guest within its reach.

"Our story begins in the merry province of Veetri," Rowlen began, "in the home of the Duke of Glenhume. Many years before the time in which our tale begins, the duke had taken into his service a woman from Dwons. Though dour and scornful, she was quite efficient as a housekeeper, and in time, Aspera Scyles earned the trust of the family. Eventually she was promoted to the position of Head of Housekeeping."

The snake uncoiled slowly, and as it rose, it took on the exact likeness of Mrs. Scyles.

Of course I had known it was coming, but seeing the Asp's face again after so long still caused me to take in a rather sharp breath.

Rowlen blew across his palm and the Asp disappeared, replaced by the image of me, looking as I did upon my arrival in Veetri, at age eight. One by one, the other members of Lord Whittier's family appeared.

It was an odd experience, looking back in time at my own life, my arrival at Mirthan Hall, and my adoption into the family there. And yet I remained strangely distanced from the memory now that I knew my true name—and the significance of my true coloring.

The black hair worn by the Story Girl had efficiently disguised her identity—*my* identity—from most of the onlookers. My father squeezed my hand. Though he had never seen me with black hair, had never known me in childhood but for one brief visit that lasted less than an hour when I was very small, he had enabled Drinius to provide me with the dangerous—and quite illegal—ebonswarth dye that made my disguise possible and more easily maintained.

"Everyone loved young Rose," Rowlen proclaimed. "Everyone, that is, except the Asp."

On the edges of the scene, Mrs. Scyles appeared again. Soon, the housekeeper shrank back into the form of a snake and coiled around the legs of the Story Girl, who now appeared as I had at sixteen. The asp struck out at her with bared fangs, eliciting gasps of horror from the audience. But the girl stood stoically silent, only wincing at the attacks, but never crying out.

"The awful Housekeeper used every opportunity to make Rose's doubts about her own worth grow, and those threats kept Rose from telling her family about the abuse. Soon, even Rose's long-cherished memories of loved ones were tainted by the lying tongue of the woman she now thought of as 'The Asp.'"

The snake grew back into the form of the housekeeper, whose satisfied laugh held an evil note. I couldn't help but flinch at the uncannily accurate impression.

"You've no business here!" Rowlen proclaimed in a perfectly nasal depiction of Mrs. Scyles's voice. *"Your father doesn't even want you. He's ashamed you were even born!"*

Although they were not the exact words Mrs. Scyles had used, they were close enough to clench a fist around my heart.

My father gripped my hand tighter. Anger and regret seeped from his thoughts.

"By and by," Rowlen's normal voice returned, "a gathering was held to celebrate two family events. The most important, of course, being the sixteenth birthday of the daughter of the house." Rowlen glanced over to where his brothers stood and shot Kinley an unrepentant grin.

I laughed aloud, drawing several eyes my way, including Kinley's. The party had not only been a celebration of my birthday, but also a recognition of Kinley having achieved knighthood.

Kinley rolled his eyes and shook his head toward Rowlen, but then gave an abbreviated bow, in deference to me. Joy quickened my heart and I laughed again. How happy I was to have my brothers with me once more!

Most of the crowd was riveted on Rowlen's tale. As I moved my gaze back to my Storyteller brother, refusing to pause on the face of Tarlo de Veir lest I need to excuse myself to find a basin and lye, I met the smile of Sir Kile, my night guard. He, too, had been at that Veetrish celebration and understood the teasing Rowlen had directed at Kinley, his friend.

Sir Kile raised his goblet to me and dipped his head in an abbreviated bow. I grinned back, offering a nod of my own.

"All three of Rose's brothers, as well as her guardian, were in attendance that night," Rowlen continued, directing my attention back to him. "Her guardian was a fearsome man whose absence had weighed heavily upon Rose, especially in light of the lies the Asp had cast about the honored knight."

Even if only for a few days, Mrs. Scyles had made me question Uncle Drinius's honor, as well as his affection for me, by implying that he was my father—and I was the unwanted, ill-conceived result of a tryst. I was glad Rowlen didn't elaborate about the content of those lies. While they might have made for a more dramatic story, I was sure neither Uncle Drinius's family, nor my father, would appreciate them being repeated.

Rowlen blew across his palm and shimmers of blue, silver, and gold trickled through his fingers. At once, the crowded Grand Hall of my Veetrish home appeared, decorated nearly exactly as I remembered it from that night. As he continued the tale, I watched my sixteen-year-old self dancing and moving about the crowd.

Suddenly, the dancing Story Rose and her companion turned, revealing the face of the man with whom my translucent counterpart spoke.

Uncle Drinius. My breath caught.

Soon, Rynnaia. My father's voice touched my mind. *He'll be restored to us soon.*

Nodding, I swallowed the lump in my throat.

"The duke's youngest son was an Apprentice Storyteller at the time, and as a gift to his sister, he engaged the crowd with a familiar tale he had adapted to amuse her."

The scene before us changed to a younger Rowlen who immediately began the telling of the story of Lady Anya as he had told it that night, allowing the heroine's form to mirror mine at that age.

It was the oddest sight, seeing Rowlen presenting a story of himself presenting the same story he'd told the night of the gathering at Mirthan Hall. Even odder, since I'd "seen" Lady Anya in a vision and knew, without a doubt, that while her hair was as black as the ebonswarth root dye had made mine, she was as petite as I was tall and her eyes— My gaze shifted to Julien. Her eyes were as brilliant an emerald hue as his.

The moment was utterly surreal. I was in awe of the enormity of my brother's gift. Every aspect of his tale-within-a-tale appeared effortlessly believable and real.

When the Story Rowlen reached the end of his tale, a shimmer of orange fell down upon the Story Anya, who looked exactly like the Story Rose. The crowd gasped as her hair turned from black to orange and they realized, at that moment, that the "Rose" they'd been watching grow up before their eyes was, in fact, me.

The Ryn.

"Well, that explains why Drinius was so angry," my father said, but quietly so that only I would hear. "Revealing you in that way might well have been considered treasonous, so great a risk did it place upon you. Had I witnessed the end of his tale, Rynnaia, I fear your Storyteller might not be with us today."

Rowlen continued. Before us appeared the darkened balcony of Mirthan Hall, inhabited by the Story People representing Rowlen, Sir Drinius, and myself. Coiled next to a flowerpot was the black form of the snake.

Well, that's new. I arched an eyebrow at the license Rowlen had taken with the story. When he glanced my way he shrugged, gave a wink, and continued with his tale.

"The hidden viper listened to the explanation given by the girl, the apology of the Storyteller, and the knight's warning, savoring the information and tucking it away in order that she might someday use it against the young girl she so despised.

"A few days later, however, the Asp's taunts fell on the wrong ears. Learning of the vile housekeeper's actions, the Duke of Glenhume expelled the Asp from his lands. Unfortunately, she took Rose's secret with her. And when she grew desperate, she sold the information to the traitorous Cobelds."

"No!" A feminine gasp permeated the thick silence.

"Yes." Rowlen nodded toward the embarrassed young woman. "Her treachery, however, was paid in full. The Cobeld took not only the information she offered, but her life.

"Just in time to avoid a Cobeld attack, Rose was spirited away, hidden in the Great Wood until such a time as her true identity could be revealed."

Rowlen's next breath produced threads of fire and smoke. "Within a few days of Rose's departure from Glenhume, the duke's lands were invaded. The Cobelds and their allies devastated the village of Glenhume as well as the home where Rose and her family had lived."

I gasped and my hand flew to my mouth as the smoking rubble of the home of my childhood appeared before me. Though it had happened two years ago, I'd only learned of the attack just before leaving for Tirandov Isle. To see the devastation like this—and to know the Asp's betrayal, fed by her hatred of me, was what had led to it—broke my heart.

Fire roared. Smoke billowed. Arrows flew from the bows of Dwonsil warriors and innocent villagers and farmers fell. Above all the visible, audible chaos, the cackling laughter of crazed old men echoed in such a way that it sounded as if there were ten Storytellers relaying the tale instead of just Rowlen. It was riveting. And entirely horrifying.

The sounds faded, the smoke cleared, and my heart broke, just a little bit more.

Mirthan Hall was a skeleton of stone. Her doors had been ripped from their hinges and rested at odd angles. Tendrils of smoke escaped upward. Windows were broken or missing. The gardens were burned down to ash and the pond, dry.

Tears coursed down my cheeks. The happy memories I had been privileged to obtain in that home, among the duke's family, were all that was left of Mirthan Hall. But at least I had that! The village of Glenhume, the families of the slain tenant farmers . . . they had lost . . . everything. Everything!

Grief tore at my chest, filling me up with its empty maw, and with it came the stark realization that this would be the tragic future of the whole of E'veria, should I fail my coming quest.

"Rynnaia," my father whispered, "it's all right now. Mirthan Hall has been rebuilt. Whittier, Capricia, and their household are safe."

Yes, my family was fine. But so many others . . .

All around me, ladies sniffled. A few loud, manly nose blows rent the air.

"*Rynnaia.*" My father's low voice held a sense of urgency.

I wiped my eyes and turned toward him. His thoughts were so drenched in gray that it dimmed the blue of his eyes, and though I tried, I could not access them. It was no small feat on his behalf that separated our minds. But why?

"You must shield your colors, child. Your grief is too vivid. I can only imagine how powerfully it is affecting those without a defense against it. It is too much for the people to accept. They cannot comprehend it."

"What?" I opened my mind to the people around us. Their thoughts were shadowed in the colors of my emotions. I had forgotten to censure the power of my thoughts. Being part Andoven, my father had protection from my grief. But even Rowlen was staring at the scene, an expression of hopeless sorrow written across his features.

I reached for the grayness I'd let slip away while distracted by the devastation of Mirthan Hall and the losses the dukedom had sustained.

As the gray filtered the passion from my thoughts, Rowlen and his audience took on slightly bewildered expressions, unsure of why they had been so moved by the destruction of the Story House. After another moment or two had passed, Rowlen cleared his throat and continued the tale.

"The King's Army came to Glenhume and restored a semblance of peace to the region, and the duke was able to return home to rebuild his estate."

A shining, new, even more charming Mirthan Hall stood where the rubble had been just moments before. The room let out a collective sigh and my father squeezed my hand.

"Rose remained hidden in the Great Wood for nearly two years. Finally, the unrest in the land forced her out of hiding and she came to know her true identity, the reason the Cobelds desired her death, and the reason her parents had resorted to such desperate measures to keep their daughter safe for nineteen years."

The edge of the wood appeared and a cloaked figure stepped out of the trees and into the sunlight. A feminine hand reached up and pulled back the hood of her cloak, revealing the black-haired Story Girl.

As the crowd looked on, the ebony hair on the girl's head was suddenly bathed in a coppery shimmer until it transformed into my natural, fiery copper. A glimmer of silver encircled her head and my mother's crown materialized. The center stone glowed brightly upon the forehead of my exact likeness.

The audience was silent as the Story Princess turned her head. From the trees behind her, the King stepped forward and took his daughter's hand. The silence continued as the scene froze, depicting a satisfied King and a confident princess who was sure of her identity and comfortable in her father's love.

Rowlen blew into his palm again and the vision disappeared in an upward-arching golden shimmer of light.

A supreme moment of silence filled the pause and then the audience burst into cheers. Even the occasional whistle could be heard amidst the thundering applause. Rowlen strode to the dais, stopped directly before me, put a hand to his heart, and bowed. Unlike his usual, showy posturing, this bow was formally reverent. When he arose, the crowd had silenced and they all either bowed or curtsied to me in a similar fashion.

My father stood. "Master Rowlen, I understand you have long desired to become the Regent's Storyteller in your home province of Veetri."

Rowlen's glance grazed my face before returning to the King. "Yes, Your Majesty."

"Would you be willing to forego that hope to serve me instead as the Royal Storyteller?"

Rowlen's pale eyebrows lifted. "I would, indeed."

"May it be so." Turning to the servant behind him, my father retrieved his sword. He stepped off the dais. "Kneel, lad."

Rowlen's knee went immediately to the green marble floor.

"Good people of E'veria," the King began, "this young man and his family have served my daughter for many years. Even should I put aside the great debt I owe Lord Whittier's family, I find this young man worthy of an honored appointment by nature of his dedication to the craft entrusted to him. Due to the exceptional effort Master Rowlen has put into learning how to use the Storytelling gifts granted him by The First, I have offered him the position of Royal Storyteller and he has accepted."

I looked at Rowlen. His head was bowed, but the hand resting on his knee trembled.

My father placed the flat of his sword on Rowlen's right shoulder. My brother jumped slightly and I held in a giggle.

"Master Rowlen de Whittier," my father's voice carried across the Grand Hall, "I knight you in the Order of Conlan, Storyteller to the Second King of E'veria, Stoenryn E'veri. May you use your masterful gift to spread truth, light, and hope throughout the Kingdom!"

The King tapped each of Rowlen's shoulders with his sword, handed it back to the servant, and offered his hand to the Storyteller. "Arise, Sir Rowlen!" he pronounced.

Rowlen took the King's offered hand and stood with an expression of utter amazement on his face. The King guided him to turn around to face the people and then lifted his goblet.

"My people, it is my great honor to present Sir Rowlen de Whittier, the first official Royal Storyteller our land has seen in several generations! Lift your goblets to toast a man who is not my son, but who has served faithfully as my daughter's brother. To Sir Rowlen!"

"Sir Rowlen!"

I wasn't surprised to hear Kinley's and Lewys's voices leading the cheer that broke out as the crowd lifted their goblets.

The disbelief I had felt upon my entrance in the Grand Hall had disappeared. Truth, as seen through Rowlen's story, had been the catalyst for that change.

I stepped forward, and throwing protocol to the wind, allowed my more Veetrish nature to reign for a moment. I threw my arms around my brother and kissed each of his cheeks. Twice.

"Congratulations, Sir Rowlen!"

"Thank you, Rose. Er, Rynnaia, I should say." He grinned. "I never dreamt of such a thing as this." Turning to the King he said, "Your Majesty, I am honored by this appointment. Utterly and entirely honored. I will do my best to serve you and E'veria in this station with all that I am and for all of my life."

"I look forward to it." The King clapped an arm around the Storyteller's shoulders. "The love and friendship you have given my daughter have served me better than any story ever could. I do, however, look forward to seeing more of her childhood through your tales."

Rowlen laughed. "I can assure you, King Jarryn, I have enough of those to fill many a quiet evening." He winked at me. "And I've no doubt that she will continue to provide many more adventures for our entertainment!"

The King chuckled and motioned to the orchestra, who had begun tuning their instruments again. I was unable to hear the rest of their conversation, though. Since protocol had been met before the orchestral break, I was instantly surrounded with young men who were grateful for the opportunity to bypass the Herald of the Dance.

The celebration continued well into the night, but eventually the crowd began to disperse. My father led me back to my chambers a scant few hours before sunrise.

Sir Kile was already there and he nodded when I thanked him for his service. The skin under his eyes was a bit dusky and I felt a little guilty that he had to stand guard, since he'd already been on duty for several hours keeping track of Tarlo de Veir. Other than offering that brief "Thank you," I did not engage him in conversation.

My father was well pleased with the way things had played out, and after accepting my good-night kiss, he continued down the hall to his own chambers.

I shut my door with a wave of my hand. Exhaustion pulled at the very hairs on my head and I wanted nothing more than to shed my beautiful gown and crawl into the island that served as a princess's bed.

I paused when I saw Erielle curled up on the settee. I assumed she had come to help me undress, but as it had taken my father and me a long time to send our guests on their way, she had likely arrived more than an hour ago.

"Dear Erielle," I whispered affectionately. She was fast asleep. After retrieving one of the coverlets from my bed for her, I found Julien with my mind.

He was in the quarters reserved for his family, speaking with Gerrias. Suddenly he held up a hand and his brother quit talking.

Erielle is staying in my chambers tonight. I thought you should know.

He nodded once.

Good night, Julien.

A slow smile revealed a dimple so deep that I wanted to reach through my mind to touch his cheek. But that, of course, was impossible.

"Good night, Princess Rynnaia," he said aloud. The look on Gerrias's face was priceless, but I left them to seek their rest as I, most definitely, sought my own.

SEVENTEEN

*J*t was a scent, borne across the filmy wave of a dream, that first alerted me to an unwelcome presence in my bedchamber. But it wasn't strong enough to pull me completely from sleep.

I was dancing . . . in Julien's arms . . . but when I caught a glimpse of my reflection as we twirled past a mirror, something was different. I was not the princess. I was, instead, black-haired Rose de Whittier. And each time Julien twirled me, my hair swept across my face, assaulting my nose with the putrid scent of the dye that had kept it black all those years in Veetri.

I wrinkled my nose at the offensive odor, but my hair swept across my face again. Hot like breath, it faded my vision to black, until suddenly, other colors filtered into my mind and my perspective switched. Or rather, I switched identities within the dream.

A goblet was placed into my hand, but when I spoke to thank the person who brought it, the voice was not my own, but deeper. A man's voice. And the face of the one I thanked was blurred, as if a fog had formed between us. As I tipped the goblet to drink, the hand clutching it was not mine, but the larger, stronger hand of a knight.

If this oddly lucid dream had me playing the part of a knight, why was the smell of the dye still present, lingering, almost as if someone had stirred ebonswarth root powder into the very goblet from which I drank?

I gasped and tasted the scent on my tongue. It was in the wine!

The conscious part of my mind screamed at myself—or the knight, rather, whose eyes I was seeing through—to spit out the poisoned wine. To alert the guard. To defend the King! But he couldn't hear me.

Moments later, unintelligible whispers tickled my ear. Instructions of some sort, but of which the lucid part of me could not comprehend beyond one particular command, "Disgrace her."

You're dreaming, I told myself. Open your eyes!

But it wasn't until ebonswarth-scented breath neared my lips that my eyes obeyed.

The scent of ebonswarth was even stronger now that I was awake, carried on the breath of the man whose face leered above me, but whose identity I could not discern in the darkness.

I took a breath to scream, but he covered my mouth with one hand and placed a dagger at my throat with the other. I ceased struggling, lest the blade break through my skin, but my racing heart echoed the power of the scream I longed to release.

Who was this man, taking such violent liberties as to approach me in my bedchamber—nay!—my very bed? What was he doing in my room? How had he gotten past Sir Kile? Past Erielle, sleeping on the settee in the antechamber?

My mind raced toward his, seeking not only his identity, but some means by which to remove him from my person, but his mind was clouded with inky black and engaged in a struggle of its own.

"Noooo," he groaned, as if in agony himself.

The dagger's pressure lightened for just a moment, and then he was shoved off me and struggling with a person whose identity was much easier to grasp.

"Rynnaia, run!" Erielle's voice was muffled by the sound of the gurgled groan produced when her fist struck my assailant's windpipe.

I tried to obey, but not having removed my ball gown before falling into my bed, I was now constricted by a tangle of ribbons, linens, and the pressure of the two bodies struggling, trapping the coverlet beneath them and on top of me.

The assailant moaned, "Forgive me, Princess," but the words were forced out like a stutter, as if spoken underwater, and he continued to struggle against Erielle. "*Please.*"

I recognized the voice, though had I not been trying so hard to discern his identity through his mind it would have likely proved impossible. Such inner torment fueled his words! The speaking of them seemed almost more than he could bear.

It was Sir Kile. My night guard. Kinley's friend.

My breath came in gasps, spots dotted my vision. Why would my personal guard, one of my father's knights, attack me? Why was he, even now, struggling against my friend?

Fractured images crossed my consciousness, finally melding together within the Andoven awareness that sleep had robbed from me.

It was Sir Kile's hand in my dream. His lips that drank from the poisoned cup. Even now, he was being controlled by the directive of whoever had drugged him with ebonswarth root powder.

It hadn't been a dream. Not entirely. While in sleep, I had seen his thoughts, his most recent memory, and now, his struggle against the poison that stole his will to resist the instructions he had been given. Instructions to disgrace me. Perhaps even to kill me?

I barely caught his next whisper. "Do . . . what . . . you must, Lady . . . Erielle," he said, spacing apart the words as if even exhaling the breath necessary to speak them caused him anguish. "Kill me before I hurt her!"

But even as he said the words, the poison and his powerful strength denied their meaning, overtaking Erielle's diminutive size. They rolled to the edge of the bed and onto the floor.

As soon as they were off me I sat up and ripped the coverlet away, tearing at the ribbons still holding me captive while gracelessly throwing myself to the edge of the bed.

But they were between me and the door. Sir Kile had Erielle pinned beneath him. With one hand he stretched her right arm above her head and pressed it to the floor. Light from a lamp in the antechamber caught on the metal of his dagger as he raised his other hand.

I gasped. One downward thrust would end their struggle—and Erielle's life.

Please! I petitioned The First with the only word that could escape my panic.

But Erielle moved faster than my mind could focus my gifts enough to try to defend her, not that I had the first idea of how to accomplish such a feat. Arching her back against him, Erielle slid her free hand behind her back and produced a dagger of her own. With a flip of her wrist, it spun in her hand until it was facing upward, and in a blur, she plunged it up and into Sir Kile's chest.

A crash in the antechamber stole my attention.

"Rynnaia!"

Julien! "In here!"

Julien rushed in, his sword drawn. With his other hand, he grasped the back of Sir Kile's tunic and pulled the knight's dead weight off Erielle.

"Rynnaia!" My father rushed in, fear blazing out through his mind so powerfully that it stole my breath. "Guards!" he shouted. "Light the lamps! Search her chambers! Rynnaia, are you hurt?"

"No." I shook my head. "But Erielle may be."

She stood and straightened her skirts. Her bodice was covered in blood, but I knew it wasn't hers. "I'm fine," she said, but her hand trembled at her side. She quickly hid it in the folds of her gown.

Julien propped Sir Kile up, but his head lolled to the side. As the lamps around my chamber were lit, the vacancy in his eyes confirmed he was dead.

"Kile." My father inhaled. His jaw clenched. "Would someone care to explain to me why the knight entrusted with guarding the Ryn is dead?"

"I killed him, Your Majesty." Erielle took a breath and wiped her hand across her skirt, leaving a trail of blood behind. "I didn't know it was Sir Kile at the time, I only saw a threat to Princess Rynnaia."

My father's eyebrows shot upward. "He *threatened* her? How?"

Erielle swallowed. "I was sleeping in the antechamber. I'm not sure how he got by me, but he did." She took a breath. "When I heard the princess scream, I woke up and rushed in here."

"I didn't scream." I shook my head, confused. "I couldn't. His hand was over my mouth."

"You did," she said. "You screamed for Julien. I heard it as clear as if it were in my—" She paused. "As if it were in my head."

"It likely was," Julien said, placing a hand on his sister's shoulder. "I heard it, too. And I was in an entirely different wing of the palace."

"I heard it as well," my father said. "I would have been here sooner, Rynnaia, but I thought, at first, it was a dream," he apologized. "But when I sought you with my mind—"

A shudder passed through his thoughts. He closed his eyes. "But Sir Kile? Are you sure he was the perpetrator? Could the villain still be about?" Disbelief coated my father's words as much as it did his thoughts.

"I'm sure," Erielle said. "When I ran in here he was . . ." she paused and looked at the floor. "He was . . . on the bed, with a dagger to Princess Rynnaia's throat." She glanced at me. "I'm sorry."

Sorry? She saved my life!

She lifted her gaze again to my father. "I tackled him. We fought. He said some strange things . . ." Erielle's voice trailed off.

"Rynnaia," my father's voice shook with his fear that I might have been violated, "were you . . . harmed?"

"No. Erielle came before he could . . ."

I took a deep, shaky breath in through my nose, but with that inhalation, the smell hit me again. *Ebonswarth powder.* It was then that I started to shake.

Julien knelt before me and took my shaking hands into his own. "Rynnaia, look at me."

But Julien's voice seemed a thousand miles away. Instead the anguish of Sir Kile's requests echoed through my mind. *"Forgive me, Princess,"* he'd begged. And to Erielle, *"Kill me before I hurt her."* Even though Sir Kile was across the room, several yards away, I could still smell the putrid trace of the evil with which he had been used—and I could still hear the echo of how bravely he had fought its terrible control.

"Sir Kile—" I began, but the quiet gasp of a denied sob stole my voice.

"He can't hurt you now," Julien whispered. "Never again."

"It wasn't him," I said. "Well, it was, but he wasn't . . . himself. Someone else is at fault. Someone poisoned him with ebonswarth root powder."

I shivered, remembering how Lord Whittier's men, the guards Mrs. Scyles had poisoned, had so long remained haunted by what they had done while under the powder's influence. I looked up and the first tears escaped my eyes. "He tried to fight it, Father, but he couldn't."

My father moved to sit at my side. His arm went around me and I leaned into him. "You are sure about the poison, Rynnaia?"

I nodded, wrinkling my nose. "Can't you smell it?"

He inhaled. His brow creased. "No. But then again, I've not been around it as much as you have."

His gaze rested on Erielle for a long moment and then his eyes closed and his hand rubbed down over his beard. "No one must know what happened here until a full investigation has been completed." His gaze rounded the room. "Understood?"

Everyone nodded.

The King looked toward one of the guards. "Summon Dyfnel," he said, "and see that a laboratory is set up to his specifications in the infirmary." He moved his gaze to another knight. "Assign guards to the kitchens, pantries, and anywhere else food or libations are stored." He spoke to everyone then. "Until Dyfnel has ascertained the safety of our food and drink, I order a fast." His gaze landed on another of the guards. "Make it known."

The three guards nodded and left.

"Julien, Erielle, you will accompany the Ryn and me to my chambers. Risson?"

"Yes, Your Majesty?"

"See to the removal of Sir Kile's body to isolation in the infirmary. Unless proven otherwise, which I do not expect to happen, he is to be given all rights and honors due him as a knight of E'veria."

I breathed a sigh of relief. *He believes me.*

"The rest of you are dismissed and ordered to silence concerning what has happened here tonight."

A solemn chorus of "Yes, Your Majesty" followed us out of my chambers. I paused in the door and glanced back at Sir Kile's lifeless body just as Sir Risson covered it with one of the linens from my bed.

Oh, the evil of it! A young knight, gone. His life forfeited to some traitor's plot. Though his actions seemed to nullify the sacredness of the Knight's Oath, Sir Kile's words had held fast to it, fulfilling his sworn allegiance to me—to E'veria—to the very end, even though it meant his own death.

Kile died to protect me.

Erielle, too, had proven her loyalty. Without regard to her own safety, she had bravely fought and killed a fully trained and vested knight of the King, a knight whose size and strength dwarfed her own . . . so that I might live.

Could I ever hope to be worthy of such sacrifice? Such love? Such wondrous, selfless fealty as these friends—one now lost to us—had shown tonight?

As I allowed myself to be led away from my chambers and to my father's, I wondered how many more friends' lives would be forfeit for my sake, in the name of loyalty. And how would we discover who was behind this evil?

For hours, my father, Julien, and a select few knights offered names of those whose loyalties were considered weak, but they could not seem to pinpoint one who seemed more likely to have arranged the treachery than another.

Word arrived from Dyfnel, who confirmed the knight had indeed been a victim of ebonswarth poisoning. As tragic and frightening as that validation was, it was not substantial enough evidence to even give direction to an investigation— and certainly not enough to make an accusation of any sort. Erielle may have dealt the blow, but she was no more responsible for the knight's death than Sir Kile himself.

But without more evidence, how would we find the villain and see justice served?

Eventually, I began to doze. I tried to fight the fatigue, but my father's voice found my thoughts.

Rest, child. I will keep watch.

And I was reminded that not only was Jarryn E'veri the King and my father, he was a knight, as well. I closed my eyes and did as he suggested.

EIGHTEEN

I awoke well past the midday mark, curled up on an oversized, cushioned bench in my father's suite. My swollen feet ached and my head—oh, my head!—raged. With the ball of one hand pressed to my temple, I eased into a sitting position.

"You look terrible."

"And good morning to you, too, Erielle," I said, punctuating the greeting with a yawn. "Where is everyone?"

When I'd fallen asleep, my father and Julien had still been in the room and had been joined by Kinley and a couple of other knights for whom I could not place names.

"They went to the War Room once they realized you were asleep. They left three guards just outside the door, though. Here." She picked up a goblet and brought it to me. "Drink this."

"The fast is lifted?"

"Yes. Dyfnel tested the King's private reserve first. He brought this himself."

"Oh." I sniffed it. Hmm. Sweet. Somewhat familiar, but . . . "What is it?"

"Eachanberry juice. Dyfnel said it would help restore your fluids and ease any anxiety you might feel due to last night's . . . events."

She paused and I detected the slightest tremble in her thoughts. "He brought me some as well," she said finally. "I found it quite soothing."

I laid a hand on her arm. "Erielle, I didn't get a chance to tell you last night, but thank you. You saved my life, and in a way, you saved Sir Kile, too."

"Saved him?" Her voice broke on the last syllable and a shudder moved across her shoulders, sending the thickness of her cloying, gnawing guilt into my awareness. Erielle shook her head as if to ward off the vividness of the emotion, but it wouldn't be borne away.

"Erielle, I know it doesn't seem like it, but you did. You saved him in the only possible way."

"How can you say I saved him? It was my hand that drove the dagger into his—" She gasped in a breath and swallowed. "Your Highness, I *killed* a *knight!*"

She made a strangled sound and looked away. Her voice dropped almost to a whisper. "All these years I have trained so that I might someday be allowed to serve the King as my father and brothers. All that time, I have known I might have to take a life someday. But to kill a knight? One of the number I had hoped to someday serve alongside?" Another shuddered rippled through her. "Kile was kind," she said. "He made me laugh." She swallowed. "I danced with him last night. And then, only a few hours later . . ."

"A few hours later, you defended the life of your Ryn," I said firmly, though I felt her pain as plainly as if it were my own. "Ebonswarth is an evil substance, Erielle, and whoever slipped it into Sir Kile's goblet is the villain responsible for his death. Not you. Kile could not control his actions. Somewhere within him, he knew that. His request of you was sincere. Were he able, Sir Kile would thank you for doing the duty he was unable to perform."

Her eyes were shut, her expression a mix of grief and disgust.

"I will never forget the feeling of my dagger entering his heart. Or the look in his eyes." Her hand lifted to her mouth. "It was shock at first, I think. But then . . . a strange sort of peace came over him just before . . . nothing." She inhaled through her nose and let the long breath out through her lips. "It was almost as if he was relieved that I'd struck his heart."

"I think he was," I agreed. "On some level, he was aware that he was being controlled by someone else's will. Asking you to kill him was his final act of loyalty to the Knight's Oath."

She nodded, but regardless of the circumstances, this was a memory she would carry with her for all her days. As would I.

"The person responsible for Kile's death is the person who poisoned him with ebonswarth," I stated again, hoping the truth of it would seep into her soul. "You, my friend, did exactly as you should have and you have my thanks."

"It is my honor to have served you," she said. "I only wish there could have been a better outcome for Sir Kile." She took a deep breath in through her nose and sighed. The colors of guilt subsided a little bit. She nodded toward my goblet. "You haven't drunk your eachanberry juice yet."

Just the mention of it caused my tongue to ache with thirst. I tipped the goblet, inwardly wincing at the memory of my dream, of seeing Sir Kile's hand make the same motion. But I pushed the thought away.

Erielle had called it "eachanberry juice," but I knew it as honeyed half-wine, a rare and dearly sought product of Eachan Isle, home of the Seahorse pirates. I had recently sampled it aboard Cazien's ship and found its taste delightful. But Cazien had warned me that the juice of the eachanberry was, in his words, "a bit wily, even prior to fermentation." In this case, it would be medicinal, I supposed. But the pirate had seemed to imply that the berries of Eachan Isle produced a juice that was, perhaps, a bit *too* medicinal, if imbibed in excess.

As I sipped the sweet, tangy nectar, I thought about the council to come. We had planned to confer about the departure from Holiday Palace, the point at which I would leave my father's company to move toward Mount Shireya, and the progress toward finding someone to act as my double along Dynwey Road. But with this new treachery, I could only assume there was even more to discuss.

A maid arrived bearing fresh clothes for both of us and drew a bath for me in my father's tub, which dwarfed my own. Even with the night's grief still pressing down on my heart, I couldn't help but reflect that as pampered as I was as a princess, it was clearly quite good to be King.

My hair was not yet completely dry when I was ready to dress, so I divided it into three sections, braiding each, and then braiding the three braids together before rolling and pinning up the excess at the nape of my neck.

That task completed, I dressed. The color of my gown reminded me of the rich, fresh soil found around a long-fallen tree in the wood. It had a subtle orange sheen when I stood in direct sunlight, but its only decorations were the green laces across the bodice. Even though I could easily get myself in and out of this gown without help, the ease of its use did not detract from its simple, earthy beauty. Truth be told, it was one of my favorites.

When I returned to my father's antechamber, Erielle was gone, but the King had returned.

"Rynnaia." He looked tired and I gathered he hadn't slept at all after the events in my bedchamber, but his voice held the special smile reserved for me. Seated across the wide desk from him, Julien took to his feet.

"I'm sorry," I said. "I didn't mean to interrupt."

"Your presence could never be an interruption," my father said. "Come. Sit." He motioned to the chair next to Julien's.

I was barely settled in the chair when a knock sounded on the door.

My father sighed. "Enter."

The door opened and the guard announced the herald.

I laughed.

Julien tilted his head and whispered, "What's so funny?"

"The herald was just announced." I giggled again.

"And . . . ?" He arched an eyebrow. He didn't get it.

He didn't get it? I explained. "Don't you see? The guard just *heralded* the *herald*."

"Ahh." He looked down, but his beard quirked.

"It was funnier in my head," I admitted. I bit my lip, wondering if my Veetrish nature had caused offence by allowing humor to escape so quickly after a tragedy.

Humor and the comfort of family was how the Veetrish dealt with difficult times. But perhaps, as in so many other arenas, the rest of E'veria dealt with pain with more solemnity than did the Veetrish. I would have to apologize to Julien and my father later, for it appeared I wouldn't be given a minute longer to muse over my probable breach in etiquette now.

"Your Majesty, the post." The herald passed my father a thick sheaf of parchments. "Twenty came with instructions of urgency."

"And are they?" My father asked, but frowned as he scanned the first page.

"That is, of course, not my place to say. But I believe you will find the urgency of their authors to be much more ardent than the need to reply."

My father flipped through the messages. With each page, the line between his brows deepened. Finally, he set the parchments down and turned his gaze to the herald.

"Is there anything here that might shed some light on the attack on the princess?"

Earlier we had agreed that Sir Kile would be remembered for having died while defending the Ryn from an attack. And, due to some unknown person's treachery, it was the truth. The details didn't matter outside our small circle.

"I'm afraid not, Your Majesty."

My father flipped through a few more parchments. "Is there a single message here that does *not* pertain to the court-ship of my daughter?"

The herald's lip twitched. "Yes, Your Majesty. Several do not speak of courtship at all but instead contain proposals of marriage."

"*What?*" I stood. "You must be joking."

At my outburst, Julien laughed aloud. I turned toward him, but he just grinned and arched an eyebrow as if to say, "*I told you so.*"

"It seems there is a mad rush of love in Dynwatre," the King said with a dry smile.

Julien snorted.

"You doubt the sincerity of these men, de Gladiel?" My father's tired eyes sparkled as he held up the pages. "Why, one claims he has been aware of her existence for years and was just waiting for—" He paused. "Wait. I'll read it." He sorted through until he found the right one. "Here it is. 'We were only waiting for the time we could declare our mutual affection and receive Your Majesty's blessing upon our marriage.'"

The sound that rushed from my throat was a cross between a squeak and a snarl. I reached across the desk and grabbed the parchment out of my father's hands. I scanned the script. "Leflin de Monnyn? I don't even recall his name! Did I even dance with him?"

"You did." Julien's laugh was so hearty he bent at the waist and put his head in his hands. When he arose his eyes danced. "He's the magistrate from Port Dyn. A short widower with three long hairs combed around his bald head."

I groaned as the picture formed in my mind. "I remember him!" I wrinkled my nose. "He smelled of gutted candles and . . . and broccoli left too long to boil!"

Julien leaned back in his chair and rested the back of his head in his clasped fingers. "I had no idea the competition would be so fierce."

The King rifled through the messages. "At least there are none here of whom I will have to lower my estimation of their character."

I lifted my chin. "Is it so hard to believe that I would merit the attention of suitable men?"

"No, Rynnaia," he replied. "But *suitable* men know a lady more than one evening before issuing a declaration of love or proposing marriage."

"Some even threaten the lady's life at the tip of a sword once or twice before requesting her father's permission to court," Julien added with a grin.

I barked out a laugh. "Indeed."

"I don't believe I'm familiar with that story," my father said.

"I am!" Erielle announced from just inside the door. Behind her, the guard stammered out an apology.

My father waved at the guard in dismissal while shaking his head at Julien's sister.

Erielle pursed her lips. "I should have waited to be announced. Sorry."

Julien let out a heavy sigh. "Nothing new there," he grumbled.

My father just chuckled. "Well, you might as well come the rest of the way."

Erielle took the third and final chair facing my father's desk and proceeded to tell him about the first time Julien had met his new "squire"—me.

This, then, is how we will make it through Sir Kile's passing, I thought. *Not by ignoring the tragedy, but by trusting that life is bigger than the pain death brings.*

Perhaps some Veetrish ways were more universal than others.

I smiled through the story, proud of Erielle for not only her actions in protecting me, but for her strength in not succumbing to the misery that might have overtaken a weaker person in her position.

In the days to come, I reflected, *evil may force us to take regrettable action, and death may rob us of friends, but neither will be allowed to steal our joy or rob us of the benefits of friendship itself.*

"Even you, Your Majesty, would not recognize your daughter in her disguise," she finished.

My father leaned back in his chair and tented his fingers at his waist. "Oh, I might surprise you."

Erielle wrinkled her nose. "Well, if not for the Andoven connection you wouldn't."

Julien nodded his agreement. "It's quite a convincing disguise."

"Of that I am glad. Unfortunately, I believe it's time we move to the War Room," my father said. "Some of the knights have likely already gathered." He stood, and although his smile didn't entirely disappear, it seemed a bit sad. "We've much to do to ready for your journey, as well as Sir Kile's honors to arrange."

At that we all sobered.

The council met again in the War Room, among them, Sir Kiggon of Sengarra, under whom my brother Lewys served.

My father outlined the plan we had discussed to rescue Uncle Drinius and Sir Gladiel. No one questioned whether I would be able to unlock the cells, but they didn't have to. Disbelief was carved in each knight's brow. Well, each but Julien's. His confidence bolstered mine and I could only hope it was well-placed.

"I've lost a good number of men and a score are still within the infirmary, recovering from their wounds," Kiggon said when my father had explained his strategy: six regiments, depending on the element of surprise, would attack and hope to draw the enemy away from the fortress while I, wherever I happened to be at the time, would unlock the cells and guide the prisoners out of the fortress and to the awaiting troops.

"If your Majesty would grant it," Kiggon continued, "my men and I would be honored to join the troops you're sending to recover Gladiel and Drinius."

My father nodded. "Granted. There is an individual member of the third regiment whose welfare must be assured in order to facilitate the knights' release. I would like to put him in your especial charge."

"Of course," Kiggon said. "It would be my honor. And might I ask his name?"

"Harbyn."

"The horse trainer?"

"Indeed. His grandmother was Andoven, and while his gifts are not strong enough to allow him to unlock the cells at the Cobeld fortress, he will be able to communicate with the princess concerning the timing of her efforts to that end. He has also been instructed to report to me periodically to keep me apprised of your progress along the way."

"Your Majesty," Kinley spoke up, but his eyes were on the maps laid out on the table. "By my calculations, the princess may well be within Mount Shireya by the time the regiments reach the fortress."

"Yes," my father said, his brow furrowing.

Kinley continued, "If the scrolls' prediction of her possible . . . incapacitation," he paused and looked over at me then, his eyes troubled, "should be accurate, I'm caused to wonder if Harbyn will be able to reach her."

My father looked down at the maps, nodding. "You're wondering if we should have a secondary plan, should Rynnaia be unable to unlock the cells."

"I think we all are," Sir Risson spoke up. "Regardless of Her Highness's condition, a secondary option would be a good idea."

Quiet descended. Faced with the prospect of figuring out how to release prisoners whose very cells were armed with hairs from a Cobeld's cursed beard, no one could think of another option.

"Between transporting the King back to Salderyn and helping the Ryn accomplish her quest," Sir Risson added, "we can hardly afford to send more troops to Dwons."

I wanted to shout, *"If it were up to me, I would send the whole army to save my uncle and Sir Gladiel!"* But my mind treaded back before that thought could take another step in that direction. *No. I would not.* And they would not wish me to. There were more pressing matters at hand, and regardless of their loyalty and my love for them, the task of finding the Remedy had to come first.

"These knights are dear to me," I said instead. "Nothing but death will keep me from answering Harbyn when he contacts me. I have to believe the plan will work."

"And if for some reason it does not," my father added, his gaze resting first on Sir Kiggon and then moving to the knight who would serve as this action's commander, "I trust you will do whatever seems wisest."

The knights nodded and my father moved on to the next topic, deferring to Julien to explain the strategy for delivering me safely to Mount Shireya.

Julien spoke with an authority that not even the older, more experienced knights questioned, even internally. I felt a tad bit guilty for looking into the thoughts of the council, but admiration for my suitor overcame the restraint I should have exercised to follow Andoven etiquette. I was curious to see where he stood in the minds of the other knights and gratified that it was at such a well-earned height.

"Sir Kile's memory and loyal service will be honored at table tonight," my father said when Julien finished. "Since we have an Andoven elder present, Dyfnel will preside over the burial rites at sunrise. You are dismissed."

The mood was solemn as we left the War Room. Beyond the treachery that had led to Sir Kile's death, other concerns abounded.

Would the woman serving as my imposter be believable enough to draw the Cobelds from Shireya? And if the ruse was successful, would the King and his army be able to thwart a concentrated attack from the Cobelds and the Dwonsil warriors? Would Gladiel and Drinius survive long enough to be rescued? These questions and more were heavy upon us all.

"I refuse to accept the possibility of failure, Kiggon." Sir Risson's low voice caught my ear as I made my way to the door, but I doubted he meant for me to hear. "Mourning the Ryn was costly the first time. Should we have cause to mourn her again, I fear the Kingdom will not survive."

NINETEEN

The last full day before our departure found nearly every occupant of the palace engaged in travel preparations. The majority of my time was spent perfecting my disguise and learning how to work the hatch in the floor of the carriage by which I would sneak out to meet up with Julien once we were well enough away from Port Dyn.

The carpets had been removed from my bedchamber but had not yet been replaced. I was relieved to avoid seeing the bloodstained reminder of Sir Kile's attack and subsequent death, but my chambers seemed colder with the stone floor echoing every step I took.

I hadn't slept here again. Instead my father ordered a bed placed in what had been my mother's personal sitting room, adjacent to his study. I was glad to be nearer to him, but I had objected to putting anyone to the task of moving my things when we were soon to leave Holiday Palace anyway. I didn't linger long in my dressing chambers when the need arose, but I couldn't see the sense in packing it all up twice.

I had just finished packing the few wardrobe items I would need to regain my identity as Rozen de Morphys when Erielle arrived with a tall young woman in tow.

"This is your imposter, Princess," she said as soon as the door was closed. "Vayle de Ellis, may I present Her Royal Highness, Princess Rynnaia?"

"Your Highness." Vayle gave me a low curtsey.

"You're blond." I looked to Erielle. "She's blond." I repeated the obvious.

Erielle grinned. "Not for long. Dyfnel has brewed some sort of concoction that he believes will make her hair nearly as fiery as yours. He'll be arriving shortly with a couple of maids to help apply the mixture."

"Oh." It was then I noticed the decided blush on Vayle's cheeks.

"Vayle, I'm sorry." I grimaced. "What an ungracious way for me to meet the one doing me and the Kingdom such a service. Forgive me. I'm honored to meet you and grateful that you've volunteered to serve E'veria in this way."

"I took no offense, Your Highness," she said softly.

"I'm going to teach Vayle how to help you dress like Rozen," Erielle said, adding, "Since I won't be there in the carriage to help."

Vayle was a quick study in learning how to dress me in the somewhat unfamiliar male garb. The task was not difficult, but it differed from the feminine way of dress, and since I expected it would take a good deal more patience when confined in a tiny space like a carriage, I would be glad of her assistance.

"You don't look like a woman at all!" Vayle exclaimed after I applied the last piece of my costume: gray-tinted spectacles that hid the brightness of my blue Andoven eyes. Her hand flew to her mouth. "Forgive me, Your Highness! That was a terribly rude thing to say."

I laughed. "That's the whole point of the disguise, Vayle! I'm glad to see it's still as believable as it was back when Erielle and I first came up with the idea."

A knock sounded on the door to the hallway and Erielle went to see who it was, though I already knew. "It's Dyfnel," I told Vayle. "Do you need a moment alone with the looking glass before your beautiful blond hair turns to fire?"

She shook her head. "I must confess I'm a little curious. Who could dream of such a thing as to undo the appearance Rynloeft granted me?"

"Thank you for doing this for me, Vayle. Truly."

"Shall I help you back into your gown now, Your Highness?"

Just then, the herald announced Dyfnel.

I smiled at Vayle. "Thank you, but I think you are about to be otherwise occupied." I turned around.

I had been wearing men's clothes when I'd first met Dyfnel, but not the rest of my disguise. He had never seen me dressed completely as Rozen de Morphys. To say his reaction was surprised was an understatement, but when he got over his shock, he smiled and nodded. "Good. Very good. Well done."

Erielle and I bid good-bye to Vayle and set off to visit my father's chambers, only to be informed that he'd gone for a walk in the gardens. Attired in my squirely disguise, I had a freedom of movement—even with the bindings around my chest—that I wasn't allowed in a gown, and it seemed to birth a certain restlessness and a desire to be with my horse.

"Let's go to the stables," I suggested.

Erielle frowned. "Do you think we should summon a guard?"

I laughed. "Do squires normally have need of a guard? Besides, I have you."

"I'm wearing a gown."

"Then we'll pretend I'm your guard."

The look she gave me would have seemed offended if not for the snort that accompanied it.

"Come on. I miss Stanza."

"Your father would want you to have a guard," she frowned, but brightened. "But there are bound to be a few knights around the stables. All right, let's go."

As Erielle surmised, there were quite a few knights about, and if they thought it odd that a lowly squire would seem so familiar with a Regent's daughter—or the princess's horse, for that matter—they didn't mention it. While several acknowledged Erielle with a dip of the head or an outright greeting, I received no particular notice. No notice, that is, until I caught site of Julien near one of the paddocks.

He was leaning against the fence with one elbow propped up on the top rung. The three men facing him were my brothers.

"Erielle, wait." I said, unable to keep a prankish tone from my whisper. "Kinley and Lewys have never seen me like this."

She laughed when I waggled my eyebrows.

We crept a little closer.

Almost as if he deduced my intent—perhaps he had witnessed my grin?—the corner of Julien's mouth twitched when I met his eyes, but it quickly settled into his former expression.

He stood up from his lean. "Men de Whittier, I'm afraid I must beg my leave of you. My sister and my squire approach and I would see what they need of me."

Rowlen was the first to turn. His gaze rested a moment on Erielle and then moved to me. He blinked and laughed. "Squire, indeed."

I looked down at the ground and kicked my foot in the dirt, trying to take attention from the amusement that filled me at Rowlen's reaction to my disguise.

"You've taken on a squire, Julien?" Kinley turned to follow Rowlen's gaze. "When did this come about?"

"It wasn't all that long after I met your sister," he said, and I almost ruined the ruse by laughing aloud, but caught myself just in time. "Knights de Whittier, may I present Squire Rozen de Morphys, late of Veetri?"

I made a deep bow and Rowlen let out a breath that held the tiniest trace of a laugh. I squinted at him through my spectacles and lowered my voice, thickening my accent to sound as much like a Veetrish boy as I could.

"Is the air too thick for you in the south, Sir Rowlen, that you should need to breathe with such effort?"

Kinley's eyebrows lifted. "Quite a tongue on the lad, Julien."

"Mmm. Yes." Julien rubbed his beard and walked toward me. "I suppose I shall have to find a way to conquer that tendency, although his quick wit is a welcome diversion when we're on the trail. You will likely come to appreciate it over the next few weeks, Kinley."

"Surely you don't mean to take an untried squire with us, Julien? Such an undertaking would be foolish!" He shot a quick glance my way. "No offense, lad, but your inexperience could put the princess at great risk."

"Oh, you might be surprised at how useful Rozen is in protecting the princess," Julien said. "And the two of them do get on quite well. You can, of course, consult Princess Rynnaia on the matter, but I'm fairly certain she'll insist that Rozen accompany us."

I could barely control my expression. The sport Julien was having at Kinley's expense was entirely too entertaining.

"Kinley," Lewys said slowly, his eyes on Rowlen's grin. "I think we're missing something. Something important."

Rowlen chose that moment to let loose a guffaw.

Lewys and Kinley gaped at him.

With a sigh, I removed my spectacles and spoke in my normal voice. "Close your mouths, boys, before you choke on a fly."

Lewys spun back around. "Ro-rose?"

"No, actually." Even though no one was within earshot, I lowered my voice. My disguise was effective, but to remain so on the journey ahead it had to stay a secret. "My name is Rynnaia." I slid the spectacles back on.

A smile gleamed in Lewys's eyes and a moment later his shoulders shook with laughter, but my attention was suddenly caught by movement just beyond Julien's shoulder. When I glanced toward it, a murky shade of red swam within my mind.

It was an emotion, a color, with which I had never before come in contact. I couldn't identify the meaning, but something about the odd texture the color took on just as it dissipated chilled me. *Had someone been listening?* But surely no one within the palace gates would wish me or my friends harm.

Unless whoever had used the ebonswarth powder on Sir Kile was still within the palace gates.

Julien frowned and stepped closer to me. "What is it?"

"I don't know," I said. "I thought I saw something. Someone, I mean. But they're gone now."

"Where?" Kinley's voice was hard, but quiet.

I nodded to the small tack building to the right of the paddock. "I think someone may have heard us."

Kinley and Julien exchanged a look and a nod.

"Lewys and I will go check it out," Kinley said.

"I'll guard the Ryn," Julien replied, his voice barely above a whisper.

Julien decided we should find the King and inform him of the possible breach. I sought him with my mind and found him still in the gardens, on a marble-railed terrace overlooking the sea. The remaining four of us headed his direction.

My father had not acknowledged my brief touch to his thoughts when I'd sought him, neither did he notice our approach, which caused me a moment's pause. He appeared pensive, yet troubled. With a hand to Julien's arm and a quick word, I decided to approach my father alone, but I knew my friends would remain close.

His gaze rested cloudily in the distance across the sea and I couldn't help but wonder if his thoughts were on my mother. Perhaps he was speaking with her, even now. I hated to interrupt if that were the case. But being that she *was* my mother, I knew she would understand.

I moved to a spot along the rail, only a few feet away from where he stood, and waited for him to notice me.

It didn't take long.

"Are you lost, lad?"

I blinked. Oh! He'd never seen me in my disguise!

"Rynnaia?" His eyes widened before a satisfied smile overtook his expression of surprise. He laughed. "Well done."

It was then that my mother's sweet laughter touched my mind. The King's gaze flew out to sea. He had heard it, too. But just as quickly as it came, it faded away.

"I thought she'd fallen asleep." The King shook his head, turned, and placed his finger under my chin, lifting my face. He inspected my disguise. "Well done, indeed."

"You were speaking with Mother, weren't you?" I cringed. "I interrupted. I'm sorry."

"I was, but we had finished. In fact, I was fairly certain she had fallen asleep. Either I was wrong," he said, "or she was awake just enough to sense your approach as I was saying good-bye." His smile fell. "You shouldn't be about without a guard."

"I'm not." I turned and gestured. Erielle twinkled her fingers at him. Rowlen grinned and nodded his head in an abbreviated bow. Julien's smile was thinner and his posture was much less relaxed.

My guard, indeed. Every muscle in Julien's body was taut and ready to spring into action.

"There may be a . . . complication," I said, motioning them forward. "With my disguise," I added.

Julien filled him in.

My father's frown grew more pronounced with every word. "Your disguise is exceptional," he said. "But for it to work it must be known to very few." He clasped his hands behind his back, paced a few steps away, and back again.

"Julien, come with me to my chambers." He paused, glancing quickly at me before he returned his gaze to Julien. "Julien, I'd like a private word. Rowlen, watch for Kinley and Lewys's return and send them to me at once. Erielle, I trust you are armed?"

"Yes, Your Majesty."

"Good. Accompany Rynnaia back to your family's wing. Rynnaia?" To everyone else he issued an order. To me, a question. "If there's nowhere else you need to be, would you stay in the Regent of Mynissbyr's rooms until I send for you?"

I nodded. "Of course

His brow furrowed. "On second thought, Julien and I will see you to the Regent's suite before going to mine."

As we followed Julien from the gardens, I glanced at Erielle. "How armed are you, exactly?"

"From toes to teeth," she said. "Or as near as possible, in any case."

I examined her from top to bottom. She wore a long-sleeved gown that matched the color of the violets dotting the grass along the path, but no belt, no sword.

Yet, I reminded myself, Erielle had slept in a ball gown the night Kile was killed, and from it had drawn a dagger when she was called upon to defend me. The way she spoke now made it sound as if she had multiple weapons at her disposal, though I could not identify a single one on her person.

She laughed at my confusion. "Trust me."

After assuring himself that Julien's family's chambers were secure, my father and Julien left us. At my request, Erielle was only too glad to show me the collection of thin daggers—and even a short sword!—she had hidden up her sleeves, down the front of her bodice, and within hidden pockets of her gown.

"Besides the other night, have you ever had to use any of them?" I gestured to the collection of eight, yes *eight*, weapons she had laid out on my bed as she put them back into their proper places.

"Once or twice," she said. "Occasionally at a ball there are men who are a little too affectionate." She arched one brow and looked at me out of the corner of her eye. "But I've never had to threaten the same man twice."

For as young as she was and as easily as she masqueraded as a boy, Erielle was a beauty. At the two balls we'd both attended at Holiday Palace, I'd noticed that she was also quite popular as a dancing partner. I was sure she'd had plenty of opportunities to fend off unwanted advances.

She shrugged and slid a dagger only as wide and long as my little finger into a hidden leather sheaf in her sleeve. "All my gowns are tailored this way."

It was a comfort to me, who knew little of weaponry other than how to mark the dagger, that at least the rest of our party on this quest would be well-equipped.

It wasn't until early evening that my father sent for me. I barely had time to divest myself of the squire's clothes and regain my femininity before we had to go to the dining hall.

Many of the guests who had attended the ball reappeared at table that night and a few of the nobles made sport of each other by steadily increasing the verbosity of their toasts. Even though my father assured me this was a normal occurrence in such company, and considered something of a game, I lost my appetite after the sixth mention of my "graceful, iconic beauty."

"And may your future and the hope of fair E'veria be as bright as the blue of your eyes and as sure as the flame of your hair."

Everyone raised their goblets and drank. When the young lord, whose name I could not remember, sat down, a hint of murky red touched my thoughts. At first, I thought it came from him, but when I focused my thoughts, I found his own to be as clear and loyal as any I'd seen.

I took my time scanning the faces and thoughts around him, but could find no trace of the strange deception that had so briefly touched my mind, but that exactly matched what I had sensed by the paddock earlier.

"Where is he?"

"Who?"

I hadn't realized I'd spoken aloud until Julien responded to my question. And all at once, I knew the answer. "Tarlo de Veir."

I closed my eyes, pictured his face, and whispered his name. *"Tarlo."*

He was moving swiftly, already out of the castle. He looked over his shoulder, as if sensing he was being followed. Suddenly he jolted. Stopped. He met my eyes and tilted his head. "Your Highness?"

I gasped. How could I have forgotten that even non-Andoven people could see me when I spoke to them over a distance? I'd nearly caused Uncle Drinius to think he was losing his mind the first time I'd spoken to him in the cell in Dwons.

In my shock, the connection was broken, but I had seen enough.

"He knows about my disguise," I whispered.

I opened my eyes and looked at my father, but his eyes were on Julien. He nodded, the confirmation of a wordless command. Julien returned the nod and rose.

"If you'll excuse me, Your Majesty, Your Highness," he said. "There are some matters to which I must attend with my brother on behalf of Mynissbyr."

"Of course," my father said.

Gerrias was a bit down the table, but he noted the exchange and rose. "Your Majesty," he said. "Your Highness."

My father nodded, excusing them from table as if he didn't know that Gladiel's sons were about to go after Tarlo de Veir.

Be careful, I whispered into Julien's thoughts. *He's already left the palace.*

His only answer was a tight smile and a nod.

Another chair scooted back, and yet another young nobleman arose and lifted his glass my direction. It was all I could do to contain my groan.

By the time the final course was served, my smile was frozen near to the point of pain and I only vaguely listened to the toasts. Following the cues of those around me, I lifted my goblet at the appropriate times and pushed the food around on my plate between speakers, but my thoughts were on Julien and Gerrias and their pursuit of Tarlo de Veir. Every time I thought I had a moment to contact Julien and check their progress, however, someone new would demand my attention.

The dinner lasted until late into the night, but Julien and Gerrias did not return. Eventually the toasting tapered off and my father declared the meal finished.

As my father escorted me to my chamber, exhaustion pulled at both my mind and my body. But anxiety over the nefarious purposes Tarlo's behavior might explain, combined with the anticipation of the adventure and danger the coming quest would hold, kept rest far from my mind.

After I readied for bed, I contacted Julien, anxious to know how their search was progressing. Unfortunately, he and Gerrias had not yet located the man. By the time it occurred to me that I might use my Andoven abilities to find the would-be traitor, Tarlo's thoughts were jumbled with drink, and since I knew so little of the area's landmarks, I was of no help in the search. It was a long night, and although I was anxious to seek the Remedy, I didn't welcome the sun as heartily as might be expected.

ᎢWENTY

Ꭲhe first half of the day came and went without so much as a "good morning" to be heard within the palace.

My father had taken Kinley's suggestion that our group split up on the first leg of our journey, and to that end, Erielle, Risson, Edru, and Dyfnel had already departed when I arose. Since Erielle would be traveling ahead, my father had hand-picked two women from among the palace staff to serve as lady's maids for me until I left his company. After, they would perform the same duty for Vayle as she traveled in my stead toward Salderyn. It was they who awaited me when I awoke, and their care of me was skilled but so much more reserved than Erielle's. They were pleasant enough, if a bit nervous, as I supervised the final packing of the gowns that would pre-cede my arrival at Castle Rynwyk in Salderyn.

Lunch with my father was a sober affair. Neither of us spoke much once he informed me that Julien and Gerrias had returned in the early morning hours—having been unable to locate Tarlo de Veir. Although there was much to say, words seemed inadequate. The gravity of our parting so soon after we'd met, especially with the possibility of sabotage hanging over our heads, rested heavy and thick within our hearts.

Early afternoon found me dressed in a traveling gown with my hair coiled around my head and the silver circlet in place. I had been instructed to await my father's escort in my chambers, but I was not surprised when I detected Julien's approach.

I'd left my chamber doors open, so he walked directly to me and took my hands. The frustration and unease he felt for having not found Tarlo was written across his face, but neither of us mentioned it. There was no point.

A sigh escaped my lips, letting a bit of my anxiety out with it. I couldn't explain how glad I was that he would be with me on this journey. His very presence calmed me on a level that sank under my skin and into my blood. Even back in the Great Wood, when we were little more than strangers, it was Julien's comfortable companionship, the way he knew just the right thing to say—or when to say nothing at all—that helped me to believe I was the Ryn. Now those uniquely Julien traits continued to offer hope that I could survive this quest, and reassurance that, even if I didn't survive, I would have done my duty.

Julien stepped back. As his eyes roved my form from tip to toe, his expression shifted. The slow build of a roguish smile sent a wisp of emerald fire up the back of my neck and it was that same heat that defined his expression.

"It will be a long time before I'll look upon my princess again."

"Hardly." I laughed and ducked my head to hide the color in my cheeks. "I'll join you tonight at my father's camp."

"No, you won't," he said, shaking his head. "Rozen will. It's not quite the same." His hand lifted to caress my cheek. I closed my eyes and tilted my face into his palm.

"Rynnaia?" he whispered.

I opened my eyes.

"I love you."

My breath caught.

"Whatever happens," his voice was low but full, "from this moment on, never doubt that my heart is yours."

For some time, I'd held the surety of his words in my heart and had felt their confirmation in the colors of his thoughts, but hearing them aloud seared my very soul with their song.

My breath left me in a rush as he pulled me close and wrapped me in his arms.

"I wanted to tell you, to say the words, without an audience," he whispered against my hair. "And I fear this may be our last chance to speak privately until after—" he broke off and pressed a kiss to the top of my head. As chaste as the gesture was, it sent a flash of heat to the tips of my toes.

Julien must have felt it, too, for he loosened his hold and stepped back. His eyes were troubled as he brought my hand to his lips, and then clasped it between both of his.

"What's wrong?"

"I have vowed to protect you with my life, but the prophecy seems to nullify my vow in places. That is hard to accept." He paused and his tender but troubled smile pierced my heart. "Perhaps I put a bit too much trust in my sword."

The memory of his arms, his kiss—even though it only touched my hair—still coursed through my blood, making my voice a bit breathless. "Do you think I should have a sword of my own?" I had always wanted a sword, but none of my brothers had been inclined to tutor me in the use of such a weapon.

Julien's brows drew together. "Can you wield a sword, Rynnaia? Has my sister given you some sort of lessons on the sly these past few days of which I was not informed?"

I shook my head. But how hard could it be, really? It was a metal stick. One side was sharp. Even a novice could do a bit of damage to an enemy if pressed, couldn't they?

Couldn't *I*?

Julien stepped back and pulled his broadsword from its sheath. Placing the tip on the floor, he gestured for me to take it.

The dawn of a grin stretched my cheeks as I wrapped my hand around the sword's hilt. I lifted it. It wobbled. I scowled. Princess or not, I was no weakling. I'd worked hard to retain the muscle I'd gained the last time I'd pretended to be Julien's squire.

But even then, I had not carried a sword. A dagger, yes. And I was proficient with it. But not a sword.

The weight of the weapon surprised me. The sword wiggled and wobbled in my grasp. I sighed. My lack of strength and nonexistent skill obliterated any advantage the mere possession of such a weapon might give me.

With a bit more speed than intended, I let the tip return to the floor.

"Next time, then," I said.

"Next time?"

"Well, yes!" I lifted my chin. "After Erielle has trained me, of course."

Julien took back his sword. Lifting it up as if it were a twig of cottonwood, he slid it into its scabbard. "I think your father would agree with me that we hope there will not be a *next time*."

"Even if the Cobelds are defeated, other enemies will arise in time. The Dwonsil warriors have proven that Cobelds do not hold a monopoly on mischief within the realm," I argued. "Even if I don't see another rebellion in my lifetime I see no reason to allow myself to become lazy, and thus unprepared."

"I won't argue with that. Although, should you decide to follow through with this threat, your father—"

"*Threat?*"

"I meant no disrespect, Your Highness," he added when I crossed my arms and glared. His eyes sparkled. "I only mean that I long for peace in E'veria and for your safety. I hope that if you train at swordplay it will be just that. A means for your own entertainment." He smiled and I relaxed my posture. "Once our current expedition is concluded, I hope you will never need to worry about defending yourself again."

He tilted his head and held out a hand. His lips quirked. "Would you indulge your lowly servant and forgive my impertinence?"

Even if I had been truly angry with him I couldn't have continued to be once I saw that spark dancing in his eyes. I slid my hand into his. "You are forgiven."

His lips brushed across my knuckles and he gently turned my hand over and opened my fingers. Bending over my hand, he kissed my palm, and then closed my fingers around it.

"To carry with you, Rynnaia."

Tears sprang in my eyes. There was something so solemn, so sacred, about his gesture. It made his love seem a tangible thing. I pressed the kiss against my heart and then reached for his hand. Closing my eyes, I kissed his palm as he had mine. "To carry with *you*, Julien. And with it, you have my heart and my devotion. I love you."

A glimmer of moisture in his eyes added depth to his smile. And then, almost as if they were pulled by an invisible cord, our kissed hands met in the space between us, upright and flush against each other. We stood like that, our eyes speaking volumes, our hands sharing our kisses, until my attention was stolen.

"The King approaches," I whispered. Our hands dropped to our sides. "It would appear our adventure is about to begin."

"Until this eve, then." Julien reached into his pocket and removed a folded square of parchment, which he slipped into my hand just before my father entered the room.

"Your Majesty," he said, bowing slightly to my father before exiting.

When I met my father's eyes a trace of humor moved across his worry-worn face, and when he reached for my hand, he noted the parchment Julien had given me.

"Ah, courtship," he said with a chuckle. Then, with a sigh, he regained his seriousness. "Vayle and her maids are ensconced in the carriage. The procession waits only for our arrival. Are you ready?"

I nodded and took his arm. He led me from the palace and helped me up the steps and into a carriage that looked like a lidless jewel box on wheels. Behind it, even more ornate, was the matching but enclosed version of the jewel box carriage where Vayle and her lady's maids awaited behind thick, black-lined curtains of moss-green silk.

I reached for my skirts but the crinkle of parchment revealed Julien's note, still in my hand. Careful not to drop it, I lifted the fabric, and allowed my father to assist me up the cast-iron steps where I then took my place upon the downy cushions.

My father squeezed my hand before letting go and then he hurried away. He was second-guessing his decision to lead the procession rather than ride with me, but he didn't change his course. I was glad he didn't try to speak to me. I was not sure my throat, as thick as it felt, would allow me to reply. Part of me wished he would ride in the carriage with me, but I feared being reduced to a puddle of tears if I was in his presence one moment longer.

Knights on horseback lined either side of the open carriage, but I was its only passenger. To distract myself from the oddness of the arrangement while I waited for our procession to begin, I unfolded Julien's parchment.

He'd neither addressed it nor added his signature, but his tidy, masculine penmanship was as familiar as the hand that had slipped the parchment into mine.

As you've no doubt noticed, I'm of an age at which I should be well-practiced in the art of courtship, he wrote. *Sadly, I am a novice, but I hope my lack of skill will not reflect upon my sincerity in this endeavor to woo.*

If I were a poet, I might find a more clever way to convince you of the fullness of my heart whenever you are near and the loss it feels when we are even a room apart. Sadly, however, that gift seems to have perished with the ancestress who now sends us forth.

I smiled. Ah, Lady Anya. I thought back to the otherworldly visitation from Julien's many-greats-grandmother and of how I'd recognized her by the bright green of her eyes—the same deep emerald hue as Julien's.

Although my suit has gained your father's permission, the method of our paths' divergence places a series of severe obstacles to conventional courtship in our immediate future. Yet I find within me no desire, nay, not even the ability to postpone my pursuit. But how to proceed?

This question plagued me until I realized that, where circumstances will prevent me from expressing my love aloud, parchment and ink will comply. Therefore, I urge you to be watchful, for while you journey you may find the odd scrap of inked parchment tucked here and there. And with it, a small measure of my heart, kept in trust for you.

For I am ever, yours.

I read the missive over and again before surreptitiously tucking the note into my bodice to carry it close to my heart.

If my smile was extra wide as I waved to the crowds lining the streets of Port Dyn, I could say it was for the relief of finally greeting my people. But truth be told, while that relief was real, it was the promise of Julien's courtship, a luxury I had not expected to enjoy while en route to Mount Shireya, that lifted my cheeks with pleasure.

It took hours to get beyond the city, so thick were the crowds, but when we were a short distance away, my father called us to halt and I was moved to the closed carriage.

Vayle and one of the maids sat on one side, but I could not see her face beneath the heavily hooded cloak that hid her newly reddened hair. I took the seat next to the other maid, and once I had finished adjusting my skirts, my gaze fell on the rug covering the hatch on the floor. Before I let my trepidation overtake me, I pulled the curtain slightly back and peeked outside.

Julien rode up beside the carriage, his face a mask with one question at its center. Our eyes met, and he had his answer: yes, I'd read his note.

A tinge of pink appeared, something I had never seen brush his cheeks on such a temperate day. Warmth flooded the center of my soul. In Julien's eyes I saw every word of his letter and more.

I've never so looked forward to finding parchment and ink, I spoke into his thoughts.

He inclined his head, the only sort of bow one could do atop a horse.

I reached out to touch Salvador's nose. The beautiful silver stallion whinnied softly in response to my touch and I sensed that he not only knew that the dynamic of my relationship with Julien had changed, but that we were not going on a peaceful journey.

TWENTY-ONE

The pace quickened for an hour or two, and the carriage, even as ornate and cushioned as it was, bounced the four of us about as if we were dice in a giant's hand. Every so often we slowed for a village. And then another. Each time, I waved at the gathered crowds, sending the assurance of my presence within the King's caravan.

We reached the village of Yeld at dusk, and although it was not nearly as large a settlement, crowds had thronged in anticipation of seeing the King and his newly revealed Ryn. Vayle remained beneath her cloak, but I, as expected, leaned out the carriage windows and waved to the people gathered along the main thoroughfare, Dynwey Road. We traveled with much fanfare, as my father had planned, revealing to all the gossiping tongues the reality of the princess and the direction of her travel.

The sun had nearly set by the time we exited Yeld. The caravan changed position, allowing my father to drop back behind the protection of the guard as night fell.

The sun had just kissed the western horizon when I felt the approach of the King's Army.

We left the road to make camp. The sky darkened and I asked the maids to light the oil lamps and draw the curtains.

"I think you can take off your cloak now, Vayle."

She did and I nearly gasped. Vayle had been sequestered in a set of chambers far away from mine and, in the busyness of readying for the journey, our paths had not crossed. I had not seen my imposter since her hair had been dyed.

Her hair was not quite as deep a copper as mine, but the color was almost an exact match to my mother's. And Vayle's eyes, while they couldn't be as blue as an Andoven's, looked convincingly bluer with the red hair than they had when she was blond. Beneath the cloak, she wore a traveling gown exactly like my own. It wasn't a perfect disguise, but it would do.

I removed the circlet from my head and held it for a moment, running my finger over the glowing Tirandite stone that usually rested on my forehead. It flared at my touch.

I closed my eyes and concentrated on the memory of words I'd heard spoken to my mind by The First as I floated in the Bay of Tirandov, among his charming enikkas, those tiny creatures of light and comfort.

You are mine.

The Voice had claimed me as his own.

I will be with you.

He had given me his word.

I opened my eyes. "This was the crown worn by my mother when she married my father. She gave it to me, and now, for a short time, I entrust it into your care."

I placed the circlet on Vayle's head. Even the dim lamplight couldn't hide the pink tinge that rose on her cheeks, but her eyes remained downcast. Her lower lip trembled.

"While you possess this crown you are no longer Vayle, the blacksmith's daughter. You are the Crown Princess of E'veria, and you must remember to act accordingly."

When she met my eyes, I recognized the disquiet within her, having seen its reflection so recently and so often in my own mirror.

Suddenly, Vayle gasped. Her hand flew to her forehead as the Tirandite stone flashed warm and bright orange for a moment before settling its warmth to a more comfortable glow.

"Truth knows you, Vayle," I repeated the words Celyse had said to me the first time the stone had warmed my own forehead on Tirandov Isle. "You are no less a daughter of The First King than I am. You will do well as my ambassador." I smiled. "Hold your head high and do not be afraid to meet the King's eyes. Speak with confidence and know that I believe you can do this and do it well."

"I will do my best to honor your faith in me, Your Highness."

"I know you will." I took a deep breath. "Now," I said, leaning down to pull a gunnysack from beneath the cushioned bench, "it's my turn. Shall we see if we can turn this princess into a wormy little squire?"

Getting dressed inside the carriage was a challenge with three other people—especially considering I barely knew them—and oil lamps burning. Vayle's help was most appreciated, but my sense of modesty was sorely tested just the same, especially when she helped to affix the binding that would hide my more womanly curves. When that humiliating exercise was complete, she held a small mirror while I adjusted the black hairpiece and squire's cap. Finally, I put on the gray-tinted spectacles Erielle had given me all those months ago.

I turned to address the maids, whose mouths were agape in shock. "It's a rather effective disguise, is it not?" I grinned.

They nodded.

"Now, I believe there will be dinner trays prepared soon. Would you mind fetching them for us?"

They scurried away and soon returned. I savored the simple but hearty meal that had been brought from Holiday Palace and warmed on the fire, with the knowledge that it would be the last such bounty I would know for a long time. The company traveling with me would rely on the forest for food, and once within Mount Shireya, our sustenance would be limited to keola, the precious mixture that served as a filling meal when steeped in water.

As I ate, I relaxed back into the cushions. The luxury within this carriage, while nothing compared to that which I'd quickly adapted to in my chambers at Holiday Palace, was something I might miss even more than the food tomorrow night—and over the next several weeks of nights—while I slept on a bedroll in Shireya's heavily forested hills.

Once our trays were removed, the sounds of the camp began to die down. The longer we sat in the silence of anticipation, the more my stomach clenched and the less I appreciated the meal I had so greedily consumed.

Rynnaia.

Finally, my father's voice reached my mind. It was time.

Are your knights in position?

I sent part of my mind to seek Julien and then Kinley and Gerrias. *Yes.*

Good. I will come to collect Vayle and address the assemblage shortly. While their attention is diverted you will be able to exit the carriage.

Father. All of a sudden it was as if every weighty word we'd left unspoken desired purchase from my lips. Or at least my thoughts. But I couldn't afford to let them loose, even silently, lest my composure leave with them.

My stomach flipped over. Tears began to burn behind my closed eyes as my father's love and worry poured into my mind—and mine volleyed back to him. Neither of us could quell our concern for the other and the flow of colors was nearly dizzying.

I love you, Father.

Oh, I love you, child. Even in my head, his voice seemed strained, pressed upon by the ache of too many years spent apart. *You will contact me when you can? To let me know you're safe?*

Of course. And after Harbyn contacts me from Dwons, I will let you know the outcome of that action as well. Even though he was nearly consumed with worry for me, I knew the recovery effort to bring Drinius and Gladiel safely home also weighed on his mind.

A subtle third presence joined our communion.

Mother.

I will petition Rynloeft on your behalf, she said.

As I will for you, I answered.

My eyes filled with tears as her whispered *I love you* faded into the night.

She was so weak! Yet it was her sacrifice that made me strong.

We have no regrets, Rynnaia. My father's voice was confident, if pained at the evidence of her continual decline.

I sensed him nearing. I opened my eyes and looked at Vayle. "The King approaches, Princess Rynnaia," I said.

Her hand lifted to her throat and she looked as if she might be ill.

"Fear not. He is a loving father and a gentle King."

The carriage door opened and I moved out of sight of the door, though my father's eyes found me.

Be safe, Rynnaia, he spoke silently and his colors wrapped around me like an embrace. *Do not take any unnecessary risks.*

I nodded. *The same to you, Father.*

He turned his gaze to Vayle then and gave her a warm smile. "Shall we?" He offered her his hand, which she took, her own shaking only a little, and exited the carriage. The maids extinguished the lamps and followed them out. I sat alone in the dark carriage, waiting for my ears to catch the silence that would mark the time of my exit.

As my father's colors receded from my mind, I shivered at the loss. My pulse pounded in my throat so that I could barely swallow around it.

I had told Vayle not to be afraid. Could I still claim a bit of courage for myself?

I will be with you.

The silence ushered in the memory of the promise. It slowed my blood and set my body in motion.

If our mission is successful, I reminded myself, *no Cobeld will ever threaten another person again. Families like Sir Risson's will never regain those they've lost, but perhaps they will find comfort in knowing the Cobelds will steal no more members of their brood.*

I moved the rug aside and felt for the latch.

And losses like those suffered in Glenhume and so many other villages will not be a constant, lurking threat.

Fortified by the need of my people, I pulled the latch and moved the panel aside. As I lowered myself onto the ground, the first muffled syllables of my father's speech reached my ears.

Stealthily, I crawled out from under the carriage and slipped into the crowd surrounding the King. I pulled a thick charcoal gray over my thoughts, hoping it would also help to disguise my physical presence. Moving quickly, but not so fast as to draw attention to myself, I skirted the assembled knights and soldiers. Slowly, I edged toward the eastern side of the campsite where Julien waited.

Julien's jaw was set, his expression grim. Without speaking, he turned and began walking. I followed. Julien's rank and status moved us quickly through the watchmen and past the roving patrols to where Kinley and Gerrias waited with our horses, but it seemed to take forever.

For me, silence was most difficult to maintain. I wondered, was this how knights always worked? Without speaking? Clenching my jaw to avoid revealing myself with the questions burning to escape through my lips, I put my foot in a stirrup and lifted myself onto Stanza's saddle. Not until we were well beyond the lights of the soldiers' fires with only the moon as our guide did our formation change. And even then, it happened without speaking. Julien simply nodded at his brother and Gerrias took the lead, sending a copy of Julien's nod my way.

As if I could tell the difference between one knightly nod and another?

Then again, I was Andoven. Maybe he thought I spoke "knight," as well. Or maybe he didn't realize that I generally tried to ask for permission before looking into a friend's thoughts. Since silence was clearly expected, I could not ask for permission. I would just have to assume his nod meant something close to, "Well, then? Let's go."

With a quick tap of my heels to Stanza's sides, I followed Gerrias. Julien moved beside me and Kinley brought up the rear.

The night air chilled my face, but it helped to awaken my senses.

I sent my father a quick message. *We are away.*

TWENTY-TWO

Regardless of the humiliation that put them in place, I was glad for the warmth of the bindings that made me look more like a boy. The breeze became colder as the night grew long.

I leaned into Stanza's silky black neck. After being cooped up in the stables and paddocks of Holiday Palace for so many weeks, he seemed more than ready to run. Being next to Salvador gave my competitive Veetrish horse even further impetus to speed.

We had much ground to cover before dawn and rode thusly for several hours before stopping at a stream. Still, no one spoke, though I followed the knights' examples and dismounted. After a few quick hand gestures and a wordless nod or two, Kinley and Julien walked in opposite directions, leaving me and Gerrias with the horses.

I held in the groan that wanted to escape as soon as my feet touched the ground. As if my legs were filled with silt where bone used to be, they wobbled and shimmied, promising the stiff soreness one can expect when returning to the saddle after too long away. I'd known it would take three or four days before my body accustomed itself to a hard ride again, but I hadn't expected it would affect me so quickly.

"How does Vayle?"

I jumped when Gerrias spoke, even though his voice was soft and low. His were the first words since camp.

"Vayle? Like a princess." I smiled. "She was an excellent choice."

"Her aunt Bess is my uncle's housekeeper," he said. "Our families have known one another for many generations."

"Bess is Vayle's aunt? Bess who works for Ayden?"

"Yes," he sounded surprised. "You know my uncle?"

I smiled, recalling Ayden's home in the Great Wood and how it resembled a giant bird's nest. "Oh, yes. Your father escorted me from Veetri to Mynissbyr. We spent the night at Ayden's house."

"I'm sure he was glad of the company," Gerrias said. "Uncle Ayden doesn't get many visitors. Mynissbyr is not a place for the faint of heart."

"I should think not," I said with a chuckle. "Where did Kinley and Julien go off to?"

"Patrolling. We can't be too careful."

"Or too quiet, apparently."

Gerrias laughed. "That's Erielle's biggest struggle, too." He shook his head. "You females appreciate chatter a bit more than we feel the need for it."

I could hardly argue with that even though I wanted to, because just then Julien reappeared. A moment later, Kinley did as well.

"All clear?" Julien asked Kinley. He nodded and no more words were spoken, although I could feel Gerrias's laughing eyes on me until the horses had finished drinking their fill and our ride recommenced.

What had been a softly rolling plain near the camp had metamorphosed into rocky hills and jutting precipices over-hanging the trail. As dawn neared, the change in topography became more pronounced and everything that had been masked by the night lost its menace.

The rock walls along the trail were sculpted from a creamy stone, subtly marbled with dusky veins of ore. I wondered if the mine from which the marble at Holiday Palace had been gained was nearby.

I should have been exhausted from lack of sleep, but speed was the constant companion of my blood, keeping me alert and ever wary now that I could see and be seen. By the time the sun was high, however, I had begun to flag. We paused at the top of a ridge overlooking a small village nestled in the valley below.

"This is the village of Canyn," Julien said, and with a nod to his brother, we were off again.

Gerrias turned his horse slightly south and the rest of us followed closely down the slope, keeping to the perimeter of the valley. We wouldn't go through Canyn, but in order to stay on course we would skirt its edges.

A strange new awareness tickled my mind a little more forcefully with every step closer we came to the village. Suddenly it took on a name: *Enemy.*

I turned in my saddle and inhaled sharply. At the edge of the village, outside a building that looked like a stable, a fig-ure stood alone but for the five horses for which he held leads. Dressed in the same sandy-brown garb I had noted when we were pursued by Dwonsil warriors on the Stoenian plains nearly two months ago, the man had a strong build and a bow on his back.

His gaze was trained, not on us as I had feared, but west. I breathed a sigh of relief that we had not yet been spotted and centered my concentration on his thoughts. My father's name flitted about his mind. The colors seeping from the man were warlike, but lacked the passion I had expected to find. Though ordered in a precise, methodical way, they carried within them a surprising tinge of sadness which caught my attention and helped me to see a more deeply hidden despair and an undeniable sense of guilt concerning the devastated lands and suffering people of his home province.

He wants to blame my father for the problems in Dwons. But he blames himself even more.

Compassion stirred within me. Was he one of the desert clansmen? For some reason I thought not. *Who are you?* I peered at him with more concentration, as if that would help me to discover more, but I came up empty. *If only he would turn around, so I could see his face!* Then I would know—

"Rozen!" Julian hissed. "Move! We must not be seen!"

Without realizing it, I'd become so caught up in the mind of the Dwonsil warrior that I had reined Stanza in and was now facing the village. By now we should have been well out of sight of Canyn, but here we were at a standstill.

"I'm sorry!" I whispered. As I urged Stanza back into formation I took one last look over my shoulder.

The warrior turned toward four men who had just emerged behind him and noticed . . . us.

My thoughts were still connected to his. Colors exploded in my mind, prickling down my arms. A memory surfaced of a man who offered information to the warriors and then accepted a bag of gold in return.

I gasped. I knew the face in his thoughts. The hand accepting Dwonsil gold had partnered mine for a dance.

Tarlo.

Whatever his allegiance, this particular man of Dwons disliked Tarlo almost as much as I did. But as I peered deeper into that memory, it was the description Tarlo had given of my disguise—and of Julien—that made him suspect the purpose of the four riders paused above the village.

In that moment, our fear of my disguise's discovery was confirmed and made a real threat. That day by the paddock at Holiday Palace, it *was* Tarlo de Veir who had overheard us and discovered my disguise. And he had used that knowledge to betray us.

My mind moved to the next warrior, but once I'd connected to his thoughts, his memories of another recent transaction with Tarlo de Veir nearly caused me to fall from my horse. For this man had provided Tarlo with the powdered root of a plant native to Dwons—ebonswarth—and had directed him on how to use that substance, which, if found in one's possession, was a capital offense.

I should have known.

Tarlo!

My mind did not have to travel far to locate the traitor, but the only response to my silent shout was a grunt, acknowledging that he had heard his name from within a deep, drunken sleep in a room above Canyn's tavern.

Murderer! I spewed the accusation and the memory of Sir Kile's blank stare into his mind. It was he, not Erielle, who was ultimately responsible for Sir Kile's death. *Justice will find you, Tarlo de Veir!* My words dripped with red anger and black grief, but they only elicited another disinterested grunt as the drunkard rolled over and pulled a pillow over his head.

Rage sizzled in my blood. *Would that my words poison your dreams every night and your memories every waking hour until my father's knights arrest you! Just as you poisoned Sir Kile's wine!*

"Rynnaia!" Julien hissed my real name, shocking my eyes open. I gasped when he grabbed Stanza's reins from my hands and forced my horse to turn back in the desired direction. Once we were in place, he tossed the reins back to me and swatted Stanza's behind. "Ride!"

I glanced back over my shoulder and found find all five warriors' eyes on us. *What have I done?*

I spurred Stanza forward. As much as I wanted to go down into Canyn and see the traitor—the murderer!—brought to justice, there was a bigger cause at stake. *The Remedy.*

Sir Kile's death was a great loss, and eventually he would be avenged. But Tarlo's treason, and even Kile's death, were small matters in light of what finding the Remedy could do for the people of E'veria.

And, should the warriors decide to follow us, my selfish curiosity might have just killed E'veria's future.

Finally we descended a small hill that blocked the village from our sight. We galloped up the far slope of the valley and kept our pace through the rocky outcroppings, unsheltered by the covering of trees. I closed my eyes and trusted Stanza to follow Gerrias—and my own skill to keep me in the saddle—while I concentrated on finding the warrior's thoughts and ascertaining whether or not they had chosen to follow us.

They had. And they were gaining.

They were not far behind us. They knew the men they pursued were knights, but as I quickly scanned each of their thoughts, only the one was troubled by the thought that the Ryn might be among those they chased.

Who was he? My father hadn't mentioned having any spies among the Dwonsil warriors. But then again, we'd been much more concerned with the quest to come than the strategies already in place.

The men from Dwons were capable riders. Each horse was a near match in size and speed to Salvador and each one was as fierce. Every second brought them closer.

The path widened and the knights moved into a more protective position around me. Julien and Kinley galloped side by side at the rear and Gerrias was beside me.

Turning in my saddle, I met Julien's eyes. His face was set and ready for battle. I turned to look at Kinley. He mirrored Julien's expression. Before I could turn back to face forward, the Dwonsil warriors rounded a bend and came into sight, closing the gap between us with unbelievable speed.

There were five of them. We were outnumbered and they had arrows at the ready, possibly wrapped with hairs from a Cobeld's beard. We had dressed for speed, not battle. My knights wore no chain mail or armor.

The warriors nocked their arrows.

"No!" I breathed.

As if of one accord, each archer fumbled and his arrow fell to the ground. None noticed the others' clumsiness. Instead, each deftly reached to string another arrow.

Did I do that? I wondered, even as the truth of it washed over me.

My great-grandfather's words coursed through my memory. *"Each time you use one of your gifts,"* he had said, *"it is only by the permission of the Giver."*

I closed my eyes and let Stanza's reins slacken in my hands as my arms dropped and my palms rose. My face tilted toward the sky.

Please, Giver of Gifts. Protector and Sustainer, I pleaded silently, *tell me what to do. Show me how to best use what you've entrusted to me!*

Sudden heat warmed the pendant hanging hidden beneath my tunic. My hand flew to where the carved Emblem of the First rested against my skin as a memory from a childhood dare danced across my mind.

My eyes flew open. Could it work?

It was worth a try.

I tied Stanza's reins to the pommel of the saddle, hoping the knights hadn't noticed the grin that had sprung across my lips at the memory of an escapade involving Rowlen and Lewys, and the dare I had accepted—and achieved—at the age of twelve. The question was: could I do it again?

I bent my left leg under me and shifted my body in the saddle. *This is so much easier when you don't have to bother with skirts!* Bending my other leg, I gripped the saddle and rotated my backside. I straightened my legs and secured my feet in the stirrups, though backward, facing Julien and Kinley.

Stanza forged ahead, unbothered by the unorthodox position of his rider. It was gratifying to know that my horse trusted my instincts, but when I finally looked at Julien and Kinley—I couldn't say the same for the knights.

"What are you *doing*?" Kinley roared. "Turn around!"

I shook my head, hoping we would live long enough for him to forgive me, and concentrated on the ever-decreasing gap between the warriors and us. Just as they let another batch of arrows fly, I closed my eyes and spoke to the shafts of wood.

"Fall."

Without opening my eyes I saw each arrow abruptly nosedive into the ground. The arrows shook with the vibration of the impact. I allowed myself a small smile at the disbelief that crossed the minds of the warriors, but did not have time to dwell on it. They had quickly reached for fresh arrows.

We galloped through a shallow canyon. My thighs ached from gripping Stanza's sides and my knuckles whitened on the back edge of the saddle as I knocked the new arrows from their bowstrings.

I turned my head. Just beyond us was a fissure in the dusky orange rock of the canyon. Its sides were steep and reached at least as far above us as the vaulted entry of Holiday

Palace, but its path was narrower even than the hallway that led to the palace's Grand Hall. Wide enough for two skilled riders to enter at a time, it would be a tight fit for a skittish horse or horseman. Thankfully, none of our group fit into either of the former categories. But would it lead us out—or to a dead end that would trap us?

I looked down each side of the canyon, but I could note no other exit. The fissure had to be the way out.

The Dwonsil warriors seemed to have an endless supply of arrows. How long would it be before one of them evaded my notice and struck one of my friends?

The gestures and nods being exchanged between my friends seemed to indicate that the knights had formulated a plan. I might not be able to interpret my knights' nods and gestures, but I could peer into Julien's thoughts to gauge their intent.

Julien met my eyes, nodded, and tapped a finger at his temple, giving me the permission he knew I sought.

His colors rushed over me the second I sought his mind. I had to push away his tension, his fear for me—even his love—to find that which I sought.

I grasped on to the thread. His thoughts were clear, warm, and true. *You are the Ryn. I trust you.*

I loosened my hold just a tad and sought Gerrias's and Kinley's thoughts in tandem.

They were of one mind and both assumed Julien was, too. And rightly so, as I'd seen the plan in his thought, just awaiting my approval.

Kinley and Julien intended to turn and fight, delaying the warriors as long as possible, while Gerrias took me through the fissure to meet up with our friends at Shiridyn Bridge.

I shook my head. Julien and Kinley were finely skilled knights, but against five Dwonsil warriors, and arrows which may or may not be wrapped in a Cobeld curse, the risk was too great. *No.* I could not, would not, lose them. Not when this predicament was entirely my fault. But how could we all escape?

I knocked the next arrows from the warriors' hands before they touched them to their bows and looked over my shoulder at the narrow way out of the canyon and then up its rocky sides. A way out was a door, right? Could I . . . ?

With a wave of my hand I sent another round of arrows to the dirt, and then spoke into the knights' thoughts.

Follow me through the fissure!

Kinley and Gerrias shook their heads.

A strange strength welled up within me, a feeling of authority I had never experienced before. The sudden swell of Julien's anger, however, directed at his brother and mine, surprised me, and although he did not voice it aloud, Julien's authority as our company's leader clearly backed mine. Whatever his next nod and gesture conveyed, it was clearly not to be argued with.

Kinley and Gerrias exchanged a quick glance, but each nodded their reluctant compliance.

Beside me, Gerrias spoke to Julien. "This is not wise. We need to draw them away from her. She must be protected at all cost!"

"Don't do this, Rose," Kinley pleaded. "Let us protect you!"

"You *are* protecting me. Now I need you to trust me as well. They will not be able to follow us."

As Kinley ground his teeth, I sent another plea for strength to Rynloeft above that my words would prove correct.

Sudden shade alerted me that we were entering the fissure. I disabled another round of arrows, and even more swiftly than I'd turned to the rear, regained a normal riding posture. Untying the reins from the pommel, I leaned forward to urge Stanza faster. It was a tight squeeze with Gerrias beside me, but soon we exited the rock-walled passageway and entered a slightly wooded glen, followed closely by Julien and Kinley.

My hand pulsed where I held Julien's kiss. Did he know how much his belief in me, his counsel, the very potency of his presence, strengthened me?

I circled Stanza back around until I faced the fissure.

Gerrias reached for his sword. "What are you going to do?"

"It's a door," I said, gesturing to the fissure. "I'm going to close it."

I closed my eyes and focused my thoughts on the overhanging rocks above the fissure. *Move,* I thought. *Close and do not open.*

A soft rumble sounded, followed by a sound like sand, raining down. Suddenly, as if they had become molten, the uppermost portions of the rock that framed the fissure broke loose and slid downward, gathering their smaller fellows with them to fill the passage.

A cloud of dust rose, as if a giant sack of flour had been pounded by an even larger fist. Even with my eyes closed I knew the fissure was now impassable. We were safe.

For now.

I focused my mind on the warriors whose pursuit had just been thwarted. The heat of anger and the denial of revenge oozed from all but one of the warriors as they fought to regain control of mounts that had been spooked by the avalanche of stone. From the warrior I had first seen, however, a sweet sense of relief echoed up from the depths of his heart. He had no true desire to harm knights of the King, and he seemed especially glad to think that if the Ryn was among them, she was safe.

He's not our spy, but he knows he's fighting for the wrong side, I realized. *He just doesn't know if he can change his course.*

The warriors fought to regain control of their animals, but his horse, strangely, hadn't spooked as badly as the others.

The hand of The First is with you. I sent my voice into the warrior's mind. *You can change. Fight for E'veria!*

The poor man almost fell from his horse, but at least I had his attention.

You do not need to stay on the path you've chosen, I said. But reading his next thought, I added, *No, you are not losing your mind. I am Andoven. Follow your heart to a new course. Choose a path of peace!*

The message had gotten through to him, but he didn't believe it. The ache in his heart pained me. *Follow your heart. Do not betray your King.*

My connection to the warrior's thoughts broke as my own were assaulted by the force of my brother's anger.

"Rose de Whittier!"

Kinley's use of that name could not be good. And although the roar accompanying it was internal, I didn't have to be Andoven to see it vibrating within him.

Julien growled my brother's name like a warning, but Kinley paid him no mind.

"You could have been killed!" he said. "What if your little plan hadn't worked? What then?"

"Well, it did!"

Our eyes locked, shooting the sort of sparks only siblings can fire.

Kinley pressed his lips together. He closed his eyes, took a breath, and a moment later his lips began to relax. One side twitched upward. And again, higher. When he spoke, the passion of an overprotective brother was replaced with affection. "And just where, might I ask, did you learn to ride like that?"

"In Veetri, of course." I gave my brother a slight bow before sobering to face them all.

"Tarlo de Veir is in Canyn," I said. "The Dwonsil warriors suspected who we were based on information their gold bought from him." I swallowed. "And it was he who put ebonswarth into Sir Kile's wine at the ball."

Julien's jaw clenched. "The King should be notified."

I nodded, closed my eyes, and saw to it.

My father was not happy to learn that my disguise was indeed compromised, as we'd feared. But he was glad that Tarlo had been located.

I opened my eyes. "My father will see to it that Tarlo is taken into custody and tried for treason and murder." I took a breath. "I owe you all an apology. It was my fault we were seen. I'm sorry I put us in danger and I'm sorry I worried you during the attack. I hope you will forgive me."

"It is I who should ask forgiveness. From both you and Julien," Kinley said, keeping his voice low, but just loud enough for us to hear. "Julien, you are in command by rank, by right, and by order of the King. And Rynnaia, ultimately, we are *all* at your command. I'm sorry I questioned you both."

"You're forgiven," I said. "But my actions near Canyn put us in danger in the first place. And for that, I am deeply sorry."

"You will always be my baby sister, but it would do me well to remember that you are the Ryn, as well. It is our job to protect you, not the other way around," Kinley said.

I shook my head. "You are citizens of E'veria as well as knights. As such, I am your servant."

A flash of rightness and purpose heated the thread of my thoughts still connected to Julien's. I turned my head toward his smile.

I tilted my head. "What brought that about?"

His smile widened. "I think you know."

And without needing to delve deeper into his thoughts, I did.

After a slow nod that practically said, *"I love you, Rynnaia,"* Julien led us away from the dust of the former fissure.

TWENTY-THREE

We followed Gerrias along the trail and farther into the wood. When we topped a hill and could see into the distance, I caught my first glimpse of Mount Shireya.

The sun illuminated the southern side of the mountain, making it appear like a lump of blue-gray stone. *It's just an overgrown rock*, I told myself. Still, I tried not to look at it too often, for each time it caught my eye, it sent a shiver through my soul.

The sound of rushing water told me we must be close to rendezvousing with our teammates. The Vorana River divided the provinces of Dynwatre and Shireya. Soon we would cross it and then our adventure would truly begin.

We rode single file along the steep banks of the swollen river and continued upriver. Now and then I peered around Gerrias, hoping to see Erielle, Sir Risson, Dyfnel, and Edru just ahead where they were expected to await us at Shiridyn Bridge. But it was a long while before they came into view. When I finally caught sight of my friends, I peered about for the bridge.

There was something there, seeming to pass over the river, but it wasn't anything I would consider a bridge. No, the bridge must be farther downstream. At least I hoped it was. But a niggling settled in my stomach. After all, Dyfnel had said they would await us at Shiridyn Bridge, and there they were. As we neared the natural structure, my fears were confirmed.

In my mind, the very word "bridge" implied a man-made construction that connected two points—a solid sort of structure on which one could traverse from one side of the river to the other. This ineptly named "bridge" was nothing more than white stone that had somehow grown out from the east bank of the river, but had refused to grab hold of the bank on this side. As soon as we reached our friends I dismounted and walked to the edge of the steep bank.

I turned to Julien, who had come up beside me. "Surely you do not expect us to cross by way of that cliff, do you?"

"It's the only bridge within several days' travel and the quickest route to Mt. Shireya," he stated.

I tried to gauge the distance between where I stood and where the "bridge" began. If three knights stood, arms spread out from their sides, that span would not reach the tip of the narrow band of arching stone.

"*That* is *not* a bridge," I said, finally. "*That* is the type of thing you read about in a book and wonder at its creation. That cannot possibly serve as a conveyance of horse and man!"

"It does, actually."

When I turned toward Edru's voice, I did a double take. I still had a hard time getting used to seeing the young Andoven teacher in the clothes of a mainlander. On Tirandov Isle he had worn the robes common to his people. Now he wore a combination of leather, wool, and linen, just like the rest of us.

"Shiridyn Bridge is so named because it connects Shireya and Dynwatre."

"Edru," I said, putting my hands on my hips, "I think your definition of the word 'connect' could use some work."

"Aw, Rozen, where's your sense of adventure?" Erielle grinned and swung up into her saddle. "I suggest you make way, squire, while I show you just how this particular bridge works!"

Julien put a hand to the center of my back and guided me away from the river's steep bank while Erielle circled her horse farther back into the trees. Surely she wasn't going to—

Erielle dug her heels into her horse's sides and leaned into the gallop. My heart froze in my chest as girl and beast vaulted over the empty air. I wanted to close my eyes so I wouldn't have to bear witness to the death of my friend, but I couldn't look away.

I needn't have worried. Erielle's landing was solid and gracefully sure. She let out a whoop as her horse galloped across the rest of the unmoving arch to the other side of the river and into the trees before circling back around to face us.

Gerrias gave his sister a quick salute and asked, "Who wants to go next?"

Julien moved to face me. His eyes narrowed, but a trace of amusement accompanied his words. "I seem to recall that you rode a horse backward just a few hours ago."

I swallowed. "Not over a bridge. Or half a bridge, rather."

"Rose—en," Kinley said, catching himself and drawing out the last syllable of my squire name just a bit. "You're as pale as cook's custard."

Julien put a hand on my shoulder. "I can take you across on Salvador."

Stanza bumped my shoulder with his nose, almost as if to say, *"Don't be a goose. We can do this."*

I closed my eyes. My horse was right. "I can do this," I said. "If I can't, then I've no use being here."

"I know you can." Julien gave me an encouraging smile. "This little jump is hardly a challenge for someone who can ride a horse like you do."

I gave him a cockeyed smile and he patted my shoulder. "I'll go ahead of you, all right?"

I nodded. In another moment he was across. I leaned my head against Stanza, but he stamped his hooves, clearly anxious to keep up with Salvador.

"All right, you overgrown shooting star," I said and pulled myself up into the saddle, "let's get to it, then." I circled back into the woods until I faced the bridge. "Rynloeft be merciful," I whispered and then took a breath and dug my heels into Stanza's sides, but he was already on the move.

Bits of dirt tossed up as Stanza raced toward the river's edge. I closed my eyes as he lunged. After a brief, disconcerting moment of silence as his feet left the earth, we landed on the narrow ledge. I opened my eyes and relief surged dizzily through my brain. Stanza reached the grass and slowed. As we circled back around to join Julien and Erielle, I couldn't contain my smile.

"Welcome to Shireya," Erielle said with a grin. "That wasn't so bad, was it?"

Although I'm sure the exhilaration of the jump was written across my face as I moved out of the way so the other riders could cross, my stomach threatened to expel its meager contents. I took several slow, deep breaths to dispel the urge to vomit.

In short order Risson, Edru, Kinley, Dyfnel, and Gerrias joined us. All made it safely, though Edru, who had much less experience with horses than the rest of us, remained pale for quite a while after.

There was no path on this side of the river, so we rode single file, trusting Risson's sense of direction when the trees blocked our vision of the mountain and the sun. Shireya was densely wooded, sparsely populated, and the farther we traveled, the higher our elevation. It wasn't a constant uphill trail, but there was an awareness of sorts of thinner, purer air and of feeling both lighter and heavier at the same time.

By the time we were four days into Shireya's foothills I was exhausted. Still, I was surprised when the knights made no move toward their horses after our midday meal. Finally, I stood.

"We should go."

Sir Risson shook his head. "We're too high. We need to stop."

"Did we veer off course?"

"No," he said. "It's the altitude. From here on out we'll rest at least an hour each afternoon. The higher we climb the more rest we'll need."

"And water," Julien added and took a long drink from his flacon.

"Indeed." Risson nodded. "Drink up, young squire," he said with a wink. "And nap if you're able. You'll be glad you did."

And indeed I was.

Each day passed in the same manner. During nap breaks and while we camped overnight, the knights alternated guard duties. At first I found the break in our progress a frustrating delay to our quest, but as the thinner air took its toll on my energy reserves, I was glad for the wisdom of those who'd traveled here before.

Risson turned out to be incredibly adept at setting snares to catch small game, and since Edru proved to be especially gifted at preparing the meat Risson provided, we enjoyed many more satisfying meals than I would have imagined when we first set out.

We had just gotten a fire going one night when a sound broke through the darkness. Somewhere between a scream and a growl, it sounded entirely animal. And all too close. Everyone froze.

"What was that?" I whispered to Julien.

"Cat." He whispered back and put his finger to his lips.

A *cat*? Surely I'd misunderstood.

While Julien exchanged a series of quick, silent gestures with Kinley, Gerrias, and Risson, I tried to figure out what rhymed with "cat" that could make such a terrible sound. Bat and rat were the only other animals I could come up with, and neither seemed a plausible explanation.

Just when I was about to break Julien's pantomimed order of silence, the knights rose with slow, silent movements and moved toward the horses. The next thing I knew, Salvador was directly behind me, but turned sideways, as if providing a barricade between me and the cat-bat-rat creature. Edru and Dyfnel slid into the spaces beside me and Erielle positioned herself directly between me and the sputtering fire. She held a bow, with an arrow nocked and ready.

A bow and arrow? Where did she get that? We had been traveling for many days and I hadn't noticed anything like that on her horse! Now all of a sudden it was in her hands?

I choked down a giggle that came out as a little gasp when the cat-bat-rat let forth another screaming howl.

It was closer now, sounding as if it came from just the other side of the fire. Erielle must have thought so, too, because she lifted the bow and drew back the string.

I turned to Dyfnel and spoke to his mind. *What is it?*

A mountain cat, he said.

A cat? But it sounds so big!

Because it is.

He sent a memory of a long, lanky creature the color of old straw into my thoughts. It had a broomstick tale and wide-set, intelligent—but wild—eyes, big teeth, and long, coarse whiskers protruding from a muzzle that was much wider and longer about the nose than any cat I'd ever seen.

Some call it a "wolfcat" due to its size, the shape of its nose, and the power of its jaws, he explained. *But it is not actually related to the wolf at all. Its mannerisms are very catlike, and physically, it does quite resemble those common creatures. But in every way, it is exponentially larger than a cat and many grow larger than even the wolves found in the Nyrland province.*

Leave it to an Andoven to take a possibly life-or-death moment and insert a lesson.

Is it dangerous?

He nodded. *Quite. Especially if it's hungry.*

"Rozen," Erielle hissed. "Can you help me see it?"

Help her . . . oh!

I broke my connection with Dyfnel and concentrated on connecting my mind to Erielle's, while somewhere beyond the fire, an odd, scratching noise sounded for a short rhythm and then stilled.

I closed my eyes, careful to keep a grip on a strand of Erielle's colors while I sought the unfamiliar, animalistic presence in the dark trees surrounding our camp.

I thought about the picture Dyfnel had put into my thoughts and my mind's eye roved the trees until a glint of reflection, that seemed almost to have its own scent, caught my attention.

I gasped. A *cat?* No, it was a *beast!*

Its muzzle wrinkled, revealing long teeth that reminded me of Julien's bearskin cloak. It sniffed the air and its long, thick tail flicked once. Other than that, it was as still as the trunk of the tree itself. In its mind was one thought:

Fresh meat.

Since the pheasant Risson had snared and roasted was nothing now but a pile of bones in our fire, I could only assume the wolfcat meant . . . us.

Its tail flicked a long, silent swoosh, like a broom across the floor, except it hung over the back of the wide branch where the giant cat perched, waiting for the moment to strike.

In the tree, I told Erielle.

"Which tree?" she hissed. "We're in the middle of a forest!"

I had no idea how to explain it.

"Timepiece!" she whispered.

Timepiece? *I don't have one,* I said to her thoughts.

She groaned, but I don't think it was aloud. Her words, however, came through her teeth like a sword. "Tell me where it is," she said slowly, "*as if* you were looking at a timepiece."

Ten o'clock.

She angled the bow to the precise angle that would have been ten on a timepiece, but it wasn't far enough to the left and was a tad too high.

Wait! Where do you want to hit it? I'd only been thinking of the general area of the cat, not a specific target.

"Kill shot!" she whispered.

Okay. I corrected my earlier instructions, *Move left and down. Er, nine and . . . a quarter.* She made a slight adjustment. *Just a bit higher.*

All of a sudden, the cat's attention was caught by movement near the base of its tree. Its head moved so quickly it was as if it there were no space between one angle and the next, as if its neck was made of fluid rather than sinew and bone.

Wait! I shouted into Erielle's thoughts. *It moved!*

I followed the direction of the cat's new interest.

"*Julien!*" I screamed his name aloud. "Don't move!"

At my scream, the cat's head swiveled back toward me and it crouched as if to pounce. Erielle let her arrow fly, but it sailed several inches over the animal's head and into the trees.

Erielle had another arrow nocked faster than I could blink.

Lower!

The animal's head was turned back to the right direction, at least. Julien was silent and still, but if it looked his direction again and decided to pounce, he was done for.

Bring it down two more inches, I told her. *Now up just the tiniest bit. There!*

I shrank back as the arrow let loose and my mind flew with it for a moment before I thought to disconnect.

The wolfcat's howl was little more than a staccato cry this time, followed by a resounding thud as it fell out of the tree and hit the ground.

A long moment stretched. Finally, Julien called out. "It's dead!" He laughed. "Erielle got him right between the eyes!"

A few moments later, the three knights dragged the beast closer to the fire. "Tonight, we feast!" Gerrias slapped Kinley on the back.

I looked at the large, limp animal. Its paws were huge clawed things and its face, even as big as it was, seemed very like the cats Lord Whittier delighted in keeping to reduce the rodent populations in the stable and barns . . . but with just a reminder around the muzzle of the dogs that herded his sheep.

"It's a cat," I said.

"Indeed," Edru nodded, grinning. "Many consider wolf-cat a delicacy. They're nearly impossible to hunt, which is why the meat and pelts are sold at such a dear cost. This is indeed a treat."

"A treat?" My stomach lurched. "No." I shook my head, vigorously. "I can't eat a cat."

"It's just meat," Kinley said. "Bounty provided us by The First."

"It would've eaten any one of us." Erielle rejoined us after examining her handiwork. "What's the problem?"

"Look at its whiskers. Its ears. Its paws. It's a *cat*. I used to play with them in the barn."

She laughed. "Not this kind of cat."

"Well, I for one will eat anything that would consider eating me." Risson pulled a dagger from his boot. "Shall we get on with skinning him, then? I've got my eye on those juicy hindquarters."

I ran for the trees and heaved, emptying my stomach of the spare portion of pheasant we had shared earlier.

I could not begrudge my friends a full and satisfying meal, especially one considered a delicacy, but neither could I partake of something that looked so like a larger version of a combination of family pets.

It was well into the night before the meat was ready to cook. While they'd butchered the animal, Kinley had whistled a Veetrish feasting tune, but when it was finally on the spit, he began to sing.

"Bring ye out the pudding, Cook. Put a log upon the fire. We've a merry tune and a goblet full and a tale to pass the hour." Kinley continued singing as Edru turned the spit, though he refrained from the usual rousing volume expected of one singing that particular tune. His voice was a tad deeper than Lord Whittier's, but Kinley's Veetrish brogue was thicker when he sang. It had to be, of course, to make the words

236

rhyme correctly. I closed my eyes as the sound recalled many happy eves at Mirthan Hall, and smiled.

Pretty soon, Risson added his rumbling bass to the song and Erielle surprised me, joining in with a pure, sweet harmony in a higher register. As vehement as she had been that I should not allow Julien to sing his courtship to me, I had assumed the gift of song to be one absent among all Sir Gladiel's children. I was glad to be wrong—and entirely too Veetrish to resist the tune's pull. I couldn't help but tap my foot now and then. Once or twice I even joined Kinley, singing the melody. But whenever my eyes strayed to the hunks of cat Edru was turning on the spit, the merriment within me curdled. Finally, I unpacked my bedroll, choked down a small wedge of cheese that argued with my stomach for a while before deciding to stay put, and turned away, purposing to sleep before my friends partook of their meal.

In the morning, no sign of the wolfcat remained and no one spoke of it. I was glad to leave the whole incident behind, and while packing up my bedroll, I was surprised to find one of the promised notes from Julien.

Like the first, it had neither salutation nor signature, but even though it consisted of only two short lines, it warmed my heart.

I'm sure my sister has warned you off my singing, but were I to present you with a ballad, it would be "So Far As Ere the Skies Have Reached."

I remain, yours.

Having been raised in Veetri, I was, of course, familiar with the song. It was the tale of a young man who learned to fly in order to woo and rescue a maiden who had been kidnapped by the moon. Unlike the lively tune Kinley had sung the night before, this song was utterly romantic. Julien could not have known how precious a place it held in my heart, but having heard Lord Whittier sing that ballad to his lady on many occasions, just the mention of it conjured the warmth of love within me.

I closed my eyes and remembered Lord Whittier repeating the chorus, the beauty of his rich, honeyed voice no match for the love in his eyes.

So far as ere the skies have reached
is not too far for me
to seek the favor of the one
whose one glance captured me.

Of all the ballads Julien could have chosen to "not sing" to me, he had chosen the best. With a full heart, I tucked the parchment among my things.

TWENTY-FOUR

*D*ays ran together like the endless view of trees as we followed the paths of deer—and sometimes no path at all—through the mountain's foothills. Risson, being most familiar with the province of Shireya, took the lead and Gerrias took the rear. When the trail allowed, we rode close enough to converse, Julien almost always on my right and Kinley or Erielle on my left.

The typical drizzle of early spring visited our journey every two or three days, and even though we were well rested, I was ready for a real bed and a long soak in a deep tub.

"Are there no inns in Shireya?" I groaned one afternoon.

"Not this side of the mountain."

I winced at Gerrias's reply, not having intended to speak my complaint aloud.

"Closer to the borders with Stoen and Dwons there are villages with inns large enough to house several hunting parties," he said. "Much like our Great Wood in Mynissbyr, this part of Shireya is sparsely inhabited."

I sighed. True, I hadn't meant to voice my complaint, but since I had, I couldn't seem to stop from adding to it. "What I wouldn't give for a warm bath and a bed with a pillow."

"Indeed." Gerrias laughed. "Risson, how close do you think we are to Fennik's Glenn?" He turned back to me. "It's not an inn, but it's a roof, a fire, and a bed."

"We're still a bit away," Risson said. "Within a week or so, I'd think."

A *week* or so? It already felt as if we had been in Shireya a lifetime.

"And how much farther to the mountain after that?" Erielle spoke up. "Are we even halfway yet?"

"By the time we get to Fennik's, we'll be almost to the Sacred Mountain's base," Risson said, adding another, "almost."

"Meaning?" Erielle prodded.

"It will be a few more days after that."

I used a bit more self-control this time and didn't voice my disappointment, because even my thoughts were tinged with a whiny sounding groan that didn't particularly suit a squire—or a princess, for that matter.

"Risson?" I asked instead. "What is Fennik's Glenn?"

"It's the home of a rather cantankerous old knight who lives like a hermit and likes it that way. He served your grandfather, King Rynitel," Risson replied. "He's not the most welcoming host, but his home is large enough and he'll share his hearth for a night." His brow furrowed as we reached a break in the trees and he angled his horse to go around the small meadow rather than through it. "If we were to angle eastward, there is a farmstead near here. A rather more humble dwelling than Fennik's. I'd meant to skirt around it, but if you—"

"Hold." Julien's voice stilled us all. "Do you smell that?"

I inhaled deeply, but only caught the scents of damp earth, evergreen, and the smoke that permeated my clothes from our campfires.

"Smoke," Gerrias said with a nod.

I took another breath. Perhaps the smoke smell was a bit stronger than I'd originally given it credit.

"Look up." Erielle pointed above the meadow to a path of dark gray puffs snaking across the blue sky. "It's coming from the northeast. It's a bit too much smoke to be a cooking fire, isn't it?"

Risson and Julien exchanged a look. Risson nodded. When I moved my gaze to the other knights, both Gerrias and Kinley wore pronounced frowns.

"We'll go north," Julien said, turning Salvador that direction rather than the more eastward direction of the smoke. "Give it a wide berth."

"But what if it's coming from that farm Risson mentioned?" I asked. "They could need help."

Julien shook his head. "Our goal is to reach the mountain. We shouldn't delay."

"But shouldn't we offer help if we can? Or at least get close enough to make sure the farmers are unhurt? That wouldn't delay us too much, would it?"

His look was pointed, narrowing his green eyes. "That fire could be deliberately set. If there are enemies about, we need to move away from whatever mischief they're engaged in. To keep you safe."

Enemies? I hadn't even thought of that. My mind had conjured little more than a cooking fire gone awry. But now that Julien had mentioned it . . .

A scene from Rowlen's story flashed through my mind. *The smoking ruins of Mirthan Hall and the village of Glenhume.*

The surrounding farms, destroyed by fires set by Dwonsil war-
riors and Cobelds.

"This farm," I said, addressing Risson, "it is operated by citizens of E'veria, yes?"

"I should hope so."

"And are there children in this family, Risson?"

He glanced at Julien before returning his gaze to me. His answer was slow. "Yes, but Sir Julien—"

"I'm sure Sir Julien would agree that it is the duty of the E'veri family and our knights to protect even the humblest citizens of the Kingdom." I took a breath in through my nose. "If they need our help, we will give it."

I turned to Kinley. "No one was there to help the people of Glenhume when the village was razed," I said. "But we're here now. We should help."

"This isn't Veetri, Rose," he said, and I knew his use of my old name was on purpose. "And this isn't Glenhume."

"This farm is someone's home! If we can be of any help—"

"Normally, I would agree with you," Julien interjected, "but on our current course, we have to think in bigger terms. In *entire Kingdom* terms. And the best defense for the Kingdom is finding the Remedy. To do that, you must safely reach the mountain."

Why couldn't he understand what I was trying to say? This was my duty!

"What kind of Ryn would ignore her people's need?"

"Lower your voice!" Julien hissed.

I bit my lip. Until my last emotionally-driven statement, our conversation had barely registered above a murmur.

Julien closed his eyes and inhaled deeply and slowly. When he spoke, his words were soft, but as firm as the ground beneath his horse's hooves. "A wise leader must choose the path of greater benefit to the whole. Even when it is difficult."

He was right. I knew he was right. But I couldn't get the vision of Mirthan Hall, destroyed, out of my mind. What if Lord and Lady Whittier had been home when the enemy had arrived?

"Would you at least be willing to investigate it? To see if there is a need?" I implored. "If we find all is well, we could ride a bit harder or longer to make up the time."

"Our company is small." Julien shook his head. "I would prefer to avoid dividing our number to go investigate. If there is trouble, it might find you with a reduced guard."

"Julien's right," Kinley said. "I understand why you want to do this, but we shouldn't split up."

"I agree that we should not split up," I said, sitting straighter. "Therefore, we will all go." I pulled Stanza's reins to the right. "Together."

"We will *not*."

Julien's pronouncement, spoken through clenched teeth, brought me up short and my eyebrows up high.

I tilted my head, locking on to his steely emerald gaze. "Pardon?"

Kinley groaned.

A long moment of silence ensued in which neither Julien nor I capitulated—and in which I clearly saw that as long as he was in charge, he wouldn't.

But neither would I.

"I am the Ryn," I said, careful to keep quiet. The words lifted my chin, cutting off the fullness of my breath. I lowered it and looked toward the smoke. "We will go. Now."

"I mean no disrespect," Gerrias said softly, "but this is unwise."

"Rynnaia," Erielle whispered, "you should trust Julien. We may be walking into a trap."

I turned my glare to her for a long moment before letting it rove the group. "I will not force any of you to accompany

243

me, but I will go with or without you. There could be people—children, even—in need of help. I will not ignore them. I don't care if it's Veetri or Shireya. I will not let another E'verian farm burn without at least *trying* to help."

All eyes turned to Julien.

His lips pressed together as his jaw worked his top teeth against the bottom. Clearly, he did not like having his orders questioned. Even by the Ryn.

Finally, he sighed and looked off toward the trees. "Tight formation. Risson, lead. If the Ryn commands it," he said tightly, "we do her bidding."

With that, we switched direction, although the quick nods exchanged by the knights assured me that at the first sign of trouble, my commands were to be ignored.

The smell of smoke became denser as we circled the meadow toward its eastern edge. Soon my eyes were watering from it. But no taste of meat rode on the breeze. This was not a cooking fire. It may have started as one—at least I hoped it had—but it must have gotten out of control.

We crossed a small stream. A tingle of something strange lifted the hairs on my neck, but I kept my eyes forward, anxious to locate the fire and see how we could best help the family. Risson rode first, followed by Julien—whom I avoided looking at directly—and Gerrias, who rode at his brother's side in front of me. Kinley was on my right, Erielle my left, and the Andoven men followed behind us. The trees were thick to either side of the path, which was wider on this side of the stream, as if traveled often. This was, most likely, the nearest source of water to the farm.

Without warning, Gerrias's horse screamed and reared on its hind legs. Gerrias kept his seat, but the horse jolted and let loose another horrific sound.

"Archer, aloft!" Julien cried.

I gasped. An arrow had pierced the right flank of Gerrias's horse. Another was embedded in its neck. Gerrias dismounted just before his horse collapsed, a third arrow having punctured its chest.

"Get down!" Julien yelled back at me, but Kinley was already pulling me off Stanza, using the combination of his body and my horse's to shield me from the attack.

I turned to make sure Erielle was safe, but she was still atop her horse, bow out and arrow nocked. She gasped and lurched away from her bow just in time to have an arrow slice the air between it and her face.

But Julien was faster than Erielle could re-aim. I saw only a flash of reflected sunlight as a dagger left his grasp and headed high into the trees, where it elicited a grunt. A spare moment later, a man fell from his perch.

"Circle up!" Julien ordered as he raced to the base of the tree.

The horses were skittish, moving around Gerrias's blank-eyed, unbreathing mount. Gerrias took Stanza's reins from my hands and stepped in front of me, allowing Kinley to guard me from the rear position. Kinley's horse was so close I could feel his breath on my neck as we made our way to the tree under which the enemy archer lay bleeding.

Julien's sword was pressed against his throat, but the man did not seem disposed to answering any of his questions. If the amount of blood soaking through the man's tunic and into the ground was any indication, the dagger wound in his chest was mortal. Julien's sword was hardly motivation to speak when death was so near.

Julien looked at me. "Can you look into his mind to see if there are others?"

"Sir Julien," Dyfnel admonished, "I must protest. What you ask of her is entirely unethical."

Edru nodded. "A complete breech of Andoven etiquette."

"This is war," Julien replied. To me he added, "But I understand if you refuse."

"I will try." I looked in the archer's eyes and sought his mind.

"He's alone," I said finally, taking a deep breath as I processed the colors, emotions, and scenes playing out from his thoughts into mine. "There were five others with him. They left a few hours ago, heading west. He stayed behind to hunt, with plans to meet up with them later. He's from Dwons. They all are. Dwonsil warriors. They came upon the farm by accident." I gasped on what I saw next in his memory. My hand fluttered to my lips. "They killed—"

"That's enough," Julien said. His command and the pressure of his hand on my shoulder broke my connection with the warrior and saved me, thankfully, from watching this man and his fellow warriors attack an innocent family.

Just like other Dwonsil warriors had done years before at Glenhume.

A gurgling sound pulled my eyes back to his face. A moment later his head lolled, and when I sought his mind again, it was if he had disappeared, leaving only a shell behind.

Kinley shook his head. "I do not envy his next journey."

"We are not to judge," Dyfnel said, though his tone spoke agreement. "Only the man himself and Rynloeft know where he goes from here."

"Julien!" Erielle hissed.

Without waiting for his reply, she pulled her sword from its sheath, ran back to the path, and crossed it into the woods. The tiny bit of sound she made was no more than what a rabbit or a squirrel might create, and even as my heart pounded, I mused that her quiet grace was likely a product of growing up in the Great Wood of Mynissbyr.

Suddenly she stopped. After a moment of complete stillness, she took a few steps back and looked around. Again,
she stilled, her gaze pausing on something a few yards from
where she stood. After a moment more, she turned and ran
straight to Julien, as quietly as she had left.

"A woman," she said. "Dead. Arrow through the neck.
And a boy. Dagger in his arm. It's not a mortal wound, but he's
dead. Cursed, you think?"

Cursed? My blood froze. Had the Dwonsil warriors'
weapons been laced with hairs from a Cobeld's beard? My lip
trembled. *What if that arrow had hit Erielle?*

"Risson," Julien said. "How many in the family?"

"Last I knew, the man, his wife, and four children. The
youngest was just an infant when I last came through, but
that's been two years or more. The oldest would be . . . near
Erielle's age now, I suppose."

Erielle's gaze turned back to where she had discovered
the bodies. "That one is younger." Her voice was steady, but
I could tell it took every ounce of her strength to keep it so.
"Seven or eight, maybe."

My heart lurched.

Children. Babies. A family. Would Dwonsil warriors have
left any alive?

Perhaps. If they didn't expect them to survive on their own.

But if they had left some of the small ones, had we gotten
here in time? Could we yet save those who may have been left
behind to die?

Anticipating the action I didn't even realize I was about
to take, Kinley put a hand on each of my shoulders. "You need
to stay here," he said, stopping my forward motion. "It's too
dangerous."

"We need to see if there are any survivors." I removed his
hands from my shoulders. "The warriors might not have used

weapons on the little ones. They might have left them to die. We have to find them."

"She's right." Julien removed his dagger from the warrior's chest and wiped it on the man's trouser leg. He stood and nodded at me. "You stay with Kinley, under guard. Risson, Gerrias, and I will scout in and around the farmstead."

"I thought you didn't want us to split up," I argued. "If my father were here, he would go with you."

"Your father has been trained as a knight."

"My father is the King," I whispered, balling my fists. "You wouldn't question him if he chose to accompany you."

"And that, my dear sister, is where your argument goes south," Kinley said, his voice kept low. "You might outrank Julien in nobility, but the King outranks you. And it was he who not only placed Julien in leadership of this quest, but ordered us to protect you above all else."

"We're near enough the farmstead now that we can return quickly if there is trouble," Risson added. "There is no reason for you to put yourself in danger."

"But I could use my Andoven abilities to help locate survivors!"

"As can Edru." Julien nodded, his eyes still locked with mine. "You will stay here. Under guard. Edru?" He turned. "Will you come with us?"

"Of course. But . . ." he paused. "My ability to see into the thoughts of those not of Andoven ancestry is not . . . strong."

"See?" I threw up my hands. "You need me along."

"No."

"No?" I lowered my hands. They clenched into fists at my sides. "In my father's absence, your orders come from me. This is the fealty you vowed, is it not?"

The reassertion of my birthright was not accompanied by the zing of purpose I expected to feel, yet each word seemed to lift my chin a small measure higher.

Julien's nod was stiff, but his tone, even whispered, remained annoyingly calm and even. "My sworn fealty to you does not usurp my pledge to see to your safety. Nor does it overrule my vows to your sovereign father and his Kingdom."

He looked beyond our position to the path we had left. When he spoke again, his tone was bland, betraying none of the emotion I'm sure would have colored his thoughts if I had sought them, but I was too angry to want that close a connection to him right now.

"Since you have chosen to take authority of our company, Your Highness," Julien said tightly, "you might also take a moment to decide which of us will ride two astride when we leave this place. As I'm sure you are aware, we are now one horse less than we are rider."

Guilt stained my cheeks as my eyes moved from the dead horse, a rare Alvarro like Salvador, to his rider. Gerrias's eyes, however, were trained unseeingly toward a random tree.

I tried to imagine in that instant how I would feel if Stanza were killed by an enemy. A shudder threatened my heart, but I stood still.

I would make amends with Gerrias for the loss of his horse. Somehow. But grief for the loss of a horse could not compare to protecting one of E'veria's little ones.

"We are wasting time that could mean life or death to a child!"

"*You* are wasting time. I am attending to your father's wishes." The green in Julien's eyes seemed to deepen in color. "If necessary to safeguard your person, *Your Highness*," the emphasis on my title could not help but be noticed this time, even at this low volume of speech, "I will not hesitate to have you restrained."

Anger opened my mouth in a little gasp. He *wouldn't!*

"I *am* the *Ryn!*" I spat, but the title fell flat and meaningless against even my own ears.

Julien closed his eyes. He took a deep breath and let it out. "Please, Rynnaia." He was silent for a long moment, but when he opened his eyes, his tone was softer, gentler, and it tugged the stubborn strands of my will. "Please allow us to attend our sworn duty. Stay here with Kinley while we assess the threat."

Just then, a high-pitched cry, like that of a panicked child, rent the air.

I turned toward the sound. "Dear Rynloeft, no!" And without another thought, I barreled through my companions and ran toward the sound.

TWENTY-FIVE

The first thing that hit me as I passed into the farmyard was the unexpectedly strong smell of animal urine, so pungent where I stood that it nearly overpowered the putrid smoke of two dying fires that had once presumably been a house and a barn. The second thing to hit me was . . . Gerrias.

He shoved me from the side as another high-pitched scream pierced the air, but this one was closer, and at this range, even *I* couldn't mistake it for human. I flew through the air and landed against a tree with a grunt, righting myself just in time to see the flash of Erielle's dagger as it spun through the air and into the side of a writhing length of fur, attached by its teeth to Gerrias's sword arm.

The shock of the weapon's hit caused the creature to loosen its hold. Gerrias had nearly pulled his arm free when it emitted a screeching growl and latched on again. Even though its size was more like that of a herding dog than the beast we'd met before, its shape, face, and ferocity left no question that it was, in fact, a wolfcat. A young one, to be sure, but its teeth, sunk into my knight's flesh, were clearly large enough to kill.

"No!" I screamed. Even with Erielle's dagger sticking out of its side, its strength was frightening and feral. Determined.

Gerrias slammed his left fist between the creature's eyes and it released its hold, dropping to the ground.

The small beast let out another cry, but it cut off abruptly when Kinley's sword sliced through its neck.

Blood wept through the punctures in the arm of Gerrias's tunic and he fell to one knee.

Dyfnel rushed to his side.

My shaking hand lifted to cover my trembling lips.

It should be me on the ground, grimacing in pain, I thought. *Me, bleeding.*

Had I but listened to Julien, or to Erielle, Kinley, or Gerrias himself, the knight would not be injured. Nay! My pride reached farther back than that. Had I been able to set it aside in favor of my knights' wisdom, Gerrias would not only be unhurt, but he would still have his horse. We would not have detoured from our quest for the Remedy, rather than consuming time here and putting more E'verians at risk with every moment we delayed.

Regret twisted my gut and stretched its tentacles into my heart. Nearly every member of our group had spoken up against our current action, but I had overruled them all. Me. The one who could not even wield a sword. Had I listened to any one of them rather than the self-important voice of my own foolish pride—had I allowed myself to be guided by the wisdom of my friends rather than the misguided sense of duty that marked me as a fool—

But Gerrias had taken the wound meant for me. Gerrias had put himself in the direct path of that wolfcat to protect his unworthy, bullheaded Ryn.

"Forgive me, Gerrias," I whispered, though too quietly for him to hear. Yet while the fault, the guilt, rested so heavily

HE REMEDY

upon my chest, I couldn't seem to find the breath to speak my apology louder.

We shouldn't even *be* here. By all rights, his injury should have been mine. I owed him an apology, at the very least. I moved to rise.

"Wait." Julien ordered.

I obeyed and hung my head.

He knelt in front of me. "Are you all right?"

My head shot up. "Me?"

He brushed a pine needle from my cheek. "You hit the tree pretty hard."

"I'm fine." How could he look at me with such gentleness when his brother lay injured because of me? I swallowed and peered around him. "But Gerrias—"

"Dyfnel will see to him. Come." He offered his hand to help me up. "Can you handle the sight of blood? I'd like us to stay close together."

I nodded, a bit confused. Hadn't I just proven that while seeking the thoughts of the dying Dwonsil warrior?

"It's different when it's someone you care about," Julien explained, as if he'd peeked into my mind.

Again, I nodded. How could I refuse to see the result of my pride's folly?

"The smell of fresh blood could draw more predators if they're downwind of us," Julien said softly. "We'll stand guard around you and Gerrias while Dyfnel binds his wounds. There could also still be villains about. Are you recovered enough to use your Andoven abilities? Could you ascertain if there is a human or Cobeld threat?"

It was the least I could do. Not trusting my voice to speak, I nodded and closed my eyes, sending my consciousness out from our position.

253

"I don't sense any unknown colors," I said finally, but my voice betrayed my fear. "But . . . I'm not . . . sure—"

Could I trust my abilities when I had so flaunted my pride in the face of Rynloeft, from whence they came?

I swallowed. *What if The First has blinded my abilities as punishment for my pride? What if he has abandoned me?*

That is not his nature, Your Highness.

I turned to face Edru, not realizing until he answered that I had, in fact, posed the question to my teacher.

Edru gave me a reassuring smile before turning his gaze to Julien. "I do not sense an enemy presence, either."

As we walked to where Gerrias sat, I avoided meeting anyone's eyes. It was my prideful folly that had injured one of my knights. A knight who had already lost his horse, his trusted companion in battle. Both were important members of our quest. One was dead, the other, terribly injured. I couldn't bear the thought of the accusations in my friends' eyes. I didn't deserve their fealty. Who was I kidding? I didn't even deserve their *friendship.*

I deserved neither my gifts nor my crown.

What sort of Ryn was I?

A self-centered, self-important one, that's what. The worst sort there could be.

But I had to speak to Gerrias. As lacking as words were, I couldn't let my apology remain unsaid a moment longer. I knelt at his side and put a hand on his shoulder. "Gerrias, I'm sorry."

"Injury is a hazard of the job." He gave me a weak smile. "I've had worse, Your Highness."

"Please don't call me that. I don't deserve the title. Not after the way I acted. It's my fault you're hurt. It's my fault you've lost your horse." My voice clogged with tears. "Gerrias, I'm a terrible Ryn."

He opened his mouth to argue, but Dyfnel spoke first. "We grow and learn from our mistakes, Your Highness. Nothing happens apart from the knowledge of The First. Neither can we make a mistake that he cannot redeem for the betterment of our character if we open our hearts enough to welcome in that change."

He lifted his eyes to offer the sympathy of a smile I did not merit, and then, although he turned his attention back to Gerrias's wound, he said one more thing. "This lesson will make you a better Queen."

A humbled Queen, perhaps, I thought.

Indeed, Dyfnel answered.

We stayed close together beneath the trees rimming the farmstead while Dyfnel treated the wolfcat bites.

How bad is it? I spoke into Dyfnel's mind.

The punctures are deep, he said, frowning, *but no sinews have been torn. Cleaning the wound will not be pleasant for Sir Gerrias, but it must be seen to twice a day to guard against infection. The bite of a wild animal is no trifling matter.*

Will he regain the use of his arm?

In time, Dyfnel said, adding, *if no infection sets in. And I will do my best to see that it does not.*

The circle around us grew suddenly smaller. I looked up. Julien and Risson had stepped from it, and Erielle, Kinley, and Edru had moved closer to make up for their absence.

"Where are they going?"

"Patrol," Kinley answered, his voice low. "Looking for signs of the enemy and for . . . survivors."

Survivors. How swiftly I had put aside my initial impetus to foolishness. How quickly I had forgotten the little ones I had been so anxious to help.

May Rynloeft save E'veria! Had there ever been a more unworthy Ryn?

The vicious animal that attacked Gerrias was only a young wolfcat, perhaps still a pup—or was it called a kit or cub? There might be more of the beasts—it's mother?—nearby. I couldn't imagine how, even had a child's life been spared, he or she might have escaped the predators who could find them simply by scent.

When Julien and Risson returned from patrol their eyes spoke of what they had found. There were no survivors. The remains of the rest of the family, which had grown by one since Risson had last visited, were just that. *Remains.* The infant, a baby girl, was found pinned beneath her fallen father. The arrow that pierced his back had been fired at such close range that it had gone through his chest and into her tiny heart.

Overcome, I covered my face with my hands.

The Cobelds were responsible for this horror. They and their allies, the Dwonsil warriors.

How could E'veria's own people justify actions that would allow such inhuman villainy and needless carnage, even in war? How had my family so wronged the people of the Dwons province that they wanted to destroy us and our Kingdom?

But how could one so selfish, so foolhardy as I, ever hope to lead this splintered Kingdom to peace?

How cocky I'd been, setting off on this adventure to find the Remedy. *Adventure, ha!* I almost laughed aloud, but had I let such an inappropriate sound escape my lips, it would have been more chilling than mirthful. I was neither a brave adventurer nor a royal sage. Stupid. Reckless. Foolish.

Spoiled.

The Ryn? Hardly. I was nothing more than a child playing dress-up in a squire's clothes one day, a princess's the next. E'veria deserved better.

"Rynnaia."

I lowered my hand and wiped an arm across my face.

Julien knelt before me, his eyes bearing the weight of what he'd found. "Kinley, Risson, and I have studied the area and . . . the dead. It appears that the attack was Dwonsil in nature, as you saw in the warrior's thoughts, and likely preceded our arrival by less than half a day. There are also signs that confirm they moved westward."

I nodded. Why would they stay? They had done their worst.

"Night draws near and we must see to the dead." He took a breath, his eyes on the ground. "Digging graves will take too long, but to leave the bodies will draw predators. If you are agreeable to the idea, I would have us build a pyre and bless their path to Rynloeft in that fashion."

I looked behind me at the smoky rubble that had been their farm. It seemed both a sacrilege and strangely appropriate that their bodies should be consumed in the same manner as their livelihood had been taken. But I was unworthy to make this decision. *Any* decision. And yet he awaited my leave.

"Do what you think best."

He rose and bid Risson, Kinley, and Edru to assist him with the grim task.

TWENTY-SIX

I forced myself to watch as each body was brought to the pyre, even those of the enemy archer and Gerrias's horse, pulled to the pyre by ropes attached to three of the other horses. The disquiet resulting from observing the consequences of my mistakes was hardly enough penance for what I'd caused, but what other service could I offer?

We had nothing with which to wrap the bodies since their possessions had been destroyed, so the knights covered them in pine boughs. It was still early enough in the season that dry wood was plentiful. The fire caught quickly.

We stood in a line, me at its center, as the crackling wood caught.

"Embral e' Veria."

I jumped when Dyfnel voiced one of the names of the First King, even though I knew he would speak a few words to honor the passage of this family.

"We know little of these souls who have taken the path to meet you in Rynloeft, other than that their last moments in this world were unpleasant. But you knew of them before even time began." Dyfnel paused. "You know each calamity that will befall us and the number of our days. The very nature of your name lets us know that you weep, along with our chosen Ryn, at the cruelty that led to this tragedy."

I hadn't even realized I was crying again until Dyfnel noted it. I wiped my face, all the while wondering: could this loss have been prevented? A mother, father, and five children, victims of a combination of Cobeld curses, Dwonsil weaponry, and likely, though I dared not ask, the beasts of these ruthless foothills. Could this loss have been prevented?

What if I hadn't paused near Canyn and delayed us? Would we have gotten here in time for my knights to have defended these people? What if I had studied harder at Tirandov Isle, and therefore, would have been able to set out on this journey earlier? What if—

"Our Creator," Dyfnel said, his own voice thick, "we thank you for these, your servants, and release them to your care."

Julien cleared his throat. "May it be so."

We all echoed his benediction as the flames reached through the pyre and toward the sky.

After a few long moments of silence, Julien stepped from the line and turned to face us.

"At dawn we will water down the fire and depart. For now, we will make camp upwind."

Kinley and Edru offered to keep watch over the fire in case it should spread, and Erielle volunteered for the first watch at camp.

My emotions had exhausted me, but my heart twisted too much over Gerrias, over the misguided pride that had resulted in his incapacity, to allow me sleep. My mind wandered and wallowed, and silently, I wept.

Julien's thoughts, even in sleep, were mired in the emotion of his dreams. I should not have allowed myself to infringe upon his privacy to look, but I didn't have the strength to block him and I had little energy left to try. Perhaps it was my selfish need to have my shame lifted by making some sort of penance that caused me to linger within his mind, for the emotions leaking across the space between us were a sad mixture of duty, anger, confusion, love, and failure, all shadowed in the orange and blue swirls that signified my presence in his mind, his heart.

Julien's honor was impeccable, and I, who should have been moved to acquiesce by my respect for him alone, should have supported his leading. Instead I jabbed a thorn into his heart. Julien's training, his inborn character, and the position of his birth had shaped him into a man worthy of following. What would become of us, of our love, now that I had arbitrarily pulled rank and so disgraced his faith in me? Would he withdraw his courtship, in light of learning I was so childish, so unworthy of the honor his suit bestowed upon me?

I forced myself to pull gray around my mind and his to block the pain. Morning would come soon enough, and with it, one look in his eyes would likely confirm that he had decided to withdraw his suit.

I must have finally fallen asleep, for it was the scent of keola that opened my eyes to dawn.

I sat up and silently took the mug Edru offered, glad that no one else seemed to desire solid food either after the previous day's tragedy. I walked a bit away from the fire to break my fast, conscious of the eyes upon me, and found a log on which to sit.

Julien was gone, likely on patrol or seeing to the watering of the pyre. And I, the unworthy Ryn, needed to alert my father as to what had transpired . . . and what might come.

I closed my eyes and found the King close to his own fire, breaking his fast.

What's wrong?

He didn't even greet me, except for the close of his eyes and the one swiftly spoken question.

Was my shame and grief so obvious?

Of course it was.

I have dishonored both you and E'veria. Even the voice of my thoughts broke on the admission that tore my heart. I explained the events of the previous day, careful not to give into the temptation to gloss over my pathetic, childish response. *I'm sorry.*

My father was silent for a long moment. When he spoke, the change in topic surprised me. *As a young Prince, I was passionate about my position and the responsibility I was entrusted with to defend my realm. Like you are now. Unlike you, however, I spent the entirety of my life being raised and trained toward the duties of that position, as well as that of a knight. But even with a lifetime of preparation toward those positions, I made many mistakes on the path to becoming E'veria's King. And even more after I was crowned.*

He smiled and the love in his eyes both compounded my pain . . . and seemed to put an arm about my shoulders.

It is a hard thing, to believe you know the path to take and to find out it was wrong. But you will be a better Queen one day because of the mistakes you make as the Ryn.

I wiped a tear from my cheek. *That's what Dyfnel said.*

Dyfnel speaks from experience. My father chuckled. *He has witnessed many of my bullheaded blunders over the years.*

But Julien . . . I didn't know how to put my fear into words, so I let the thought hang, drenched in the colors of my emotions.

Julien loves you. My father's voice was much surer than my heart. *Loving an E'veri Ryn cannot be an easy thing for a knight like Julien. For anyone, actually. I'm sure your mother* _would agree._ He paused and a flash of memories showed me that in the brief years before the Cobeld curse forced my mother to convalesce on Tirandov Isle, arguments between my parents were frequent and fierce. Yet it did not seem to have marred their love.

Like you, Julien was born to lead, he continued. _But he was trained to it within the confines of a Regency and a youth spent training under me. The honest fact is that you outrank him. The hard truth is that his experience outweighs your rank._

I choked back my desire to weep. _I realize that now. But the damage has been done. Apart from injuring his brother, I have damaged his opinion of me. With cause._

You worry about the future of your courtship.

I nodded. _I do._

If you love him, do not be so quick to discount his love and commitment to you. Beyond his duty to you as the Ryn, Julien loves a beautiful young woman with a charming Veetrish accent. It was you who won his heart, Rynnaia, not your title. Have faith. Julien will not relinquish his love for you due to one argument. His heart is stouter than that.

I sincerely hope you're right, I sighed. _But I am also concerned about the outcome of this quest. I am unworthy to have so much of it resting upon me._

It rests on you, does it? He arched an eyebrow. _And in whose hand do you rest? On whose strength do you depend, Rynnaia E'veri?_

I closed my eyes and let out a long breath. Though my heart felt like it was drowning in a deep ocean of fear and shame, his gently scolding reminder was a buoy I could cling to.

I rest in the palm of the one whose strength is inexhaustible.

You are the Ryn. He gave one solid nod. _More importantly, you serve The First. Now serve._

Thank you, Father. I blew him a kiss with my mind and he faded from my view.

When I opened my eyes, Julien had returned, but everyone else had gone. So intent was I on speaking with my father that I hadn't realized how much time had passed. The fire had even been snuffed.

"Where is everyone?"

"With the horses. If you've finished your keola, we're ready to break camp."

I stood.

"Rynnaia." Julien's voice was suddenly thick. He took three strides toward me and took my hand. "I—"

"Forgive me," I interrupted him. "I was impetuous, prideful, and foolish. I shouldn't have fought with you. I shouldn't have asserted my position above yours. I shouldn't have gotten your brother injured or his horse killed. All those things are entirely my fault and I take full responsibility."

The words fell out of me, as if a flask had been uncorked and upended.

"I understand if your respect for me as the Ryn has dwindled to the point of finding me unworthy of further courtship, but I do, most heartily, give my word that I will try to earn back your respect, even if I must give up your heart."

He lifted our joined hands, and with them, raised my chin until I met his eyes.

"Should a thousand Dwonsil warriors try to remove my heart from where you keep it, I would fight them and prevail." He let go of my hands then and wrapped his arms around me. "Even should, as my sovereign future Queen, you order me to relinquish your love, I would disobey and, instead, hold fast to it until I could convince you otherwise."

"But Gerrias could have been killed because of my pride."

"I love my brother, but even had he been lost, I would forgive you. As I have already."

I pressed my trembling lips together and then took a breath as I leaned back to look up into his face. "How can you overlook such an offense?"

"I love you, Rynnaia. And it is the calling of love to forgive." He smiled and brushed a tear from my cheek. "We will disagree again, I'm sure. But love is stronger than any argument and is designed to outweigh any offense if we allow it to do its work within our hearts."

"But I'm so foolish."

"I will only agree to that statement if you choose to spurn my suit. And even then," he said, offering a sly wink, "I shall do so silently so as to remain loyal to my future Queen. Now give me your hand. It would seem that you need a reminder."

He opened my fingers, just as he'd done in my chamber at Holiday Palace, and kissed my palm. "You'll keep that close?"

I pressed it against my heart. "Always," I pledged. "And Julien," I swallowed, "thank you for seeing to the bodies and for keeping us safe."

He nodded, his expression solemn at the reminder of the lives lost to our enemy. "Then by your leave, I would have us quit this place."

"Lead on," I said. "I will follow."

TWENTY-SEVEN

We rode without stopping for a midafternoon rest that day, in silent but mutual agreement that we wanted to put as much distance as we could between us and the losses suffered at the ruined farmstead. Having offered Gerrias my horse, I rode with Julien upon Salvador's ample, strong back.

The next day we resumed our usual routine, and little by little, we regained our former camaraderie and humor. Soon we had ridden another week through mindless stretches of green, but we had not yet reached Fennik's Glenn and Risson's promise of the opportunity to bathe. Though I kept my complaints to myself, inwardly I began to despair over my own stench. Not that my companions were any better off, of course.

Time stretched with little to differentiate the view from one day to the next, but at last we reached a long, wide valley which reminded me that there were colors other than green and brown in E'veria. I couldn't help but lean over and pick one of the tall yellow wildflowers that added such brightness to our view. I lifted it to my nose and—

"Don't—!" Julien's warning came a moment too late. The instant I inhaled, I regretted it.

My nose burned. Fire reached down my throat and inflamed a tickle that sped back up my nose. I tossed the flower aside and covered my mouth as sneeze after sneeze wracked my frame. Julien pulled a handkerchief from his saddlebag and doused it with water from his canteen.

"Here." He handed it to me. "Wash your face and hands. It will help."

I took the cloth and rubbed it over my hands and face, pressing it hard against my eyes, but they had already begun to swell. Gritty and full, as if someone had poured sand over my face and then injected the skin of my eyelids with molten lead, they itched and ached.

"Hold the cloth over your face," Julien said. "We need to get through this."

I just nodded. Within minutes, several of my companions had begun to sneeze or sniffle. Even the horses' noses were irritated by the blooms.

"We'll go slowly, as to not disturb any more pollen than necessary," Julien's voice was muffled.

I looked over my shoulder and lifted the cloth to see that he'd tied a kerchief around his face, over his mouth and nose.

"We'll keep a steady pace. Cover your face," he reminded me. "It will help." I did.

As the day wore on everyone's voices grew rough and I heard one or two complaints of itchy eyes. The flora that drew the buzz of bees around us was no friend to our journey, but no one had been as foolishly enamored by the flowers as I.

By midafternoon I vowed to never like anything yellow again.

When we finally reached the other side of the narrow valley, I welcomed the endless green. Or would have, had I been able to see it. All I could note was the dimming of light and the slightly cooler temperature under the evergreens' shade. My eyes were completely swollen shut. I had given up the spectacles to my saddlebags days ago, but when I reached up to touch my face, I found only a tightly stretched, bulbous, and foreign shape beneath the cloth. Almost numb in places from swelling, I could only imagine how truly horrible I looked.

And the sound of my breathing! That alone was all kinds of ugly. A disgusting mixture of wheezes, hisses, coughs, and gurgles, it seemed especially grotesque this close to my own ears. And Julien's were just behind me.

We rode for hours with little conversation and everyone's sneezing eventually stilled, even mine. But I guessed it was only because my nose was too clogged and swollen to allow any further irritants within. So wrapped up in my own misery, I barely noted when the horses slowed, Julien dismounted, and the knights began conversing in hushed tones. Instead I regretted every day I'd taken my health and appearance for granted, pressed the damp cloth to my eyes, and vaguely wondered if I should wish for a swift and merciful death.

"Can you see well enough to dismount?" A low voice spoke beside me. I hadn't even realized we'd stopped.

"Kinley?" My voice rasped in a low and unfamiliar pitch. "Is that you?" I angled my head down and the cloth fell.

"Ohhh." He cleared his throat. "You can't see at all, can you?"

I bit my lip and wanted to cry.

"Are you crying? Or are your eyes weeping of their own accord?"

"I don't know," I croaked and a little sob escaped. But I did know, really.

"Aw, Rose. Don't cry. It'll pass."

The tenderness in my brother's voice elicited another disgusting, thick-bubbling sob.

"Give me your hand," he said.

I held out my left hand, holding to the pommel of Salvador's saddle with the other for balance. How keenly I missed my sight!

Kinley placed my hand on his shoulder. "Now allow your weight to rest on me and I'll lift you down." He put his hands about my waist and a moment later my feet were on the ground.

I rested my forehead on my foster brother's shoulder. I needed a hug in the worst way, but I only stayed there for a moment before taking a wobbly step back, right into Salvador, but he stood like a stone pillar, supporting me through the offense.

"Oh dear," Erielle's voice came from the left. "You look terrible."

"Erielle!" The hissed reprimand came from either Gerrias or Julien, I couldn't tell. "You forget yourself!"

Ahh. Julien, then.

"Oh, calm yourself Sir Stiffness. Rozen can take it."

"How bad is it?" I angled my question in the general direction of her voice. Since she didn't answer, I assumed she had moved on, but my hand was still on Kinley's shoulder. "Did she go?"

"No, I'm here," Erielle replied. "I was just trying to think of a diplomatic way to answer your question."

I groaned.

"Let me put it this way," she said slowly. "Be glad you already have a suitor, because otherwise you might end up a very lonely Queen."

I think I heard Julien's teeth grate against one another just before he growled her name again.

"Is it . . ." another abbreviated sob slipped between my lips, "permanent?"

"No." Kinley's voice was soft. "You'll be fine in a day or two, most likely."

"Most likely?"

"You'll be fine," he repeated. "I promise."

"On a brighter note," this came from Gerrias, "at least we don't have to worry about Fennik recognizing you."

"*I* don't even recognize you," Erielle laughed. "Um, sorry."

"Fennik? Are we near?"

"Yes," Gerrias said. "Risson went ahead to alert the old man to our arrival. He's not one you want to surprise."

"Then I hope Risson warns him about Rozen's face!"

"*Erielle! That's enough!*" I wasn't sure I'd ever heard Julien so angry. "You claim you want the honor of knighthood, yet you cannot even censure your own tongue?"

"Julien, I was only—"

"Enough! Consider your silence for the rest of the evening as your gift of penance to us all. You may spend the air you might otherwise spoil with your impertinence in the task of filling Fennik's tub. You will be the last to bathe and find your rest tonight, I think. Perhaps tomorrow's fatigue will help to tame your careless words."

As Erielle's friend, I wanted to stick up for her and argue with the punishment Julien doled out. But with his father away and Erielle still a few months shy of seventeen, he was the head of their family. I would not question his leadership again. And he was right, in a way. Her teasing had hurt me when I was vulnerable. Even if my vulnerability was steeped in vanity, it still hurt to have my gruesomeness flung in my face—especially in front of a group of men, one of whom I wanted to find me beautiful above all others. I wouldn't hold it against her. Perhaps when the swelling went down I might even find it funny. But at the moment, it stung, and Julien was in the right to point it out.

"Your Highness—"

"*Shhh!*" About six voices shushed Dyfnel at once.

"My apologies." He cleared his throat. "I've gathered a few herbs to make into a poultice. Once we've reached Fennik's Glenn I'll crush them, mix them with a bit of water, and apply it to your face." He paused. "Of course, if Sir Fennik would happen to have spirits available it would make it all the more effective."

"Oh, I don't think that will be a problem," Gerrias said with a chuckle.

"He's not a drunkard, is he?"

I could almost see Dyfnel's brow crease with concern, just by the tone of his voice.

"Oh, no. Not Finnick. He doesn't touch the stuff. He does a right fine business selling it, however."

Risson soon returned and we continued on toward Fennik's Glenn.

Before the sun hit my face, the smell of rotting grain permeated the clogs in my nostrils. By the time the brightness of sunshine came through my swollen lids, it had faded.

"What was that awful smell we passed?"

"That's the smell of money, pretty boy." The gruff voice was unfamiliar. "You passed by my distillery."

"Rozen," Julien said, "this is Sir Fennik de Selwen."

"Gums, boy. You're a sight. Must've near stuck the bloomin' yellowhocks up your nose to come out like that," Fennik said. "Well, come along, then. Sir Risson said you'd need a wash off and I got a tub ready for you. Foolish boy."

"Errol." Julien's use of Erielle's squire name was telling. He didn't even want Fennik to know that his sister was along. "You go with Rozen. Fennik, why don't you help us with the horses?"

The old man grumbled something about pompous Regents ordering him about his own home, but he complied.

Julien dismounted and then helped me down, and Erielle took my hand to lead me to the house. I stumbled about six times before I hollered back at Julien, "Sir Julien, would you please allow Errol to speak before I break a leg?"

There was a moment of dead silence in which I assumed Julien made some sort of gesture that gave Erielle permission to talk to me because she said, "There's a tree root three steps ahead. Easy, easy. There. Good job." Finally, we made it into the house.

"Wow. It's nicer than I expected," she said, then laughed. "But the tub is right here by the fire! Here, sit." She led me to a chair. "Thank goodness there are curtains, but we'd best make this quick or I'm afraid the old knight will walk right in and see how not-a-boy you are."

I groaned. Would the humiliation of this day know no end?

"Ah, but there's a bolt on the door. Good." The metal slid home and she returned to my side to help me undress and guided me to the tub.

"Oh, Rynnaia. It's cold."

"Is it clean?"

"Yes, but—"

"That's all that matters." A moment later, when I cramped my long legs getting into the short, narrow tub, however, I wasn't so sure. My teeth chattered. "L-let's make this quick. No hair."

"I wondered, since you left the hairpiece and cap on." Erielle gave me a rag and said, "Here. I've soaped it for you." I scrubbed at my skin faster and harder than I ever had before. A few moments later, I stood. She said a quick, "Sorry!" and poured a bucket over me to rinse. And again.

She shoved a towel in my hands. "Look on the bright side. Our next baths will be at Castle Rynwyk. And warm."

"Not if we follow the scrolls," I said. The scrolls promised more than one opportunity to get wet within Mount Shireya.

"That's not exactly my idea of a bath. And I'm fairly sure the water of which Lady Anya wrote didn't include soap or towels," she said. "But maybe our swims will help get the stink out of our clothes."

I groaned. "I forgot I'd have to put those same filthy clothes on again."

"Unless you want me to get your spare set?"

"No. I'll want them clean and dry later," I sighed. "We all agreed."

"Yes. How idiotic was that?" She was quiet, helping me keep my balance while I did my best to dry off with the scratchy towel.

"All right, wrap me back up."

She had me bound and dressed in no time, which was no small feat considering how I shivered throughout the ordeal and kept losing my balance since I couldn't see.

"Now you just sit here by the fire," she said, guiding me to a chair that was surprisingly soft and comfortable, given the man who owned it. "I'll get Dyfnel and see if he has that poultice ready yet." She paused. "Rynnaia?"

"Yes?"

"I once met a girl in Stoen who suffered many of the same symptoms you are going through." She paused. "The difference was that her ailments were caused by the curse of a Cobeld and there was no hope for their reversal." Her voice grew quieter. "Her name was Nella. She was the daughter of a Sengarren Earl. Shortly before she was cursed, she had been betrothed to the heir to a dukedom in Stoen, but when he saw the result of the curse, the agreement was broken."

I gasped. "She's better off without him, if his love was that shallow."

"Yes. Well, no actually." She was quiet for a moment. "What I'm trying to say is that I'm sorry I made fun of you. It was cruel. Especially when I consider Nella's pain."

"Thank you. I forgive you," I said. "And when we get the Remedy, perhaps you can be the one to deliver it to your friend."

"I'm afraid that's not possible." There was a slight tremble in Erielle's voice and I wondered if I could see her face if there would be tears. "Nella took her own life a month after her betrothal was broken. She could no longer take the pain and humiliation the Cobeld's curse had brought about."

My hand fluttered to my heart. "Erielle, I'm so sorry," I whispered, suddenly feeling like such a whiner. "My face isn't nearly as sore as my vanity. I've been so worried about how monstrous I must appear that I didn't consider the passing nature of my ailment." My mother's face flashed through my mind. "The discomfort of a day or two hardly excuses my whining when compared to that of your friend, or that which my own mother has suffered."

"There were rumors at Holiday Palace that she is getting weaker."

"She is," I admitted. Father, Julien and I had admitted it to few, hoping to keep the Kingdom's hope alive. "I tried to contact her about a week ago, but she could barely—"

I paused. The memory was fresh with pain. "It seemed all she could do just to hear me. She could not respond in kind."

"Perhaps you contacted her during a bad spell and another day might find her in better health?"

"Perhaps." But I knew better. And if my face wasn't so grotesquely swollen, Erielle would have seen the falseness of my response.

"You will find the Remedy, Rynnaia. And I'm sure Dyfnel and . . . whoever will be traveling with him," she paused on that mystery of the scrolls, "will get it to the Queen in time. And as for your worries about your appearance?" She laughed. "Don't bother to include a fear that you might lose Julien's affection. My brother thinks you're an angel. His opinion of me, on the other hand . . . ?"

I laughed. "I imagine it will be a long night for you."

"Indeed." She sighed. "I'd best fasten my lips and seek out the physician now. Rest easy. Dyfnel will have you looking yourself again in no time."

TWENTY-EIGHT

The nightmares began almost as soon as my eyes closed that night. I awoke screaming, fighting anyone who came near, until Kinley, Julien, and Erielle were finally able to convince me of who they were and that they meant me no harm.

With the help of Dyfnel's poultice, day by delaying day, the swelling slowly receded. But the dreams did not. Each bit of sleep I caught was plagued with restless images and deep, haunting laughter that taunted me, challenged me, and caused my mouth to fill with the taste of fear.

"They're like traps," Fennik said of the yellowhock fields after dinner one night. "I've mapped their locations and come up with no other conclusion but that their positioning is meant to keep people from coming too near the mountain."

"I thought yellowhock was a native plant," Gerrias said.

"Aye, it is," Fennik replied. "But it doesn't grow that way naturally, taking over an entire space like that. It has to be cultivated to that end. And neither does the inhaling of a

277

native yellowhock cause that like what your young friend has experienced. No, only the crop fields do that."

"Crop fields?" Kinley spoke up. "Who would be able to stand being within that field long enough to harvest a crop?"

"Cobelds." Fennik's tone grew dark. "It's harvested twice a year. But try as I might, I've never been able to catch the little demons at it."

"Then how do you know it was them?" This, from Erielle.

There was a long pause with no noise but the crackling of the fire. Finally, Fennik spoke. "Have you ever suffered from night terrors as your friend does?"

"Yes." The admittance was hard won from Erielle.

"Do you remember the feeling you had upon waking from such a dream? The creeping of your scalp and the clenching of your insides that said you'd just escaped a great evil? The surety that, had you awakened a moment later, you would surely have died from the fright in your sleep?"

His description sent a shiver through my bones, and though blurred, I noted the slow nods of several members of our group.

"That," he said, "is how I knew it was them that gathered the yellowhock when I came across a recently harvested field."

No one argued with his assessment. Instead quiet descended as we all wondered what use the Cobelds would have for such a toxic substance, or if they were somehow immune to its pollen.

We stayed at Fennik's for four days in all, but from the first, terror-filled night, Fennik implied that my dreams were a side effect of my reaction to the yellowhock pollen. But in his thoughts I saw that, although he considered it a possibility, it wasn't a symptom he had ever seen before. Why he lied, I could only imagine was to soothe my pride, because although he continued to address me as "Squire Rozen," I think he began to suspect my true identity as the swelling went down.

How could he not, with a quartet of knights, two Andoven, and a squire hovering so? Still, the act of kindness surprised me from such a gruff old knight.

But then again, as a young man Fennik had sworn fealty to my grandfather, King Rynitel, and later to my father before retiring to his solitary home in Shireya. Perhaps it was the Knight's Oath itself that made him able to recognize the Ryn.

Even with Fennik's ready supply of spirits, the poultice wasn't powerful enough to perform a miracle. My features had nearly returned to their normal size, but the bruising around my eyes made me look like I—in Fennik's words—had "tried to steal from a pirate."

I'd have to share that comment with Cazien the next time I saw him. Then again, if this was just the first of the booby traps set to keep us from finding the Remedy, there might not be a next time.

The last night we spent at Fennik's found me awake more than an hour after the deep breathing of my companions proved their passage into dreams. I was anxious, fearing the visions that would come in my sleep. And even more pressing than that was the mire of embarrassment my vanity had delivered me to. Having finally convinced Fennik to allow me a glance in his looking glass, I had been expecting a sense of relief. But it was not to be. Most of the swelling had receded, but my nose was red and chapped from dripping and wiping, and a yellowish ring around my mouth still remained as evidence of the bruising caused by my swelling lips. But worse still, the skin around my eyes was mottled with purple, black, and green. I looked nothing like a princess. An apt description of my face might even allude to an ogre out of a child's storybook or a Veetrish tale. Even the ugliest Cobeld would likely find me so repulsive that he would flee.

When I said so, Kinley had joked, "Well, we won't be complaining about that now, will we?" But his humor had faded when he noted the tears gathering in my eyes.

I was ugly and I was vain and I was exhausted, but the promise of sleep wasn't as alluring as it might have been had it not seemed to guarantee a wealth of terror. I stared at the fire, watching the flames dance. Since everyone else was asleep, I figured I could wallow a bit.

A tear rolled down my cheek and I swiped it away, cursing my vanity as well as the stupidity that put me in this position in the first place. Grinding my teeth, I rolled over. As I slid my hand under my pillow, however, my fingers touched a scrap of parchment.

My heart lifted. *Julien.*

The light from the fire was dim, especially since I was facing the opposite direction, but his few words imparted more warmth to me than any that might have made its way to me from the hearth. It was the shortest note I'd yet received from him, which wasn't surprising given our close quarters, but somehow, in those spare lines, Julien expressed exactly what my wounded vanity needed to know.

Never doubt.

My heart is yours.

I read his note over and over until my eyes began to droop. Carefully, I folded the parchment and stuck it into the binding under my tunic, close to my heart.

The nightmares were longer in coming that night, but they eventually found and captured me. At first I was aware that I was dreaming, but too quickly the dream became too real to allow me to know anything but the terror from which I could not escape. Regardless of my sleepy prison, however, my screams roused everyone else. When Julien's voice finally broke through my dream, the look in my friends' eyes told me that no more sleep would be had by anyone that night.

Dawn had just crept into the woods when we finished our breakfast of deer sausages and fried bread. Shortly after, we packed the horses, bid Fennik good-bye, and resumed our journey toward the ever-looming mountain.

With four days lost to the Cobelds already, we resumed our path toward the Sacred Mountain.

TWENTY-NINE

I was alone, standing in the middle of a yellowhock field. The only light came from the tirandite torch in my hand.

"Julien?" I whispered his name again, but my voice only echoed back on me, almost as if I was surrounded by walls of stone.

I looked down at the flowers. Tears, caused by their pollen, streamed down my face. All at once, the bud of each flower quivered. A moment later, a pair of black eyes blinked from each center. Another moment passed and the stems became bodies, and the leaves, arms and legs.

And then, appearing on the very edge of each bloom, a long, gray beard.

Was that a breeze, rustling these strange-featured flowers? No, it was a whisper.

"Fail." Followed closely by another. "Die."

Suddenly, the blooms weren't flowers anymore. They were wrinkled old man. Cobelds!

I was surrounded by Cobelds!

Screaming, I turned to run, but in my path, one of the flow-er-turned-Cobelds stretched taller, taller than my lucid mind could allow a Cobeld to be, taller, even, than me.

Other Cobelds grabbed my arms, my legs. They pulled me down to the ground. The giant Cobeld leaned down and leered at me. A drop of spittle stretched from his lips and landed on my cheek. When his beard was only a breath away from my face, he laughed.

I opened my mouth to scream, but all that came out was a whimper.

"I'm here." Julien's whisper was close. Too close.

No. No! He can't be here! They'll kill him, too!

The Cobeld backed up, looking around as if searching for the knight.

"Rynnaia," the whisper came again.

Where was he? Why couldn't I see him?

But maybe it was good I couldn't see him. Maybe the Cobelds couldn't see him, either.

The giant Cobeld met my eyes and smiled. He didn't speak, but a promise, a threat, haunted the laughter that ensued.

"Rynnaia, wake up."

I struggled against the Cobelds holding me down. "Julien!" I screamed. "Julien!"

"I'm here." His voice was strained. "It's just a dream, love. I'm here."

I opened my eyes to find myself in his arms. A trickle of blood dripped from his nose.

I winced. "Did I do that?"

He loosened his hold on my arms to wipe his sleeve across his face. "It's nothing."

"I'm sorry." I looked around the circle of concerned fac-es. I had hoped that my nightmares would stop when we left Fennik's Glen. "I'm sorry," I sighed. "Would that my sleep was the only sleep disturbed by these terrors."

"Would that I could take them from you," Julien said in a low voice.

"Is it nearly dawn?"

He shook his head. "You couldn't have been asleep more than a quarter of an hour this time," he said. "I'll stay close. Try to go back to sleep."

For the rest of that night, at least, the dreams stayed away. I mused it was because Julien kept a tight hold on my hand and that I drew peace, even in sleep, from his love. Or perhaps it was the soft lullaby Kinley hummed, one his mother had often sung to me when I was a little girl, awakening from a bad dream.

The next night, however, the dreams returned, and neither my Bear-knight's strength nor my brother's song could keep them at bay.

Just over five weeks had passed since we left Holiday Palace. My father and Vayle were still a few days from Salderyn, their journey having been slowed by a battle or two with Dwonsil warriors along the way. And my mother, while I sensed she could hear me, could no longer open her eyes when I contacted her. My heart was heavy, but it kept my feet from flagging. There was no time to waste, and since sleep wasn't something I looked forward to, knowing what nightmares would come, it was often my voice urging our group to cover just a little more ground each night after the sun had set.

Finally, Mount Shireya loomed before us as a fearsome gray adversary, but a smaller one than I'd expected, especially considering the way the nightmares had engraved it in my mind.

For so long, the Sacred Mountain had seemed so high and so far away. But now that we were nearly there, we found that our gradual ascent over weeks traveling through the foothills had shrunken her. I had expected the mountain to be larger, somehow. It was, after all, the highest point in E'veria. I had not expected, seeing it from lower elevations, that it would be *less* spectacular close up.

Regardless of its size, I still had to go *inside* it. And I wasn't looking forward to that.

Of course I knew that the mountain itself wasn't working against us, but my dreams argued against logic. There was evil inside that mountain. Evil that had crept into my dreams.

Evil that knew I was on my way to meet it.

The scenes in my dreams varied, but always they were accompanied by the same malevolent laughter. It wasn't the cackle of an old man, like one would expect from a Cobeld. It had an ageless quality to it. And even within a nightmare, it seemed both an echo of the past and a portent of the future.

I dreamed of drowning in a river of rolling rapids. Of falling from great heights. Of feeling my insides catch fire. My nightmares took me to the very tip of a sword . . . and sank it into my chest. They forced me to watch my friends die horrible deaths, one by one—or all at once. And the most terrifying dreams of all found me deep within the darkness of the mountain and completely alone, but for the unseen source of that hideous laughter.

It made no sense. In all our weeks of travel through Shireya, the only sign of Cobelds we'd come across was Fennik's assertion that the yellowhock fields were tended by them, and the cursed arrows of the Dwonsil warriors who had murdered an innocent farm family. Julien assured me that the Cobelds' camps were generally to the north and east of the mountain, and since we'd come from the southwest, seeing them was unlikely. But I thought my father's all-too-successful campaign to make the Cobelds think I had traveled with him toward Salderyn was a more likely explanation for our lack of confrontation with the enemy.

Periodic updates from my father, which I could only assume he sanitized to ease my worry, were frequented by the mention of Cobeld and Dwonsil warrior incursions with our army along Dynwey Road. As of yet, neither my father nor Vayle had been injured, but friend and foe alike believed she was the Ryn. The ruse put her in regrettably great peril, but it was effective.

Thus far.

The night we reached the mountain, we camped just inside the cover of trees at the very base of the rock face. Numerous caves dotted the southern side of the mountain and none of us had a clue which cave was the right one by which to enter.

"Do you think the horses will fare well in the forest while we're within the mountain?"

Julien gave me a small smile. "As long as they keep with Salvador, they'll be fine."

"I hate leaving them."

My Andoven abilities could help the horses to find us once we exited the mountain, but depending on how far they wandered in the meantime, it could take days for us to meet up. None of us could guess whether our journey within would take hours, days, or even weeks.

"I wonder if we've passed any of the nine marks yet," Erielle mused.

"I don't think so," Edru answered as he turned a rabbit on a spit. "I don't think the marks begin until we're inside."

Risson and Kinley took the second watch that last night, but none of us slept soundly. Shortly before dawn, a commotion just beyond the fire shook the last vestiges of irregular rest from our minds. We all arose in a flash, and without speaking, Julien, Erielle, Gerrias, Dyfnel, and Edru surrounded me and drew whatever weapon was closest.

My heart beat a wild rhythm, but I had to smile a little when I realized that Erielle alone had a weapon in *each* hand. A moment later, Dyfnel and Edru parted to make room for Kinley. His quick but silent entrance within the circle made Risson's much louder appearance all that more shocking.

After all this time unhindered by the enemy, were we now to come face to face with a Cobeld?

At the tip of Risson's sword, an oddly attired, filthy, but mostly beardless man was prodded into the center of our camp. His height matched Risson's.

I breathed a sigh of relief. *Not a Cobeld, then.*

"I found him attempting to lead away Kinley's mount." Risson sounded impatient, almost disappointed, as if he'd been aching to engage an enemy and was frustrated that the first person he encountered this close to the mountain should be a mere horse thief.

I couldn't blame him. After little sleep and much worry, I was more than a little irritated myself. Not that I'd wanted to meet a Cobeld, of course. I had simply wanted to delay the start of the day a bit longer. Like until after the sun was up, rather than just casting an upward glow from the horizon, as it was at this early morning hour.

I pushed through the spot between Gerrias and Erielle and approached the pair. "Have you a name, thief?" I asked, "Or a ready defense of your actions?"

He tilted his head at me, an odd expression on his face. "My Lord Squire knows my name, though he does not know what he knows."

I took a step back. I'd forgotten for a moment that I was dressed as a squire, especially since Julien and Kinley had come up along either side of me and taken a defensive stance toward the stranger.

"My apologies, Sir Julien," I said, as a squire should. As the Ryn should, to the man charged with her safety . . . and her heart.

Julien didn't respond to me, but spoke to the thief instead. "What acquaintance would a squire from Veetri have with a Shireyan horse thief?"

"No acquaintance but with knowledge, Your Lowliness. Knowledge of my name, of course. But the squire does not know it."

What?

Dawn was dim, but if he thought he knew me, especially in Rozen's clothes, he must have me mistaken for someone else. Just in case, I looked closer at the man. I studied his face, but from the double notches of his receding hairline to the scruff on his chin that looked to be as much dirt as beard, nothing about him was familiar.

"He must have me confused with someone else," I said, deferring to Julien. "I've never seen him before."

"That's because we've not been introduced, though you've already called me by name," he said, nodding as if his statement made perfect sense. "A wonder, that, isn't it? But it makes an introduction at this point little more than a formality."

"My squire has called you naught but a thief," Julien said. "Tell me now, what is your name and with whom does your allegiance lie?"

The man spit into each hand and gave great show to smoothing his greasy, thinning hair with the spittle as if it were costly oil. "E'veria is much changed since the die was cast, but had I known the knights were now the squires and the squires were now the lords, I would have sought to breed a squire while a wife would still have me."

Julien took a small step forward. "You will answer my question, or you will answer my sword."

The thief licked a finger of each hand and smoothed his bushy, graying eyebrows before making a dramatic bow to Julien.

"I have both a name and a defense, Your Worthy Slaveness," he said.

Julien growled. "*What* did you call me?"

The air was taut as we awaited his reply, but the horse thief seemed entirely relaxed. Could it be he was just one of a gang of bandits and that we were soon to be outnumbered? Julien must have had the same thought.

"Gerrias. Erielle," he said. "Perimeter."

I didn't hear their movements as they left the camp, but I knew the younger de Gladiel offspring would quickly discover whether or not this thief was working alone.

The thief gave me an indulgent smile as he used a fingernail to dislodge a food particle from between his yellowing teeth.

"Speak," Julien ordered.

"It would give me great pleasure. But I can't decide to whom I should address my address." He waggled a finger between me and Julien. "The squire serves the knight . . . who serves the squire, but it is unclear to whom I should presume to ply my defense."

His elocution was perfect. Refined, even. But the direction and meaning of his words was . . . less than.

Kinley and Julien exchanged a quick glance and one of their mysterious nods. Kinley then took a step toward the thief. "You may address me," he said, "as it was my horse you were attempting to steal."

The greasy man nodded. "I will if you insist, Second Knight of the Boy, though it does your Lord Squire little honor to his station." He bowed. "I am Taef de Emwyk and I am no horse thief. I prefer to think of myself as a diplomat to the equine citizens of E'veria."

The sun chose that moment to send its first rays into our camp and its westward glow helped to better delineate the stranger's filthy features.

He had looked more appealing in the darkness.

"A diplomat, you say?" Kinley arched an eyebrow. "To . . . horses?" His tone was curious, but cautiously so. Like the rest of us, he was trying to discern whether the man was a calculatingly shrewd criminal or simply insane and deserving of our pity.

"Yes, indeed! Your horse and I—a fine specimen, I might add—negotiated an agreement this morning. My alliance with him is now sure."

He smiled at us, the picture of blinking innocence. None of us knew how to respond.

"My liege desires a guide and the worthy steed desires oats. We bargained," Taef de Emwyk explained, "and I am pleased to say we reached a mutually beneficial agreement." He nodded at Kinley and added, "A skilled deal weaver, that one."

Taef closed his eyes and kept nodding with a smile of sublime satisfaction on his face, as if he had been impressed with the horse's business acumen.

"You say you came to an agreement with . . . my horse?" Kinley prodded.

"Yes," the strange man replied. "I have need of serving and he has need of guiding. Also, a desire for oats."

"Truly, sir, your cleverness exceeds my own," Kinley said.

"You are humble beyond your years, Lowly Sir, to so readily admit to your deficiencies. Although the agreement benefits us both, I do believe the steed receives the better end of it. He is a tougher negotiator than I."

Erielle strode up behind Risson. With a nod toward Julien, she said, "All clear." And then, pushing a surprised Kinley aside, she moved to stand directly in front of the would-be thief. At once she took a step backward, tucked her head to the side, and wrinkled her nose, making me glad I was farther away and upwind of the man.

"Thief," she said, facing him again, "I would ask a question of you."

The stranger folded his hands in front of him and inclined his head in assent.

"In return for allowing you the temporary care of Sir Kinley's worthy horse," she said, "will you show us which cave contains the ruins of the cells destroyed by The First?"

The smile fell from the man's countenance as if a heavy cloth had washed it away.

"My Lord Squire," he sounded unaccountably offended, "indeed I know the place of which you speak, but I would not divulge its location for all the horses and oats in E'veria, be they the property of Enslaved Knights or," he turned his gaze to me, "Majestic Squires." He took a breath and rubbed a shaking hand across his brow. "Only one may take the rise."

A collective intake of breath was the only sound that permeated our camp. Stepping close enough to the scoundrel that I was forced to swallow the bile that rose in my throat at his stench, I locked eyes with him and spoke the next line of poetry from the scrolls.

"With mane of fire and sky-jeweled eyes?"

His eyes widened.

"Nothing for it, then," Erielle grinned at me. "Show him the fire."

I ripped the squire's cap and hairpiece from my skull, wincing a bit for the hairs that were sacrificed to that hurried action.

The would-be thief fell to his knees.

"Ryn Naia!" he cried. "I have lived to see the Ryn Naia!" He rocked back and forth, weeping as he sang the words. "Ryn Naia. Ryn Naia!"

My breath caught. The joy and relief in his words stung my eyes with sudden emotion.

"It would seem we have found our scoundrel ally," Julien said softly. Turning to Erielle, he asked, "How did you guess?"

"His manner of speaking was strange and," she interrupted herself with a laugh, "annoying! Even walking the perimeter of the camp, I found myself so wearied of his nonsense that I wished to gag him, chain him to a tree, and leave him there." She shrugged. "Then when you called him 'thief' the poetry came to my mind."

"His name!" Dyfnel had a strange look on his face. "I should have known."

"Indeed." Edru looked as if he wanted to strangle himself. "In the Ancient Voice, Taef de Emwyk means *thief descended from a seat of power.*"

"Not descended from," Taef said, shaking his head sadly. "Stolen. The thief was stolen. By a servant of the worst horse thief E'veria will ever know. And the least equine of them all."

Silence reigned as we tried to make some sort of sense of that statement.

"Regardless," Edru finally said, "I doubt he would have made away with the horse. He was sent to us by The First."

Risson sheathed his sword, grinning. "We begin!"

We welcomed Taef into our company, though we were careful to sit as far upwind as we could without causing offense to our strange new guide. After building up the dwindling fire, we invited him to join us in finishing off the rations of dried meat, cheese, and hardened biscuits Fennik had sent with us, along with a pheasant Risson had snared and cooked. It was a good meal, if gamey, but we were well used to forest fare by now. Besides, it would be our last real food for . . . we didn't know how long.

Much more important than food, we wanted to make sure to be able to shoulder the torches I'd been gifted from the Andoven on Tirandov Isle. In addition, we had each hoarded one change of clothes, tightly wrapped in oiled and waxed skins, to wear after we'd gotten through the wet and cold the scrolls promised us.

As we left our camp, Taef had a spring in his step, and even though part of me wanted to drag my feet all the way to the cave, my heart was eased when he offered to take our horses to the northern side of the mountain where the scrolls had predicted we would eventually exit once our task within was completed.

If our task within was completed, that is.

If we survived.

I shook my head to dispel the morbidity. That sort of thinking wouldn't help any of us.

"A horse in the company of the Ryn Naia would rather serve her in starvation than eat the best oats my Regent's horse-house has to offer," Taef spoke up.

"Your liege is the Regent of Shireya, then?" I asked.

"You are my liege and my hope, Ryn Naia," he answered vaguely. "I claim no other allegiance, though an allegiance may have claim on me, and I on it in days long past."

I nodded as if I understood him. Julien shot an amused glance my direction.

I placed a hand on Taef's shoulder, hoping that nothing that might reside within the fibers of his clothing would decide to change address when given the opportunity. "Your service to us will be well rewarded if we survive our quest."

"I, too, appreciate oats," he said with a shy smile.

"Oats?" It took quite a bit of effort to keep the serious expression on my face. "Then oats you shall have, Taef de Emwyk," I replied. "Oats in abundance."

"You are a generous and worthy future Queen, Ryn Naia," Taef said, wiping away a tear. "Oh, yes," he repeated. "Such a wise and generous Queen you will be." And then, with a little skip in his step, he said, "Follow me," and led us onward.

PART II:
THE RYN NAIA

⁂HIRTY

orth and east of Mount Shireya, the clansman from Dwons seemed grotesquely large as he stood among the gathered Cobelds. But for his face, not a bit of flesh shone through the leathers he wore—a wardrobe that had become a necessary fashion among Dwonsil warriors since they had formed an allegiance with the Cobelds.

The five Seers circled the Dwonsil warrior, waiting.

"The one traveling with the King is a fraud," he finally said. "It is confirmed."

Tension lit the air with a hiss. One of the Seers took a step forward. "If the one traveling with E'veria's King is false, where is the Ryn Naia?"

"We don't know."

The Cobeld Seer gestured to his fellow. "Kill him."

"There is more," the Dwonsil warrior added as his hand reached for a sword that wasn't there. It had been removed from his possession when he arrived among them.

The Seer held up his hand to pause the curse-wrapped dagger a Cobeld guard had aimed to throw. "Go on."

Winter had taken much of the color from the warrior's desert-darkened skin, but in the last few moments he had paled even more.

"A contingent of knights was discovered near Canyn Village some weeks past," he said. "I only recently received the report. They managed to elude our men, but they were headed for Shireya."

"Knights? Bah. We seek the Ryn Naia. A woman. Was there a woman among them?"

"Not that we could tell, but one of the knights was identified as Julien de Gladiel, the Regent of Mynissbyr's heir. He ranks high and should have been with the King."

The Seer spun around. "You. And you." He pointed at random Cobelds from among those gathered until they numbered an even dozen. "Go to the mountain. If they are within, kill them. Bring me the flame, and the head attached to it, to prove it is done."

The Seer turned back to the Dwonsil warrior. "You will live another day. Tell your men we retreat to our base camp near Shireya's northern steps. Your job," he said, "is to keep the E'verian King's Army far enough back that we can protect our interests near the mountain."

The Seers formed a line and shouted a command that set an army of shriveled old men to their feet with a speed that blurred the air.

"Cobelds!" the Seers cried as one, "To the Shrine! Guard the well and protect the source of our power!"

THIRTY-ONE

Flattening our backs against the southern face of the Sacred Mountain, we followed Taef de Emwyk, inching up a nearly invisible trail to an even less visible cave.

Relatively low on the side of the mountain, it was camouflaged by the natural progression of brush and climbing vines so common to the region. Even had its precise location been mapped on one of the scrolls, we would have had a difficult time finding it. Until Taef grabbed hold of a vine and yanked, it was entirely invisible. It took a good dulling of the swords before the cave's opening was passable.

While Erielle and the men took turns cutting away at the vines that concealed the cave's entrance, I busied myself removing our tirandite torches from our packs. A gift from the Andoven people, these torches required no fire and could be extinguished by nothing but time. I set them on a flat rock where the sun seemed brightest, knowing it would only take a brief time for the torches to absorb enough light to allow us several days' illumination. And if the darkness peeking through the thick vines was any indication, using the torches would be necessary almost immediately upon entry.

Finally, a hole was roughed out just wide enough for one person to pass through at a time. But even then we could not enter. The swords and daggers used to cut away the brambles and vines had to be painstakingly cleaned and sharpened. Since no one was inclined to allow me to help, I vacillated through the occupations of sitting and pacing. No one talked, but Taef shadowed my movements, and as strange as it was, his company was a bit of a comfort.

Thoughts of wolfcats, bears, and other carnivorous beasts flitted through my mind. For some reason I had given no thought at all to what dangers we might face beyond those promised by the scrolls. But now our encounters with the wolfcats seemed an ominous promise. What else might lurk within the unknown passages of this mountain? Now that I was about to cross its dark and eerie threshold, nightmarish visions of predatory creatures large and small crept into my thoughts.

"Small creepers there will be," Taef said with a nod, almost as if he had seen my thoughts. "But the bears have already awakened and left their winter homes. The cats don't like these caves. Too wet."

As I had already tried several times throughout the day, I focused my attention on our "scoundrel ally," but his mind moved in such randomness that I could not discern a single coherent thought amidst the chaos.

Taef's eyes were blue, if cloudily so. I supposed he could be a bit Andoven. But what most struck me about his thought patterns was their similarity to Salvador's. In some ways they seemed more animal than human, yet in others . . . even less organized.

"Have you been inside the cave, Taef?"

"Not far," he replied. "I'm no fish, just a bridge builder."

Kinley looked up from his sword. His lip twitched. "But I thought you were a horse diplomat, Taef," he said, "not an architect or engineer!"

Taef inclined his head. "I have witnessed the building of bridges between diplomats and architects in the course of my duty, but I wagered not that they would collapse under strain."

"Who are you, really?" Kinley pressed, but his smile was friendly.

"I am ever your humble better," Taef bowed lowly, "and as such I give you my fealty."

My brain began to feel the strain of trying to discern what his conflicting words meant. I gave up trying to see his thoughts and excused myself to spend a few last minutes with Stanza and Salvador.

Soon everyone's weapons were back in shining order and Julien secured Taef's promise to conceal the cave as best he could after we had entered the mountain. Shortly thereafter, we—all but Gerrias, of course—bid a solemn good-bye to our horses, now in the care of the strange fellow The First had sent to accomplish that part of his purpose. Right before we parted ways, we clasped hands in a circle and raised our faces to the sky as Dyfnel spoke a benediction over our quest.

"Light of Truth, Sustainer of Life, and Author of Hope," he began.

His words gave me a moment's pause. The last was a title I had never heard concerning the First King. Yet upon a moment of reflection, it seemed just.

"Our Mighty First King," Dyfnel continued, "we seek your guidance to help us achieve the wisdom by which we will be enabled to see with the eyes of our hearts and our minds as we enter this place and time of darkness. Light our way with the truth that has brought us here and carry us on your strength when our own fails us. We ask that you protect our King and Queen as they fight your battle on different fronts and guide this company and our Ryn in the humble care of all you have entrusted to us. Thank you for allowing us to see this time come to pass, and thank you," he paused and I heard a smile in his voice, "for the ways you continue to surprise us by your wise provision for our needs."

"May it be so," we whispered. And then, torches aloft, we entered Mount Shireya.

THIRTY-TWO

Inside the cave, the light of our torches was much better than I had expected. Stronger than lanterns and with nearly the same coloring as daylight, our vision was hardly impaired by the cave.

"Look!" Erielle gasped. "The cells!"

Less than twenty paces inside, we came to the remains of the ancient cells which had once imprisoned the knights of the First King. The bars were off-kilter and bent wide enough to fit through. None of us could resist the temptation to go into the cell and back out at least once, reenacting, as it were, our own history. I'd heard the story as a child, told in the dramatic style of the Veetrish Storytellers with whom I was raised, but only recently had I learned the tale was true.

In the ancient time of Loeftryn de Rynloeft, his knights— including my ancestor, Stoen, who was eventually renamed Stoenryn and crowned as E'veria's second king—were captured and imprisoned here by the traitor, Cobeld. But a miraculous explosion of light, brought about by the power of

The First, released them from their cells and shrank Cobeld's traitorous warriors into shriveled old men.

As we gazed upon the evidence of that ancient story, silence descended. And with it, hope seemed to whisper, *You are not alone.*

This quest was set for us the day these bars were broken, perhaps even before then.

No matter what happens, history joined hope to speak, *you will not be abandoned.*

We took a moment to pause and then, reverently, moved on.

We walked a fairly straight path for some time and then, like a fork in a road, the cave split.

"Gerrias, Risson, you stay with the princess," Julien said. "Kinley and I will scout ahead and come back to report."

"Don't say 'princess'!" Erielle hissed.

Julien quirked an eyebrow. "We're inside Mount Shireya, Erielle. I think we can use her real name."

It wasn't long before the knights returned. Julien's path led to a gradual incline; Kinley's to a series of downward platforms.

"They look like steps," my brother said, "except they're enormous, as if made for the feet of Gaganti the Green!"

I was the only one who laughed.

I looked around at my companions. "You don't know that story?"

"Not all of us grew up in the house of a Storyteller, Your Highness," Erielle said. "Perhaps you'll get a chance to tell it to us someday. But for now," she said with a grin, "I believe your Veetrish brother has found our way."

I nodded. The scrolls said our path would lead downward into the deep center of the mountain.

The giant stairs curved in a nearly perfect helix, graduated by the largeness of each individual step. As we descended, small rodents and insects, unaccustomed to such brightness as our sunlit torches conveyed, scuttled away from our intrusive lights. After a time I looked up, but the shadows the torches threw, though wavering only from our movement, were too eerie. When I trained my gaze forward again, it was just in time to let out a squeal. I shrank back to avoid a spider web directly in front of my face.

"Whoa," Kinley chuckled behind me when I stepped onto his feet. "Perhaps you will keep your eyes more focused on the future than the past now, eh Princess?"

"Very funny." The spider itself was only as big as the cork of my flask, but when it came to spiders, fact and logic couldn't combine well enough to allow the matter of size to remove their threat from my mind. Forcing myself not to look at the web's small but heavily furred resident, I ducked and held my breath until I was clear of the sticky trap.

The only sounds were our own footsteps and an occasional sigh. Eventually the spiral ceased and the platform formation leveled off until the delineation of steps disappeared entirely.

We paused to take stock of our surroundings. Everyone spread out and walked around the chamber in which we had ended our descent. Again, I was glad for the torches that made our way bright, but the shadows they cast from the jutting rock formations did make me jump every now and then.

Several openings revealed passageways, possible exits, in every direction. But nothing stood out as a clue from the scrolls. I spied a large rock that seemed to have several sturdy footholds and decided to climb up on it to take a better look around.

I tucked my torch through a belt loop and began to climb. The stone was surprisingly cold under my hands and slightly slippery, making the ascent a bit of an effort. Finally, I made it to a level place where I could sit. Dangling my legs over the side, I pulled my torch free and shined the light all around. Nothing caught my eye or sent even a vague surge of poetry to my memory.

I was about to climb back down when I noticed Risson. He stood just a few paces in front of my perch, rubbing his chin with his thumb and forefinger. He took a few steps back and struck the same, pensive pose. Suddenly, he moved around the rock formation.

"A-ha!" he exclaimed. A moment later he was back where I could see him, grinning. "It's not Castle Rynwyk, Princess," he said, "but it appears you've found a throne!"

Everyone stopped what they were doing and came our way. I stood up and lifted my light higher to better examine the rock. It didn't take very much imagination to see that the formation of this particular rock had the shape of a chair. I stood on the giant seat. The ledge I'd climbed over to get here was an arm, which had its lumpy match on the opposite side. The back of the rock, like a throne, reached higher than the arms until it came to a rounded point.

"Mark one," I whispered.

"Not necessarily," Edru mused. "We've found the broken cell doors and the stairway. The throne could be the third mark already."

"If so," Kinley said, "may Rynloeft grant we pass the remaining six marks as swiftly." But his tone betrayed his doubt that we would be that fortunate.

By the time I finished my inspection, everyone else had gathered with Risson and was examining the back side of the rock. I climbed down, but took Julien's offered hand to jump the last few measures.

Dyfnel rubbed his hand over the rock. "There is a stronger sense of humidity to the rear than the front."

Erielle moved to the front of the group and Gerrias lifted her up to a thin precipice that she was able to balance on and look directly into the pit behind the chair. "Listen! Can you hear the water?"

We fell silent, barely daring to breathe.

It was there, a faint rushing sound, almost river-like, though it sounded far away, masked and insulated by layers of mountain stone. It was impossible to gauge the distance from here to there.

"Hold my ankles, Gerrias," Erielle said. "I want to see what's down there."

The space was narrow, only wide enough for Erielle and her brother to fit. We all waited, watching the curious sight of her legs twisting as she shined her light in different directions, held only at the ankles by her much larger brother.

"Lower me a bit, Ger," she called up, her voice slightly strained. "It's water!" she exclaimed a moment later. Gerrias pulled her back up and she turned around.

"The water starts right there! It's very still, though. We'll have to jump in from here and wade through. Maybe swim, if it's deep. It was so dark and dull I didn't realize it was water until I touched it. It didn't reflect the light as it should have."

She took a breath and lifted a hand. A slimy material clung to her fingers. When she spoke again her words came just as quickly and were infused with every bit as much excitement. "There's a mossy substance on top that camouflages the water, but it is very, very cold. 'Should the fish skill not be known,'" she grinned and quoted the scrolls, "'do not continue past the throne.' Well, we're in back of the throne, and there's water, so I guess it's time to swim!"

"Where does it go?" Julien asked.

"There's a stone arch that seems to lead on from here. I think there's just enough room between the stone and the surface for us to be able to keep our heads above water. This stuff might be a challenge to disengage ourselves from, though." Erielle shook her hand, and then again more violently, but the slime wouldn't come off her fingers. "This could be a problem."

"I'll go first," Risson said, bending to unbuckle his boots. "I'll go ahead and make sure it's safe to venture beyond the arch." Risson tucked his torch and boots inside his small pack and secured it to his back before dropping over the side. Even inside his pack, the torch still gave off enough light that we knew exactly where he was.

There was a muted splash and then a moment of silence.

"It's deep," Risson said, his voice strangely muffled. "And this moss is thick. It clings to the skin." He sputtered and spit a bit. "I'll swim under the arch, look around, and report back."

Erielle kept her torch aloft as we waited for Risson to return. The rest of us removed our packs and carefully stowed our boots, stockings, and torches. I was glad my pack was light. I didn't need dead weight dragging me down into deep, slimy water.

As soon as I finished with my pack, Julien reached again for my hand and gave it a soft squeeze. I stepped toward him and turned so I could lean my back against his chest. His arms came around me and a slight pressure to the top of my head left a kiss behind.

I had found another of Julien's notes when, after revealing myself to Taef, I'd packed the squire's cap and hairpiece away. As if he knew how my vanity still pained me, it had simply said:

No disguise can hide the beauty of your heart. Likewise, no cruelty of nature or time will ever dampen the fire of my love for you. Steadfastly, yours.

Cruel nature, indeed. The bruises around my eyes had gone green, according to the admission I'd coaxed from

Erielle. And my hair, on which Julien's chin now rested, probably smelled like the hayloft above a pigsty. But it was nice of him to ignore it. To be able to feel his tenderness right now was exquisite comfort. And this particular posture, a backward sort of hug, was how he had held me the night I met the enikkas, those beautiful creatures of light, in the bay on Tirandov Isle . . . a lovely, cherished memory.

But for the recent nights when he'd held my hand to try and keep the nightmares away, traveling disguised through Shireya had not lent itself to physical tenderness between us. After all, a squire should not receive such attentions from his mentor! The unpredictable discovery of his notes was sweetness itself, but I had missed Julien's touch.

A tear spilled down my cheek and landed on Julien's arm. He released his hold to gently turn me around.

The light was much dimmer now that all torches but Erielle's had been stowed. Julien brushed his thumb across my cheek. "What's wrong?"

Although opportunities to be held by the man I loved had been few, and each much shorter-lived than suited my fondness for his affection, the memory of each stolen moment in his arms was a comfort only eclipsed by the feeling of being held within them now. I spoke words into his mind so no one else would hear. *I have missed your arms.*

He smiled and turned me back around. As his arms returned to their place, he whispered in my ear, "As they have missed you."

"He's back," Erielle announced.

With a sigh, I stepped out of Julien's embrace.

"This is almost like a tide pool," Risson said, treading water. "But it's deep. We'll need to use caution beyond the arch. It leads to a shallow river that has a steady current. The sounds are much louder beyond this chamber. I have no doubt the current, and the depth as well, will increase not far downstream, but there was a curve in the passage and I could not see beyond it."

Risson went back through the arch and Erielle was the next to enter the water. I had to smile at her spirit. Whereas Risson had allowed himself to gently slide into the mossy pool, Erielle didn't even hesitate before taking the plunge into the frigid water. She did sputter a little as she came up, but in less than a minute her strokes echoed off the stone walls as she swam through the arch. Dyfnel, Edru, and Kinley followed in quick succession.

And then it was my turn. Rather than imitating Erielle, I chose Risson's more sedate example and allowed myself to slide into the water. Though I knew it would be cold, the shock of its frigidity nearly opened my mouth. The water closed over my head and I kicked my feet until my face breached the surface again.

I opened my mouth and the foul moss stretched over my lips, so I clamped them shut. Breathing through my nose was no more pleasant. The moss smelled as if boiled cabbage had been mixed with soil and left in a sheep's pen overnight. It was cold, earthy, and altogether rotten. I treaded water, snatching at the smelly moss and wondering what sort of miracle it might take to remove it from my hair when our adventure was through.

Julien slid into the water beside me and I reached up to catch the lone, unpacked torch Gerrias had held above us.

Now that I had light at my disposal I couldn't help but laugh when Julien surfaced, covered in moss. Gerrias slid down and came up looking much the same.

I laughed. "You two look as if you've been sneezed upon by an ill giant."

Julien smiled as he wiped the moss from his face. "Might I remind Your Royal Highness that the one holding the torch is the one on whom the light most rests?"

I reached over to cuff his shoulder and started to sink. He put a hand under my arm and took the torch from me before my head submerged.

"I think," Julien said, laughing, "your arms would better serve you by swimming than by throttling me just now."

The arch took about ten strokes to clear with Julien and Gerrias close behind me. It finally widened and dumped out into a shallow stream. The rest of our party had unbound their torches and stood shivering in the waist-deep water waiting for us. Without another word we unpacked the rest of the torches and began wading downstream.

The noise in the cavern grew louder by the second and I wondered if our small river would be meeting up with a larger, faster current soon, as Risson had surmised. Every few steps seemed to increase the river's depth a little more. Soon after we went around the bend I was forced to hold my torch above my head. Erielle, lacking the height to be able to keep her head above water, attached her torch to her belt loop and swam instead.

Sound bounced against the base of my neck. It echoed off the smooth stone walls and through my bones. My teeth chattered with the cold and my limbs stiffened. How long could we withstand the freezing water without suffering ill effects from it?

A sudden current came from the right, taking me off my feet. My head ducked under. The torch began to slide from my fingers. I grabbed its tip with my other hand just before it would have been taken. When I regained my feet, the sting of water having gone up my nose and down my throat was fierce, but I coughed a few times, rubbed my nose as if scrubbing a stain, and moved on.

A precipitous drop met my next step and the depth of the stream reached my neck. I took a few difficult steps back to make movement easier, and secured the torch to my belt. It illumined the water at my waist and gave off some light, but the water was murky, dimming its brightness. By the time I was finished, mine wasn't the only light stowed. In fact, it was so dark now, that I couldn't even tell who belonged to which murkily submerged light. But at least each bobbing glow gave me some idea of where everyone was.

My neck muscles soon tired from the effort of holding my head above water, so I took a deep breath and began to swim. The extra movement warmed my muscles some, but I feared the ache in my legs would turn into a cramp. The only thing I could do was continue swimming and be grateful for the current that was increasing its strength as it pushed us along.

Forward, forward. I repeated the mantra, and tried to think of warm things like hearths and steaming mugs of keola while I followed the path of bobbing lights ahead of me. I tried not to think about what would happen if one of my friends should cramp or tire and go under. If anyone succumbed to the cold of the water or the fatigue of the swim I would have no way of knowing or helping. A cry for help would not be heard and the torch light would continue to bob in the current even if its bearer's face was submerged.

I could no longer feel my fingers and toes, but hoped our swim would end before the numbness stole up my arms and legs.

One light suddenly disappeared.

A wave of dread, colder than the water around me, shivered through my mind. I closed my eyes to concentrate on those closest to me. I sensed Julien, as well as Gerrias, Erielle, and Kinley. My mind stretched a bit farther and found Dyfnel and Edru.

Risson, I thought. *Risson's light is missing.*

I sought him with my mind. His colors were intense with sudden shock and struggle, but everything was happening to him so fast that even his mind couldn't form it into something I could understand.

I opened my eyes. But when I looked ahead, it was only to see two more lights disappear simultaneously. Edru and Kinley.

Princess! Waterfall! Prepare yourself! Edru's frantic thought found mine.

A waterfall? I almost inhaled part of the river.

I remembered following Sir Gladiel down a treacherous trail beside the steep, multi-level Brune Falls in the Great Wood. Could anyone survive going over something like that? I couldn't imagine how.

A line from the scrolls tapped against my memory. *Take a breath but don't expel. Brace for descent, ride its swell.*

A *waterfall.* We should have known. I had to warn the others! Closing my eyes, I called out to them.

Waterfall ahead! Ready yourself and hold your breath! I opened my eyes just as Erielle's and Dyfnel's lights disappeared.

I was no longer swimming so much as working just to keep my head above water in the strong current. Without warning my feet surged ahead of me, as if someone had grabbed me by the ankles and pulled. I took a huge gulp of air just before my head was dragged under the water by the force of the current.

And then I was falling . . .

Falling!

Thousands of strong, watery fingers pushed me down, down, down. Other than the fleeting hope that whoever had already gone over the falls was out of the way before I reached the bottom, there wasn't a single thought that could usurp the panic invading my mind.

My back slammed the surface of the water as if it were a metal plank. My legs surged up, but the pounding torrent pushed me deeper and deeper.

My head throbbed with the need to release the breath I held. Water pummeled my stomach and chest like a gang of murderous thieves. It took every pin from my hair and ran its claws through my braid, releasing its coil and wrapping my hair around my face as if it wanted to smother me. The force turned and twisted me, shifting my direction to assault whatever part of my body had not yet received its lash.

I could not tell which way was up, down, or sideways, so I just kicked as if my life depended on it. Because it did.

Where is the swell? I'm supposed to ride a swell!

What good was the poetry if it didn't deliver? Every time I thought I was close to gaining my freedom, the pressure beat me down again. I could not perform even the smallest stroke with my arms, worthless as they were in the onslaught. The extra toweling I wore under my clothing had absorbed water to capacity, weighing me down even more than my pack. The strength in my legs was my only hope of survival, so I kicked until my thighs burned as much on the inside as they were bruised on the outside.

Out of nowhere, a forward current slammed into me from behind. It arched under my back, lifting me up and out of the downward thrust of the waterfall. My hair was dragged away from my face as I surged forward on the current, riding the swell that had been so long in coming. But I was still deep, deep beneath the surface.

I released a small stream of air to give my lungs some relief from the burn that threatened to consume me. I opened my eyes, but the blackness remained as an uncanny reminder that I had no idea if I was kicking myself toward the surface or the depths. Deciding to trust the prophecy, I curved my body in so that my head would lead me along the swell rather than my feet. I pressed my hands together and pushed them apart, each stroke releasing a bit more of the precious breath that could be my last.

Blood pounded at my temples. Nausea threatened my throat. But finally, a faint glow appeared ahead.

A torch!

Dizziness stole my vision. I had little time before I lost consciousness or was forced to inhale water.

I exhaled the rest of my breath and surged ahead, pushing the water behind me with my arms in wide strokes, aiming toward that beacon of hope.

A sudden roar exploded in my ears and air—sweet air!— hit my face. I gasped, taking in equal amounts of water and air, but a sudden cramp pierced my side and I was too battered, too tired, and had inhaled too much water to know how to recover. I went under again.

THIRTY-THREE

Just as I feared the current would drag me so deep that I would never find air again, something hooked on to the straps of my pack and pulled me up until my face breached the surface. The initial contact from my rescuer was a tad violent in its swiftness, but a gentler hand hauled me the rest of the way to the side, hefted me up, and deposited me on a cold, hard—but thankfully dry—surface.

Gasping for air, I coughed, sputtered, and collapsed on the rock floor.

Princess Rynnaia.

I held up my hand. I couldn't speak yet. I opened my eyes between coughing fits. Everyone was accounted for. Julien, even, was there. He knelt at my side. How was that possible? I had gone over the waterfall before him or Gerrias. How had they beaten me to the bank?

Princess Rynnaia.

The voice was more insistent, but I couldn't put a name to it. Water had pressed deep into my ears, dulling my ability to hear. Besides the roar of the falls, I wasn't sure I could make

319

out a word. My vision blurred. I closed my eyes as my name was called again.

How could I hear a voice so clearly with my ears clogged and the waterfall thundering so strongly behind me?

Blood pounded against my temples as if it would break through my skin. Nausea assailed me in a hot-cold wave. Pushing Julien aside, I crawled to the edge of the bank and leaned over the side of the rock, gagging at the force of the fresh air I gulped into my lungs.

When I finished heaving up parts of the river I hadn't even realized I'd taken in, Julien pulled me into his arms. Even then, I continued to cough so violently that I feared my chest would explode. My throat burned. My head throbbed as if the hilts of ten swords were being pounded against it at once. I was barely aware of movement when Julien stood and carried me down a passageway and away from the sound of the waterfall.

The coughing gradually subsided. But it was then my body remembered the cold. I began to shake. I drew my arms from around Julien's neck, pulling them in as if to cocoon myself inside his arms. Julien stumbled when even that meager assistance of carrying me was withdrawn, but quickly regained his footing and tightened his hold.

The sound of the waterfall was muffled by the mountain passage that separated us from it when Julien finally stopped and sat down.

He cradled me in his lap, attempting to warm me, though his skin was nearly as cold as my own.

A random thought surfaced. *Oh, what I wouldn't give for his smelly old bear cloak right now.*

"Rub her feet and hands." Julien's command was soft as he rearranged my position in his lap. "Get the blood moving again."

Tremors shook me from head to toe. I bit my tongue and another spasm of coughing robbed me of my breath, but as Julien rubbed my back I allowed his colors to envelope me while I tried to regain a normal cadence of breathing. Other hands joined his, rubbing my legs, arms, even the lobes of my ears.

Princess Rynnaia.

"Who is t-talking?" I pushed away the hands at my ears and rubbed my temples. "Why d-do you sound s-so s-strange?"

"No one has spoken, Princess," Dyfnel said. He leaned toward Julien. His eyes were filled with dread. "Do you think she hit her head?" His hands moved over my skull.

"N-no," I said, jerking away. "I didn't."

Princess Rynnaia.

"There! There it is ag—" I gasped. "Oh."

I closed my eyes. *Who-who is in m-my head?*

It is Harbyn, Your Highness. We are in position at the fortress in Dwons. We are ready to attack as soon as you open the Cobeld-cursed cells.

I-I-I. Even my thoughts shivered. It was hard to concentrate with five different sets of hands vigorously trying to warm my blood. *Harbyn.* It took me a moment before I placed the name as the half-Andoven horse trainer accompanying the regiments that had been sent to free Uncle Drinius and Sir Gladiel from the Cobeld fortress in Dwons.

Harbyn, can you wait for a m-moment? I just f-fell over a w-waterfall and I'm c-c-cold.

There was a pause in which the picture of Harbyn's face in my mind trembled to the point that I feared I'd lost the connection, but then it steadied.

Oh, dear! Harbyn's eyes grew wide. *Are you . . . injured?*

I'll be fine. I just need a few moments. I had to wonder if his alarm was due to my statement, my explanation of circumstances, or the bruises still marring my complexion from my run-in with the Cobelds' yellowhock.

Please let me know when it is safe for us to proceed, Your Highness. We have not yet been detected, but if we don't act quickly we may soon be.

I-I will unlock the c-cells, I said, *as soon as I have changed into d-drier clothes. I-I-I have to b-be able to c-concentrate and I c-can't do that while I'm shi-shivering like this.*

We await your command.

I opened my eyes.

"H-Harbyn is r-ready," I said.

"No." Julien's voice was fierce. "Not now. It can wait."

"They're in p-position." I almost bit my tongue again from shivering. "Now."

"The timing could be better," Kinley growled.

"Indeed." Dyfnel nodded. "We must find a way to warm you, Princess. And quickly."

"Erielle," Julien said, "will you be able to help the princess change?"

"Y-yes," she replied, her own voice quivering with cold. I turned my head. Gerrias had taken his sister into his arms much in the same way Julien now held me. She stood up and shined her torch around the space. "We-we'll go over there." She pointed and my eyes followed her gesture to an outcropping of rock that would afford us some privacy.

Julien helped me to my feet and removed the pack from my back. When I swayed a bit he wrapped an arm about my shoulders to hold me up.

"H-how did you get out first?" I asked. "I went over the fall before you did."

"I don't know," he said. "I dove and the swell of the water took me immediately forward and up. I think the pressure forced you down instead of out like the rest of us. You were under so long, Rynnaia. I honestly don't know how you survived." His voice was husky with emotion as his grip tightened on my shoulder. "I thought I'd lost you."

Julien kept hold of me as we walked around the big rock where Erielle waited.

I willed myself to stand on my own two feet as he gently set me down. He was barely away when Erielle began ripping at the buttons on her shirt. I followed her example, knowing that I would not be wearing it again anyway.

Erielle used her dagger to cut through the twine that bound my clothes, tightly wrapped in oilcloth that had been rubbed with beeswax to help keep the dampness at bay. Whereas everything else in my pack was soaked, my clothes were only slightly damp.

"I can do this," I said. "You get your own."

"Are you sure?"

I nodded and she moved to retrieve her own similarly packed clothing.

With my extremities numb and shaking, it was no easy task getting dressed, especially considering my skin was wet. The big rock hid us from view, but knowing a group of men was on the other side made me feel incredibly exposed. I moved as quickly as I could. The clothes were not warm, but they were mostly dry and, as such, were almost as good as warmth.

The dry stockings soothed like a blanket to my feet, but as soon as I put my wet boots on, they were soaked.

"At least the next water will be warm," Erielle said. "'A dive through water strangely warm,' remember?"

"And yet I can't bring myself to look forward to it," I answered in a tone much drier than the rest of me. "The phrase 'strangely warm' is too mysterious for my taste."

I squeezed the water from my hair as best I could. Except for an occasional shudder, the shivering had let up and I was only cold, not frozen. Erielle had braided her hair, but she left the braid hanging down her back. I followed suit. The tangles would have to remain until, if The First allowed, I arrived at Castle Rynwyk in Salderyn.

$\mathcal{T}$ H I R T Y - $\mathcal{F}$ O U R

$\mathcal{I}$ bent to retrieve a few small sticks of kindling from my pack. We each had a few, wrapped snuggly within waxed oilcloth, for building a fire. Now seemed as good a time as any to use them.

A prickling sensation lifted the hairs on the back of my neck. My hands fumbled and I dropped the sticks.

Enemy. I recognized the warning this time.

"Wrap them back up," I said to Erielle, hastening to do the same with mine. "We need to keep moving." I rolled the oilcloth around the kindling, tucked in the ends, and tied the twine.

The men were all changed and had piled some of their own kindling together. Kinley knocked a spark with his flint.

"Put it away," I said. "Enemies approach. We don't have time." Without thinking to explain myself, I lifted my torch and walked the circumference of the room.

Besides the point at which we had entered, three deeply shadowed passageways led away from this chamber. To my left was the best passageway, wide and secure-looking. As I approached it, however, the prickly sensation increased.

I quickly moved to the other two and groaned. Both looked as if they might cave in at any time. I turned back toward the men and Erielle.

I pointed toward the perfect cavern passage. "Enemies approach from that direction. We must pick one of these two tunnels. And fast. I will try to unlock the cells in Dwons as we flee."

"Are you sure?" Julien sounded dubious, but stilled at my look. "Of course you're sure," he amended. "Which way seems best?"

"What's the next mark in the scrolls?"

"Well, we've ridden the swell," Kinley said, "so that's the fourth mark, I guess. We're on to the night-drenched caverns, yes?"

"You're assuming the scrolls are chronological," Dyfnel argued. "They may not be!"

"I think they are," Erielle spoke so quietly that I doubted anyone but me could hear. I started a bit at her tone, for in that moment, the quiet confidence in her voice reminded me of Lady Anya.

"You have a better idea?" Risson arched an eyebrow at Dyfnel, but the physician shook his head.

"'Through night-drenched caverns of silence dimmed,'" Erielle quoted the poem, her voice louder now, but it echoed the frustration of trying to decipher that particular rhyme. "Well, without our torches," she said with a scowl, "they're all as dark as midnight. But how do you dim silence?" She threw up her arms. "It's already as dim as it can be!"

Princess Rynnaia. I closed my eyes to receive Harbyn's message. *We have been spotted. The enemy has engaged. I'm*

326

sorry, Princess, but we must act now. Our opportunity to rescue Sir Gladiel and Sir Drinius will not come again.

Unlocking the cells would be easy as long as I was able to fully concentrate on the task, but I couldn't allow myself to become distracted, not even by the scrolls and the marks to which they led.

"Julien," I said, "the regiments have been spotted. Hurry!"

Julien strode between the caverns, shining his light down each. "Both look more than a little treacherous. There is a strange noise coming from this one. Like hail on the roof," he said, and then moved to the next. We were all silent while he listened. "Nothing." He scowled. "Which could really be nothing . . . or could be something worse."

"Worse than hail inside a mountain?" Gerrias crooked an eyebrow.

"I didn't say it was hail. Only that it sounded like it."

Risson rushed to the corrupted entrance where Julien had noted the sound. He listened for a moment.

"How do you dim silence?" He turned around, grinning. "With sound! You can only dim silence by making it *less* silent!"

"Of course!" Julien said. He drew his sword. Kinley, Risson, Erielle, and the Andoven men also drew their weapons.

Gerrias stepped forward. "I will carry you, Princess," he said.

"What about your arm?" The wolfcat's bite had gone deep.

"It's healing." He shrugged. "But I'll shoulder most of your weight on my left side if it makes you feel better."

"Are you certain it's wise? I don't want to—"

He silenced me with a shake of his head. "You concentrate on your task, Princess, and allow me to attend to mine."

Without waiting for my reply, he scooped me up in his arms and gave me a tentative smile imbued with hope. "And while you're at it, tell my father 'hello' for me, would you?"

THIRTY-FIVE

$\mathcal{G}$errias followed Julien and Dyfnel through the noisy door with me in his arms. Everyone else was behind us with Kinley as the rear guard. I settled my head against Gerrias's shoulder and closed my eyes.

Uncle Drinius. I pictured his face and my mind raced out of the cave and across landscapes at a gut-wrenching speed.

"Rose?"

I shuddered at the name and almost lost my concentration. "Rynnaia." I said aloud. *Rynnaia.*

"Of course. I'm sorry."

There is no time. I am going to unlock the cell doors now and you must escape. Regiments from Nyrland and Sengarra have engaged the enemy outside to distract them. Whatever you do, do not touch the locks or the cell bars. I will open the cells from here.

"You can do that?"

Yes. Be ready to help those around you. I will free as many as I can.

"There are few left. Most have died trying to escape. Only four cells remain occupied."

My heart clenched. *And Sir Gladiel?*

"I'm here."

Thank Rynloeft.

I changed my focus from his face to the lock on the bars and felt the presence of the coarse silver strand of beard before I saw it. Wrapped firmly around the bars, it was implanted into the locking mechanism. *Amazing,* I thought, though it caused a shiver to rove my form. The curse had been spoken in such a way that its evil seemed to infiltrate the very metal the hair touched.

As my mind entered the hole of the lock, my ears rang with a sound like freshly forged metal scraping against the teeth of a rusty saw. Searing pain shot through my temples as the Cobeld magic resisted me.

I gasped and felt Gerrias's arms tighten around my body. But a spare second later, agony exploded in my brain and I lost awareness of Gerrias, of everything, except the lock . . . and the pain.

My goal argued with my need for relief. If I looked away and severed the connection, the pain would go away. But if I severed the connection, I would consign Drinius, Gladiel, and the other prisoners, perhaps even the regiments fighting outside the fortress, to death. *No!* I refused to move my gaze from the lock.

As if sensing my determination and deciding to thwart it, the level of pain increased. I fought against it, but if steel bonds had been wrapped about my body, I could not have felt more trapped within the pain. I twisted and struggled, but the hair, that shimmering silver hair, had me in its thrall.

Move aside! I commanded. It only glittered in response, almost as if the curse itself was denying my request. At the glimmer, another burst of ice-cold agony struck my mind. The pain was nearly unbearable.

Move aside! If I moved my eyes from the lock, the connection would be broken and the knights would not escape. *Move . . .*

The rest of the command failed to form as agonizing torment seized every nerve in my body.

I was failing. The curse of the Cobeld beard was too strong for my mind. Even my mother's blessing was not enough to protect me from it.

My heartbeat slowed. A searing, cold numbness stole over me. *Am I still breathing?* I wondered, unable even to access whatever allowed me to know.

I've failed. I. Have. Failed!

Something hot and wet traced a path across my face, but I was unable to see, hear, or comprehend anything beyond the shining strand of hair. Even if I wanted to, I couldn't break the connection now. The curse held me firmly in its grasp.

Despair seeped into and around every thought. I was filled with utter desolation and a loneliness so deep that it was as if my last friend had finally abandoned me to die alone in this dark and frightening place. I was entirely alone, but for the ancient evil that was so much stronger than I could have imagined.

I could not even see the lock anymore. Only the hair. That cursed silver hair. It was dark and cold. So very cold.

Where is the light? Where is everyone?

With a chilling sense of unendable torture, agony sent claws of dread into my soul and I lost all comprehension of time. How long had I been in this battle? Moments? Days? Years? I could no longer sense Drinius or Gladiel. Perhaps they were already dead. Perhaps my efforts had killed them, rather than saved them.

All is lost.

A fresh, stabbing glimmer came from the hair and more pain shot through my skull. Surely I would be released from the anguish soon, even if only through death. Freezing, but unable to shiver, I wished the pain would numb with the cold, but it only grew stronger as my will to outlast it weakened.

I tasted blood. And I knew it was mine. The tang of copper and salt filled my mouth until I was drowning in it, and death seemed so near that its breath brushed against my heart.

Just as I was about to admit defeat, sudden spots of warmth touched my body. Warmth! I reached toward it.

Specks of light, like stars in a velvety sky, broke through the sinister night that had invaded my mind. Colors, like tiny sparks, invaded my thoughts, but the torture was too severe to put names to them. Drops of liquid fell on my face, accompanied by the strange awareness that they were tears, but unlike the blood that filled my mouth and threatened to drown my breath, they were not my own.

The darkness eased just a touch. The despair gripping my soul lifted slightly, as if lightened by a brute force of excruciating consolation. Suddenly, a memory pierced through my pain-filled consciousness like a dream, a memory to which I had only recently gained access.

I was a child again, cradled in my father's strong arms. I sat in his lap and he had an arm around my shoulder and the opposite hand resting on the top of my head, his own face lifted toward the ceiling. His rich, tender voice spoke a name over me . . .

Embral e' Veria.

Unlimited power, governed by unending love.

The vision faded, and in that moment I understood what I lacked. I understood the reason for my failure.

The voice of my thoughts was faint and strained, but with everything in me, I called on that name.

Embral e' Veria. Help me.

A singular beam of pure white light rent the darkness. It seemed far away at first, but grew brighter and nearer the more intensely I focused on it.

A rumble of warmth shook the remaining darkness in my soul. The words it formed, words of fathomless power, bathed in limitless love, caressed the center of my despair.

I am with you, Rynnaia E'veri.

The Voice. *The Voice!* I was not alone. The First was here and he would help me defeat this wretched curse.

I gasped. It was the first breath I'd taken in some time and it carried a sweet aroma of which I had never caught scent of before, but I knew from whence it came. It was a scent of deeper, stronger, older power than any rotting curse the Cobelds could create.

I focused on the hair again.

Move aside!

The whisker quivered but it did not move.

By the power granted me by The First, I command you to be gone!

At the utterance of that name, the hair disintegrated and fell, becoming nothing more than a shimmer of powder on the dungeon floor.

Gratitude humbled me. Rynnaia E'veri had presented no challenge to the evil Cobeld curse, but its limited power was obliterated by the infinite dominion of Embral e' Veria. The First. The Highest Reigning who had descended from the Reign Most High . . . to rescue me.

With the hair out of the way, my mind entered the locking mechanism. It clicked and I flung the door open.

Hurry, Uncle Drinius! Gladiel, hurry!

I moved my focus to the remaining cells, but as if each silver thread had sensed the power of The First as clearly as I had, the remaining hairs disintegrated at a glance. The prisoners clamored after Drinius and Gladiel.

Take the left passage and up the stairs!

I guided the prisoners through the maze of the dungeon passageways. Even weakened as they were from months in captivity, surprise enabled them to overtake the few remaining guards who had not joined the battle outside the fortress.

Once they were safely ensconced within the ranks of our men, who had taken a clear advantage in the fight, I disconnected my mind from the rescue effort and tried to find my way back to the rest of me, still within Mount Shireya.

But that proved more difficult than I could have possibly imagined.

T H I R T Y - *S* I X

*W*here am I?

I could not yet open my eyes, but the sounds of battle seemed too close. Too close, that is, for my consciousness to have returned to my body within Mount Shireya. Had I not removed my mind as entirely from Dwons as I had thought?

I tried to speak, but couldn't. Numbness still trapped most of my senses and functions. It stole my voice and set my heart—which had nearly ground to a halt while battling the lock—beating at a frantic, frightened pace.

Could my senses have stayed in Dwons against my will? And if so, why couldn't I open my eyes? I couldn't see—or even sense—anything but the dim sounds of a battle.

My mind was exhausted. My ears, confused. Why did the sounds of war still echo around me when I felt wholly within my body? It was as if I was suspended between places, my ears still trapped on the battlefield in Dwons, but the rest of me restored—yet inaccessible—to my friends within Mount Shireya.

Little by little, sensation returned to my skin. Wherever I was, Gerrias no longer held me. Instead I was on my back with a cold stone floor beneath me.

A swish of air passed over my head. And another. But I could not seem to move or open my eyes. Had the battle I'd fought against the Cobeld curse paralyzed me? I tried to move my fingers, but I wasn't even sure they were still attached to my body. I only hoped my paralysis was a temporary disability. The Remedy was not yet in my grasp!

A sense of urgency pulled at my mind with the colors of my friends and truth rushed in.

I was in the mountain.

The battle was *here*.

The enemy had found us.

A groan sounded nearby, followed by a *thud*. A warm object landed beside me and one set of colors flashed brightly—so brightly that my mind ached with their beauty—and then disappeared from my mind.

Risson! I searched, trawling my mind for the threads of color that were uniquely him. *Risson!* It was no use. He was somehow blocked from my mind and I refused, at the moment, to face what that might mean.

I put all my energy, such as it was, to the task of simply opening my eyes. Finally they complied, if only by a slit at first.

I faced the ceiling of a large circular chamber. Dampness clung to the air like thick, invisible sheets, but the room was bright, illumined not only by tirandite torches, but . . . by fire?

My mind was so weakened by the Cobeld curse that I could move no part of my body, save my eyes. Another breeze passed over my face, brought by the blur of an object I couldn't identify. Was it a bird? If so, it moved more swiftly than any bird I had ever seen.

Encircling the perimeter of the ceiling, a formation of stalactites pointed downward. The mineral deposits within each icicle-like form glittered as if they had never before been touched by light and were determined to show off their beauty in case the chance never came again.

I took a deep breath and reached for my other senses.

My hearing was the next to strengthen, but it seemed to favor one ear over the other. I had a sense of hearing, at least partially, from the moment I had returned, but sounds were now more easily distinguished from one another.

Metal clashed against metal and a twangy zing of arrows had a rhythmic regularity that revealed that Erielle was not the only one with a bow in hand. When I noted the guttural voices amidst the noise, and my mind translated their muttering curses, I feared what might accompany those arrows.

"Death! Death! Suffer! Die!" The Cobeld voices rang through the room, grating on my eardrums. Had I been able to move, I'm sure I would have trembled as the Cobelds named each curse before letting it fly at my friends. But paralyzed as I was, I couldn't even turn my head.

I searched my memory for something from the poetry that I could draw from to help me help my friends. As verses went through my mind, the circle of stalactites picked up bits of light and proudly cast shadows around the room as if they were the jeweled crown of Mount Shireya herself.

What was the last bit of the scrolls we had identified?

Through night-drenched caverns of silence dimmed.

Yes. That was it! *What comes next?* I had to repeat the whole stanza in order to remember it.

The Ryn must travel deaf and blind. Well, I'd not seen or heard anything between when we entered those night-drenched caverns and now, so I guess that qualified as traveling deaf and blind.

Unsheathe the swords as arrows fly. My friends, even now, were in the midst of that.

Casting spears from halo's rim. I gazed up at the stalactites and repeated the stanza again. *It's not a crown*, the realization dawned slowly, *it's a halo!* This chamber was Halo's Rim.

Fire returns from foreign lair to call down defense unimpaired. There was fire on the Cobelds' torches, but perhaps the poetry referred to a more proper noun.

Me.

But how could I do what it asked? Never in my life had I been so impaired!

The answer was, I couldn't. Not yet.

My uselessness grated against the desire to help my friends. Above me was a rim of spears that, with a little help, might serve as a most effective weapon if only I could fully regain my faculties.

Embral e' Veria . . . my heart whispered the request.

A tingling sensation traveled from the base of my skull to the tips of my fingers and down my spine, tickling slightly as it passed through my knees and into my toes. Little by little, my strength returned. I sat up.

"Stay down!" Julien shouted.

I fell back into my previous position, but when I turned my head, I met the blank stare of Sir Risson, who lay beside me with a Cobeld arrow through his heart. His expression, in death, was so reminiscent of Sir Kile's that I gasped and recoiled.

"Get down!"

I obeyed and my gaze touched the stalactites again. Offering another quick request toward Rynloeft, I shouted, "Julien! Let them surround us!"

He did not turn. "If we do that we block our only route of escape!"

"Look up, Julien! This is Halo's Rim! Trust me. I know what to do!"

I tried to look beyond my protectors, but they had blocked me well enough that I couldn't even see the Cobelds.

Julien's head tilted slightly upward. I felt his hesitation, but finally he shouted out the command, "Surround the Ryn!"

The Cobelds shrieked, as if hearing the proof of my existence caused them physical agony.

Pushing to my feet, I stood within the center of my protectors, whose swords and bodies insulated me from the threat. On Julien's command they tightened the circle so that we were just inside the rim of spears hanging high above our heads.

"Edru! Dyfnel!" I shouted. *Help me call down the spears on our enemies!*

Loosen your hold, I synchronized my thoughts with Dyfnel and Edru, who, at the same time, were using their minds to repel the Cobelds' arrows. We repeated the command to each individual spear, and as we did, the glittering stalactites quivered. A shower of dust sprinkled down.

On my signal, I said to the Andoven men. I took a deep breath and quickly checked to make sure all my friends were out of the path of Shireya's spears.

Now! I signaled the Andoven men and then turned my attention to the spears. *RELEASE!*

A great renting of stone made me cover my ears as the naturally formed spears fell from the ceiling.

I flinched. I guess I must have closed my eyes, too, because I found myself having to open them.

I was covered in glittering dust, as were my companions. The circle of them loosened and I finally saw the enemy.

There weren't as many as I had feared. Only about a dozen. The stalactites had impaled several of the Cobelds, killing them on impact. The rest were imprisoned either beneath or behind the glimmering bars, but none still had a weapon in hand, other than their cursed beards, of course. And at this distance, they were not a threat.

Someone coughed, and then all was quiet but for the soft falling of a few dislodged stones.

We pulled up the necks of our shirts to cover our mouths and noses from the cloud of dust that filled the air. The few Cobelds who still lived were safely out of reach, but when I looked to the left, one passageway was miraculously clear of both Cobelds and fallen stalactites. I closed my eyes and sent a word of thanks to The First. When I opened them, Dyfnel crouched by Risson's body, his fingers to the knight's neck.

Tears filled my eyes as he glanced at Julien and shook his head.

"This way is clear." Erielle's voice shook as she moved toward the opening. She coughed and a tear traced a path through the dust on her face.

I took a step toward her and stumbled. I looked around. Each one of my fellows had also lost their balance for a moment. A shower of pebbles fell from the ceiling. The floor rumbled.

Julien sheathed his sword and grabbed my hand. "The ceiling's going to collapse! Let's go!"

Edru looked behind us. "What about Sir Risson's . . . body?"

Julien glanced at me and squeezed my hand. "It would appear Rynloeft has arranged for his burial. We must go. Now. Risson would not have been happy to think he slowed our passage to safety."

Edru nodded. We picked up our torches and, with Erielle in the lead, sprinted down the passage, followed by the high-pitched shrieks of the dying Cobelds.

Moments later, another vibration shook the floor beneath our feet, followed by a crashing roar that left no question in any of our minds concerning how narrowly we had escaped.

Julien kept a firm grip on my left hand as we raced after Erielle, but I was forced to wipe my right arm across my eyes several times to be able to see the path ahead. Our group of adventurers had become a family of sorts these past weeks, and although he was not the highest ranking knight among us, Risson had become the unofficial patriarch of that family. Even though I knew it was not Risson, but only the shell of him that would be buried with the Cobelds, sorrow chased me as we ran from his tomb.

I hated that we had left Risson's body to be buried alongside the traitors he had so valiantly fought, but I was comforted to know that while his body might be entombed among them, the knight himself had already been borne away. As evidenced by the departure of his colors, the bright and joyful passing of his very essence into the next realm, I was comforted knowing that Sir Risson now served a greater King than Jarryn of E'veria. Now and forevermore, Sir Risson de Sair would serve as a Knight of the First.

In my mind, I counted marks we had passed. Two of those six marks had been identified as such by Risson. What would we do without him when there were so many left to find? We'd yet to find the strangely warm water, the lone voice chorus, the brine, the pool, or . . . the place where I would be forced to go on alone.

Risson was not only a careful, intelligent, and observant knight, he was my friend. And I would not get the chance to thank him for his service this side of Rynloeft.

Before that moment I would not have thought it possible to run and weep at the same time, but it was. It was some consolation to know that Sir Gladiel and Uncle Drinius were safely out of the enemy's grasp, but that relief was tempered by wondering who else we might be forced to leave behind before our journey was through.

THIRTY-SEVEN

We came around a corner of the passage and the height of the ceiling dropped dramatically. Julien let go of my hand. It was hard to keep our balance, having to bend over as we were.

Like an icy needle had been driven into it, sudden pain stabbed my inner ear. I gasped, switched my torch to the other hand, and pressed my right hand against the pain.

"Rynnaia, what is it?" Julien paused and turned to me.

"My ear." I closed my eyes and grit my teeth as the invisible needle jabbed me again.

"*Breathe*, Rynnaia."

There was a slight edge to Julien's words, almost as if he thought I couldn't obey his command.

I inhaled through my nose and the cold, dusty air of the passage went straight up, pinching my temples with razor sharp claws. I exhaled with a wince.

"What's wrong?" Kinley said behind us. His voice held the same dangerous and fearful tone as Julien's.

"Pain in her ear," Julien said tersely.

As suddenly as it had come, the pain left me. I pulled my hand away and held the torch up to my fingers. "Is that . . . blood?"

"Yes."

A vibration tickled the bottom of my feet.

"Go!" Gerrias shouted from the rear of our line. "The passage is collapsing!"

Julien nearly ripped my arm out of its socket as he pulled me forward. Even bent over as we were, urgency drove us faster, though our velocity was rather awkwardly won. Soon we had nearly caught up to Erielle. Dust clouded over us so much that we didn't even notice the ceiling had risen again until the passage doubled in width, allowing the explosion of dust to effuse throughout the larger space.

The passage twisted and turned, widened and narrowed, but we continued to run until a splash sounded directly ahead of us, stealing Erielle from sight.

"Erielle!" Julien stopped short at the edge of the water.

Erielle's head bobbed up. She flailed for something to grab on to and found Julien's hand. He pulled her up with such force that, had the ceiling been any lower, she might have been slammed against it.

She gagged and coughed. When she pulled her hand away, she looked at it. "Blast! I dropped my torch." She coughed again.

Julien peered into the water and I joined him at the edge. Erielle's tirandite torch was little more than a tiny line of light at the bottom of this small but deep pool.

When everyone else caught up, they circled the water.

Whereas the stream and river we had swum through before was mossy and murky, this was, quite possibly, the clearest, cleanest water I had ever seen. It was as if a perfect cylinder had been drilled out of a vertical vein of white marble and filled with warm, melted snow. Were it not for the ripples Erielle had caused by falling in, the pool would have been entirely still.

I stuck my hand into the water and then I pulled it out and rubbed my fingers together. This liquid water had a slickness to it that was unlike the other waters we had found inside the mountain.

"It's warm," I said. "And slick. Like the sea."

A dive through waters strangely warm, I thought. Yet another verse of Lady Anya's poetry, another mark along our quest.

"Another landmark," Edru agreed, nodding.

Julien cupped a handful of water and brought it to his lips, but immediately spit it out. "Saltwater."

Gerrias made a face. "Warm saltwater in the middle of a mountain?" He shook his head. "Shireya certainly does not shirk from the odd, does it?"

"This could be the 'long-sought brine,'" Dyfnel said, peering over the side. "Bless Anya's quill, it's deep, though."

"Well, we couldn't very well dive if it were shallow," Kinley shrugged. Before he'd finished speaking, his boots were off and on their way inside his pack. "I'll go look around."

Taking a deep breath, Kinley dove. He swam a circle and then paused to kick himself deeper, where he repeated the circle. When he came back up he took Julien's hand to get out of the pool.

"I've found an opening," he said after he had caught his breath. "It's on the right, about as far down as the distance from the balcony to the floor in the Grand Hall at Holiday Palace. But it's very narrow. We can only hope that it isn't too lengthy."

A narrow, underwater tunnel. I fought the chill that crept across my shoulders. *At least,* I thought, gazing at the tiny line of light at the pool's floor, *we won't have to swim as far down as where Erielle's torch rests to reach it.*

"I'll go first and see where it leads," he said. "After I catch my breath, I'll come back and report."

I swallowed. "Kinley, what if . . . ?"

If the passage was long, Kinley might run out of breath before he found open air again.

"If it looks like I won't be able to make it to the end, I'll come back and we can look for another opening." He put a hand on my shoulder. "I promise. But I'm going to try to make it."

I nodded.

"Two should go," Gerrias said and then sat down to remove his boots and stow them in his pack. "One of us will stay and guard the passage exit, the other will come back to lead you to it."

He didn't wait for approval, but dove in and headed straight for the opening and disappeared inside. A moment later, Kinley dove back in and followed.

Warmth radiated up from the pool, but I found myself shivering. So much had happened in such a short time. In truth, I had no idea how much time had passed while I was engaged in opening Drinius and Gladiel's cell, but in that time we had not only come across a band of Cobelds, but lost a member of our group. In that time we had also found two more distinct markers toward finding the Remedy.

I mentally checked the list of landmarks we'd already encountered against the scrolls and then sighed.

"Do you think helping with my father's rescue was one of your tasks?" Erielle asked.

I had been so caught up in counting the marks—nine marks, of which, if my count was correct, we'd found seven—that I had nearly forgotten about the promised three tasks that would, according to the scrolls, "prey" upon me.

I was slow to nod. "Perhaps," I said finally. "The process of disengaging the Cobeld's hair from the lock had a very . . . predatory feeling about it. And speaking of your father, I'm going to contact Harbyn to make sure he and Drinius are safe."

Not only were the knights and other prisoners safe—even now they were in the care of medics—our forces had taken the fortress. Everyone cheered when I relayed the information, but it was Erielle's whoop that made me wince. My hand rose again to my bloody ear. Not because it hurt, but because that ear, which was closest to Erielle, had not registered the sound as clearly as the other. It throbbed and ached, to be sure. But I couldn't tell if it had *heard*.

I covered my unaffected ear to gauge the damage. Had I entirely lost my hearing in that ear?

No, there was still at least a little registry of sound. I could just make out muted hints of Dyfnel and Edru's quiet conversation, but it wasn't until I uncovered my "good" ear that I could discern actual sense from their words.

So I hadn't come away from that battle as unscathed as I'd thought. Was my injury permanent? Were any other parts of me damaged? I wrapped my arms about my middle as my insides quivered, remembering the cold that had almost taken my life.

When my teeth chattered, Julien pulled me away from the edge of the pool and wrapped me in his arms. He ran a hand over my hair. "Shh," he whispered, though I knew he wasn't telling me to be quiet. "Shh."

I turned and buried my face in his chest. His arms tightened around me and a mild tremor passed through his frame. I looked up.

"I should never have let you try to unlock those cells," he whispered.

"It was worth it. Your father and Uncle Drinius are free."

He ran two fingers down the side of my face, pausing near my ear. "I thought I'd lost you," he said. "Your breathing grew shallow. Your body seized, thrashing so violently that Gerrias could no longer carry you. It took all of us to restrain you."

He took in a ragged breath. "When the seizures finally stopped, blood ran from your ear, your nose, and your mouth. Even Dyfnel didn't know what to do. Finally, at Edru's suggestion, we petitioned The First. We joined our hands and placed them on you and called for help, but—" Julien's voice broke. "You stopped breathing."

"And then the Cobelds were upon us," Erielle said. "We had to fight." When I looked over at her she tilted her head. "Rynnaia, what happened to you?"

A brief sensation, a memory of the torture the Cobeld hair had inflicted upon me, made my knees go weak. Julien's embrace was the only thing that kept me from falling.

"I received a Cobeld curse," I said finally. "But it doesn't matter now. I was rescued, your father is free, and The First has been proven faithful once again."

"Just don't do it again, all right?" Erielle's eyes filled. "You scared me to death."

Julien lifted my chin. "Are you still cold?"

"A little." I wasn't sure it was cold that made me shiver, but Julien's arms were welcome. When he touched his lips to my forehead, the light kiss drove the chill away, replacing it with comfort.

As we waited for Kinley or Gerrias to return, I followed the example of my friends and petitioned The First on their behalf. *Give them strength*, I begged. It seemed like an eternity had passed, but as I waited, my own strength returned. *Give them breath enough to make it through.*

I took a deep breath and loosened my hold on Julien's waist. Restlessness drew me to the edge of the pool.

I gazed at my reflection in the now-still water. Streaks of dried blood traced a rusty path from my nose and ear, even from the corner of my mouth. They jagged across my face and neck in a macabre pattern of death denied.

The swim to come would surely wash them away, but I couldn't wait to rid myself of the reminder of the agony I had suffered. How had my mother endured nineteen years of a Cobeld curse? No wonder she was so weak. It was a miracle she was alive at all.

Dipping my hand into the water, I rubbed it across my face and neck, washing away the blood. I grit my teeth against the salty sting where unknown abrasions announced their presence.

"How long has it been?" Edru voiced the concern on all our minds.

"Too long," Julien frowned and began unlacing his boots.

"No," Erielle put her hand on his arm. "Give them more time before you go chasing after them. What if you met them head-on in the tunnel? What would you do then, swim backward?"

Julien clenched his teeth, but nodded. "We should try to be ready, though. We don't want to leave anyone alone for long." He glanced sideways at me. I knew he wouldn't mention the Cobeld attack or Risson's death, but like me, he wondered if more of the same awaited us farther in.

We each removed our boots and put them in our packs, and then the five of us sat on the edge of the pool with our feet dangling in the warm water. It was a soothing, almost stolen luxury after all we had faced in the last hours. But still, it was difficult to relax not knowing if Kinley and Gerrias were safely through.

"Look!" Erielle cried. "I think there's something down there!" And then, "It's Kinley!"

A moment later, Kinley burst from the surface. Julien and Erielle each grabbed one of his hands and hefted him out of the water. For several long moments he simply lay face down on the stone floor and gasped. Finally, he rolled over onto his back.

"That," he gasped, "was much less fun," he paused to cough, "the second time."

He didn't speak again for a long time, but once his breathing regulated he sat up.

"As I'm sure you've surmised, the tunnel is long," he said and then quirked a smile. "But it's much longer the second time through. Hopefully no one else should have to come back here."

"Where does it lead?" Julien asked.

"It dumps into another warm pool, fed by a stream." His smile widened. "And there is light!"

"Light?" Erielle asked. "From outside the mountain?"

"No." Kinley shook his head. "Its source seems hidden within the very walls. It's a strange thing, perhaps akin to our torches."

"'Isle stone no hand has mined lights the path to long-sought brine,'" Edru quoted the scrolls. "Tirandite stone? In Mount Shireya?" He shook his head and looked toward Dyfnel, who nodded.

"It must be," he said. "Won't the Elder Council be surprised to learn it exists somewhere besides Tirandov Isle!"

Julien met my grin. We both got a bit of a wicked thrill from anything that could befuddle the stodgy majority of the Andoven Elder Council.

"I thought that verse was about our torches," Erielle said, wrinkling her nose.

"So did we," Dyfnel said, tugging on the end of his beard. "But we were wrong. I would wager to say that the stream Kinley found will lead to—"

"The living rain," Erielle interrupted. "'A pool that teems illuminate precedes living precipitate,'" she quoted.

"The poem's riddles have surprised us before," Julien's said, and his tone darkened, "I only hope that whatever falls on us is something friendly."

I grimaced. Like Erielle, I had always thought of "living precipitate" in terms of rain, not anything dangerous. Julien's thought that the words could simply be a metaphor for something that would literally *fall* on us—something *alive*—sent creepers back and forth between my shoulders.

Living precipitate. Living precipitate. My mind conjured any number of unpleasant things that could fall from above.

"Water is necessary for life," Erielle stated with a tone that said she'd made up her mind. "Living precipitate," she repeated the phrase echoing in my mind, "could simply be water. Condensation, even. You must admit that's likely, given the warmth of this pool."

"Indeed," Dyfnel nodded.

"Well, we might as well get on with it." Julien stood. "Kinley, I think we all have a good idea where the tunnel is. Why don't you go last so you have time to breathe a bit longer, eh?"

He nodded.

"Erielle, you go first, followed by Edru and Dyfnel. Rynnaia will go next, then me, and finally, Kinley."

Erielle threw a cheeky grin in her brother's direction. "There you go again, barking orders and assuming compliance." She stood and curtsied. "Ever at your command, Sir Julien." With that, she winked, took a deep breath, and dove into the pool.

As soon as she breached the tunnel, Edru dove. We followed, one by one. Erielle's torch was, of course, left in the depths of the pool. It looked so tiny down there that I couldn't imagine any of us having the breath or strength to retrieve it.

The warm water delighted my aching muscles, but the salt stung my eyes. As the brine soaked through my clothing, I became aware of each tiny cut, each miniscule abrasion on my skin. It prickled with the sharp tingle of warm water running over a bad sunburn.

I swam down, down, until I found the tunnel. I couldn't pause, but a moment of panic made me want to when I first entered the circular waterway.

It was close. *Too* close. A chilling tingle chased up my arm when my elbow banged into the side. I adjusted my strokes and kicked my feet harder to make up for the lack of propulsion from my arms.

Ahead, the subtle outline of Dyfnel's torch within his pack kept me moving forward, but I tried to think about other things, things that brought me comfort.

Lady Whittier playing one of her instruments.

Riding Falcon across the Veetrish countryside.

But each time I allowed myself a brief reminder of where I was, and that I couldn't see the end of the tunnel, panic roared and threatened to steal my breath.

Swimming in the Bay of Tirandov.

Meeting my mother.

Meeting my father.

Dyfnel's light disappeared.

Julien.

If I didn't make it through, neither would he. Neither would Kinley, who had surely dived in again by now. He had to be exhausted, doing this for the third time. His life depended on my speed. I kicked harder.

The tunnel brightened and my last exhale was forced out as the passage suddenly widened. I spread my arms to propel myself farther and . . . it shot me into light.

"*Wobfdm!*"

Still underwater, the exclamation bubbled forth as my cheek kissed the gravelly bottom of a pool much shallower than that into which I'd dived. A second later, strong arms hauled me to the surface and placed me gently onto dry stone.

THIRTY-EIGHT

J panted and blinked, gulping in air as if it were the finest banquet and I was a starving dog beneath the table. My vision was dotty for a few minutes, but when I finally caught my breath I became cognizant of the welcome warmth of the stone beneath me.

It had a faint glow that was strangely brighter under the water of the stream coming into the chamber. The air was hung with humidity that reminded me of Tirandov Isle. It was bright enough in here to almost dispel the fact that we were deep inside a mountain, far from the light of the sun.

A low grunt announced Julien's arrival. A few moments later, Kinley arrived, though experience gave his entrance a bit more grace. His nod took in each member of the group, counting to make sure we were all accounted for. A brief flash of sorrow passed over his face, the only mention of Risson's loss any of us could bear.

"Have you ever seen anything like it?" Erielle whispered as she came to sit by me.

"It reminds me of Tirandov Isle," I whispered back. "But different."

"It's like we've entered another realm," she said. "One out of a dream."

"Why are we whispering?" I asked. But as my full voice echoed back at me, a verse of the prophecy came to light: *a lone voice chorus takes its form.* The echo was the result of a lone voice, multiplied by the acoustics of the room. A chorus of one.

Was this another mark?

From then on we spoke in hushed tones, but even our whispers echoed a little bit off the smooth, rounded walls of the long illumined cavern.

The chamber was about half the size of the dining hall at Holiday Palace, and its stone walls glowed with rosy light. The stone itself was a brownish-pink color that had veins of white. Every now and then, a streak of yellow-brown ore crisscrossed in jagged, semi-vertical veins.

The stream I had been dumped into ran barely as deep as my knees and it flowed through the room like a lady's ribbon, curving its shallow path and doubling back, only to curve again. Beneath the water, the pink floor shadowed darker than the walls above, and every once in a while I thought I saw a little flash of light, but I couldn't be sure.

The saltwater and humidity helped to clear the dust from our noses and lungs. Breathing was easier here, and the longer I sat on the warm stone, the sleepier I became.

"We should eat," Kinley whispered as he unwrapped his kindling and tinderbox.

"You mean drink," Erielle said and made a face as the chamber's echo taunted her, *"Drink, drink."*

I grinned and reached for my pack to add my own kindling to the pile. So far, Erielle had shown remarkable restraint in voicing her dislike of keola. Unlike Erielle, I enjoyed the spicy-sweet drink. Even the thought of it now, after so much activity and strain with no sustenance, set my stomach to rumbling.

As I unwrapped my kindling from its protective waxed oilcloth, a piece of parchment fluttered out. I hid it in my hand while I delivered my kindling to the pile.

How long we had been in the mountain was anyone's guess, and mine would be the least accurate, having been unconscious, or at least removed from any sense of time, while my mind was in Dwons. But even at that, I was sure at least one full day had passed since we paused in our journey to rest or eat. Somehow, I had not even thought about it. But now that a meal, even a liquid one, was not only a possibility, but already being prepared, the ache of emptiness in my gut and the weakness of hunger in my limbs made the passage of time more real.

Kinley struck his flint several times before a spark caught. A few strikes later, a tiny, starving flame sprouted. Slowly and silently we each added half of our remaining fresh water into the small pot Edru produced from his pack. When it boiled, he added a measure of the dried keola mixture, wrapped in thinly woven cheesecloth, to steep.

While everyone's attention was diverted to the fire, I turned my back and opened the parchment.

I cannot pinpoint the day my love for you became known to me, only that its arrival seemed the natural progression of the sweetest friendship of my life. My heart is, and shall ever be, yours.

Julien's breath tickled my skin, but without a quick peek into his mind, my injured ear would not have discerned that his breath against it held meaning.

He had whispered, *"I love you."*

I leaned toward his ear and returned the sentiment.

The warmth of his love and the creativity of his courtship combined to soothe me, but the damage to my hearing was a cold reminder that I had not yet faced the worst this quest had promised.

"Thank you," I whispered, unwilling to share my infirmity, or the disquiet it caused my spirit, lest its admittance mar the sweetness of Julien's latest note.

"It's almost ready," Edru called out at a normal volume, forgetting for a moment that his last word would come back to him several times. We all laughed then and that sound, too, rounded the room as if there was a much larger crowd than the seven of us.

My mug was drained too soon, and as much as I enjoyed the taste of keola, the lack of having something to chew left me less than satisfied, even though I was no longer hungry. With full stomachs and drooping eyes, we decided that time spent resting would not be wasted.

I was only too glad to be denied my turn at keeping watch. Bone-deep weariness tugged at my mind, rendering the strength from my body as well. I curled up on the warm stone floor, closed my eyes, and fell instantly asleep.

The dream began instantly, or so it seemed.

The cloying sweetness of yellowhock filled my lungs until they were so thick with it that each breath was but a gasp. I ran through the field, panic sweeping my feet through the flowers. I couldn't stop, lest my pursuer overtake me. Casting glances over my shoulder only slowed my progress and made the terror grow, for although his face and form were hidden from me, his laughter—that same evil, twisted laughter that had poisoned my dreams since I'd first inhaled the pollen of the yellowhock flowers—chased me without mercy.

I ran and ran, but the field only stretched longer before me. Somewhere beyond the range of my vision, I knew Julien waited, but he was immobilized somehow, and unable to come save me.

"*Rynnaia.*"

A voice called. A man's voice. But it wasn't Julien.

"*Rynnaia!*" It was my father's voice.

What was he doing here? I wondered in that barely lucid place that was able to think within a dream. *He was supposed to be nearing Salderyn!*

I turned my head to look behind me, but I couldn't see him in the sea of yellowhocks. Suddenly, I tripped and fell, lurching as the ground seemed to drop away, taking my midsection with it.

I gasped and opened my eyes.

Rynnaia.

With a start of guilt I acknowledged my father's voice—his real voice, heard through our Andoven connection—and the love that was so strong it had overcome the boundary of a nightmare to find me.

As the vision of his face touched my sleepy mind, the tension there spoke his worry without the need for words.

I'm sorry, Father.

Where are you? It's been days since we last spoke!

Guilt woke me further. I should have contacted him sooner. *We are well within Mount Shireya. We only just stopped to rest a while.*

I'm glad you are within the mountain. Relief came with his sigh. *Our enemy discovered our ruse. Three days ago they made a sudden retreat. Toward you. We have, of course, pursued them. We're in the northern foothills. We expect to have engaged them by dawn.*

How can you get here so fast?

We were already in Stoen. The mountain is much closer to the Stoenian border than it was to the Dynwatre border. We had less distance to cover than you did coming from the south. Are you well?

I hesitated. *Yes.*

He didn't say anything for a moment, but his gaze pierced through mine. *No . . .* he said finally, and his brow furrowed a bit deeper. *I think, perhaps, you are not.*

A fresh wave of grief crushed my chest. *We lost Sir Risson.* I quickly explained what happened at Halo's Rim, including freeing Gladiel and Drinius, but left out the details about my impairment.

My father was quiet for a moment. *Risson was a loyal knight and a good friend. I'm sorry you had to bear witness to his death.*

I didn't actually witness it, I said, *since I was unconscious at the time.*

Unconscious? Rynnaia!

Exhaustion fought against my desire to keep those details from him. *I will tell you more of it later, but suffice it to say that unlocking Drinius and Gladiel's cell was much more difficult than I anticipated.*

Are you recovered?

Well enough, I sighed.

I could tell he didn't like my answer. *How many marks have you identified?*

The next thing we will likely see is the living precipitate.

Wisps of poetry danced through his mind. Concern colored his words. *You will soon face the foe. Alone. I do not like this.*

Neither do I, but the suffering caused by the Cobeld curse must not continue to plague our people. What they do with those cursed beards . . .

Without my permission, my memory replayed part of that still-too-fresh experience and I brought my hand to my ear. It still throbbed every now and then, but the pain was much duller now.

Oh, Rynnaia. My father saw the memory and winced as he witnessed a moment of my torture. I reached for gray, but even the thick swirls I found couldn't hide it completely.

Tell me what happened.

I didn't have to. The memory was still so fresh, so frightening, that it transferred to him almost instantly—and entirely without my permission. I hadn't wanted to burden him with the details, but the fog of interrupted sleep limited my control.

A torrent of angry, protective colors flew into my mind as the King fought to gain control of his thoughts. *I had no idea the curse could prey on your mind at that distance! I thought there would have to be physical contact. It was a foolish risk that I put in your lap. Forgive me.*

No one knew, Father. And you are not responsible. Besides, I survived.

Has Dyfnel examined you?

No.

There could be other injuries, he said after I explained my hearing loss and the pain that still throbbed. *Internal injuries that affect more than your ears. Dyfnel should examine you.*

I can't see the point of it. Even if I have other injuries, how could we treat them here? I asked. He couldn't answer. *We don't have time. And besides, I'm not telling the others about my hearing loss. It will only worry them.*

My father paused and then nodded. The look in his eyes, even though I saw it only with my mind, was as comforting as if he'd put an arm about my shoulders. *You are weary.*

Yes. I inhaled and imagined resting my head in the crook of his arm. He smiled at the image. *I am weary beyond anything I've known,* I admitted.

Rynnaia, I— He broke off for a moment and the colors he sent next turned that arm around my shoulder into an embrace that forced the breath from my lungs and his abiding affection and care deep within my soul. *I love you, Rynnaia.*

I love you, too, Father.

Sleep, Rynnaia, he said, even as I drifted there on my own. *Sleep.*

THIRTY-NINE

Whether my father had somehow stayed in my mind to guard my dreams or sheer exhaustion had not allowed them entrance, I didn't know, but the nightmare did not recur. When I awakened, it was gently. And I held on to the lazy calm as long as I could before opening my eyes.

Julien's face was what greeted me first. Propped against the rock wall, he sat next to where I lay with his legs drawn up, one elbow cocked on his knee, and his smile made me wish I'd reached wakefulness sooner.

"Good morning, Princess," he whispered.

I reached over to caress his cheek. "Good morning, Bearknight," I said, and then laughed at the memory of the first time I'd done that at the Bear's Rest in the Great Wood of Mynissbyr.

His smile widened when I relayed the memory. "That seems a long time ago," he whispered. "I thought perhaps you wouldn't remember. You were half-asleep when you said it. And disoriented from reading your father's letter."

He chuckled and the sound echoed around the cavernous chamber. "But I knew, even then, that I would cherish that moment."

"Even then?"

He nodded. "And I have. Every moment after."

Oh, yes, I sighed. *I love this man.*

My back popped as I stretched. In that instant I became aware of each aching joint and strained muscle in my body. I tried to suppress the groan that threatened, but it wasn't easy. I hurt. Everywhere. Even the roots of my hair seemed to have been pushed beyond the limits of what they'd been designed to endure. Then again, I had traversed the inside of a mountain, gone over a waterfall, almost drowned, and nearly died while my mind was in Dwons. After that, I ran through tunnels at a breakneck pace before swimming through a narrow tunnel that required more breath than my lungs could provide. Yes, I supposed, it was bound to cause a few aches and pains. But what could I really complain about? I was alive, and as far as I knew, I was whole. I was surrounded by people who loved me.

"How long has everyone else been awake?"

"Awhile," Julien answered. "But none of them almost died freeing two of E'veria's finest knights, either. You needed your rest, Rynnaia, and I, for one, am glad you got it."

Edru was tending a small fire with what was surely the last of our precious kindling. "Is that keola I smell?" As if it could be anything else.

"I'll get you a mug," Edru said. "The rest of us have already partaken."

Julien put his arm around my shoulders. I scooted closer to him and leaned my head against his cheek. Erielle caught my eye and gave me a long wink, which was punctuated by a low chuckle from Julien.

"It would seem my sister approves our courtship, Princess."

"As does your brother," Gerrias added softly. "Though I doubt our approval means much to you one way or the other!"

"On the contrary," I replied, pretending he had been speaking to me instead of Julien. "If you, as my dear friend and loyal knight, opposed Julien's suit, I might reevaluate the matter! However, since you so readily approve of him, I suppose I must continue to accept his courtship."

Kinley looked up then with a mischievous gleam in his eye. "But what of your own brothers' objections, Princess? If Lewys and Rowlen and I had our way you would be bundled up and carted back to Veetri to live the life of a happy maid, never to be bothered by the attentions of any men at all!"

Kinley had forgotten to whisper the last few words and his words bounded back. I grinned. "It is a shame the King has ordered me to consider the knight's suit," I said, inserting a melodramatic sigh that echoed around us all. "The peaceful existence of an old maid might better suit my gentle temperament."

I shifted position and my laughter cut off with a gasp. A sharp pain stabbed between my shoulders again and again.

"What is it?" Julien gripped my left hand with his, but I didn't miss the motion of his other hand, drawing Dyfnel to us.

"I don't know." The admission came out with a groan I couldn't contain.

I squeezed my eyes shut, suddenly aware that a semblance of that pain had been there since Halo's Rim, but since it had not been as sharp as the ache in my ear I had not paid it as much notice.

"It's my back," I gasped as pain stabbed me again. "And . . . through it."

Had the pain shifted to my chest? Perhaps it was only strengthening and making itself known. Another sharp stab stole my breath. I pressed my hand into the space where my neck met my chest, as if that could stem the pain.

"Lie her down. Carefully," Dyfnel commanded. As soon as I was flat on my back, he knelt by the crown of my head and placed two fingers of each hand on my collarbones. He closed his eyes. Even though his request was silent, I heard it.

Show me, he petitioned Rynloeft for guidance.

The pain stabbed stronger and I did not even attempt to see his examination of my internal workings.

After a few silent, tense moments, the pain subsided to a dull throb and I was able to breathe regularly.

What you just felt was a muscle spasm that appears to have caused constriction of the nerves, he said to my mind. *It was made more severe by the damage your organs have sustained. Your heart is weakened, I'm afraid. Your lungs and kidneys are bruised as well.*

I was glad to have not known of this before speaking to my father. *The damage is from the Cobeld hair on the cells, isn't it?*

He nodded. *I would assume so. But the deprivation of air during the swim through the tunnel certainly didn't help. It is not immediately life threatening, but . . . our situation could increase that risk.*

But why am I just now feeling it?

His brow furrowed. *It makes no sense, medically. I can only assume The First wanted you to be able to swim through that tunnel.*

I swallowed. *Then he will enable me to complete the rest of my tasks as well.*

I kept my eyes closed, afraid Julien would see the truth in them.

Dyfnel, I spoke silently, but the tone of my thought left no room for argument, *we will not tell the others. All they need to know is what just happened. A muscle spasm.*

Dyfnel nodded, at least in his thoughts. I opened my eyes and he helped me sit up.

"The princess has suffered a muscle spasm," he said. "She'll be fine."

There was a nearly collective sigh of relief from our friends, but Julien's eyes narrowed on the physician and then me. He said nothing, but I had no doubt he suspected there was more to Dyfnel's diagnosis than what we let on.

Everyone was quiet for a bit. Finally, Gerrias spoke, "So what do we do from here?"

"Follow the stream to its source, I guess." Erielle shrugged. "And after Rynnaia . . ." she paused, "when she's finished, I suppose we can only hope that one of these passageways can lead us to the three doors we saw earlier, because the scrolls tell us that's our way out."

"When the time comes," Julien spoke up, "something will make it clear which is the way we should go. We can't lose faith, especially now that we are so close to our goal."

Edru's eyes rested on me.

You will soon be alone.

No. I shook my head. *Not truly alone.* If The First had brought me this far, he would not abandon me now.

You are right, of course, he said, moving on. But his words lingered in my mind, adding a bit more trepidation to my already queasy stomach.

Dyfnel brought out his copy of the damp scrolls and Erielle read them again to us, but we all knew them so well that the echoed hisses of her whispers didn't hinder our understanding.

A frown soon furrowed her brow as she continued her recitation and got to the part about me facing the foe alone.

Every eye in the room rested on me and I was forced to pull swirls of gray around my thoughts to protect me from their worry. I stared at my hands when she finished.

Julien squeezed my shoulder. "Remember, Rynnaia, the scrolls also have a role for you to play outside the mountain," he said. The rest of our company nodded in a way that seemed like a benediction, a promise that I would return to them.

"When I get back," I said the words slowly, careful to make them positive, as if victory was assured, "I'll have the Remedy in hand. If someone went ahead and found the way out, maybe we could get on to the next part of the prophecy faster."

Julien nodded. "Once the princess is . . . on her way," he paused, "a pair of us should double back here and try to ascertain which of these passageways," he gestured around the cavern, "is the best path by which to leave."

"I'll go," Gerrias said.

Julien nodded. "Who else?"

"I will," Dyfnel offered.

"No." Julien shook his head. "I want you here." He glanced at me. "In case the princess has need of a physician when she returns."

Dyfnel and I avoided each other's gaze, lest we give the truth of that need away.

"Send me," Edru said. "That leaves two knights to protect the princess. Well, three," he said, directing a smile toward Erielle.

I returned Erielle's grin, hoping it didn't look as forced as it felt. Suddenly, the keola was not sitting well in my stomach, but it was fear rather than infirmity that caused it to quiver so.

Swallowing hard, I tossed the remaining contents of my cup.

"If everyone's ready," I said, forcing a bit of bravado into my voice as I bent to pick up my pack, "I'm rather anxious to find the Remedy."

We packed up, extinguished the fire, and waded into the stream. The water was warm and soothed my aching joints. Walking against its gentle flow did not cause further strain. The water never reached higher than our waists—well, a little higher on Erielle, of course—but, although the current grew stronger around every winding bend, it didn't hinder our forward motion.

Our tirandite torches were unnecessary and stowed in our packs, which freed our hands to help us balance against the current. The farther we followed the stream, the less marbled and brighter the tirandite walls were, but a growing noise reminded me of a waterfall. The direction of the current implied we were at the bottom of the waterfall, and while that was some comfort, it was limited. The memory of going over the huge waterfall was still fresh in my mind. And the battle to come, whatever form it might take, was an even more pressing concern.

We rounded a corner and quite suddenly entered a chamber that was so bright we had to shield our eyes until they adjusted to it. The whole chamber glowed as if we'd stepped out of a shaded glen and into the center of a meadow at midday that was graced by not one, but two suns.

However, it seemed we had reached a dead end. There was no way out except the way we came in.

At least no way we could yet see.

The glowing walls were even warmer here. At the far end of the room, water poured so smoothly from a slit in the rock that it was like a wide ribbon had stretched out from the wall and into the small pool below. The pool fed the stream up which we had traveled to find this chamber.

From where we stood, the ribbon of water looked to begin no higher than what Julien's fingers would reach if he stood on his brother's shoulders with his arms extended upward. A slight foam bubbled where it hit the surface of the pool, but the sound was more of a hum than a roar. This waterfall was drastically smaller than the immense, plummeting cliff we had crashed over earlier. But even so, I was relieved to already be on this side of it.

A spark caught my eye. And then another. The more my eyes adjusted to the room, the more I realized that it wasn't just the walls that glowed, but the water itself.

The water . . . glowed?

I tilted my head. The falling water sparkled with a glittering luminescence that was so familiar and so . . . precious.

But we're inside a mountain! I reminded myself. *It can't be . . .*

My breath caught in wonder as I raced toward the waterfall, only stopping when I reached the edge of the pool at its base. I flattened my body to the ground. When I placed my hand in the water, a swarm of tiny illumined creatures rushed up to meet it.

"Careful!"

I gasped as Kinley's hand reached in and snatched mine out.

"We don't know what those things are, Rose! Er, Rynnaia," he corrected. "They could be dangerous. Poisonous!"

I shook my head. "It's all right, Kinley. They're enikkas." I smiled as a familiar awe filled my center and spilled out through my voice. "I know them. And they know me."

"Enikkas?"

"Yes." Julien's voice sounded as full as mine.

I pried my hand from my brother's and slid it back in the water. From the depths of the pool a vortex of tiny lights rose to brush against my skin. "Greetings, sweet enikkas," I whispered. "You are lovely, as always." The lights brightened and dimmed for a moment in response to my praise.

Erielle was soon by my side, her hand in the water. An uncharacteristically girlish giggle bubbled from her lips. "I've heard of them," she said, her voice full of wonder, "but what are they, really?"

"They are a gift from The First," I replied, my throat tightening. "A reminder that we are not alone."

Tears pooled in my eyes and escaped down my cheeks when I blinked. I didn't try to wipe them away. The utter beauty of the tiny creatures, and of their Giver, astounded me. As each tear fell into the pool, the enikkas swarmed it as if they drew sustenance from the gratitude captured in the substance of my tears.

The men joined us then, circling the pool, each with a hand in the water. For a time we just lay on our bellies, drawing strength from the comfort found therein.

I looked across the pool at Julien. His eyes were closed and his lips moved around the wonder of his smile, speaking silent words to his Creator.

A swarm of enikkas moved toward him. Like my tears, Julien's silent exaltation to Rynloeft was simply a reaction to the overflow of his heart. The enikkas, being emissaries of The First, couldn't help but respond to him.

As I watched the delight of their comfort play across his features, a tender emotion seized hold of me. I had known for weeks that I loved him, but never had I loved him more than I did in that moment. Julien had taught me so much about truth. About love beyond what a man feels for a woman or a woman for a man. While we were on Tirandov Isle he had expertly extracted truth from the folktales of my childhood and had shown me how to apply it to the historical fact recorded in *The Story of The First*. He'd spoken of time and tide, and of stars and stories that illustrated the greater love beyond us. The love that encompasses us. Bathes us.

An infinite consolation wrapped itself around my heart. I closed my eyes to savor it. *Thank you. Thank you.*

Finally, I whispered my affection to the enikkas and withdrew my hand.

I turned my gaze to the ribbon of water above. It poured from a narrow fissure in the rock wall and seemed to act as a transport of sorts for the enikkas. I guessed that somewhere beyond the source of its cascade was a hatching-ground for the sweet creatures of light.

Sparkling as they plunged downward, the enikkas were music in motion. Surely this was the *living precipitate* we sought.

"There are no shadows in this room," Erielle stated, bringing all our minds back to the scrolls.

I looked around. She was right. Light poured from the walls and water. It came from every direction, even the floor. *But . . .*

I pointed to the waterfall. "It's darker back there," I said. "The waterfall must hide the door."

Indeed, the fall of the water seemed to shadow the light of the stone. Not for lack of light, being as the water itself was illumined by enikkas, but the rock behind it was, upon closer examination, of a different, darker stone.

I stood and walked toward it, and then pressed myself against the wall and gazed behind the falling water.

"There's a cave," I said. "It's small. Barely wide enough for one person to fit through at a time."

But then again, only one had to fit through.

Me.

I retrieved my torch from my pack and pushed the illumined stick through the water to the dark rock behind it.

Erielle joined me. At her sharp intake of breath I knew there was no mistake. "I guess this is it," she said and quoted the scrolls, "'the Remedy rests through shadowed door.'"

"Yes." I nodded. Taking a deep breath, I turned around and apprised the rest of the group of our discovery.

Of one accord, the knights strode forward to see for themselves and I silently watched as their shoulders drooped.

"Do you so soon discard your hope?" I asked when they stood before me. "The First will not abandon us now, not when we need him the most."

I stepped forward and embraced each member of our party in turn. Then, taking a deep breath, I removed my dagger and handed it to Erielle. She took it with wide, blinking eyes. I removed my pack and set down my torch.

Julien stepped forward and put his hand on my shoulder. Everyone else followed suit, placing a hand on my back or shoulder, surrounding me with a silent show of loyalty and love. In their thoughts, each one petitioned The First on my behalf.

After several silent moments, Dyfnel spoke. "May it be so." His words echoed throughout our group.

Julien squeezed my shoulder, and as soon as everyone else's hands had been removed from my person, he pulled me fiercely to his chest. His breath tickled my ear. "I love you, Rynnaia E'veri."

"I love you, too."

"Come back to me."

I closed my eyes and pressed my hand to his cheek. I wanted to promise him that I would return, or at least that I would try, but even though the scrolls might have a job for me outside the mountain, they didn't promise I would survive long enough to complete it. My focus had to be on finding the Remedy. I had to survive just long enough to see it into my friends' care. Beyond that, who could know?

Julien set a soft kiss on my brow, and as his lips lingered there I closed my eyes, committing the feeling of that moment to my memory.

Julien released me. I bent to retrieve my torch and fastened it at my waist. With one last look encompassing the faces of my faithful friends, I turned my back on them and walked toward the waterfall.

Settling my feet on a narrow, wet stone ledge, I inched my way behind the fall. Just over halfway across the back of the ribbon of water I was able, with only a slight reach, to stretch my arms and pull my body up into the small passage cave that would lead me to the Remedy that could save the lives of my people.

And to the unknown foe, who, if I failed, would consign my Kingdom to a slow but certain death.

$\mathscr{F}$ O R T Y

$\mathcal{M}$y first impression of the tunnel was . . . sharp. Formed of a rough, pumice-like stone, the entrance dug into my fingers as I pulled myself up and into it. Once inside, it caught on my clothes, my hair, and even my skin. With some effort, and more than a few unprincess-like grunts, I moved the torch to a rear belt loop so the light would not be blocked while I crawled through the narrow aperture. The cramped space necessitated I drag my body forward with my arms. As I slithered over the gravelly, pocked stones that caught on my clothes and skin, abrasion upon abrasion scraped into my hands and arms. I cringed at the thought of immersing them in the return trip's salty water.

I crawled thusly for what seemed like a very long time, and in truth, it must have been. I could no longer hear even the slightest hint of the waterfall or the muffled voices of my friends when I finally paused to rest my forehead on my hands. After a few minutes I resumed my forward trek.

It was a good thing I had been forced to overcome my fear of tight spaces in the underwater tunnel. Otherwise, panic would have surely paralyzed me here.

The tunnel curved sharply to the right and I paused. Looking forward pained my neck and upper back, strained as they were from being arched up and out from my body's prone position, but beyond the stretch of light my torch provided, an orange glow danced on the dull black of the tunnel wall ahead. As I rounded the corner, the light was joined by strange, musical sounds coming from somewhere beyond my vision.

I closed my eyes and listened. The sound was pleasant, like Lady Whittier's favorite stringed instrument, but somewhat deeper. Music was certainly not what I had expected to hear. Taunts, yes. Curses, certainly. And that terrible laughter? Absolutely. But not music. My dreams had been filled with evil Cobeld laughter, not sweet notes of song.

Urgency pressed me forward, but the weight of fear made me cautious. Just as I was about to move on, a sudden muscle spasm in my back and chest made me wince and hold my position.

"Embral e' Veria." I dropped my head into my hands and whispered the name so dear to my heart. "Be with me. Make me strong."

I stayed like that, breathing shallow, careful breaths so as to avoid irritating my already-pinched nerves with the expansion of my lungs. Finally, the spasm passed.

I tried to focus my thoughts on a pleasant memory—the enikkas—but as I wriggled forward, the face of Aspera Scyles flew into my mind instead.

I paused. What could have possibly brought her to mind?

With the exception of the Cobelds, the sour disposition of Lord Whittier's housekeeper was as far a thought from the sweet enikkas as my mind could reach. Why, then, when I searched for peace and comfort, had the Asp, the antithesis of those very things in my childhood, come to mind?

It made no sense.

Mrs. Scyles was long dead, having been killed by the Cobeld to whom she'd betrayed my location in Veetri. And the way she appeared now in my memory was with an expression she had never sent my way. No, Mrs. Scyles had despised me. But try as I might, I could not conjure any expression but that which she'd always bestowed upon Lord and Lady Whittier. The expression which had deceived them into thinking she did not have such a serpentine nature.

I shook my head as if to send the image on its way. Perhaps it was simply my snake-like crawl through the cave that brought her to mind now. The boys and I called her "the Asp" and I was wriggling through this tunnel on my belly, like a snake, so . . . yes. That must be it.

I squeezed my eyes shut against the emotions the memory invited to rise within my heart. *Focus, Rynnaia!* I needed to think about the foe I would soon face, not a long-dead enemy from my past.

With renewed vigor, I tucked my head and continued forward. I slithered around a tight corner, scraping every bit of exposed flesh against the rough tunnel walls, and without warning, the tunnel sloped downward and abruptly—

Ended!

Unable to stop my forward motion, I spilled out of the passageway, screaming as I fell headfirst into a deep chasm.

In that instant of knowing death was upon me, I scrambled and twisted, trying to arch my back, or lean somehow so that my knees or belly could grasp on to the tunnel's rough stone. But even my clothes, which had before fought against my forward motion, gave in to gravity's greater strength.

SERENA CHASE

This wasn't in the scrolls!

Had there been another tunnel behind the waterfall? Or, in keeping my head down so much, had I missed a fork in the one I'd taken and gone down the wrong path?

Eventually I would hit bottom, and—

I'm going to die!

The rapid succession of thoughts was halted by the impact of my face smashing into a hard, transparent barrier.

I barely had time to gasp against the pain rendered to my already-bruised face when the rest of my body tumbled painfully onto the invisible floor and . . . it trembled beneath me.

"When *I* came through the tunnel, I was a little more graceful about it."

My head snapped up and I quickly gained my feet, scanning the space for the source of the deep voice that had spoken.

"Who's there?" I reached for the dagger I usually kept at my belt, but clenched at empty air.

No sword or dagger at her side, The First alone will be her guide.

Oh. I'd left it with Erielle.

"You might want to use a bit more care, Ryn Naia." The friendly voice was accented by a benign chuckle that echoed through the space. "The floor seems to hold weight without issue, but I am not certain whether it was designed to withstand force."

The voice was unfamiliar, but it lacked menace. Where was it coming from?

A giant boulder protruded up through the center of the chamber. I couldn't see around it to identify the speaker, but one thing was clear: *he knows who I am.*

I looked down then and almost lost the scant bit of keola I had consumed. Whatever the transparent material I stood on was made of—glass? An undiscovered ore?—it lidded a chasm

378

so deep, so dark, that it seemed to go on forever. Perhaps to the very center of the world.

Reminding myself that I wasn't alone, I looked up and tried to regulate my breathing as I scanned the circular chamber.

The space was lit by several torches, hung in ornate sconces carved directly from the reddish-brown stone of the walls. At the far side of the room, a good twenty paces away, was a table, complete with golden candelabra, a crystal decanter that appeared to be filled with wine, and two goblets.

A table? A set table? I gaped at it. *What—? How—?* I blinked several times, but the table remained. I finally tore my gaze away.

Between the table and me, the boulder—which was really more like a wide rock platform, now that I looked at it more closely—was made of the same sort of reddish stone as the rest of the cavern. It jutted up from somewhere deep below the floor, effectively blocking my view of the rest of the table.

And whoever had spoken to me.

Like a living beast of a thing, the platform grew up from the center of the chasm. I put my hand on the wall behind me and took a deep breath to remind myself that I was standing on a solid surface. But the fact that I could see nothing but empty air beneath my feet was, at the very least, disconcerting.

My heartbeat pounded with the frantic rhythm of one awakening suddenly from a dream of falling. My chest tightened, whether from another spasm or sheer panic I couldn't be sure, but I forced my eyes to move from the depths under my feet, lest I be taken unawares by an enemy whom I had yet to see. What I did see then, however, almost brought another scream from my throat.

A small body rested, facedown, to the left of where the platform met the glass-like floor. Unmoving.

Peeking out from beneath the body, a dirty gray beard was caked in blood. The body appeared lifeless, but I couldn't assume it was. The Cobelds were known for their trickery.

I took a cautious step forward, sliding my foot in case it should meet less glass and more air. A small pool of blood seeped out from underneath its head, seeming to float on the transparent floor. Cautiously, using the toe of my boot, I flipped the body over.

Bile rose in my throat at the gory wound that parted the long gray beard and opened its throat. Yes, it was a Cobeld, but it was no longer a danger to me. Apart from the mortal wound, a gauzy, blank stare marked it as dead.

But if my foe was dead, who had spoken to me?

Without ever lifting my feet from the floor I couldn't see, I slowly skated around the large rock.

The table loomed before me, set as grandly as if the King himself was expected to dine. At the head of the table sat a knight wearing a tunic of light chain mail that looked as if it had been fashioned from pure gold.

Silly, I thought. *Gold is too soft to serve as armor.*

And then I saw his face.

Beyond his armor, everything about the knight was golden and beautiful. Radiant skin glowed with health. The knight's blond hair caught the light in such a way that it brought out golden flecks in his amber eyes. I blushed as his eyes met mine, feeling as self-conscious as a girl at her first ball. Though I was sure I'd never met him, there was a familiarity about this knight that beckoned my curiosity.

"Welcome," he said with a gentle, friendly smile that relaxed my shoulders. "At long last, welcome."

The knight held a stringed instrument in his hand. It was beautiful and it sang a haunting, lovely song as he ran a bow across its strings.

I blinked. Music? A banquet? A knight? These were not mentioned or even hinted at in the scrolls! I struggled to recall anything of the poetry that would show me what to do next. I came up with nothing and contemplated the "wrong turn" idea again.

"Who are you?" I finally asked. I wanted to sound forceful and confident like my father, but the voice that escaped me was little more than a whisper. "What is this place?"

He stopped playing and set the instrument on the table. "I am that which you have sought, Ryn Naia." He rose and his smile was so warm it heated the tips of my ears. "This, my dear, is the place of your triumph. Welcome."

His voice was soft and he moved with a patient grace that eased my mind. Were those tears in his eyes?

He placed a hand over his heart and bowed. As he rose, my breath caught again at the beauty of him. Even the golden chain mail he wore couldn't hide the sculpted perfection of his form.

"Who are you?" I repeated.

"I know it is difficult to understand, but I have waited a long time for you, Ryn Naia. Now that you have finally come to me, we can fulfill the destiny given to us."

"Us?" I tilted my head. The destiny given *us*? "Wait. I—"

But words failed me when he reached for my hand and lifted it to his lips. "I, Ryn Naia, am that which you have so bravely sought."

"You?" My mouth dropped open. I shut it. "*You* are the Remedy?"

His smile widened. "I am not quite what you expected, am I?" He chuckled. "Prophets tend to speak in riddles. It is to keep us humble." He sighed. "Although I suppose if we were allowed to easily meet our goals, we might very well die of boredom!"

"But what about the Cobeld?" I pointed toward the dead creature, thinking of what the scrolls said about my foe. "I was supposed to fight him and lock him up."

"Death is an eternal cage for those who don't rally to the cause of The First King, is it not?" He tilted his head. "But you need not worry about him. I am your champion, Ryn Naia. I have vanquished the foe in your name, as any truly worthy knight would do for his future Queen."

"But I thought *I* was supposed to do it."

"Do the scrolls say that, exactly?" he asked. "They informed you to leave your friends behind, yes? To move onward alone. But do they specify that you will *remain* alone?"

I thought about it. "Not . . . exactly. Well, no!" The realization hit me like a blacksmith's hammer. "They don't."

"Precisely." Still holding my hand, he led me to the table and pulled a chair out for me. "Please, join me. You have had a difficult journey and have done well. The prophecy is nearly fulfilled." He poured wine into both goblets. "You deserve a moment of peace, and I must admit I am curious to know you better. As I am sure you are curious about me. Now that the prophecy has brought us together we must put our inhibitions aside to let it complete its course."

I wasn't hungry, and although the food looked delicious, I couldn't help but wonder how it got here, so I asked.

"The Provider gives us all we need."

The Provider. A name listed in *The Story of The First.*

"He gave us the scrolls, did he not?" The knight took a sip from his goblet. "And through them he provided the path by which you and I, together, will heal E'veria. For one who cheated death and walked away unscathed from his own funeral pyre, I should think something as simple as the provision of food and a table, even one such as this, would be but a trifling thing, don't you?"

"I . . . suppose."

The golden knight continued to speak of the prophecy and our shared destiny. I only half-listened, still so overwhelmed that the Remedy was, in fact, a *person*, not a *thing*, that I could barely move, let alone process all he said. But I was snapped back to the present when he said, "With me at your side as your prince and champion, we shall not only heal E'veria, but expand our borders beyond even the wastelands of Dwons."

"Expand E'veria's borders? Why?"

He blinked. "Because truth must prevail."

He rose from the table and knelt beside my chair with an earnest expression that spoke not only of sincerity, but of a powerfully infectious sense of destiny. He then reached into his pocket and brought forth . . . a ring.

"For you." His warm golden skin caressed my palm. "For me." He lifted my hand and placed the large emerald stone upon my finger. "For the renewal of E'veria." He brought my hand to his lips and kissed the large green stone.

I pulled my hand away. "You are too familiar, sir."

"Am I?" His eyes mirrored the confusion in his voice. "But the prophecy has declared our bond necessary to save E'veria. According to the prophecy, we are already betrothed."

I blinked. Already betrothed? How . . . ?

"For years I have known the name of the one to whom I would be bound," he said, "but nothing else. It is a pleasure to finally meet you. To seal our bond."

"Our bond?"

"Yes." He reached for my hand again. "I am to be your prince. To fulfill the prophecy, you must marry me, Ryn Naia."

"Marry you?" My windpipe constricted. I shook my head. "No. I'm sorry, but . . . no. I can't. That's not right. I—" I swallowed hard, completely out of words.

His smile fell and he closed his eyes. When he opened them, he nodded sadly. "I forget that you have not lived with the reality of the prophecy for as long as I have. I will help you understand. Examine the words."

One at a time, he spoke each line of the prophecy in the Ancient Voice, and then again, translated. The words were beautiful and without rhyme in their original form, but when said with the emphasis on certain words, and translated . . .

"'Emerald bonds to seal the Ryn. Their toast expels curse taken in,'" he quoted. "Our marriage toast, the final act of the marriage ceremony, expels the curse." He rubbed a finger over the stone. "You wear my emerald, already. To complete the prophecy, we must marry."

My heart sank. It was right there, in the words of the prophecy. My fate, my future, my . . . husband?

"This is our shared destiny, Ryn Naia. To rule E'veria and lead her to a golden age!"

He wore an expression of vulnerable adoration as he quoted more lines from the scrolls I had memorized. His impassioned delivery revealed layered meanings to the words that had never occurred to me or to the Andoven. At least not that they had shared with me.

My stomach turned over and I blinked rapidly to quench the fire of tears, surging up to my eyes from my breaking heart. The prophecy was unfolding before me in a way I had not considered, taking my heart and my future down a path that would sever the ties I had hoped to forge with Julien.

I shook my head, unable to reconcile myself to this strange turn of events.

"You and I are bound together by the prophecy." He pointed to the ring on my finger. It wasn't a gift. It was a bride-price. "I have waited over a thousand years, and now circumstances have finally aligned to bring you to me. Our bond, our marriage, will break the curse, Ryn Naia. It was foreseen as that which will remedy the ills plaguing E'veria."

"If you've been alive for a thousand years, how is it that you appear so young?"

His smile was caught somewhere between indulgent and amused. "A good question, but one I cannot answer. All I know is that I was given this task. I know not how my needs have been provided for, nor why my youth remains. I can only believe this was allowed to achieve a purpose beyond our understanding. A purpose that will benefit E'veria through our union."

I covered my face with my hands. Truly, this was something beyond my comprehension. *Was this what Lady Anya had foreseen?*

Why, then, had the prophecy made such strange allusions to food and gifts when the Remedy was, in fact, a knight I was expected to wed? How had Dyfnel and the other Andoven scholars missed something this important in the translation? How had I? Why was there no mention of this knight? Of why he'd been left here—for a thousand years—awaiting my arrival?

I had studied the prophecy, but only the translations. Why had I not asked to see the original copies myself? If I had, maybe I could have caught some subtlety that might have prepared me for this strange turn of events.

I lowered my hands and examined the exquisite jewel the golden knight had placed on my finger and thought about the promise he offered with it. Marriage now. Soon, the destruction of the Cobelds and peace and healing in E'veria.

I flinched. I couldn't imagine loving anyone but Julien.

What would happen if I *did not* marry this knight?

The way he'd explained the meaning of the prophecy made the answer too quick in coming: if I didn't marry him, the curse would not be expelled.

My mother's face swam before my eyes and then the faces of so many who had shared their stories of loss with me. As the Ryn, the Kingdom's well-being had to come before everything, even my own heart. Could I put aside my own happiness and sacrifice it in this way?

He was gentle. He seemed kind. And there was no denying he was beautiful.

But he wasn't Julien.

Could I give up Julien so my mother could live? Would I give him up for my Kingdom?

The responsibility of my birth gave me no other option. Could I do it? Could I really give up Julien? Could I, instead, marry this stranger, and by so doing, expel the Cobeld curse from E'veria?

My eyes closed, loosing tears to streak my cheeks.

Something about his interpretation of the prophecy bothered me, but I feared it was only my emotions causing my distrust. He had recited the prophecy and explained the meanings of phrases that I had never considered. But still, a niggling doubt remained. Yes, it bore Julien's face and it whispered of dreams that would be lost should I accept this knight's words—and his hand in marriage. But could I trust a misgiving when it was so influenced by my aching heart? Or should I believe the word of this unaging golden knight who had known of the prophecy much longer than I?

My breath caught. I was sent here to find the Remedy and I could find no logical explanation for this golden knight's presence, but that he was that which I had sought. Thinking over his translation of the prophecy's meaning, it made so much sense it broke my heart. This knight was the Remedy. And I was the Ryn Naia, prophesied to . . . wed him.

A cloak of acceptance settled heavily over my heart. I could not be selfish. I had to think of the entire Kingdom. Regardless of personal cost, I would do what was right for E'veria.

I took a deep breath, opened my eyes, and lifted my chin.

I am the Ryn.

FORTY-ONE

J lifted my hand and examined the gem. Its facets glowed with green fire, the same spark I had seen in Julien's eyes when he told me he loved me.

I tried to hold back my emotions, but tears fell like water through a sieve. Oh, why had I let myself fall in love with Julien? How would I ever explain this to him?

"Ah." The golden knight saw the pain in my eyes. "There is another?"

I nodded.

"I'm sorry. I had hoped you would yet be unattached when you finally came to me. This will be even more difficult for you since your heart is otherwise engaged. But you know the prophecy, Ryn Naia. You know our bond, our union, is necessary." He sighed. "I only hope, one day, you will allow yourself to care for me."

I sniffed. "The E'veri family has always married for love."

"True," he said. "But what is love, in essence, but a common goal and an affectionate, determined pursuit? These things we share. Already we are friends, yes? It is not such a big leap to love."

I knew the truth of that from my friendship with Julien.

"Time has not given us the luxury of courtship," he continued, "but the prophecy has foretold of our union, and as you well know, no one can thwart the will of The First King."

His jaw stiffened slightly and, as he finished, a bitter color touched the surface of my mind. But even so, his tone had not betrayed that emotion. I blinked. Had I sensed his bitterness . . . or my own? Certainly, the thought of giving up Julien caused me pain, but though I searched my heart, I found only sadness, not its darker cousin.

Andoven etiquette demanded I seek permission to see his thoughts, but how could I even consider marrying a man, even one such as this, without knowing beyond the shadow of a doubt that he had E'veria's best interests at heart? If he was lying, I had no compulsion, Andoven or otherwise, to restrict myself thus.

But why would he lie? His recitation of the prophecy was so sure. And his interpretation made sense. Besides, he'd done nothing to harm me. In fact, he had killed a Cobeld on my behalf!

What to do?

With a twinge of misgiving, I decided not to use my gift. Instead I sought its Giver.

The moment I closed my eyes the face of Aspera Scyles slid through my thoughts. A shiver moved across my shoulders as the vision passed, replaced by the warmer memory of the last advice my mother had given me before I left Tirandov Isle.

"When you are in doubt, or when fear itself seems as if it will overpower you, concentrate on his names, the many titles of The

*First King that you have studied these past weeks. You will be
reassured by them.*

"My dear?" The knight interrupted my thoughts. "Are we
agreed? We should proclaim our vows and leave this place."

"I understand your urgency, sir, I do." Indeed. The
Kingdom needed to be freed from the Cobeld curse. "But I
need a moment to absorb this. You are asking me to forsake
another and bind myself to you, a virtual stranger, while the
weight of the Kingdom's future lies at my feet."

"It is not me who asks," he said. "It is what the prophecy
demands."

I sighed, lowering my lashes to release the tears that had
built up at the thought of losing Julien. With eyes closed, my
mind turned page after page of Loeftryn de Rynloeft's names
and titles, finally coming to rest on the one I needed.

Truth Barer, I silently called, wrapping my plea in gray
camouflage. *Truth Barer! Please make this clear!*

Aspera Scyles's deceptive look of subservience pierced
through my consciousness again, surrounded by a field of
pure white light.

I'd asked for the truth to be bared, but had been given a
vision of . . . deception?

All at once, the picture was joined by an echo of poetry
from the scrolls. *Ryn Naia's past on future bears and memory
serves to foil the snare.*

A gasp sounded silently in my mind. The Truth Barer had
been speaking to me all along. I had not been listening.

"It pains me to see your tears," the knight said. "It will
not be easy for us at first, but love will grow in time. Of that I
am sure."

I opened my eyes as he ran a soft, beautiful palm along
my tear-stained cheek. "Does the thought of marriage to me

repulse you?" he asked. "In time, could you grow to find me attractive? Someday?"

The vision the Truth Barer had granted me of the Asp gave me fresh insight into the knight's question. His sincerity was tainted, somehow. And his eyes bore the look of one who was supremely confident in his own loveliness.

And who willingly used it for his own gain.

Suddenly, I knew why he looked familiar. I had seen him before. He had come to life in my mind through the pages of *The Story of The First.*

The First King had overcome the bonds of time, ink, and paper to show me how the Emblem of the First came to be. This very knight had been on the battlefield when Loeftryn de Rynloeft's body was burned at the base of the Sacred Mountain.

He was the traitor, Cobeld. The one from whom E'veria's greatest enemies had taken their name.

He was not the Remedy. He was the foe.

I had to suppress a shiver when he stroked the back of my hand. It took every ounce of strength within me to keep my face from betraying me as I silently expressed my thanks to the Truth Barer.

"If you find me even the least bit attractive, Ryn Naia," he said in a tone that was now more syrupy than vulnerable to my more discerning ears, "that attraction could grow to love."

I opened my eyes. "You are the most handsome man I have ever seen."

I spoke honestly, even though admitting it left a vile taste in my mouth and made me feel like I was committing an offense of disloyalty to Julien. But it was that taste that assured me that somewhere beneath the knight's—no, *Cobeld's*—beauty, was the rancid ugliness of an ancient lie.

"Regardless of the cost to me," I said, "I will do what is right to fulfill the prophecy. But," I paused and forced myself to smile at him, "my father would be disappointed if I accepted your proposal too readily. Allow me to walk a bit. To take a few moments to acclimate myself to the idea of our future together. I would not wish the King to think I spoke my vows too hastily."

"Perhaps that would be wise," he said, chuckling. "You are his only child. He is bound to have some reservations to our match, even if it is clearly necessary from the scrolls. I am, after all, much, much older than you."

Indeed. I fought the shiver that threatened to shake my spine. If he'd been trapped in this chamber for a thousand or more years, how did he know so much about me? Did the Cobelds know he was here? Had they told him? Did they worship him as they would a god?

Or was this, like my visitation from Lady Anya, some strange magic that ripped the very fabric of time?

I disregarded that last thought. He was here. Exactly here and exactly now. But how? And why didn't he look like his namesakes? How had he retained his youth?

Truth Barer, I petitioned while trying to keep my companion's steady gaze. *Why have you allowed him to remain young that he might lie in wait like this for centuries?*

There was no answer to my question, but as I pondered it, I realized I didn't need one.

I already had truth.

Whatever power had enabled Cobeld to keep his youth, whatever window he had to the rest of the world, Cobeld was trapped inside this mountain.

No, Cobeld was not as powerful as I'd feared. His power would not even register when measured against that of the Warrior King who had sent me to defeat him.

And defeat him I would.

I gazed at the glittering emerald on my finger, but pictured Julien's eyes instead. "It is such a beautiful color, this ring," I said. "I will think on your proposal and give you my answer in a moment." As an afterthought, I pulled every ounce of Veetrish charm I could to the surface of my smile, hoping it appeared both genuine and slightly besotted, something he would likely expect, given his apparent confidence in his beauty. "I will not keep you waiting long."

With that, I turned from him and began what I hoped looked like a thoughtful stroll around the room, careful to keep my thoughts and expression masked while dearly hoping the transparent floor would remain solid beneath my feet.

I paused here and there to examine the carved sconces and other artful objects that made the chamber so lovely. I barely noticed them, though, so intent was I on surveying the room for a hint of the two things I truly sought. First, the Remedy. And second? A weapon.

Guide my eyes, Truth Barer, I pleaded. *Please show me what to do. Voice of Truth, be my guide.*

Again, I turned my gaze to the engagement ring, its color so like the eyes of the man I loved. But while my heart sent a continuous stream of requests to Rynloeft, my thoughts raced through the poetry.

For Ryn alone must foe engage and settle in eternal cage. Must foe engage. Is that what the scrolls meant? That I had to accept the ring? Something about that seemed wrong.

When I looked down at the floor again I had to steady myself by grasping the nearby sconce.

It was a truly dizzying view. If the transparent floor gave way, how many leagues would I fall? It had trembled when I fell out of the tunnel. Perhaps if it was struck just right . . .

It might not take much of an impact to cause it to give way, I thought. *It would just have to be at a point of weakness.*

I looked around for a crack or a hole, some evidence that one part of the transparent barrier was less sturdy than the rest, but found none.

I will have to create the point of weakness myself, I thought. *But not yet.*

It took a moment to regain my equilibrium when I looked away from the chasm. As soon as my stomach returned to its original position, however, my gaze was drawn to the rock formation in the center of the room. The rock was nearly flat at the top, but had a lumpy growth of some other kind of stone in the middle of it.

I lifted up on my tiptoes, grabbed a torch from a sconce on the wall, and held it up toward the rock. The lump in the middle cast a strange shadow. "What *is* that?"

I hadn't meant to speak aloud. Silently, I chided my foolishness when Cobeld hurried around to my side of the rock.

But I didn't need an audible answer to my question. As if Rynloeft had shined a light reflecting its name, I knew I had found the gift. The sustenance.

The Remedy.

The hairs on my neck tingled at Cobeld's nearness.

"Please, Ryn Naia," he said. "You cannot understand how agonizing these years have been, waiting for you. How often have I longed for death! But now you are here and my life has reason again. There is no time to waste. Let us be married at once! Let us exile the curse and save the Kingdom!"

Silence stretched the scant air between us as I rethought every word the traitor had spoken. A burst of righteous anger consumed my thoughts at his knowing manipulation of the scrolls.

And not a little rush of humiliation that I'd almost fallen for it.

For *him*.

Sir Cobeld had been one of the First King's knights. A *friend*. But he had betrayed his oath and his King. Cobeld had no intention of exiling the curse.

He *was* the curse.

I closed my eyes and thanked The First for allowing me to see through this golden deception and then humbly petitioned for permission to use the gifts of my heritage and the extended power of my mother's blessing.

I trained my eyes on a place on the floor, though it looked like air.

Weaken and crack, I commanded.

Directly in front of me, a jagged stripe appeared. It snaked across the glass-like floor between us. A slight sizzling sound broke the silence as the stripe fractured off in several different directions across the floor, multiplying in size and sound as it weakened the only support which kept us from a terrorizing fall and death.

It had to be done, but it sent panic swirling in my core. When I looked over my shoulder I was relieved to find that the crack had not yet made it completely around the rock. It was moving fast, but there was still time. Taking a step back, I looked up and was met by the golden knight's furious gaze.

"*You* did that?"

I nodded, my heart pressing against my throat.

"You are not only the descendent of Stoen, but of . . . Andov?"

He knew so much about me, but he didn't know that? Again, I nodded.

A sudden and horrible change worked over the traitor knight's glorious face. He took a step toward me and I stepped back. In a moment of panic, I threw the torch at the floor near his feet, hoping it would make a crack large enough for him to fall through.

But even after more than a thousand years, his reflexes were still knight-quick. He caught the torch just before it would have crashed onto the weakened floor.

FORTY-TWO

My heart almost stopped. Throwing the torch was a gut-level reaction to the threat he posed to my person. But had the torch hit its mark, I likely would have fallen into the chasm along with my enemy.

Think, Rynnaia! I chastised my foolishness. *Think!*

Torch in hand, the golden knight stood stock-still, but for the change overtaking the loveliness of his form. In a matter of moments his beauty melted away to reveal centuries of living death and a feral countenance of pure hatred even more terrifying than the chasm beneath our feet.

I fled back toward the rock platform and ran my hands over it, seeking a hold for my hands or feet. Finally finding a grip, I climbed as fast as I could, but just as my hand reached the top, he started to laugh.

I almost lost my hold at the frighteningly familiar tone, the same bone-chilling laugh that had haunted my dreams over the last several weeks. Fear threatened to paralyze me. My breath came in short gasps and my heart beat a frantic pace. When a spasm gripped my chest, I cried out, but I willed myself to keep moving toward the Remedy. I had just pulled my torso over the top of the rock when a searing pain tore through my leg.

Twisting at the waist, I grasped at the dagger he had thrown, now embedded in my calf muscle. I wrapped my fingers around its handle and ripped it free.

The blade was covered in my blood; the pain, agonizing and all too familiar. A closer look at the knife revealed what I feared: a coarse silver hair was tightly wound around the tip of the steel blade.

His laugh was almost a shriek now. I turned my shocked gaze to him and recoiled at the drastic change in his appearance. His golden armor hung on shrunken, wrinkled skin and a silver-gray beard fell past his waist.

"I have been waiting over a thousand years to have my revenge," he said, but his voice was as changed as his appearance. Its tone was guttural, like that of his servant, the Cobeld who had tried to kill me in the Great Wood. "I have parceled it out over the centuries, using those who pledged to be my subjects against the progeny of those who refused. But no matter how much death the curses I designed rained upon E'veria, it never sated my appetite for more. How could it while E'veria still had the hope of *you*!"

"How did you 'design' the curses?" Curiosity forced questions from my lips, but the first was followed by a gasp and the second, preceded by a groan. "How did the curses get inside the hairs of their beards?"

"Water," he spat with glee.

Pain swelled to a pitch I had known only once before. Opening the cell doors had nearly killed me, but I had a feeling this curse was meant to be drawn out longer. And it didn't have to enter me through my mind. It was already in my blood. I tried to hold back my scream, but the curse forced it from my lips, leaving the taste of greed and evil behind.

His laugh conveyed the pleasure he found in my pain. "Shireya was mine. The land, the mountain, the vineyards, and the springs. All gifted to me by Loeftryn de Rynloeft for my *loyal service*," he sneered. "Did you know, Ryn Naia, that the watered wine of Shireya was once E'veria's most lucrative export?"

"Watered wine?" My question came out through the clenched teeth of another chest spasm that had come too swiftly after the last. My knees ached, but below them? Nothing. It was almost as if the bottom halves of my legs were not there.

"Yes. It was purported to contain the healing properties of Shireya's mountain springs, and, indeed, it did. But it was I who discovered what could result when the water of the springs was combined with things other than wine. Things like yellowhock pollen." His laugh contained the very essence of evil. "And extract of ebonswarth root."

My brain swam between pain and horror. Yellowhock caused distress to the lungs, the eyes, the nose. And it might have contributed to my nightmares. And ebonswarth root was not just the effective dye that had kept my hair black while I'd lived in Veetri, but a powerful substance that, when ingested, caused people like Sir Kile to act in ways contrary to their convictions. Combined, I could only imagine what terror and devastation they could cause in a person's mind.

"You're a—" My throat suddenly spasmed and I choked. "Monster!"

"And you will soon be dead," he replied darkly. "But lest you think your death will be quick, Ryn Naia, let me assure you that I will not be satisfied unless I am allowed to savor this triumph. No, your death will not be swift, but it is sure."

His tone changed, then—almost back to that of the knight he had been before. "It is a shame, really," he said. "You could have had the beautiful knight as husband, you know. I would have never needed to reveal this cursed skin to you."

I wasn't sure he was capable of feeling grief, yet his voice held the smallest tone of regret.

Almost as if he'd become aware of that weak emotion, he made a sound that morphed from a growl to a shriek. "You could have had more power than you ever dreamed!"

The sound he made next reminded me of the young wild-cat that had attacked Gerrias, it was so feral, so shrill. "You are more foolish than even your ancestors," he screeched. "Andov was filled with the capacity for power, but refused to claim it for himself. And Stoen?" He expelled the name with supreme distaste. "An idealistic slave! He had no ambition, no real power of his own!"

He was wrong. Stoen—Stoenryn, rather—had a gift that, had Cobeld sought it, would have changed the course of history. "Humility is a purer power," I whispered.

But he didn't hear me until another scream was yanked from my throat, and by then his eerie laugh was building again.

"Stoen always saw himself through the eyes of a servant, a slave. I was a *leader* of men. When I spoke, people listened and obeyed. But that tainted history no longer matters. Once you are dead—and I do enjoy hearing the sounds you make as my curse takes hold of each new piece of you—I will have won. At long last I will be freed from this prison. And I will kill your friends with as much slow but certain pleasure as I have now in killing you." He laughed again and even the sound seemed to speed the path of the curse. "I will then dispatch your father," he said, "and take E'veria as my own. As it should have been all along."

My head pounded from the poison snaking its way through my blood. The baneful venom infiltrated every cell of my body, one drip at a time. *Help me!* I cried out to The First, even as he sent reminders of poetry to my thoughts.

Shale of flour from the loaf, in water dropped, a moment soaked.

I had no feeling left below my waist. Using my arms, I dragged my body closer to the protrusion at the top of the rocky platform. I could no longer see Cobeld. I only hoped he hadn't decided to climb the rock himself, because if I was forced to fight him, the curse would numb my heart before I reached the Remedy.

I breathed through another chest spasm. One more inch and I could just reach the rounded protrusion.

With Cobeld's dagger, stained red with my blood, I reached toward the lumpy growth on the stone. I pulled the blade across it and a fine powder, as white as a cloud on a summer's day, fell from its surface.

I set the dagger down and swept the powder—the shale of flour—into a small pile. Now . . . I needed water. But where would I find water?

There was plenty of water on the other side of the tunnel, so much that I had been forced to wade through it. Could there yet be enough still in my garments after this much time?

I grabbed hold of my sleeve. It was damp, but not wet. I squeezed and squeezed until my hand shook, but only one small drop landed on the pile of powder. I squeezed the other sleeve, and then painstakingly pulled my legs forward to wring the cuffs of my pants. A filmy white stripe on my pant leg reminded me that the water was salty.

Would saltwater work? I wondered. *Or did the Remedy require freshwater?* Water was water, right?

But it didn't matter. There wasn't enough.

The pain increased with every second, so much so, that even though my hands seemed to be working of their own accord, I could barely think. My senses were failing. I could see nothing but a pinprick of the scene in front of me. My eyes burned with tears.

Tears.

Tears are just saltwater, I thought through the pain pounding in my head. I cupped my shaking hand under my chin.

Excruciating torment reached deep within my bones, a torture so constant that I couldn't imagine my eyes ever being dry again. But would even my tears be enough? Would it work? Or would I die here, the prelude to Cobeld's imminent invasion and the death of E'veria?

Numbness stole past my waist. It wouldn't be long before my arms were paralyzed. Already they tingled with the pins and needles of reduced circulation.

Unseeing, I pressed my finger into the palm cupped under my chin to catch my tears. It might be just enough.

Blindly, I reached toward the powder and pinched a tiny bit between my finger and thumb. I released it into my tear-filled palm. My hand shook so that I feared I would spill the Remedy. If I did, I would surely die from Cobeld's curse. I raised my palm to my lips and tipped the chalky, salty mixture into my mouth.

Just as it touched my tongue, my spine seized and the curse took hold of a fresh part of me. I swallowed and concentrated on keeping my hand at my mouth. Only with utter concentration was I able to push my tongue through my lips. With slow, meticulous motions, I licked whatever remained of the Remedy powder and tears off the surface of my palm until my arm fell useless on the rock beside me.

"It won't be long now!" Cobeld cackled with glee as I fell over on my back. "I can feel the curse moving through your blood, Ryn Naia. You are as good as dead."

I feared he was right. My limbs were heavy and disconnected from my control by the curse's paralysis. It could be mere minutes until my heart gave out or my throat closed off to breath, but at least for the moment, my lungs still took in air and I still had my voice.

Although the pain was strong, there was a strength beyond it to which I had access.

Embral e' Veria . . . Even as my power to think began to stall, I silently called out to The First. I imbued my request with everything I believed about him and everything I knew to be true about that particular and precious name, knowing that, even at the cusp of death, I would be cradled in the arms of unquenchable love, whether they bore me to health . . . or to Rynloeft.

Beneath my tunic, hanging from a chain around my neck, the Emblem of The First began to warm the skin on which it rested.

My tongue was swollen, my lips numb, but somehow, my next words came out clearly. And even as I uttered them, peace stole a bit of my agony.

"I belong to The First, Cobeld. With all that I am and for all of my life, I am his. And I am loved. Even your curse cannot take me from his care."

"His *care*?" Cobeld laughed bitterly, mocking me. "You're dying. I *have* thwarted his plan! I have defeated the prophesied Ryn Naia, and in so doing, I have defeated the First King!"

His shout of triumph echoed around the chamber. "I knew his power would someday be mine! You could have shared it with me, but you are a fool!"

"I never wanted the sort of power you desire, Cobeld," I said more softly, each word scraping painfully through my lungs and throat, "I only wanted the Remedy. I only wanted to accomplish the task assigned to me by The First."

"You are nothing but his slave. Just like Stoen was." Disgust coated each syllable he uttered, only to be replaced with a sheen of pride. "I gave you that pain! *I* spoke the curse over that hair that is killing you! I am your master now, for I have all the power over you!"

My chest tightened. Pain shot down my shoulder, curling the fingers I could barely feel. My breath curdled in my throat.

Embral e' Veria . . . I called out to one whose unlimited power was drenched in unquenchable love. *I am yours.*

I would soon lose consciousness, but even then he could bless the Remedy I had ingested and save my life.

But even if he didn't, even if this next, liquid breath was my last, I would remain steadfastly *his.*

Pins and needles sparked to life in my numbed arms, leaving a blessed, awful throb in their wake. My spine relaxed. My jaw unclenched. My lungs cleared.

The stimulus worked its way down my legs, prickling and kneading its way through every sinew, every joint, every bone and muscle. I gasped as the skin on my calf sizzled and stretched, melting back together in a series of excruciating moments that cauterized the wound Cobeld's cursed dagger had rent there.

One of my fingers felt suddenly heavy and I met it across my stomach with the other hand.

The engagement ring, I thought.

Ryn alone must foe engage and settle in eternal cage.

A sweet, searing sensation, as if pure light had shot through my veins, shocked another gasp from my lips. And then . . . the pain was gone.

Utterly. Gone.

I sat up and peered over the edge of the rock platform to meet his beady black eyes. "It would appear this power you're so proud of is rather limited."

Cobeld's ancient face drooped with shock.

Concentrating the full expanse of my gifts and my mother's blessing, I spoke to the cracked floor, aimed the offensive ring at a spot just in front of Cobeld's feet, and let it fly.

The ring made a high, tinkling sound as it hit the glass-like floor, but the impact sent millions of fissures racing around Cobeld. He looked down and, just as he lifted his face to send one last, loathing look my way, the barrier above the chasm cracked all the way through.

The floor opened beneath Cobeld's feet and swallowed Everia's most ancient enemy in its gaping mouth.

"*Nooooooo . . . !*"

Cobeld's shriek of disbelief was followed by a string of vile curses directed not at me, but at The First himself. They echoed off the walls like an evil refrain, singeing the air as he fell into the depths of his fathomless, eternal cage.

FORTY-THREE

shocking length of time stretched while Cobeld's screams echoed up from the depths into which he had fallen. Eventually, I covered my ears and hummed a monotone buzz to block it out, to cancel the reality of how deep, how incredibly, frighteningly deep that chasm was. When the ancient traitor's shrieks were far enough into the chasm that I could pretend he wasn't still falling, I took stock of my situation.

Not good.

Yes, I had found the Remedy. I had even used it successfully.

Thank you, I whispered again. Without that tiny bit of powder, scraped off the surface of the Remedy stone, I would be dead.

But even though I had defeated my foe and found the object of my quest, what remained of the Remedy—and that was most of it, since I could barely even note where I'd scraped the knife—wouldn't do anyone else any good unless I found a way out of this chamber. The transparent floor was gone. I'd defeated Cobeld, but I was trapped in the center of the chasm. Unless I could find a way out, the Remedy wasn't going to be able to serve its purpose and heal those afflicted with the Cobeld curse.

And neither was I.

Death and failure were still very real possibilities.

The distance between my perch on the rock platform and the tunnel entrance was too far to even try to jump. I closed my eyes.

Where's a bridge builder when you need one? I thought ruefully, picturing the filthy form of Taef de Emwyk. I had no wish to join Cobeld in the abyss.

My feet were level with the tunnel entrance, but even if I stripped to the skin, tied my clothes end to end, and bent the dagger into some sort of rudimentary grappling hook, there was no way I would make it. I sighed. One thing at a time.

I put aside the thought of how to make my escape and took a moment to inspect the Remedy more closely. I gave it a gentle shove and . . . it moved.

The gift will rise when the way is sure.

Well, good. It was ready to go. But even if I could jump and manage to make it far enough to scramble up, I couldn't do it carrying the Remedy, and it wasn't worth trying to leave without it. Retrieving the Remedy was the reason I had come on this quest in the first place!

I picked it up easily. For its size, the Remedy was surprisingly light. I laughed. It did look a bit like a large, round loaf of bread now that I thought about it. And when I had run Cobeld's dagger across it, the powder that resulted and healed me did resemble flour.

I rested it on my lap. When I stretched out my legs, it nearly covered the span from my hips to my knees and overhung my legs on both sides. I had no pack, but I doubted that it would have fit inside mine anyway. And unless I figured out a way to cross the chasm, it didn't matter.

I let out a deep breath and then sucked it back in when a drop of something hit my head. I reached up and felt moisture. *Ting.*

A small, wet something landed on the rock. *Ting.* Another drop hit my hand and . . . glittered. *Ting-ting-ting.* Glimmering water droplets danced upon the rock, picking up the rhythm of their song until there were so many coming at once that I could not distinguish one raindrop from another.

Rain? I held out my hand, catching the evidence within it. *But I'm inside a mountain!*

I lifted my gaze upward. Far above me, the cavern's domed ceiling glowed as brightly as if the moon itself had fallen from the sky and lodged in a hole atop the mountain. As the drops of water fell from the glow, they streaked across the space like thousands of miniscule stars.

Puddles began to gather on the surface of the rock and on the porous surface of the Remedy. The puddles glowed as if made from light itself. I looked up again and then down. I leaned as close as I could to the surface of the rock and discovered . . .

Enikkas! Each drop of rain transported a small swarm of enikkas!

I would have been content to sit there and let myself be drowned in it, but reality burst through my brain. What would happen to the Remedy if it got wet? Even my tears had dissolved the powder I'd scraped from its surface. As quickly as I could, I unbuttoned my tunic, untucked my shirt, and pushed the Remedy between the fabric and my skin to give it some protection against the rain. It was tight, but not cold as I had expected. In fact, it seemed to almost put off warmth. It stretched the fabric and grated against my skin, but at least it wouldn't dissolve.

At least not right away.

As the puddles filled, they grew brighter and brighter. With each glittering drop from the glowing ceiling, more enikkas graced the rock, filling the puddles and covering everything on the rock, including me.

Their heat was stronger here than what I had felt from them within the Bay of Tirandov or in the pool by which my friends awaited my return. There were so many of them! And their population was so concentrated that after only a few minutes I could barely suffer look at their beautiful brightness.

The waterfall was not the living precipitate after all, I smiled. *It was real rain. Enikka rain!*

Without my consent, my body shifted position. I gasped as the top of the rock formation tipped—and continued to tip!—at an ever-increasing angle. I rolled onto my stomach, or rather, on top of the Remedy still under my tunic, and grasped for a hold to keep from sliding off the now-slippery top of the rock platform. My fingers met water and enikkas before they sank into a thick mud.

Mud?

The top of the rock had turned into clay—and into something I could sink my fingers into for a hold, at least for a little while. The moisture and heat of the tiny creatures was changing the very composition of the rock platform!

I lifted my head and looked behind me. The structure was now bending ever so slightly toward the tunnel. Huddling over the Remedy, I pushed my knees, feet, and hands into the soft clay to hold on as the rock formation continued to bend by nearly indiscernible increments, gently leaning and curving toward the tunnel opening.

Where my hands held, the enikkas moved away and, without the wet heat, the clay hardened around each finger. I couldn't wiggle a single digit, so firmly were they encased in the rock.

The platform shifted faster, as if now that they had ensured that I wouldn't fall, the enikkas had burrowed inside the rock itself and were heating and melding it from within. A short time later, my body was at a nearly perpendicular plane to the chasm, but, although my stomach protested what my head knew to be true, the rock around my fingers and feet and knees was so hard that I knew I would not fall.

I am with you.

The Voice of The First sang a song of rescue in my mind. His proclamation, so true it might have been audible, echoed comfort through my blood as enikkas dripped though my hair and down my neck, tickling me with their warmth. My joy bubbled up with laughter.

"Of course you are with me!" I shouted, tilting my head back so I could better see the beauty of his illuminate provision. "I am yours!"

Myriad colors washed over me with one thread common to them all: *love.* Enormous, unquenchable, amazing love.

Suddenly, my joyous laughter was stilled by the overwhelming awe of being within the protective embrace of the very one who'd created not only me, not only the enikkas, but the very stars. I stayed like that, reveling in the care of The First, until the enikkas moved back toward my hands.

The clay loosened around my fingers—and my stomach dropped somewhere near my knees.

"Uhhhh . . ." My voice quavered. What were they *doing?* If they loosened my fingers I would fall!

Still huddled around the Remedy, I suddenly realized that there was a firm surface pressing against my backside. I twisted my head just slightly to find the bottom of the tunnel entrance directly behind my shoulders.

The enikkas' warm bodies never stopped moving. They loosened the clay around my fingers, knees, and the toes of my boots so that I could move, but my body—and the Remedy—were still supported by the pliable rock.

I took a deep breath, and supporting the Remedy with one hand, leaned back. My breath came in short but deep bursts as I pulled my right knee free of the warm clay. A slurping sound accompanied the release of my knee, and again when I pulled out my foot.

I pressed the flat of my freed right foot against the clay. Ever conscious of the chasm below, I used that foot for leverage and pressed my back even harder against the rock wall behind me. When I felt moderately secure, I eased my left knee free and then the other foot.

The sound of my panting echoed louder than the screams of Cobeld, now barely discernable below. Fear of falling, combined with the effort of keeping my precarious grip, marred my vision with dizziness.

If I was going to have the strength to get the Remedy and myself into the tunnel just above my shoulders I would have to regulate my breathing and restore my balance—or whatever semblance of it I could have while my seat was dangling over fathoms of empty air.

I pressed my back into the wall just below the tunnel entrance and my feet against the hardening rock that the enikkas' heat had tipped toward my escape, and then concentrated on calming my mind with comforting memories.

Riding Stanza across the Veetrish countryside.

Swimming with the enikkas.

Julien, pressing the first of his notes into my hand.

Dots receded from my vision as my breathing calmed. I wiped as much of the slippery clay as I could from my fingers onto my pants and carefully, so very carefully, pulled the Remedy out from under my shirt.

But it slipped!

"No!" With a gasp, I lurched left to grasp it back from where it seemed destined to slip off the tips of my fingers. The Remedy bobbled on my slick hand. As I slapped the other on top of it, my right foot slid in the opposite direction and the majority of my weight was redistributed to my left hip and shoulder.

Using every muscle in my abdomen and legs, I jammed the Remedy against my neck for support, and wrenched myself back to an upright, more supported position.

When my blood slowed to an almost normal velocity, I lifted the Remedy above my head and pressed it against the rock wall. Carefully, I lifted it up. . . and up . . . until gravity pulled the "loaf" into the tunnel entrance. I cringed as precious flour sloughed off into my eyes, but I gave it one good shove and sent it farther into the tunnel.

I let out a sigh and smiled. The Remedy was safe. If I didn't return, Julien would come down the tunnel to find me. And though he would see the chasm, guess my fate, and grieve, he would recognize the Remedy for what it was and ferry it back to our people.

Yes, the Remedy was safe.

But I was stuck.

From the other side of the tipping rock, a sudden glow appeared as enikkas swarmed to a space just a handbreadth beneath my feet. The rock stayed firm where it supported me, but just below my feet it grew slick again and so bright with enikkas that it hurt my eyes. Still, I couldn't look away, as curious as I was to see what the sweet creatures would do next.

Brighter and hotter they glowed until sweat dripped down my back and all I saw was light, with blackness ringing around it. Slicker and slicker the clay grew until the light itself seemed to be sliding on it, arching down and out. My body contracted with the pressure of the rock until my knees, which had been almost extended as they braced against the rock, were bent so severely that they were level to my chin.

The enikkas moved away.

As my eyes readjusted to the dimness, my gaze caught upon a shelf of sorts jutting out beneath my feet—a ledge I could use as leverage to turn and face the tunnel entrance, and hopefully, pull myself inside.

If I never again had to perform the contortions my body was forced to execute in order to do as the enikkas desired, it would be too soon, but somehow I managed to turn around. With the pumice of the tunnel digging into my fingers, I shoved off the tilting rock and used the strength of my arms to pull my body up and into the tunnel's mouth.

FORTY-FOUR

Once inside the tunnel, I cringed at the trail of white that had been left behind when I had shoved the Remedy across the sharp, porous surface. Mindful of what a precious substance I was transporting, I used an immense amount of care, lifting the Remedy and moving it forward, before wriggling behind it a little at a time. I did not want to risk losing any more of the priceless "flour" when I knew so many people were in need of its healing properties.

My torch from Tirandov was still on my back belt loop, but the tunnel was also illumined by the enikkas clinging to my hair and clothing. They kept me company and kept me warm, lighting the long trek back to my friends.

Finally, the sound of the waterfall bubbled over my ears. By the time that gleaming ribbon was in sight, my cheeks ached from the breadth of the smile that lit my face. Joy poured out of my mind, and rather than censuring or saving it, I set its course with a specific destination in mind.

Just inside the mouth of the tunnel, still behind the waterfall, I paused, closed my eyes, and pictured my father's face.

As soon as I made the connection I let my colors fly without the need for words. My joy soared beyond Mount Shireya and north through the mountain's northern foothills to the King.

When I opened my eyes I felt more alive than I had since the night I met the enikkas for the first time in Tirandov's bay. I stuck my head through the tunnel entrance that now, thankfully, also served as an exit.

I could sense my friends beyond the waterfall and knew they were as of yet unaware of my return. *I'm back!* I sent the words to Dyfnel and Edru, who were less likely to be shocked to find my voice in their heads. *I have the Remedy!*

A moment later, Julien's head appeared in the tunnel entrance.

"Thank Rynloeft, you're alive!" Julien reached over the Remedy and pressed his palm to the side of my face. "I feared . . ." he trailed off and closed his eyes. "There are no words, Rynnaia."

"I know of three that would soothe my ears."

His brow constricted in concern. "Does your ear still pain you?"

"No." The admission surprised me. In light of what Cobeld's direct curse had inflicted upon me, I had nearly forgotten about the injuries I'd sustained while freeing Drinius and Gladiel. I took a moment to mentally examine myself and then grinned. "In fact, I believe it's been healed!"

It appeared the Remedy had worked on both curses I'd received.

He blinked. "Your face," he said, reaching in to run a hand over my cheek. "I was so happy to see you that I didn't notice it at first, but your bruises from the yellowhock are . . . gone."

I could only thank The First and the Remedy he had provided. There was no other explanation.

"Take this." I lifted the Remedy and set it in his hands. "And be careful, please." I winked and coated my words with the thickest version of a Veetrish brogue I could conjure. "That's precious cargo, it is!"

"I'll be right back." He grinned, took the Remedy, and disappeared.

I twisted a bit, but the tunnel was too narrow to allow me to turn around. In this headfirst position, getting out was going to be . . . interesting, even with help.

I had just about decided to follow the path of the waterfall and hope there weren't rocks below—or some strange force that wanted to drown me again—when Julien reappeared.

"Ah, there's my Story Girl."

"Story Girl?"

"You're covered in enikkas." He chuckled. "That's why I called you Story Girl. You shimmer like something out of a Veetrish tale."

"I suppose I do," I said with a laugh of my own. "But without Rowlen here to assist, I'm not sure I know how to get out of here on my own."

Julien examined the tunnel, the ledge on which he stood, and the waterfall behind him. "This isn't going to be easy. But first, about those three words you mentioned?"

Something warm and delicious stirred in me when he held up the palm of the hand where he'd kept my kiss back at Holiday Palace. I placed my hand, the one he'd kissed again only days ago, to his.

"I love you, Rynnaia."

"That was four words," I said, quirking a grin. "But since I love you, I'll forgive your rotten arithmetic."

With his guidance, I stretched my arms. He leaned in so I could latch them around his neck. As our faces neared, it was as if an uncharted sense of destiny pulled our lips closer to each other.

Our noses brushed and Julien turned his head so that our cheeks pressed tightly against one another rather than our lips. I couldn't help but feel a little disappointed, but all things considered, especially his precarious balance on the ledge, it was probably best.

"Careful, now," he said, his voice low and rough. "Slowly, slowly . . ." He inched down the ledge. "Now curl your upper body to wrap around me." I did. He inched another step and—

"Julien, wait. My boot's caught on something." I wiggled my foot. "Okay, try again."

He took another step to the side, but my boot caught again.

"Errgh," I growled and yanked my leg. The pumice loosed its hold on my boot, but I knocked Julien off balance. He started to fall backward into the waterfall. I reached for him and caught the edge of his tunic, but when he couldn't regain his balance, we both fell. Before we hit the water, his arms surrounded me.

Always my knight, he never let go. In fact, he pushed me to the surface of the pool a second before his own face met the air.

"Some men will do anything for the chance to hold the princess in their arms, won't they?" Kinley's dry comment was followed by a laugh and an offer of his hand. "Here you go now, Princess. Up and out."

For some unknown reason that I could only blame on growing up in Veetri, I took hold of Kinley's offered hand and pulled him into the water.

Erielle burst out laughing. Soon everyone else did, too— and we laughed even harder when Kinley came up sputtering.

"I can't believe you did that!"

"I can't believe you fell for it!" I treaded water, laughing. "But what are little sisters for?"

"Little sisters," he said with a grin, "are for dunking, I think."

"Oh, no you don't!"

His lip twitched and when he moved forward, I knew what was coming, having experienced the same thing at Rowlen's hands many, many times.

I took a deep breath and dove out of the way. When I came up on the other side of the pool, he laughed. I looked up and caught the eye of Julien's brother. His shoulders shook.

"Gerrias, what is the punishment for dunking a princess, do you think?"

"A regular princess?" he asked. "Or the Ryn?"

"The Ryn, of course."

"Hmm. Beheading, I think. Yes, most definitely beheading."

I grinned at Kinley. "Well, then."

"Indeed," he said with a chuckle. He turned to Gerrias. "She goes and finds a little rock we've searched centuries for, and all of a sudden she's too good for a dunking."

I caught Erielle's eye. She gave the slightest nod toward Kinley, who now had his back to me. I ducked under the water and opened my eyes. As soon as I was right behind him, I sprang up. Latching my fingers together on the top of his head, I pushed him under. Swift as I could, I swam to the edge, took Gerrias's offered hand, and let him pull me out of the water.

"Well done, Princess," Erielle said, giving me a quick hug. "You've made little sisters around the world very proud today."

"So," I said after the moment of levity passed and Gerrias had pulled both Julien and Kinley out of the pool. "How do we get out of this mountain?"

"It's surprisingly easy, from here," Gerrias said. "At least as far as the chamber of the three doors. From there it's anybody's guess."

"Well, what are we waiting for?" I pushed to my feet. "Let's go!"

"Wait." Dyfnel put a hand on my shoulder. "We should contact your parents."

"I already contacted my father," I said, looking around the group. "He is within half a day's ride of the mountain. Do you mind if I take a minute to try and speak with my mother?"

I moved to the side of the room, took a deep breath, and closed my eyes. *"Mother."*

My mind raced to Tirandov Isle and deep into the castle where she slept.

But she did not awaken.

FORTY-FIVE

he Remedy was safely stowed in Dyfnel's larger pack. After I bid farewell to the enikkas, we waded back down the stream and toward our exit route.

"Oh, one thing," Gerrias paused just before the passageway he and Edru had discovered during my absence. "Remember how we chose the one tunnel from the three? The one that took us to Halo's Rim?"

"Yes." I nodded, remembering Risson's proclamation. "Silence was dimmed by sound. Julien said it sounded like hail was falling in that one passage."

"Exactly. But it wasn't hail."

Gerrias had carried me through that passage and my mind had gone so quickly to Dwons, to help rescue Drinius and Gladiel, that I had never learned what had made the sound. With all that had followed after, I hadn't thought to ask. It hadn't seemed important.

Now, however, it seemed . . . ominous.

"If it wasn't hail," I asked, "what was it?"

"Bats."

"Bats?"

"Yes. And there are more of them in this particular tunnel."

The reassuring way Gerrias smiled made it seem like it was nothing, but my mind flew directly to his bandaged arm and the memory of what had given him that injury. Bat rhymed with cat. Were the bats in Shireya as different from elsewhere as the cats were?

"Are they regular bats?" I asked. "Or some insanely large and scary version that wants to eat us?"

Gerrias laughed. "Just bats. Little brown bats. They're a bit more active than what I've seen elsewhere, scuttling between nooks and crannies about the walls and ceilings and such, but they seem content to keep their distance. I don't think you have anything to fear, but they do get a bit noisy in places and their droppings make the floor rather slippery in spots. I just thought I should warn you because I didn't think you'd noted them in that other passage."

I hadn't. And I was glad. I took a deep breath and nodded. "Lead on," I said and tried not to think about just how "active" bats must be to sound like hail inside a mountain.

At first there was little sound but for our footsteps. Edru took the opportunity to question me while the memory of my time away from them was still fresh.

As the official scribe of our quest, Edru was responsible for recording our journey for historical accuracy. Although I knew I would have to repeat the story of my encounter with Cobeld many times, there were some more delicate, regrettable bits of the tale I wished I could leave out. For the sake of truth, however, I couldn't. Therefore, it was with disjointed phrases and halting words that I recounted my tale.

Although everyone in our group was curious for details, Julien asked one question and one question only.

"You would have married *Cobeld*?"

My throat, already constricted with the regret of what I had just admitted, nearly closed at the sense of betrayal—*my* betrayal—in his tone. It took every bit of strength within me to meet his eyes.

"I thought he was the Remedy, Julien. Had I been convinced of his interpretation of the prophecy, of it being necessary for E'veria and required by The First, then yes. I would have married him."

The words came out in a steadier cadence than I expected, but still, nausea threatened to send me to my knees. I pulled more gray around my thoughts to keep them hidden from Edru and Dyfnel, as well as to keep my emotion from spilling out onto my friends. That I'd allowed Cobeld to twist the words of the prophecy so much that I had believed, even for a moment, that I was to be bonded with him in marriage, made me sick. But whatever the damage to my future with Julien, I could not, in good conscience, lie. And to gloss over the truth to make it easier on him would be no better than a lie.

"I love you," I said after a long pause in which he had looked away. And it was then my voice failed me and I had to swallow several times before continuing. "But I am the Ryn. The good of the Kingdom must be placed before my own heart."

Julien nodded, but without meeting my eyes. An uncomfortable silence descended on our group and Julien gradually retreated to the end of the line, as if distance could lessen the pain of my betrayal.

Could I blame him, really? While my heart well knew the grief I had experienced, thinking I was destined to marry the golden knight rather than the man I loved, I had not, nor could I, put those emotions into words. As with the rest of our group, all Julien likely heard in the tale—if he was able to process anything after the sting of my betrayal—was a broadly defined sense of regret and shame.

But what did his *heart* hear about the nature of my love, that I would so easily abandon him for another?

Sudden sound and movement up and to my left caused me to turn and lift my torch.

"Ugh." I squirmed in my skin. Part of the wall seemed as if it was crawling up onto the ceiling. A furry brown part of the wall.

Kinley turned around. "They're more afraid of you than you are of them," he said. But that was the most anyone said for a while, for the farther we went, the louder the scritching, scratching, and tapping of the bats' tiny claws became.

I concentrated on watching Kinley's back rather than the creeping creatures to either side of the tunnel, but from the rear of our group, thick colors of betrayal fell off Julien like waves bearing my name. Even had the bats decided to attack, the intensity of his colors would have rendered me mute to scream.

I longed to speak into his thoughts, to try and discern if it would be possible for him to forgive me for my near betrayal, but something inside me said that he needed time to process this on his own. The constant barrage of his pain, however, was more than I could take. I reached into myself, pulling more gray around my mind with which to insulate my heart from his reaction to what I had almost done.

As I had answered Edru's questions, I'd sensed some shock from the others at how Cobeld had twisted the prophecy's words, and even a bit at how I had almost fallen for his lies. But if they hadn't already accepted my words and forgiven my near-calamitous mistake, they would in time. To Julien, however, it was a much more personal injury. Would he forgive me? Could he?

I could hardly blame him if he didn't. I had come so close to rejecting him. Rejecting *us*. Even though truth had prevailed in the end and the Kingdom's future might soon be secured, the sting of what *might have been* could prove fatal to his ability to trust in my love.

As we walked on through the bat-domed corridors of the tunnel, my chest ached and throbbed. Not from any injury sustained to my person or from a Cobeld curse, but from having to accept that, by telling the truth, I may have lost Julien.

Misery clawed at my heart and I was forced to pull a bit more gray to my thoughts to keep that toxic emotion from leaking to my friends.

This was not some simple argument, or even a matter of me challenging Julien's authority or him challenging mine. This was a life-altering, possibly trust-killing truth. If he continued to court me, if we were to marry, he would always carry the memory of how willingly I'd considered discarding his love to marry a stranger. Would he ever be able to trust that my affection could be faithfully his?

My breath shallowed and my eyes burned as I tried to picture my life without Julien's love. The tunnel seemed to close in around me. My hand itched with imagined ugliness where Cobeld had kissed it, and I longed for water and lye to rid myself of his taint.

How could I keep company with Julien as simply a knight, a future Regent, when every moment my heart would be crying—no, *screaming*—that he should be a prince? *My* prince!

I sniffed and wiped my eyes. *I could ask my father to assign him duties farther away,* I supposed.

No. I couldn't do that to Julien. He deserved every honor the King had given him and more.

Suddenly dizzy, I paused as my field of vision became narrower even than the path. How would I bear going back to being little more than strangers?

May it not be so! I entreated Rynloeft. *I love him!*

I was thankful for the bats, that their skittery feet would hide the tiny series of sobs that gasped just enough air into my body that I could walk again. I wiped the wetness from my cheeks with my sleeve and tried to steady my breath.

I will never love another like I love Julien, I thought, and wiped away a fresh stream of tears. *If necessary, I will remain a maiden Queen.*

I tripped when that strategy was borne away by reason. If there was to be an E'veri on the throne, eventually I had to marry and produce a Ryn to lead the next generation of the Kingdom.

And the E'veri family always married for love.

A sob jolted my chest while recovering from my stumble and my foot slipped on bat droppings. I reached out for something to break my fall—something that wasn't a winged rodent—and managed to snag the back of Kinley's pack. My knees hit stone, but Kinley turned and caught me before my hands touched the disgusting floor.

When he met my eyes, Kinley frowned, somehow knowing that my tears had not been caused by my fall. He looked past me, as if searching for the one who had caused my distress, that he might avenge his sister, his friend.

I squeezed his arm and shook my head, gesturing for him to keep moving. His frown deepened, but he complied.

Despair sank blackened pegs into my heart, but I continued to wrap my thoughts, reaching for a gray so dark that it was nearly charcoal. My friends needed to remain unified. They needed me to stay strong, to see this quest through to its end. I reached for more and more gray, making sure my thoughts were available to none but myself, but my heart cried Julien's name over and over.

I would not trespass into Julien's thoughts, but I looked over my shoulder, thinking that if I caught his eye I might gain some idea of where he stood as he processed what he had learned. But my view of Julien was blocked. Even had Edru not been directly behind me, there would have still been Dyfnel between us. I could not see Julien. And without the further betrayal of looking into his thoughts without permission, I had no way to know if there was any hope for us.

I faced forward, but paused when Edru laid a hand on my shoulder.

"You did nothing wrong, Princess," he said, leaning toward my ear so that I could hear him above the scratching of the bats.

Edru's voice was so kind that I couldn't help but turn and look up into the matching gentleness of his rare smile. The compassion I found there was so pure, so full of friendship, that it brought fresh tears to my eyes.

"It is only his pride that is wounded," he said. "Not his love. He will come around."

Directly in front of me, Kinley snorted and threw a scowl over his shoulder. "He'd better." He angled his gaze down to me. "I will not tolerate his jealous pride making you weep."

I could hardly believe Kinley had been able to hear my quiet tutor above the noise of the bats. I was gratified by his loyalty, but I could hardly support his desire for vengeance.

"His pain is justified," I said, "and I bear the responsibility of causing it, for my actions gave him cause to doubt my love and fealty. We must allow him to choose the path it will take. And I must accept whatever will come."

My tears slowed then, and though gloom dogged my steps, I recognized the truth of what I had told my brother.

Whatever conclusion Julien reached, I would have no choice but to accept it. Even if he chose to end our courtship, I wouldn't stand in his way. He deserved love with a woman whose fealty to their union he could trust.

If only he could get beyond what I had almost done and believe that I was still that woman.

FORTY-SIX

We reached a fork in the tunnel. Gerrias took us down the passage that veered right, and though it was absent of bats and their slippery droppings, our path became more arduous. The passage was so strewn with rubble that by the time we finally reached the chamber of the three doors, we were ready for a rest.

This was as far as Gerrias and Edru had searched. After having so much of our journey within the mountain fraught with things new and strange, it was rather odd to have returned to a place we'd been before. The door by which we had left this chamber, the one in which silence was dimmed by sound, was no more. It had caved in, most likely from the resulting tremors when the ceiling of Halo's Rim collapsed.

Just looking at that caved-in passage brought Sir Risson, and the grief of our loss of him, to mind. I had tasted from the rim of death's goblet three times now on this journey, but I had never been forced to tip the cup. I drew some comfort that the cursed arrow Risson had received led to an instantaneous death. At least he had not suffered.

After we had rested for a few minutes, Erielle pointed toward the well-formed, solid-looking tunnel. "What do you think, Rynnaia?"

I walked to the opening and closed my eyes, searching with my Andoven gifts for any hint of unfriendliness, but there was none. Our way was clear.

"It's safe."

The best door of the former three, north and out it will you lead. Out. That sounded absolutely divine.

"Good. I feel as though I've been underground for a year," Kinley grunted.

The pathway was easy to follow, but I hadn't fully appreciated how deeply into the mountain we had descended until "up" was our path out. All conversation stopped as the passageway grew steeper and narrower. We were forced to travel two abreast and then single file to give our complete attention to the rigorous climb.

"Look!" Erielle stopped, panting as she pointed upward. "Daylight! Is that the way out?"

"Yes," Kinley said. "I believe it must be."

"Finally!" Erielle was silent for a moment and then she let out a sound of supreme irritation. "*What* was she *thinking*?"

"Who?" I asked.

"Lady Anya!" She repeated the sound, but in a more staccato fashion. "Why did the scrolls take us over waterfalls, into battles at Halo's Rim, into a deep pool, and through underwater tunnels?" She shook her head. "This way is so much easier!"

"Easier now, perhaps," Kinley said. "But the Cobelds we met at Halo's rim likely came in this way. Remember when Rynnaia sensed the enemy from this path? Had we come around to the northern side of the mountain we might never have made it inside."

"True." Dyfnel shrugged. "But even had the way been clear, we cannot blame Lady Anya. She was only the vessel through which the prophecy flowed. And who are we to question The First?"

"Indeed." Gerrias's low voice rumbled, but I didn't have to be Andoven to know his remark was aimed at his brother much more than his sister.

"Hey! I just had an idea!" Erielle turned and grabbed my arm. "You killed Cobeld. With him dead, will the rest of the Cobelds die, too?"

"First of all," I said with a slight shiver, "I'm not even sure he's dead yet. For all we know, he could still be falling."

Erielle blinked. A moment later she mouthed the words, *"Eternal cage,"* followed by the whisper, "it never said he would die, did it?"

I shook my head. "But the prophecy said we would have a battle soon, outside the mountain, remember?"

She nodded. "So . . . unless it's just Dwonsil warriors out there . . ."

"I doubt it," Kinley spoke up. "That would be too easy."

I shot him a look. "Too *easy*?"

He winced. "Not that what you did in getting the Remedy was easy," he said, shooting a frown in the direction where Julien stood at the end of the line. "I meant after. The King will be there with his army, according to the scrolls. If it's just Dwonsil warriors, no Cobelds," he clarified, "our numbers alone will make it a swift battle. And if we've learned anything," again, he paused and glanced Julien's way, "it's that the scrolls don't promise victories to come without cost."

We trudged on, my heart shadowed in Julien's silence.

The cave again grew steeper until it felt like we were making an almost vertical climb. We didn't speak much for a while. Like our inward trek, a winding upward path spiraled toward the light of day, but it was much more contracted than the cavern chamber by which we'd entered.

"Gerrias. Kinley." When Julien called from the rear of our line, I almost choked. "Go ahead and scout the exit. Make sure it's clear."

Gerrias moved forward and Kinley angled around Erielle to join him. Only Gerrias returned, but when he rejoined us, he squeezed by me and the two Andoven men to report to Julien. "Kinley's standing guard," he said. "It's clear."

We weren't that far from the cave entrance. And Gerrias's deep voice carried well. He would have barely had to raise his voice to make it reach his brother's ears, but instead he had felt the need to go directly to his brother.

I hazarded a glance back. With Edru and Dyfnel still off to the side, having moved to allow Gerrias passage, I caught a glimpse of Julien's perplexed scowl.

He nodded. "Let's go, then."

"A word?"

Gerrias phrased the question as if he expected no other response but acquiescence. Even without using my Andoven abilities, I sensed the word he wished to share with his brother required privacy. I moved a bit farther up the tunnel, toward Erielle, who had nearly reached the exit.

"Princess Rynnaia." Julien's voice called out. "I would prefer you proceed no further until at least two knights are outside."

I swallowed. "Of course."

"Erielle, go ahead. Edru, Dyfnel, also."

Erielle, of course, had started up the last turn as soon as Gerrias had announced it was safe. At Julien's command, Edru followed her.

As Dyfnel passed by me, a few of Gerrias's words reached my ears. Though I tried not to listen to what he clearly intended to be a private conversation with his brother, in such a confined place it was impossible not to catch some words here and there. His first word was my brother's name, followed by something that sounded like, "And I agree." But as low as he spoke, I could not entirely define the context, only a random phrase here and there.

"Jealous pride . . . thwarted duty . . . cannot possibly comprehend . . . love her or not . . . does neither of you honor."

Heat flooded my cheeks and I wanted to flee, if only to lessen the sting of Gerrias's words. Julien's younger brother was dressing him down on my behalf. Even though I appreciated Gerrias's loyalty to me, clearly he did not understand how justified Julien was in feeling betrayed.

"By your leave, then, brother," Gerrias spoke in a normal volume now, "I will go out and guard our friends."

"Go." Julien answered.

Gerrias squeezed by me and moved up toward the daylight, only pausing long enough to turn and spear his brother with a long, hard gaze.

As Gerrias disappeared into the outside world, I glanced toward Julien. His eyes were fastened on the tunnel floor, his every muscle tensed as his fingers flexed, released, and flexed again. He took a deep breath and let it out through his nose. Finally, he lifted his head.

"I have failed you."

I blinked. "No." I shook my head. "Never."

"I made you weep."

I pressed my lips together to try to stem the renewal of tears. "You are justified in your feelings," I said finally. "I should have seen through Cobeld's deception earlier, that I didn't . . ."

He shook his head, stilling my words. "I should have been there. I should have protected you from his lies."

"You couldn't have. The scrolls forbid it. It was up to me. And . . . I did not see through him soon enough to prevent you from doubting my love." I took a shaking breath. "The fault is mine and I shall do my best to bear the natural consequences of my faithlessness."

Julien raked his fingers through his hair and fisted them around a clump at the crown of his head before the hand returned to his side, only to lift again a moment later and repeat the action.

"Everyone is waiting for us," I said. "Perhaps even Taef has arrived with the horses. We should go."

Julien nodded stiffly, but his frown deepened. "Wait. Remember what the scrolls say? 'To end the curse you must endure the perils out Shireya's door that lead to poisoned reservoir.'" He quoted the poetry, wincing a bit at the irregular phrasing, and then pointed toward the exit. "That's the door. Beyond it, the scrolls promise a battle. The imagery of war 'raging,' of poisons that must be ingested, of curses that must be received and expelled . . ." He paused. "These are not words that make me want to rush ahead. Especially when there is so much that must still be decided between us."

My breath stalled. This was it, then. He was going to withdraw his suit.

"Your Highness—"

"Stop calling me that!"

My hand flew up to cover my lips. Would I be so selfish as to deny him the dignity of formality?

"Forgive me. I should not have interrupted you." I closed my eyes for a moment. "Julien," I said when he remained silent, "I will not argue what you intend to say, but please understand that whatever action I might have been willing to undertake on behalf of my Kingdom, I could not renounce the claim you have on my heart, not even when I was convinced I would have to give you up to bond myself to Cobeld."

He flinched, more in his eyes than the rest of him, but it burned a fresh wave of tears in my own.

"That my actions hurt you is my deepest shame, and I shall carry it all my days."

My tears spilled then and my voice was reduced to a whisper that exerted so much pressure along my throat that it was as if each word, each breath, was passing through an iron fist.

"I love you, Julien. I—" A sob nearly forced its way through my lips, but I choked it back. "I understand if you hate me now. I will accept the consequences for my betray—"

"Rynnaia."

Not *Princess Rynnaia*. Not *Your Highness*. Just *Rynnaia*.

When I looked up, he was directly in front of me.

"Rynnaia, I'm sorry."

Grief for what could have been, had I not been so gullible to have let Cobeld twist the words of the prophecy, filled me with a dead sort of acceptance. "I understand, Julien. You must withdraw your suit."

"That is not my intention."

It . . . wasn't? "But how will you even look at me and not see me as one who scorned your devotion?"

I gasped as he gathered me into his arms, but I pressed my face into his shoulder, knowing it might well be the last time I was able to draw such comfort from him.

"Julien, please do not remain entangled in this courtship if your only desire is to prevent causing me dishonor. The dishonor is already mine. You've no need to take it upon yourself and continue your suit as if nothing happened. I betrayed you!" The sob would no longer be contained. "Julien, I'm sorry. I'm so, so sorry!"

His hand pressed against the back of my head, stroking my hair. "You have nothing to be sorry for, other than that you've allowed yourself to love the chief of fools."

"But—"

"Please. Let me finish." His voice rumbled with an ache, a longing grief that made my chest constrict even more. "When I think of what you had to face, and that you had to figure it out all alone . . ." He took a shaking breath. "I will never fully comprehend the magnitude of what you experienced in that chamber with Cobeld and his cunning knowledge of the scrolls' contents. He threw a cursed dagger at you! You could have died!" His voice broke.

"I'm a knight, Rynnaia. *Your* knight. And it burns my soul and scalds my oath that I could not protect you from that fiend." He took a deep breath. "I understand the concept of duty to the Kingdom. I may have allowed jealousy and pride to blind me for a while, but that does not erase the fact that 'duty' is exactly what you were prepared to perform, even against your own heart.

"I love you, Rynnaia. I cannot imagine a life without you. Can you forgive me for being a jealous suitor and a prideful knight?"

"You—" I hiccupped. "You do not wish to withdraw your suit?"

"Quite the contrary," he said. "Will you forgive me?"

My throat was so tight and my heart so full that it took me a long moment before I found the words—and a few moments more before they were given passage.

"It is the calling of love to forgive," I parroted his own words, words spoken to me weeks ago at the devastated farmstead. I lifted my face to meet his eyes, which shined with a love I feared I would never see again. "I would forgive you anything, Julien. Anything."

His expression grew pensive. "Would you?"

Even the shadows couldn't mask Julien's intent. I closed my eyes as his face lowered and his lips met mine. His kiss was soft, restrained, but colors bloomed in my mind.

Like seeking hands, strands of green and blue reached through the gloomy gray protection I had placed between us, joined a spare second later by gold and orange. Once our colors met, they grasped on to each other and entwined. The gray despair turned to mist and simply faded away, leaving the beauty of forgiveness, love, and peace in its wake.

Our lips parted too soon, but Julien rested his forehead against mine for several breaths.

"I have long dreamed of kissing you," he said at last. "I had hoped that our first would be sweet."

I swallowed, and sudden shyness turned my words to whispers. "And was it?"

"Can fire be sweet?" His smile said it could. "Before today, I would have said no."

"And now?"

"And now I know that it is."

He dipped his head and touched his lips briefly to mine once more before taking my hand and leading me out of the mountain.

FORTY-SEVEN

We were standing just beyond the cave, my hand clasped in Julien's, when Taef arrived. In truth, he looked no worse for the journey, but considering his normal appearance, that wasn't saying much. Taef's eyes roved the group, but when they found me, he dropped the reins of our horses, ran, and fell upon me, sobbing my name.

I patted his back, but when I thought I saw something crawling in his hair, I quickly disengaged from his embrace.

In an instant, his tears turned to song, a silly sort of tune that seemed it might have been birthed in a child's nursery. "Cobeld's in his cage," he sang, dancing around and among us. "The Ryn Naia is victorious! The pit for the pit. The pit for the pit! Cobeld's in his cage."

The pit for the pit? I had no idea what *that* meant, but . . . he seemed happy, so I didn't give it too much thought. After being so long within the earth, the feeling of the morning sun made my skin rejoice, even if I could not number the days it had been since I'd felt its caress. I lifted my face to capture as much of it as I could, and let him ramble on. But just when it seemed Taef's refrain might never come to an end, he collapsed into a cross-legged position from which he seemed content to gaze adoringly in my direction.

Julien held my hand. From our lofty vantage point we could look down at the surrounding foothills and valleys.

"What requests does the Reigning Lady have for me?" Taef asked suddenly. "Your equine companion is a great secret keeper. Though he was tempted by the fine oats I provided, he has remained ever true to you, Reigning Lady."

"Stanza is indeed known for his loyal silence," I said. Kinley met my eyes for just a second and then coughed and turned away. "I appreciate your service, Taef, and I trust you as a most worthy diplomat and friend."

"Stanza?" The strange man tilted his head like a dog who had just heard a high-pitched whistle. "It is not the black shooting star of which I speak. Though he is loyal and is well-acquainted with speed, he knows little of secrets." He nodded and smiled in Stanza's direction and then turned back to me. "It is the mighty silver whose whispers make him truly yours. Besides, what is his belongs to you."

"You are mistaken, Taef," I corrected the odd man. "Salvador is Sir Julien's horse. He is a fine animal, and though I do care for the horse with more than a passing affection, he does not belong to me."

"Yours he shall be and already is in his heart," Taef said resolutely. "For what is his shall be yours and what is yours shall belong to him."

I blinked. Taef was no longer speaking of horses. I looked at Julien and met his smile.

"I have fulfilled my diplomatic duties," Taef announced, "and I am yours to command, Ryn Naia."

"Thank you, Taef." I turned to Dyfnel. "You are willing to accompany this man back to Tirandov?" I asked.

"And speedily so." Dyfnel nodded. "It will give me great pleasure to deliver the Remedy to your mother." Dyfnel removed his pack from his back and attached it to his horse's saddle.

He was just about to put his foot in the stirrup, when Erielle's shout stopped him.

"Wait!" she cried. "We must break the loaf and retrieve the stone!"

Dyfnel's face blanched and I think my heart might have ceased beating for a moment. We had nearly forgotten an integral part of the prophecy.

"Thank Rynloeft our princess insisted you come, Lady Erielle," Dyfnel said with a shake of his head. "The Queen does not require the entire amount. Nor would she be pleased if I had brought it to her when so many others are suffering here on the mainland."

I thought of Risson. Of the son his family had lost to the Cobelds. Of the family we'd come upon in the south. Of the farmers and villagers who didn't make it out of Glenhume before the Cobelds attacked. Of Erielle's friend Nella, whose death, while not the *direct* result of a Cobeld's curse, was a tragedy, just the same. It was too late to help them. But many still survived, still lived in pain and anguish. It had to stop.

Dyfnel removed his pack and the Remedy from within it. He set it on the ground and we stood unmoving in a circle about it.

"What do we do now?" Kinley rubbed his beard.

Taef stood and joined our circle. Nodding at the stone, he said, "The pit for the pit." And then, confident as if he had done it a thousand times before, he walked from the circle, retrieved two smaller rocks, and holding the point of one at the center of the Remedy, he raised the other and hit it with a resounding *crack!*

The stone split into two perfect halves. Fallen between them, like a peach pit, was a perfectly circular stone, clear as a woodland spring on a summer day.

Or as an invisible floor above a chasm. I shuddered. Perhaps the stone and Cobeld's transparent floor were formed of the same substance.

I scooped up the pit. It fit easily in the palm of my hand, and as I gazed at it, the crystal absorbed a ray of sunshine and seemed to catch on fire. I gasped, even though it was not hot in the least, and would have dropped it if not for Julien's quick hand steadying mine.

"It's surprisingly cool," I said, handing it off to Julien.

The fire was alive, moving like a campfire in the breeze, but round, mimicking the shape of the outer stone. The globe passed from hand to hand, until Erielle gave it to Taef, who passed it immediately back into my hands.

"The pit for the pit," he said. "Follow the mountain's scar and you will find where she keeps the puss of her wound."

I wrinkled my nose at his description of the poisoned reservoir.

"Truly, Taef," Erielle said, "your words are most picturesque."

Taef bowed.

Trying not to grimace, I put my free hand on Taef's shoulder. "Might I ask a favor of you?"

"You may ask anything of me, Ryn Naia, and I will most readily follow you unto death, or even, Rynloeft forbid it, to comfort."

He would . . . what?

Kinley snorted.

I tilted my head and then shook it slightly. There was no hope that I could possibly learn to speak "Taef" in such a short span of time as we had been given.

"Very well," I said finally. "I need you to take charge of this worthy beast." I indicated Sir Risson's horse. "See that he is returned to Sir Risson's family in Canyn, before accompanying Dyfnel to Tirandov Isle. There you will be asked to suffer many comforts. I trust you will bear these duties well."

Dyfnel met my eyes and gave a slow nod. *If there is help for his malady of the mind, Your Highness, I will see that he receives it.*

Thank you, my friend.

A moment of trepidation passed over Taef's face. "As you command, Ryn Naia. And may I live a thousand years and never graze another meadow should I fail to find joy in your service."

When Kinley snorted again it took everything within me not to laugh, but I kept my eyes on our trusty thief's somber face.

"In addition," I said, "I ask that you join the Queen's escort home. When you reach Castle Rynwyk I will, once again, depend upon you to suffer many comforts while we discuss the manner by which I will provide the oats of recompense for your loyal service."

"Oh, most worthy future Queen!" he exclaimed. "I would suffer the pain of all the comforts of the world to prove to you my fealty!" He fell to his knees and grabbed my hand, covering it with wet, stubbly kisses. "I am beyond grief in my pleasure that you would remember the request of your humble mage!"

I could only imagine the horror that must have filled my face as Taef's kisses continued with no end in sight.

I looked up. Erielle alone did not sport a grin. Instead she looked as if she might be ill at Taef's slobbery display. Julien, who I thought would be offended by Taef's show of affection, was barely controlling his laughter. At my glare, however, and after giving a pointed nod toward my hand, now slick with Taef's kisses, Julien cleared his throat.

"Arise, worthy servant of the Ryn," he said, "and be on your way. The Queen awaits the Remedy."

Taef stood, releasing my hand, which I surreptitiously tucked behind my back and rubbed against my tunic to dry the remaining saliva from it. I refused to make eye contact with anyone but my horse.

I retrieved my cloak from my saddlebags, put it on, and dropped the glowing "pit" into its deep pocket while Dyfnel packed half of the Remedy in his saddlebag and Edru put the remaining half in his. The fiery stone would remain with me until the time came to drop it into the well.

I embraced Dyfnel. "Be patient, my wise friend," I whispered. "There is truth within our trusty thief, even if it is hidden far beneath layers of insanity."

Dyfnel laughed, and with a quick nod to Taef he mounted his horse. The hapless would-be mage mounted Risson's horse and trotted ahead of Dyfnel, in the opposite direction from that which he'd advised us to take.

"'Withdraw the Healer and the Cur,'" Erielle quoted with a sigh. As she watched them go, a small smile played at her cheeks.

"It was kind of you to send Risson's horse back to his family," Julien said softly.

"They deserve to know the truth and Dyfnel will tell them. Besides, I didn't think Dyfnel would be too thrilled to have to share his saddle with the likes of Taef. At least this way, they will only need to share from Risson's home to Port Dyn. Gerrias can continue to ride Stanza."

"I take it that you plan to ride your *other* horse?" He patted Salvador's flank. "But where does that leave me?"

"You will not be a burden to my overgrown lamb." I parried his words from the long ago night on which I'd first met his beautiful horse. "You may ride with me."

FORTY-EIGHT

Gerrias stared down the mountain face, rubbing his beard with his thumb and forefinger. As we came up beside him, he pointed to a pathway. "I can only surmise that this is the mountain's scar," he said. "That must be the same road that the Cobelds used to ambush us."

We followed the path of his finger.

"There appears to be a clearing of sorts in that valley."

"Looks less than an hour's ride," Kinley said. "Is it a Cobeld camp, do you think?"

Gerrias nodded. "We'll need to use extreme caution. Their camps are plentiful in these northern foothills. And they might have a Dwonsil guard, perhaps even a full company of warriors at the ready."

"Indeed." Kinley nodded. "We can only hope the King has drawn enough of them off that we might reach it unmolested."

"Speaking of the King," Edru turned to me. "Perhaps you should inform him of our progress?"

I nodded. "I will as we ride."

Julien took my pack from me and affixed it with his own to Salvador's saddle before helping me up.

Climbing on behind me, he whispered in my ear. "You could have kept Risson's horse for Gerrias and ridden your own, but selfishly, I'm glad you chose otherwise."

I shivered at his breath on my neck. "You are?"

"Without a doubt. This arrangement gives me the perfect excuse to hold you close."

We rode down the pathway's twists and turns, reaching the bottom of the mountain by the time the sun had risen to the noon mark. I closed my eyes and tried to contact my father, but he was riding hard, and battle was soon to come. Other than relaying our location, I didn't distract him with details.

"The army is only a few miles farther to the other side of the clearing than we are this side of it."

Julien shouted the news to everyone else and we gathered speed, hoping that, as Taef claimed, this path would lead us to the poisoned reservoir—and that we would have time to fulfill the rest of the prophecy before the battle reached us.

We entered the clearing in less time than Kinley and Gerrias had predicted. It seemed deserted, but at Julien's request, Edru and I used our gifts to discern life, but found little other than rodents.

The camp was larger than a village, but more primitive. By sheer size it could have been considered a small town.

"Look how squat the huts are built!" Erielle exclaimed. "I might be the only one of us who could pass through the door. And even I might bump my head!"

The smaller scale of the poorly constructed shelters left no argument against the fact that this was indeed a Cobeld settlement.

We held our weapons at the ready riding through the camp, expecting attack at any moment. A prickle creased my shoulders.

"What is it?" Julien's arm tightened about my waist.

"They're getting closer," I said at the same time Kinley shouted, "Look there!"

He set his horse to a canter and we followed.

At the center of the camp, a huge mound of earth was surrounded by rough-hewn wooden scaffolding. The scaffolding leveled off midway up the steep slope, but the mound continued up, even more steeply, until it ended with a ring of piled stones atop its crest. Above the stones, a wooden arch was built with a bar hanging beneath it, supporting some small objects that I couldn't identify from my position so far below.

At the bottom of the mound, piles of . . . something . . . were neatly arranged as if for decoration. Kinley slid off his horse and walked toward the mound. When he reached the bottom he bent forward to touch one of the offerings, but stopped short.

He stood and faced us. "Bones," he said.

"Bones?" I blinked. "Animal bones?"

"Maybe." He glanced just behind me, where Julien sat. The look they exchanged said it all.

Not animal.

His gaze darted to me and back to Julien. He gave a quick nod and sighed as he knelt beside one of the piles. "They're small," he said. "And the sculls look fairly . . . human."

I gasped. "Children?" *Oh, please. Not that.*

"If I had to guess, I'd say Cobeld." He looked up. "Wait here. I'll climb up and see what's there."

Kinley reached for a handhold and swung up onto the scaffolding. After he reached the landing, a good twenty feet above our heads, he just kept climbing, digging his hands into the earthen mound as he crawled up the side.

"I'm going to keep looking for the reservoir, or well, or whatever it is," Erielle said.

Gerrias spoke up, "I'll come with you."

"Hold." Julien dismounted, his eyes riveted on the piles of bones. He walked up to them, and then stepped back, rubbing his beard with his thumb and forefinger. His lips moved, and I wondered which lines from the scrolls he was reciting. He turned.

"It's a shrine," he said. "'Cobeld's minions of one mind must feed their beard from cursed shrine.' This is it. This is the reservoir. The well."

"That's ridiculous." Erielle made a face. "Wells are dug down into the ground, not built up from it."

Holding my hand up to shield my eyes from the sun, I watched Kinley's progress. When he reached the apex, I was surprised to see there was enough flat area for him to stand.

Kinley leaned over the circular rocks and turned to the side, as if there was something in the center of them he was trying to listen to.

"What is he doing?" I wondered aloud.

He stood like that for a few moments more, then abruptly straightened and climbed back down the slope to the landing.

"It's a well!" he said. "Come on!"

"Surely you jest?" Erielle slid from her horse, shielding her eyes as she looked up toward him.

"No." Kinley shook his head. "I dropped a pebble and heard it hit water."

Edru, Gerrias, and I slid from our horses.

Julien stood just to Salvador's side and made a few hand motions. "Go," he said softly, pointing to the tree line near the edge of the Cobeld camp we had entered. "Stay."

Salvador whinnied at the other horses and trotted off toward the trees. I stared, open-mouthed, as the other horses
followed.

"He'll keep the horses out of sight until I call for him,"
Julien said. When he saw the disbelief on my face he gave me
a lopsided grin. "Truly. He's never failed me yet."

Of course he hadn't. Salvador was no ordinary horse.

"Come then," Julien said, giving me a wink that made my
insides quiver. "I'll give you a hand up."

He cupped his hands and I set a boot in. He hoisted me up
to the first level of scaffolding as if I were as small as Erielle,
who, without any help at all, had reached the landing before I
even started to climb.

When we reached the level where Kinley waited, we followed his gaze out to where we could see above the trees. The
wind came from the south, carrying the sound away, but the
battle was nearly to the northern edge of the camp.

"They're almost here!" I cried. "What do we do now?
What's next?"

We were so close to finishing what we had come here to
do. But we'd not yet solved the final riddles.

"We need more time!"

Why I had expected to have more time to figure out the
last bits of the poetry, I didn't know. Nothing else had come
upon us with much warning. Why should it now?

I closed my eyes and concentrated on the poetry. Around
me, the words swirled through everyone else's thoughts as
well. I opened my eyes, looking about for clues to the riddles
we had yet to solve. All nine marks had been met. The Remedy
had been retrieved.

But was retrieving the Remedy my first task . . . or the second? It all depended on whether or not rescuing Gladiel and

Drinius was considered among the tasks, I supposed. So what was left but to—

A bugler's call sounded, strong and sure. The metallic whir of three swords leaving their scabbards tingled in my ears.

I looked at Julien. "What was that?"

His jaw was set, his sword ready. "Advance."

"From our army?"

He nodded.

It was almost upon us.

But so many lines remained! The third task, as I figured it, was to destroy the Cobelds' well and shrine. But there were so many riddles left to explain how it could be done! And of the seven of us remaining, which four would comprise the council that would "strike the pyre" and accomplish it?

"Rynnaia, here." Erielle interrupted the rush of panic that threatened to consume me. She held a sword in one hand, a dagger in the other. *My* dagger. "I forgot to give this back to you," she said with a smile. "I figured now was probably a good time."

I nodded, but dropped the dagger into my pocket. It clinked against something.

The stone.

My mind raced through the riddles, but the only phrases that stuck out to me were: *Oracle's daughter scales the slope, takes the mantel, and drops the stone to nullify Cobeld's dark curse and purge the poison from its work.*

A few things were easily identifiable: the slope was right above us, and the stone, glowing in the pocket of my cloak, would need to be dropped into the well. But what of the other elements in the rhyme?

The poison. It must speak of the evil concoction of ebonswarth, yellowhock, and who knows what else Cobeld had added to his "miracle" spring water. The stone must have medicinal properties that would cancel the negative effects of the plants.

The mantel. I looked up at the well. Was the thing hanging above it a mantel, of sorts, like that which rests above a hearth? Was I supposed to knock it down? I couldn't be sure, but since I had a stone in my pocket, a stone that came from the center of the Remedy itself, I was almost sure that it was supposed to be dropped into the well.

The Oracle's daughter. As Erielle had mused back at Holiday Palace, I supposed Lady Anya probably felt a bit maternal toward me. And since so much else of the prophecy spoke of the Ryn, I could only concur that this part did, too.

But if I was wrong about even one of these things, how would we retrieve the stone once it was dropped? We had come so far, but so much was still layered in mystery. If we misinterpreted even one bit of the prophecy, would the well continue to be an available source of power to the Cobelds? A legacy of evil, even though Cobeld himself was no longer a threat?

The knights gazed northward, toward the sounds of war cries and clashing swords, now too close to be carried away on the wind. Edru had also drawn a sword, but his gaze was focused upward, as if seeking some sort of sign that would tell us what to do.

I closed my eyes and sent a silent plea to The First for enlightenment, but the skies remained silent, as if waiting for someone below to provide the key that would open them and reveal the mysteries of the riddles to us.

Father.

My mind reached out to the King, but when I found him, I almost retreated. Never had I seen such a fierce visage. Gone were the genteel expressions and courtly mannerisms to which I'd so briefly been accustomed. Jarryn of E'veria had transformed into a Warrior King.

I distanced myself just enough to avoid distracting him and watched his grace, his skill, with wonder. Pride surged within me. *That is my father!*

A corner of his mouth lifted. He had felt the color of that affectionate emotion and knew it came from me.

Julien's arm curled around my waist the moment the battle became visible. Within seconds of the first glimmer of shields, the area just beyond the tree line teemed with the movement of combat. Swords and armor caught fragmented rays of sunshine. E'verian shields, dulled by spattered blood, met blows from Dwonsil swords and poisoned Cobeld arrows.

"What should we do?" I turned my face up to him.

"We fight. Beyond that?" He shrugged. "We'll just have to figure it out as we go."

"How can you be so calm?"

"You think I'm calm?" He tilted his head. "I'm not calm. I'm a knight, therefore I am . . . controlled. It is necessary."

"You look calm." There was something else in his eyes as well, but I waited for him to speak rather than trying to read his thoughts.

"Rynnaia, when you were with Cobeld, you put E'veria before me."

I swallowed hard. "I did." Was he having second thoughts about our reconciliation?

"You did the right thing," he said, allowing me to breathe. "If the need arises, I need you to promise that you'll do it again." Julien's eyes narrowed with concern. "You've never seen this sort of battle. Things happen swiftly. People die." He paused. "You cannot. You are the Ryn."

"But if it were to save E'veria . . ."

"You are not alone here." He shook his head. "Remember the oath I swore at the Bear's Rest?"

I nodded.

"I pledged my fealty, my sword, and my service to you with all that I am and for all of my life. Kinley and Gerrias did as well at Holiday Palace. If necessary, we will die to protect you. We are knights and it is our duty and privilege to fight."

"But—"

He shook his head and put a finger to my lips. "You are the Ryn. It is *your* duty to survive. There must be an E'veri on the throne and your father has no other heir. E'veria needs you alive." He paused. His eyes softened, yet became brighter at the same time. "Rynnaia," his voice broke and the last word came out as a whisper, "*live.*"

His words seemed final. Sure. And they sounded like good-bye.

My fingers gripped his arm and my voice came out as little more than a breath that felt like my last. "Don't leave me, Julien."

The pain in his eyes was as tight as that in my throat. "Give me your word, Rynnaia, that you will not put yourself in harm's way for our sakes."

"I cannot." I shook my head. "You are E'veria, too. But I will remember my responsibilities and pledge to accept whatever task The First assigns to me, even unto death."

"I can ask for no more than that." Julien's nod was stern, but the corner of his mouth twitched. "And yet I find that I can't help myself. There is one more pledge I would speak and one more request I would pose to you, Rynnaia."

Julien turned to face me and lowered the tip of his sword so that it speared the platform between us.

One by one, as if conscious of a turning tide, our companions aimed their gazes away from the battle below and toward us instead.

"In E'veria, courtship is used as a means to test the strength of love, to ensure it is more than attraction and flirtation, and that it has the fortitude for a lifetime," he said. "Our courtship has been anything but conventional, but I pledge by my sword and these witnesses that I will spend the rest of my life, whether it lasts for only the next hour or for the next hundred years, proving the depth of my love for you."

Julien reached for my hand, placed it atop the hand resting on the hilt of his sword, and then covered it with his own as he knelt on one knee.

"Rynnaia E'veri, I love you. With all that I am, I love you. Should Rynloeft allow us safely forth from this battle, it would be the greatest honor of my life if you would consent to be my bride."

FORTY-NINE

*J*ulien's eyes locked with mine and his love flooded my mind with green and gold, filling the core of me with the intense truth of his commitment. I opened my mind entirely to its sweetness.

"I love you, Rynnaia," he repeated. His whisper stole my breath. "My heart is yours for the taking. Marry me."

Yes! I let my colors wash over him. *Yes, I will accept your heart, but only if you fill its place with mine.*

Julien stood and his head bobbed in one solid nod. "Done."

At once, something intangible and bright spilled out of me . . . and into him. Julien sucked in a breath. His eyes widened. A moment later we were lost within an explosive wonder, a sense of two destinies, met and melded, that reset the world.

On some level, I was conscious of the sounds of battle coming closer. Primal yells, the sound of swords hitting flesh and shield, metal on metal. But the noises of war were secondary to the trumpeting emotions that caressed my heart from Julien's loving gaze.

"Ah, not to spoil the moment, Julien." Kinley cleared his throat. "But this is the Crown Princess of E'veria to whom you just offered marriage. There is the little matter of seeking permission from the King."

Julien didn't take his eyes off me, but said, "He's already given it."

"Oh," Kinley said. He drummed his fingers across the flat of his sword. "Well, then?"

I looked over at him and scowled. Leave it to my brother to dump a bucket of water on romance. "Well, *what*?"

"Well, answer the man!"

"She already did." Julien grinned.

"She did?" Erielle spoke up. "I didn't hear anything."

"Neither did I," Gerrias said.

"I did." Edru favored us with a rare chuckle. "She said yes. Quite forcefully, as a matter of fact."

Erielle let out a puff of air that sounded a bit like, *"Andoven!"*

"Did she?" Kinley prodded. "If I'm to serve as witness, then I think I'd like to hear it for myself."

"As would I," Gerrias said, giving his brother a sly grin. "Otherwise, I'm inclined to disbelieve that our fair princess would tie herself to such a beast as my brother for the rest of her days."

"In that case," I said, cupping my hands near my mouth and shouting with all my might, "let it be known this day that I, Rynnaia E'veri, have agreed to wed this Bear-man of Mynissbyr, Sir Julien de Gladiel!"

With a singing whirr, Julien's sword returned to his scabbard. "Did you hear it that time?" He laughed. "She said yes!"

Without another word he crushed me into his arms. As his lips laid claim to my soul, I was drawn into his. Whatever had happened when I'd accepted his proposal had bound our hearts and minds, roping emerald and gold around me and blue and orange around him. The kiss only deepened our bond, sealing it with fire.

"Huzzah!" Erielle's cheer was immediately echoed by Gerrias, Kinley, and even Edru, but I barely noticed. My mind and my heart were too full for my ears to make sense of their joy. Strong as it was, it paled to invisibility next to my own.

Our first kiss, just a few hours earlier, had been sweet, filled with the relief of forgiveness and the perfection of a gently shared promise. This embrace overflowed with passionate truth and furious love that sought to singe the very skin from our bones.

Perhaps a kiss so scorching would have been best shared in private, but privacy wasn't afforded us right now. And since not even my own brother was protesting, I wasn't about to argue with the timing. How could I? I was utterly lost within Julien's love.

Emerald bonds to seal the Ryn and toast the curse they've taken in.

The phrase of poetry burst in amidst our combined colors. The blazing green onslaught became suddenly more intense. Another presence, one of similar green, but streaked with lustrous strands of ebony, joined us. Though our breath yet mingled, I lost conscious awareness of the kiss itself.

Souls conjoin, a third concurs. Hope consumes Cobeld's saboteurs. The words sang through my head.

Suddenly, though Julien and I had not moved from our physical location, the boundaries of time were loosened and our conjoined consciousness traveled to another plane. Again, I stood behind the desk at Fyrlean Manor, watching the young oracle work her quill. But this time, I was not alone.

This was an ethereal moment, a meeting realized through means beyond my power, beyond Julien's, and beyond Anya's. Something only attainable by The First.

Lady Anya turned and pierced me with her gaze. She was older than the last time we had met. Years older, though it had only been months for me . . . yet centuries . . . since we'd last met upon this plane.

"*Ryn Naia.*" Lady Anya had an urgent tone to her voice. "*You and your betrothed must do this together.*"

She gestured to Julien, who stood at my side behind her chair. When the bright emerald eyes they shared connected, Lady Anya caught her breath. Her hand moved to her belly and I noticed it was swollen with child. When she looked up, her eyes shone with recognition of one of her progeny.

"*A Bear-man King?*" She laughed. "*Serve well, my son. Or my son's son.*" She laughed again. "*However many generations may come between this little Bear-man,*" she patted her belly, "*and you, knight, walk in truth and serve well.*"

Julien nodded. "With all that I am and for all of my life, I will."

"*You will, indeed.*" Joy lit Anya's features, and as she faded from our view, her last words echoed across the colors swelling again in our minds, "*You are bound. You are sealed. By your toast, speak as one.*"

My eyes flew open. Our lips disconnected. A mixture of wonder and understanding lit on Julien's face that I could only imagine was mirrored on mine.

Suddenly it was clear what we had to do.

"What. Was. That?" Erielle spoke. "It was as if you were frozen! Like you weren't even *here!*" She groaned, spread her arms wide, and looked to the sky. "May Rynloeft save me from romance, lest it render me frozen as a fool's statue!"

Our attention was abruptly drawn by a piercing shriek. Cobelds poured through the tree line and into the camp with E'verian soldiers close behind.

"We need more time!" Gerrias growled.

"Or a distraction," Kinley said as he effected a battle stance. "Something!"

"A distraction?" I turned from Julien. "That, I can do."

I untied my cloak and dropped it on the floor of the scaffold platform. Next, I pulled the leather tie from my hair, doubled over at the waist, and snaked my fingers through the braid until it flowed free. I flipped my hair back over my head and stood straight.

"Well, I'm distracted." Julien shot me a grin that brought some of the red of my hair into my cheeks. Gerrias cuffed his shoulder.

I looked up at the sky, moved about three feet to the left and stepped into the path of the sun.

"Whoa." Erielle breathed. *"Fire."*

Kinley blew a long whistle. "Your hair looks as if it's made of flame itself." He nodded and resumed his battle stance. "Yes, I believe that should slow them down for a minute or two."

I planted my feet and faced the enemy. When the first Cobeld noticed me, a cry pierced the air.

The Cobelds stopped dead in their tracks. Another shriek lifted from the battlefield. *"The Ryn Naia!"* In tones of gasping horror, others joined in, little by little, until their shrieks of *"The Ryn Naia!"* were barely distinguishable as words.

The distraction I provided gave the King's Army a momentary advantage against the combined Cobeld and Dwonsil forces. They pressed forward. I couldn't see my father yet, but he was there. I sensed him.

Erielle turned a wicked grin in my direction. "That was effective!"

Unfortunately, the Cobelds were quick to recover from their shock. Having seen me for themselves, and so close to achieving my goal, their desperation increased.

Could they sense I'd defeated Cobeld? A quick brush against the mind of one argued against it and made me wonder if perhaps they'd been unaware of his presence, trapped as he was inside Mount Shireya all these centuries. He had known about them, of course. But had it been part of his curse to not only know the prophecy of his doom, and that his followers benefited from his well and the proliferation of the botanically-derived curse he'd left behind, but to know he had only *one chance* to prevent its destruction?

Ah, something to wonder on when my Kingdom's destiny was not so imminent.

Regardless of what the Cobelds knew of their former leader, they knew the prophecy as surely as we did. Maybe better. And they believed that to foil it would allow them to take E'veria for themselves.

Cobelds began clawing their way up the shrine. Julien pushed me behind the line of knights. He joined Erielle, Kinley, Edru, and Gerrias in using their swords to knock the Cobelds from the scaffolding, but the sheer number of the enemy was staggering. For each that was killed or knocked down, another took its place. They were as desperate to reach the well as we were to ensure that they didn't. The Cobelds needed to get to the well to save the source of their power, but they still held poison-tainted weapons, ready to strike. We had to figure out what to do to end their curse.

"Rynnaia!" Erielle shouted. "Go! Throw the stone into the well!"

Forgetting that I'd taken off my cloak, I felt for my pocket and then fell to the ground, seeking the stone in the pocket of my discarded cloak. Finally, its warmth touched my fingers and I pulled it out. The light of the stone was brighter, now a piercingly bright orange that filled the entire core of the sphere. As I closed my hand around it, Lady Anya's voice reverberated in my head, speaking the prophecy she had inscribed.

The Oracle's daughter must scale the slope, take the mantel, and drop the stone.

Lady Anya called Julien her son. Her son's son. In the two hundred years since the prophecy was penned, there had not been a female born to the Regent of Mynissbyr's family. At least not until . . .

I gasped. The moment was upon us and the riddle was finally unmasked. *I'm not the Oracle's daughter!*

"I'm hit!" Gerrias cried.

Switching his sword to the other hand, Gerrias wrenched the dagger free of his already-injured sword arm and sent its point into the neck of a nearby Cobeld. As if he'd always fought with his left arm, Gerrias continued to knock Cobelds away. But his face grimaced with an agony I knew only too well.

"Rynnaia, go!" Kinley urged.

The Oracle's daughter . . .

"But I'm not the Oracle's daughter!" I shouted, even as Julien pushed his sister back toward me. "It's you, Erielle!"

$\mathcal{F}$ I F T Y

$\mathcal{E}$ rielle stopped for just a moment to look toward her brother and an arrow narrowly missed her head. Scrambling to duck down, she quickly covered the rest of the distance.

"Are you sure, Rynnaia?" she asked, sheathing her sword.

"Yes," I said. "You are Anya's descendant, Erielle, the first female in your line since the Oracle herself. You are the *Oracle's daughter*!"

I grabbed her hand and pressed the stone within it. As soon as it touched her palm, it flashed blue and brightened even more until it glowed white. I closed her fingers around it.

"This is why you had to come, Erielle. Do it now!"

With a nod, she scaled the rest of the distance up the slope. She stepped up to the circle of stones and peered down into the well.

Erielle held the stone in her open hand. It glowed brighter, whiter, by the second. Her shoulders rose as she took a deep breath and . . . tipped her palm. The glowing orb rolled off her hand and into the well.

The pit for the pit, I thought, holding my breath.

Erielle screwed up her face, took a step back, and flinched as if she expected an explosion of some sort.

Nothing happened.

Although I'm sure the stone made some sort of sound as it hit the water, I couldn't hear it above the sounds of the battle, now all around the foot of the shrine. Erielle looked down at me, lifted her hands, and shrugged her shoulders. Unsheathing her sword, she slid down the slope and landed beside me.

"I suspect the rest is up to you, Princess," she said.

My mouth gaped open. "Erielle."

"What?" She swung her sword to the right and cut an arrow from the air before glancing back at me. "Why are you looking at me like that?"

"Erielle, your eyes," I said, blinking in disbelief. "They're . . . they're *green.*"

"What?"

"Your eyes aren't blue anymore. They're green. Bright green. Like Julien's." A vision of the Oracle of Mynissbyr flooded my thoughts. "Like Lady Anya's."

"A trick of the light," she said. But from somewhere deep within her thoughts, I sensed the tremble of a memory. And it smelled a lot like the sea, conjuring the face of a young man in her mind. A young man, a boy, really, who looked quite a bit like . . .

Cazien.

I shook my head. "It's not a trick of the light."

She blinked. "My eyes are . . . green?"

"Rynnaia, go!" Julien called. "Erielle! Fill the hole."

Without another word, she rushed to rejoin the fray. I turned and began climbing up the path Erielle had just come down.

Edru's voice shouted into my thoughts. *Princess, down!*

I ducked and an arrow embedded itself in the soil just above my head.

I continued the climb. Several arrows flew my direction. Thanks to Edru, none hit their mark. I was exceedingly glad to have another Andoven still in our company, otherwise I'd be dead. No one could be *that* unlucky at hitting their target.

Finally, I reached the crest of the shrine. If he could, Julien would be beside me shortly. If he could not, there would be no one with whom to drink the toast from the well.

No one else would do. Regardless of how Cobeld twisted the prophecy to make me believe otherwise, Julien de Gladiel was the emerald. Our colors had sealed the bond of our betrothal. And Lady Anya had made it clear that the toast we drank would end the curse. But it would have to be spoken together. As one.

I kept my head down and looked at the bar hanging over the well. It held several cups as well as a rope which was used to raise and lower a bucket into the cursed, poisonous water. Water I would soon drink.

Growing up from the murky depths—and oh, was it deep!—a strange vine clung to the inside walls of the well with stringy leaves, and thorns so dark a green they were almost black. A yellowish flower-like growth protruded from various points along the vine, but my eyes were drawn back to the talon-like thorns.

I'd never thought a plant could seem so sinister, but this, Cobeld's hybrid of ebonswarth, yellowhock—and was that some sort of freshwater kelp?—sent a chill through my blood.

The water might kill me—might kill Julien—but in order to remove the Cobeld curse from E'veria once and for all, we had no choice but drink it.

If he came in time.

I crawled to the edge and stole a glance at my friends.

Gerrias had fallen. He was still alive, still blinking and breathing, but it appeared paralysis had taken over. Kinley and Erielle formed a shield of sorts for him with their bodies while fighting off the Cobelds trying to make it onto the platform. Edru's sword was raised and he used it, though not with the same skill of his companions. Instead he used his Andoven abilities to knock away the poisoned arrows being sent up to us by the Dwonsil warriors and the Cobelds. He was flagging, though.

I peered toward a line of archers, and drawing my hand through the air, swept their bows from their grasp. They would soon retrieve them, but at least it would give Edru a moment to regroup.

Julien's sword arched a blur, its every angle poetry, his every strike a silent song. A dagger in his hand kept perfect time to the dance his sword performed. Not a moment was lost, nor a stroke wasted. His face shone with purpose, yet his expertise gave each turn a detached sort of grace that could only be achieved through years of training to an inborn call.

For every Cobeld knocked from the scaffolding, two more took its place, but while none were able to get beyond my fearsome knight, there was no opening, no moment in which he could turn to join me.

The coppery scent of blood tainted the air as much as the deafening sounds of battle. Horses, knights, and warriors roared furious battle cries. Ancient, shriveled men shrieked curses. Arrows flew, sword brushed against sword, shield, and with a dull slicing hiss, flesh. And underlying every harsh cry were the echoed agonies of the dying.

I focused on the Cobeld nearest Julien. *Fall.* And he did, only to be replaced by another bearded face. And those beards were too close for Julien to be able to turn his back. If he did, even for a moment, the Cobelds would gain the platform. A brush of the beard, or a jab with a tainted dagger, and the fetid old men would easily overpower my friends, finish Gerrias, and head for me.

Father. My eyes found him the same instant my mind did. He was atop his horse, sword flying in precise and deadly strokes.

Yes, Rynnaia, I'm here.

Can you press harder so that Julien can break away from his position and join me at the well?

We're doing all we can, Rynnaia. We will continue. The enemy is still strong.

It was going to be up to me.

No, not me.

"Please," I whispered, furtively seeking guidance from The First. "Please show me how to honor my mother's blessing and the gifts you've granted me."

I thought of the rocks that had fallen on my command near Canyn Village and the stalactite spears at Halo's Rim. Peace stole over me.

I focused just beyond the scaffolding to the front rows of battle. Whatever I did would affect not just the Cobelds, but the E'verians in my sight as well.

Be ready! With as few words as possible I communicated my plan to my friends. I waited until each of them nodded their understanding and then sought the King.

Do you trust me, Father? I asked.

Of course!

I took a deep breath. *Then call a retreat . . . now!*

A moment later the bugler sounded the retreat. As Julien stepped back, Kinley, Erielle, and Edru spread apart to fill the gap. Gerrias was left vulnerable as Julien sprinted up the slope to me, but I could only hope his motionlessness would make the Cobelds think he was already dead.

An arrow narrowly missed Julien's shoulder. Anger turned me to the archers again and I swept my hand through the air and spoke directly to the bowstrings, "Break!"

The E'verian Army's retreat gave the Dwonsil warriors an advantage and they pressed my father's forces back, just as I had hoped, moving them farther away. I supposed it was too much to hope that my distraction would send the Cobelds after the army, too. It did the opposite. The Dwonsil warriors were moving away from the well, but the Cobelds were focused entirely on me. And why wouldn't they be? With the Ryn Naia atop their cursed shrine, what mattered of an army? I was the prize they sought. Or my death, rather. And they were plenty motivated to achieve it.

Without bowstrings or the Dwonsil warriors' aid, however, the only weapon that remained at the ready for the Cobelds was their beards.

I focused the power of my mind on the Cobelds and as many rows of Dwonsil warriors as I could stretch it to take in, which wasn't as many as I would have liked. But considering the width of the enemy's forces, I didn't want to press my luck.

Now! I sent the order to my loyal companions. Kinley, Edru, and Erielle closed in around Gerrias, as far away from the edge of the platform as they could get.

Julien had just gained the top. He immediately flattened himself on the dirt.

I severed the mental tie to my friends, closed my eyes, and pressed my focus just a little bit wider than I'd been able to with my mind doubly engaged.

With a great shove, as if all the winds of E'veria had gathered to await my command, I pressed my arms forward, palms out, and shouted.

"FALL!"

I opened my eyes. The force of my command sent no less than ten ranks of Cobelds and Dwonsil warriors hurtling toward the tree line. Some were picked up and tossed into others. The sound was tremendous as armor smashed into armor.

Above the din, another bugle call sounded. I recognized it this time: *Advance.* The King and his army rushed forward and took the advantage.

Julien jumped to his feet. A grin stretched his triangular beard wide across his face.

"And you thought you needed a *sword*?" He laughed, but sobered quickly. "Are you ready?"

I nodded. "'One Name of Power in purest form removes the stain of Cobeld's thorn.'"

Julien met my eyes and nodded before turning his gaze to the well. "And the name we are to use?"

His thoughts concurred with mine. I nodded.

Julien pulled the rope to draw the bucket up from the well. I peeked down at our friends.

"Julien, hurry."

The enemies were rising, but not as fast as the E'verian forces were taking them down again. Erielle, Kinley, and Edru climbed down the scaffolding and stood in a circle at the foot of the well shrine, their backs to us and their swords drawn and ready. Gerrias alone remained on the scaffolding. My thoughts found him unconscious, but still alive.

"I've got it," Julien said.

I peered into the bucket. I expected it to be dark and murky, like the vine and the black thorns that fed its poison, but it wasn't. "It looks like regular water."

"But we know better." He removed two cups from the rack, dipped them into the bucket, and handed one to me.

"It's to be a toast, then," he said. I nodded. He lifted his hand, as did I. We interlocked our arms as if performing our wedding toast, and with cups at our lips, looked into each other's eyes.

"I love you," we said at the same time.

We tipped the cups. Higher and higher, we drank the cursed Cobeld water until the cups were drained. And then, joining hands, we raised them as high as we could, and tilted our faces to the sky.

With all the purity of a knight's honor and the honest plea of a Ryn's request, we shouted the name by which the depth of love could only be fully known by having experienced the suffering that preceded its comfort; the name that would break the curse of envy and hate that had been born within Cobeld and then spread like the disease that it was to his followers; the name that described his Unlimited Power and how that infinite power was kept pure by the Beautiful, Unquenchable Love that surged through it.

"EMBRAL E' VERIA!"

The volume of our cry soared across the legion of enemies below as the love of Rynloeft rang over and through us. But if the sound of their shrieks was any indication, their agony was acute—much worse than anything I had experienced due to their curse.

A searing heat lit at my chest. My hand flew to the pendant. I pulled the chain up and out from under my shirt, lest it burn my skin. At once, the pendant glowed brighter . . . whiter. Another gleam caught my eye.

"Julien, your sword!"

Like my pendant, where the Emblem of The First was engraved upon Julien's sword, it sent forth a pure, white light.

"Look, Rynnaia! It's spreading!"

On the battlefield below, every sword, every shield, and each vestment that bore the Emblem of The First shot rays of white light out and up. Even the dark red stains of war could not quench the power of the display.

Those bearing the glowing implements seemed to garner strength from the light. Our army pressed, slashed. With their purpose renewed, there was no stopping them.

Smoke snaked up from the Cobelds' faces as their beards dissolved into nothing. The shrunken, withered old men writhed in agony as their curses rebounded and time reached out to grasp and retrieve their ancient breath.

A rumbling vibration moved our feet. "Uhh . . . Julien?" I grabbed his arm as the bucket, which had been balanced on the edge of the well, toppled into the water below.

"We'd better get down from here. And quickly." Julien took my hand and we mimicked Erielle's earlier grace, sliding down the side of the shrine as if it were made of greased glass.

The rumble increased and was soon accompanied by a hissing sound. A moment later there was a resounding *crack!* and an orange-red flame leapt from the depth of the well.

"The pit?" Julien asked.

"It must have been."

The heat was intense. We needed to get as far away from the well as possible. As soon as we reached the scaffolding platform, Julien rushed to his brother's side.

"Gerrias!"

"He needs the Remedy!" I said. "But it's with the horses!"

Julien gave a nod, scooted to the other side of the platform, and with two fingers in between his lips, let out a long, shrill whistle.

"They're coming," he said. "We've got to get him down from here."

"I cans sfeel my fingeths." Gerrias's words slurred together.

"Good." I nodded. "Then the poison hasn't made it all the way through you yet."

"No. Get. Ting. Better. Couldn't sfeelf them a muhment go." He paused. "Feel them now. Couldn't talk. Now . . . I . . . can."

Julien raised his eyes to me. "Do you think . . . ?"

I reached into my mind to gather the right lines from the scrolls. *"The stone will nullify the Cobeld curse and purge the poison from its work."*

I gasped. "It's retroactive? So all who've not yet died from the poison will . . . recover?"

"It would appear so," Gerrias said, his words no longer slurred. "Look at my wound." He grinned. "I'd wager it's not even there."

Julien ripped open his brother's sleeve where the dagger had entered.

He shook his head and blinked. "There's a scar and a bit of redness, almost as if it had been cauterized, but the wound is closed."

"That would explain the rather intense burning sensation I felt a few moments ago," Gerrias said.

"Wait." Julien's eyes were still focused on his brother's arm. "The bites are gone." He looked up. "It was this arm the wolfcat bit, wasn't it?"

"It was."

I leaned over and peered at Gerrias's arm. It was as if the beast had never set its teeth to his skin. "Even the new scar is fading!" A moment later, his arm was entirely unblemished.

"Julien." My hand trembled as I brought it to my lips. "My mother."

Julien's eyes widened. "Do you think she's—"

Just then, the scaffolding shuddered. Gerrias's knee suddenly rose, knocking me off balance. I sprawled across his lap.

"Sorry, Princess. I guess my leg's working."

Julien laughed. *"Working* implies you can control it."

The earthen mound shook again. A low, disturbing growl came from within it.

"But whether you can control it or not," Julien said, "you are coming with us. Now."

$\mathcal{F}$ I F T Y - $\mathcal{O}$ N E

$\mathcal{T}$ he platform shook as Edru and Kinley climbed up it. With Erielle guarding below, I watched to make sure nothing came at her that I couldn't stop. But even the Cobelds who were not already dead were dying, and the Dwonsil warriors who had not been captured were fleeing.

Much of Gerrias's strength had returned, and with the help of the three other men, he was soon on the ground.

But the ground near the base of the shrine was no place to be.

Gerrias gained his feet and pulled a stringy white object from his sleeve. "Well, would you look at that!" he said. "It's a hair from a Cobeld's beard."

My stomach dropped as my hand flew to my mouth.

He grinned. "It's just a hair, Princess. No curse left in it."

"But there were only two of you up there," Kinley said. "Three if you count Erielle dropping the stone. Wasn't there supposed to be a council of four?"

Julien looked at me. "Lady Anya," we said together.

Kinley gaped. "The dead Oracle herself? She was there?"

"In her way," I replied. "The First isn't limited by the same constraints as we are. Somehow, for just a moment, he brought her into our time and us into hers."

Another deep rumble sent Gerrias's still-weak knees to the ground. Edru and Kinley each took one of his arms and draped them about their necks.

Hot breath brushed the top of my head and I swiveled around to find Julien's horse. The others were right behind him.

"I'll take Rynnaia on Salvador." Julien tossed me up into the saddle. "Erielle, follow. Kinley, Edru, get Gerrias onto Stanza and make for the King. Go!"

The rumble built as we fled from the shrine and the ground was bathed in the reddish glow of the pit's fire as it reached its flames toward the clouds.

The army had pulled back to the tree line when the rumbles began. Salvador slowed as we reached them.

"I think we'll be safe here," Julien said, "but be ready to go at a moment's notice if need be."

He slid off Salvador's back and then lifted me down. Moments later, the rest of our party arrived. Gerrias was even able to dismount on his own. His strength had nearly returned in full.

Although we could still hear the thunder of the earth, it no longer shook our feet. We gazed at the fire, shooting up into the sky, but dropping nothing, not even a spark or piece of ash. Its sole job, it seemed, was to consume the curse within the well and to leave it dry, clear to the source.

Julien stood at my back with his arms wrapped around me. "I think it's almost over," he said.

The well shrine trembled violently. The scaffolding collapsed and the flames turned blue, and then white. I looked away just before the mound imploded and collapsed in on itself. Dust flew into the air and silence reigned.

When the dust cleared, what had been a fount of death and pain was reduced to an innocuous pile of rubble. An ancient well of suffering, at long last, had been dried up and destroyed by the infinite power of love.

My father reined his horse in beside us. The King's elation over the victory was second only to his relief at seeing me safe. Raising his sword, he shouted with a volume that came from the power of his mind as well as his voice. "All glory to The First!"

"To The First!" Julien echoed, raising his fist in the air.

"To The First!" I returned, with my people.

From deep within the rubble, a familiar tone caught my ear. Symphonic in the depth of its beauty, it was powerful, yet soft and reassuring. It caressed my mind. Clear, strong, and unmistakably powerful, it restated its claim on my devotion.

Still, Rynnaia. Still I am with you. You are mine.

I closed my eyes and lifted my face and hands toward the sky. *Yes! I am yours!*

Peace stole over me as the thoughts of others assailed my senses.

I heard my name, they thought. *He spoke my name!*

The ecstasy of being known by The First was echoed in each heart left standing under his emblem on the battlefield.

As I turned to face Julien, I found the peace of my soul reflected in his eyes. But there was something else there, too. Something bright and full of a fire nearly as pure as that we'd just seen cauterize the Cobeld well.

He pulled me to him. The noise of the battlefield and the thoughts of those around us melted away as the passion of his kiss seared my soul with the truth of his love and the wonder of the new connection that had been forged upon the scaffolding.

My hands stole up around his neck and our thoughts swirled together in righteous bliss.

A horse beside us stamped and whinnied. Julien broke off the kiss and I rested my cheek against his shoulder.

I sighed.

Julien tensed. "Your Majesty," he said.

My eyes flew open and heat rushed into my face. I would have stepped away from Julien's embrace but for a brief, soft pressure to my lower back that disabused me of the notion.

"Julien." My father's voice held a strange, perhaps even mildly dangerous, note. He cleared his throat. "Rynnaia, is there anything in particular you would like to tell me?"

Julien released me. I bit my lip and looked up into the eyes of the King. Was that . . . amusement lurking in his bright blue gaze?

"Congratulations on your victory?"

"Hmm. Thank you." His eyes clearly laughed at me now. "But I had a different sort of news in mind. The sort that precipitates the need for me to issue an official announcement."

His gaze moved to Julien. "Perhaps young de Gladiel here would like to address the issue."

"With pleasure, Your Majesty." Julien's voice was respectful, but infected by a grin. "Since you so graciously granted your permission before we left Holiday Palace, I, this very day, asked your daughter to be my bride."

"And did she consent?"

"She did."

I nodded. "Most assuredly."

"Well, then." My father's face shone with love and joy. He raised his head and addressed the troops. "Sir Julien de

Gladiel seeks to wed the Ryn," he announced in a loud voice. "And both she and I have consented!"

The cheer that broke out resounded throughout Shireya's foothills. After the shouts and applause died down, the King dismounted and threw his arm around Julien's shoulder.

Leaning in closely, so that only Julien and I could hear, the King said, "You know, de Gladiel, had anyone else kissed my daughter in that fashion, I likely would have run him through."

My cheeks grew even warmer at that, but a sudden commotion stole our attention.

Two knights came forward with a Dwonsil warrior held at sword point between them. One of the knights addressed my father.

"He requested an audience, Your Majesty." The other knight added, "He surrendered his sword willingly."

My father nodded toward the man. "Speak."

When he lifted his eyes, I gasped.

I recognized him! This was the warrior from Canyn Village. The one from whom we had so narrowly escaped! He was much younger than I had thought from that distance, and the remorse I had sensed that day was even more prevalent in his thoughts now.

"Your Majesty," he began, his voice low with emotion, "I was once a loyal son of a noble E'verian line, but I allowed myself to believe lies that took me down paths I knew in my heart to be wrong. Many have suffered for my gullibility." He paused. "My actions leave no room for mercy and I will not presume to ask it of you on my own behalf."

"What do you ask, then?"

"I ask that mercy be granted to the innocent people of Dwons who have been the victims of false leadership and lying tongues."

"You say you come from a noble line," my father said. "What is your name?"

"I am Bryge de Taef," he said. "Former heir to the Regency of Dwons."

"Your father's name is Taef?" Kinley said, then took a step back. "My apologies, Your Majesty."

My father dismissed Kinley's apology with a wave of his hand and tilted his head at the young man. "I consider myself something of an authority on how nobility and title are attained in E'veria," he said. "How came you to be the *former* heir to the Regency of Dwons? I issued no decree to that end."

"My father became ill several years ago," he said. "A malady of the mind. One day he simply disappeared. I was young and unworthy of the duty thrust upon me and the Regency fell to the clans while under my care."

"How old are you?"

"I've passed nineteen summers, Your Majesty."

"And how many years have passed since your father disappeared?"

"Six."

"Six," my father repeated. "And in all that time, did you not think to petition me for aid?"

"Not soon enough, Your Majesty. And for that I deserve death. Had I sought help from Salderyn, many lives would have been saved and the cursed alliance with the Cobelds might have been avoided."

I had to respect the way he met the King's eyes. If I stood in his place I doubted I could look anywhere but the dirt at my feet. But to think that he had become the Regent of Dwons at the age of thirteen? At that age, I was still pulling pranks with Rowlen and doing my best to talk my way out of arithmetic homework.

But Bryge had become Regent at thirteen. And it was clear from my father's thoughts that he had not known of the change in leadership in Dwons.

"I did not fight for my birthright as I should have," Bryge continued. "I betrayed my family, my province, my King, and the memory of my father." His eyes shut for a moment, but he did not hang his head. "My people deserve better. The people of Dwons need help, Your Majesty, so before my sentence is carried out I would, however briefly, fulfill the role assigned to me by birth and make you aware of their need. That is all. I commit myself to your justice and to death, as I rightfully deserve."

The King was silent, his gaze thoughtful but intense. Even I, secure in his affection, would have trembled a bit had it been me on its receiving end. But Bryge held fast, yet humbly so, as if waiting for some assurance of safety for his people before reporting to the King's executioner.

I blinked. Did the King *have* an executioner? An executioner who would someday report to me? I suppressed a shiver. I didn't want to think of that right now.

"Your Majesty," one of the knights who had delivered Bryge spoke up, "it should be noted that, while he appears to be a Dwonsil warrior, I myself witnessed him fighting on the side of E'veria in this particular battle."

My father's eyebrows rose. "Is this true?"

Bryge nodded. "I saw the Ryn upon the scaffolding, Your Majesty, and I could no longer fight against that which I knew in my heart to be right."

Silence pressed upon us.

"Bryge de Taef." My father finally addressed the young man who had not once quailed under his gaze. It made me wonder what Bryge had been through as a young man in

Dwons to build such humble confidence in him now. "Tell me, what did you hear right after the shrine collapsed?"

"A song." The young warrior's answer was swift, but if he was surprised at the question, he seemed even more astonished that he had an answer to give to the King. As he spoke, his voice thickened with wonder. "I heard a voice that clearly saw the traitorous depths of my heart, yet still sang my name with joy."

Bryge cleared his throat, but his eyes were alight with the marvel of it still. "I believe it was the voice of The First, Your Majesty. That is what gave me the courage to seek you out on behalf of my people."

A satisfied expression smoothed the lines from the King's brow. "It has been my experience," my father said, rubbing his beard, "that it is when we least deserve it that mercy seeks us. And it is mercy that I shall grant today. Not only to the people of Dwons, but to you, her rightful Regent."

The hold Bryge had on his composure threatened to give way. He blinked and swallowed. Confusion furrowed his forehead. "Pardon?" He tilted his head as if an echo had rounded his ears and caused a sharp twinge of pain.

"Correct. A *pardon* is exactly what I offer. You were born to the Regency, Bryge de Taef. And you are repentant for the mistakes that allowed it to fall into other hands. Under the circumstances, it is not for me, and certainly not for some pilfering clansman, to remove you from that office. For the role you played in your province's downfall, you are forgiven."

My father took a deep breath and a sudden shift in his emotion squeezed my heart. When he spoke again, his voice was grieved. "As I pray you will forgive me for the role I neglected to play as servant to the Dwonsil people."

Again, Bryge's eyelashes fluttered with a series of confused blinks. "Your Majesty?"

"It is a grievous flaw of the E'veri family that the governing of Dwons has rarely received the priority it should. I intend for that to change. Once we have regrouped from this battle, I will support you with troops to reclaim your birthright from those who took advantage of your youth. Together we will reestablish peace and leadership in Dwons."

"I am honored at the offer, Your Majesty, and I humbly accept your aid to that end. If it is forgiveness you seek, of course I grant it," Bryge said softly. "But I am most humbled to do so."

"I thank you," my father said. "Now kneel, son of Dwons." The King unsheathed his sword and knighted the young Dwonsil warrior. "Arise, Sir Bryge de Taef, Knight of E'veria and true Regent of Dwons."

The moment was full, but curiosity tugged me to top off the cup.

"Sir Bryge," I said as he arose, "could I ask you something?"

"Anything, Your Highness."

"Is your father, by chance, Taef de Emwyk?"

"Yes! Well, in a way." Sir Bryge's eyes widened. "His real name is Taef de Quinn, but he began to refer to himself as *de Emwyk* when he became ill. Have you met him, Your Highness? Does he yet live?"

"He lives," I said. "His ailment is most diverting, but he was used greatly in our quest for the Remedy. Even now, he serves as my ambassador, completing an errand on my behalf." I smiled.

"Bryge." Kinley said softly. "*Bryge.*" He repeated the young Regent's name, but didn't seem to be addressing him. His brow narrowed. "Taef said he wasn't a fish, he was—"

"A *Bryge* builder!" Gerrias finished, barking out a laugh. He lifted his sword to point at Bryge. "*He's* the bridge built by our trusty thief!"

The laugh building within me spilled from Erielle's lips first. As if the pent-up anxiety of the last several weeks had decided to explode out of each member of our team at once, we laughed so heartily that tears rolled down our cheeks.

I'm sure some of the spectators wondered if the six of us had suddenly lost our collective minds, but there was nothing for it. When Kinley could finally catch his breath, he slapped Gerrias on the back and gasped out through his laughter, "A *Bryge* builder! Our horse diplomat was telling the truth after all!"

A sudden and salty breeze touched my senses with the sound of my name.

Rynnaia.

Still smiling, I stepped back from the group and closed my eyes. *Cazien?*

Indeed.

I could almost feel the breeze that blew my cousin's hair at the helm of his ship.

Would you care to tell me why, right after every Emblem of the First aboard my ship shot light toward the sky, nearly frightening my men into jumping into the sea, I've been summoned to Tirandov Isle by your mother?

My eyes flew open as if by a force of joy. I closed them again. *Mother!*

Yes, dear one?

She stood—stood!—on the shore of the Bay of Tirandov, her face to the sun. A flush of health, though not as vibrant as I sensed it might soon be, caressed her cheeks.

Ahem.

Cazien, again.

Colors poured out of my mind, nay, out of my very heart. They stretched out toward both my mother and my cousin,

THE REMEDY

exulting. Soon threads reached from my mind and pulled my father and Julien into the revelation.

I don't know how long we remained in that cocoon of joy, but finally I allowed my colors to retreat. Just as the scent of the sea began to fade from my mind, however, I snatched Cazien's attention back.

The pirate arched a black eyebrow. *Yes, Rynnaia?*

Erielle's eyes turned green today, I said. *Bright, vivid green. I thought you should know.*

His jaw clenched. He gave a curt nod. *That would follow,* he said, but he didn't elaborate, not that I particularly expected him to. Still, I did admit to some curiosity.

I wish I could tell you all, but the Seahorse Legacy—my Legacy—forbids it. Cazien sighed. *Suffice it to say that Erielle's path will likely soon diverge from what's expected of her. And when it does, please remember that I am your friend. And hers.*

Only on the subject of Erielle had I ever heard Cazien so solemn. *I will remember.* I gave him my word. *I will see you at my wedding then, Captain Cryptic?*

Perhaps. His lip quirked. *Any chance you might move it closer to the sea?*

I shook my head.

Ah, well. For you, I suppose I can make the sacrifice. Expect me to arrive with your mother. He paused and made a face. *Ach! Enough! Rynloeft save me from lovesick fools,* he growled through a grin as the anticipation of my joy threatened to consume both of our thoughts again.

Leave off, Princess! He laughed. *Go pester that knight of yours. I've a ship to captain!*

489

$\mathcal{F}$ I F T Y - $\mathcal{T}$ W O

One month later

$\mathcal{I}$ sat at the desk in my chamber at Castle Rynwyk, puzzling over a matter of diplomatic correspondence when the trumpets blared at the gates, announcing the approach of the Queen. I sprang from my chair so suddenly that I knocked over the inkwell, ruining the entire parchment.

Without thinking, I reached to catch the flow of ink with my hands, but Vayle, who now served as my lady's maid, spoke up.

"Allow me." She grabbed a blotting cloth and stemmed the flow with one hand while setting the inkwell upright with the other. "We can't have your hands as stained as Lady Erielle's when you join them to Sir Julien!"

I tilted my head. "How did Erielle stain her hands?"

"Forgive me," Vayle's cheeks turned red. "I spoke out of turn."

The trumpets sounded a second time. I wished to question Vayle further, but instead I thanked her for cleaning up my mess and hastily excused myself. My mother was almost home!

Home.

As I hurried down the hall, I wondered at how quickly Castle Rynwyk had achieved the distinction of 'home' in my heart, but I could not deny that it had done exactly that.

Built on a small rise at the very center of the city of Salderyn, Castle Rynwyk rose above the city like a scowling gray giantess. Her square towers, harsh-angled windows, and battlements growled an austere warning, drenched in the memories of wars gone by. Indeed, the first glimpse of my new home had left me so aquiver that I nearly asked my father if he might consider relocating us to Holiday Palace on a permanent basis! But once I was led inside and shown to the luxurious chambers that being the Crown Princess of E'veria granted, my trepidation drifted away and I was glad I had kept that particular request to myself.

Outside, Castle Rynwyk was fearsome. Inside, thanks to generations of E'veri Kings and Queens, it afforded its residents and guests an entirely different experience. In the month since I had arrived, my affection for it had grown. How much more perfect it would be now that my mother was nearly here!

Having been a victim of the Cobeld curse for so long, it took her a bit more time to recover than it had Gerrias and the other wounded at the Battle of the Shrine, as it had come to be called. But like Gerrias, her healing had begun the moment Julien and I had drunk our toast and proclaimed the name that broke the curse. Now, a month later, not only was she well, but she thrived. I could hardly wait to see her.

Picking up my skirts, I increased the speed of my steps and—

"Rynnaia!"

I nearly ran into my father, who was exiting his chamber in much the same haste as I.

His warm smile filled my heart. "I was just going to meet your mother's carriage."

I looked at him and paused, second-guessing my intentions. I knew how badly he had wanted to ride forth and meet up with my mother's retinue weeks ago, but in these first few weeks following the war, the Kingdom needed him here at Castle Rynwyk. Plans had to be made toward the reconstruction of E'veria, and although it pained him—and me, to see him so torn between his duty as King and his longing for my mother—he was, after all, the King, the people's most trusted Servant.

But finally, after all these weeks—no, years—of waiting, she was almost home!

"May I offer you my arm?"

I reached my hand forward and then stopped. It had been almost three years since he had last visited his wife on Tirandov Isle. For me, it had been less than three months.

"No, I think not," I replied. "I will leave you to attend the Queen alone, as is fitting. I find I have some rather urgent business with the delegation from Mynissbyr."

"Delegation, eh? Well, I suppose they do seem a delegation now that Gladiel is back among them." He smiled. "We three will sup together tonight, then. As a family," he said, choking up just a bit, "in my chambers."

"I will look forward to it. Please give the Queen my love," I said, and then laughed. "If it even occurs to you when you've finished giving her your own!"

The King lifted an eyebrow, but chuckled as he leaned down to kiss my cheek. "I will. Thank you, Rynnaia." He gave my hand a quick squeeze, and with a boyish smile, he hurried down the hall, barely acknowledging the tall, blond knight with whom he nearly collided in his haste.

Julien's grin matched mine as he strode forward. "I was just coming to see if I could escort you to meet your mother's carriage, but I think your plan is better."

Since our kiss on the Cobelds' shrine, my betrothed had been able to read my thoughts almost as well as an Andoven.

"Might I steal you away for a while?" he asked. "Or do you have other obligations?"

"Lead on, Bear-knight," I said. "We can infringe upon your mother's hospitality for a while."

"You know my family is always happy to see you, even if their son is not quite so willing to share you with them." He sighed. "I confess I tire of protocol when it comes to you."

"Just a few more weeks and we can bid farewell to our chaperones," I said. Our wedding was set to follow my formal installation as the Crown Princess.

"I plan to bar the door to our chambers and not let another soul near you for a month."

"Only a month?"

He squeezed my hand. "Were we to steal away and marry this moment it would not be soon enough for me."

I enjoyed the afternoon with Julien and his parents, but when a page arrived at their door bearing a request from the Queen that I join her and the King in their chambers, I became nearly giddy.

My family was to be reunited at last.

Mother was nestled into the crook of my father's arm, her hand clasped in his.

"Rynnaia," she said, patting the seat beside her.

"No, I'll sit over here I think," I said, taking a chair across from them. "This way I can see you both better. Together." A grin broke through that almost hurt my cheeks. "Together! My mother and father."

Suddenly my vantage point was too far away. I stood and took the place she'd offered.

"My heart has never been so full," my father said. Leaning in to embrace us both, he chuckled and added, "Nor my arms."

"It has been a long wait." My mother smiled up at him. "But this moment makes sense of the pain, does it not? And we have the rest of our lives to enjoy our daughter. And soon, the man she's chosen to be our son as well." Her sigh was dressed in realized dreams and hopes yet to come. "Yes, Jarryn. My heart is also full."

"As is mine," I said, leaning into them both and resting my head against hers. "Welcome home, Mother."

"Thank you. And although you beat me here, I suppose I should say the same to you. Welcome home at last, Rynnaia. Are you finding Castle Rynwyk to your liking?"

"I am," I sighed, happily. "I'm finding it to be home."

FIFTY-THREE

*J*ust three weeks after my mother's arrival at Castle Rynwyk, she sat in a chair in my dressing room while I stood in front of the large mirror. A new crown, designed for me by Julien, had been presented to me that morning during the formal ceremony that officially instated me as the Crown Princess of E'veria.

"I would have never thought to put a bear on a crown. A bear, of all things!" My mother laughed. "But it is strangely right."

Similar to the crown I had received on Tirandov Isle—a crown that had once been my mother's—this circlet was an intricate weave of roses, but there the likeness ended. This crown was made of gold and the vine was broken at my forehead by two golden bears, supporting the Emblem of the First, in glowing tirandite, between them. It was the ideal representation of my past, present, and future.

"It's perfect," I agreed. "Absolutely perfect."

It was a rare event to have my mother all to myself. The King had rarely let her out of his sight since her return. But we enjoyed the entire afternoon following my installation together, just the two of us, as she helped me ready for my wedding.

My mother rose and I watched her approach in the mirror. One thick strand of white stood out amid the bright copper curls piled atop her head, but it looked much less prominent than it had during her illness. Now fully recovered, Queen Daithia E'veri's face radiated the fullness of health and joy. Her bright blue eyes, so dimmed by pain before, fairly sparkled now.

"You look beautiful, Rynnaia. I daresay Julien might faint when he sees you!"

"Then I hope he rouses swiftly," I said with a laugh, "for I intend to marry him today! Should he not, it would be a terrible waste of this beautiful dress."

"Go on," my mother urged as she read the girlish desire in my thoughts, "twirl. I would, if it was my gown."

I spun a slow circle, and then again, a bit faster. The bottom of the wedding gown flared out and up, but not so much as to be indecent. Commissioned from Tirandov's seamstresses by my mother, the gown was light and airy, allowing for a full range of movement without sacrificing elegance.

With a little giggle I twirled once more and then paused, facing the mirror. I ran a finger over the V-shaped neckline and the golden Emblems of the First embroidered here and there among rose vines. Made of a rich white fabric, the fitted bodice hugged my frame to a position just below my waist where a band of embroidered golden roses encircled my hips. From there, a layer of shimmering, translucent gold streamers flared out on top of the white skirt, reaching to the floor and making it appear as if I floated rather than walked.

My mother peered over my shoulder. Not for the first time, I wondered at how truly uncanny our resemblance was.

I could hardly believe that even when I'd had black hair no one had made the connection.

"Your father is coming."

I grinned. "I know."

I followed my mother out of the dressing room, through my bedchamber, and into the receiving chamber beyond. I didn't want to risk wrinkling my gown to sit, so I stood by my mother's side. When I sensed the King had reached the door, I waved my hand and it opened.

His hand was suspended in the air as if ready to knock. "Someday you will cease to surprise me, Rynnaia," he began, but paused. "Today is not that day. You are breathtaking."

His eyes grew moist. "I am the most blessed of fathers," he said as he walked toward us. "Today, I give your hand to a man I trust and love like a son, but I get to keep you in my house rather than sending you off to Mynissbyr."

Pulling both my mother and me close, he lifted his face and spoke a blessing over my coming marriage.

"Everyone has assembled in the Grand Hall," he said when he stepped back. "One knight, in particular, is quite anxious for our arrival."

With my father on my left and my mother on my right, we left my room with Julien as the only destination I cared to claim and made our way to the Grand Hall—and my wedding!

On some level, I tried to appreciate the work that had gone into creating the elegant floral arrangements and decorations made for my wedding ceremony, but once my eyes met Julien's all else faded from my view.

He was resplendent in his wedding attire, made by the same Andoven textile artist and in the same white and gold as mine. Though his smile was subdued—no, *controlled,* I corrected myself—due to the gravity of the vows we were about to speak, his eyes radiated joy that swept down the aisle to join my own.

Julien's family was lined up on his left. With some effort I broke my attention from his eyes to give a fond smile to each of them.

Wearing a rich, dark red robe that accentuated his bright blue eyes and white hair, my great-grandfather Lindsor stood just behind and a little to the right of Julien.

The space reserved for my parents and I was empty of course, but I nearly stumbled when I saw, just beyond that space, the *rest* of my family.

In order of how they had come into my life were Uncle Drinius and Aunt Alaine, with their daughter Lily, and Lord and Lady Whittier, Kinley, Lewys, and Rowlen. I had known they would all be in attendance at the wedding, but I had not been told that their contribution to my upbringing would be so honored by my parents.

My tears threatened to spill over as we took the final steps toward the front. When my parents each lifted the hand of mine they held and set it in Julien's grasp, my lids gave up the fight. Her own cheeks wet, my mother paused to dab mine with her handkerchief.

Lindsor read beautiful words about the bond of marriage from *The Story of The First*, but I had to admit that had I not read the words previously, I would not have remembered a single syllable. My soul was completely entranced with the knight who stood facing me, holding my hands and my heart.

"Princess Rynnaia E'veri," Lindsor intoned, causing both Julien and me to jump.

It was time to speak our vows.

"Do you pledge your love, faithfulness, and friendship to Sir Julien de Gladiel? Will you promise to respect him as your husband and honor him as the future King of E'veria? Will you cherish him above all save The First?"

I knew my heart. Now the rest of the world would as well.

"With all that I am and for all of my life, I pledge my honor to that course."

Julien's grin was the widest I had ever seen.

I continued the rest of the vow in the Ancient Voice, as I'd been instructed. "Rynnaia al Julien E'veri, E'veria."

"Sir Julien de Gladiel," Lindsor no longer tried to hide the pleasure in his voice, "do you pledge your love, faithfulness, friendship, and service to Rynnaia, Crown Princess of E'veria? Will you lead her with honor, respecting her worth as your wife, as the Ryn, and as your future Queen? Will you cherish her above all others save The First?"

"With all that I am and for all of my life," Julien's voice carried to the farthest reaches of the ballroom. "I pledge my honor to that course!"

A sudden and raucous cheer rose from the knights in the audience before he was able to continue. My cheeks ached from smiling by the time the noise died down enough for him to finish his vow.

"Julien al Rynnaia E'veri, E'veria."

"Let it be known," Lindsor proclaimed, translating the vows we'd spoken in the Ancient Voice, "that Rynnaia, Crown Princess of E'veria and Sir Julien de Gladiel are hereafter bound to each other and to the Kingdom of E'veria."

Julien squeezed my hands.

"Julien de Gladiel," Lindsor continued, "do you renounce your claim as heir to the Regency of Mynissbyr, accepting that your brother, Gerrias de Gladiel, will inherit that birthright?"

"I do hereby renounce my claim as heir to the Regency of Mynissbyr."

Lindsor reached behind him where a small platform held the golden crown I had designed for my prince. Knowing Julien had yet to see it, my grandfather held it in front of us for a long moment before he spoke again.

Ropes of copper, bronze, and gold entwined around one another to meet at the fierce face of a bear. The bear's eyes were inset with emeralds as green as my groom's eyes, and his bared fangs held a tirandite stone, carved in the Emblem of the First, between them.

Perfect. Julien's thought drifted toward me. I beamed and squeezed his hands.

"Taking this crown," Lindsor continued, "do you vow to uphold the cause of The First throughout E'veria, to defend the Kingdom from her enemies, and to accept the responsibilities expected of you as the Ryn's prince and E'veria's future King?"

"I do so vow." Julien released my hands and knelt. Lindsor placed the crown on Julien's head and stepped back. My father took his place.

The King drew his sword and lightly moved it from one of Julien's shoulders to the other. "Arise, Prince Julien de Gladiel E'veri!" My father pronounced Julien's new name with resounding pride. "May you and Rynnaia be guided by The First and may your union become a force by which our Kingdom is blessed for generations to come."

Lindsor produced a pair of goblets and gave one to me, the other to Julien.

"As is tradition," he said, "a toast will seal the bond."

There would be no awkward shuffling of arms, I thought, grinning at my prince. We had done this before.

The toast completed, Lindsor took the goblets back and my father stepped up.

The King's eyes shone and love poured from him to us. He took a deep breath and lifted his arms. "Arise, Good People of E'veria!" he commanded. The crowd took to their feet. "Tonight, we celebrate the bond of love and the bright future of our fair Kingdom!"

"Huuzz-zzah!"

It was Kinley's voice that led the cheer, but Lewys, Rowlen, and Gerrias filled the space before the last syllable.

Julien swept me into his arms and dipped me so fast and so deep that I gasped. But his kiss caught my breath, and it was over too soon.

After a short speech by my father, the benches were cleared from the space and the revelry began.

Only that rendered to me by the hair of Cobeld's beard could have exceeded the torture I endured at the celebratory dinner and ball following our wedding. I was allowed only one dance with my prince before protocol dictated we allow others to offer their congratulations.

Having danced with all the Regents, their heirs, and surely half the dukes in E'veria, I was ever grateful for the Herald of the Dance, who took the guesswork out of who my next partner would be. Although protocol dictated who I partnered with, it didn't promise that partner would be skilled. My toes had been trod on more than a dozen times and my current partner was responsible for at least three of those missteps.

I pasted on a smile as best I could, but the middle-aged duke from Nyrland was not only a head shorter than me, his eyes seemed to pay an inordinate amount of attention to the neckline of my gown, even given it was in his line of sight.

Suddenly, a couple bumped into us, both carrying goblets of wine.

I watched in horror as the bright red liquid jumped out of their cups and careened through the air, miraculously missing my wedding gown, but soaking the front of my partner's tunic.

I looked up at the graceless pair, surprised to see my never-clumsy sister-in-law dancing with the youngest of my three Veetrish brothers. By the look in Erielle's eyes, I was sure some sort of mischief was afoot.

I didn't have to look at Rowlen. With him, mischief was to be expected.

The duke let go of my hand, took a step backward, and threw a loathsome glance at the couple. "Nicely done, de Whittier," he managed through gritted teeth.

"Oh, I do apologize!" Rowlen replied. "I suppose you'll need to change. Pity you'll have to miss the rest of your dance with the princess."

"Indeed."

The liquid on my partner's tunic had a strange shimmer to it that I hadn't noticed when I had drunk mine earlier. My gaze flew back to my brother's seemingly innocent face.

The duke cleared his throat. "If you will excuse me, Your Highness."

"Of course." I inclined my head in assent, but the thought of his imminent departure caused me to smile at him more warmly than I yet had. "I do hope my brother's clumsiness has not ruined your tunic."

He sniffed, nodded, and turned to leave.

Rowlen's eyes followed him until he had left the room. As the Storyteller exhaled, the goblets he and Erielle held in their hands glittered brightly before dissolving into the nothingness of a Storyteller's mirage.

I started to laugh, wondering at my former partner's reaction when he looked in the mirror and found no stains whatsoever on his tunic. Rowlen winked at me as the Herald of the Dance brought forth my next partner, and then laughed and spun away with Erielle.

"Your Highness, may I present Cazien de Pollis, Monarch of Eachan Isle, Admiral of the Seahorse Fleet, and Captain of," the herald paused and swallowed, "the pirate ship *Meredith*."

The pirate offered me a quick bow, and then his hand.

Cazien was, as I knew from the jigs he'd spun with me aboard *Meredith*, a fine dancer. But I had not spoken with him since our brief conversation following the Battle of the Shrine.

"You know I'm quite royal and famous," he said. "I should probably be offended that your father had me wait so long for my turn to dance with the princess."

"He thought it was more appropriate that his own people be honored first," I began to explain, but Cazien's wink let me know he was not truly offended.

"I jest. I may live upon the sea, but I know how these things work."

A question burned in my mind, and since I assumed he would see it there anyway, I gave it voice. "Will you dance with Erielle tonight?"

"Not if I can help it."

The coldness of his swift answer took me aback. It must have shown on my face.

"It's not that she's not lovely. She is. I would just prefer to keep my distance. For now."

For now. Hmm. "Then will you tell me why you have been so concerned with the color of her eyes?"

"I'm sorry, but . . . no."

"Why not?"

"Because I prefer to keep your friendship awhile longer."

"You will not lose it, cousin." His words troubled me, for they seemed to bode ill for my sister-in-law's future.

"Ah, perhaps not." His smile held a trace of sadness. "I only hope you are able to exert that influence over your husband when the time comes."

Captain Cryptic, indeed.

Cazien glanced at my crown and then offered me a sly grin. "I've heard that men from the Great Wood can become rather *bearish* when riled."

The Herald of the Dance tapped my partner's shoulder.

"Until we meet again, Rynnaia," Cazien said, and bowed before placing my hand into that of another foreign dignitary.

And so the night continued, Julien danced every turn, as did I, but for that one dance together when the ball had commenced, not once did protocol allow us to partner each other again. After what felt like years spent apart from my newly wedded Prince, my father finally stept up to the dais to begin the final toasts of the evening.

"It cannot escape our attention," he said, "that this wedding would not have been possible but for the willing sacrifices of the friends who accompanied the prince and princess to Mount Shireya. Tonight, I lift my glass to honor them and I ask that they step forward as I call them."

One at a time, Edru and Dyfnel came toward the raised dais and accepted the honors and orders due their brave service, followed by Gerrias and Kinley.

After a moment of silence commemorating the loss of Sir Risson, the King glanced over at me, his gaze yet unsure.

It is the right thing to do, I assured him.

A smile twitched at the corner of his mouth as he turned back to face the crowd. "And finally," he said, "Lady Erielle de Gladiel."

Erielle stepped up to the dais.

"Lady Erielle, you have proven your bravery, intelligence, and loyalty to be equal to that of any knight in my service. Therefore, it is the honor of knighthood you shall receive."

A gasp filtered through the Grand Hall. Erielle's eyes widened and her gaze flew to mine. I gave her a quick wink.

Kneel, I said to her mind. Immediately, she dropped to one knee, though it was decidedly awkward in her full-skirted gown. Erielle bowed her head as the King's sword touched each shoulder.

"We have no title for a female knight in E'veria," he said, "so I have chosen to borrow one used in the Island Realm of Nirista."

A flash of indefinable emotion touched my thoughts with the scent of the sea. My eyes roved the Grand Hall, hoping to catch a glimpse of the pirate.

Cazien stood near a side door with his arms crossed, his feet planted shoulder-width apart, and a decidedly dark scowl upon his face.

You do not approve? I asked.

No. He met my eyes. *I do not.*

Just because she's a lovely young woman does not mean she cannot serve as a knight. I lifted my chin. *Your own mother was captain of the Seahorse fleet!*

Indeed. But E'veria's knights have certain . . . sensibilities . . . that are thankfully lacking among Seahorse pirates.

Our knights are honorable! And Erielle is well worthy of the honor given her by being added to their number.

That I do not doubt, he replied.

I had to work very hard to keep my face impassive. *Then why do you disapprove?*

I appreciate the sentiment behind this honor you bestow, Rynnaia, but have you considered how such a commission could become a stone around her neck? By knighting this girl, you have cast a jeweled dagger into a sea of swords.

The sigh in his heart was so profound that I could almost feel the breath of it upon my face, though he was at the opposite corner of the hall.

*Never fear, even with this . . . complication . . . I will do my
duty and rescue her from being swallowed by the deep, as it
were. But now, I leave you.*

Cazien, wait! I called, but he was gone.

"On behalf of my daughter, the Ryn," my father's voice brought
my attention back to the moment at hand, "I knight you Dirme
Erielle de Gladiel, First Knight in the Honorable Order of Anya."

Erielle's head flew up.

My father smiled. "Dirme Erielle's ancestor should have
received that honor long ago. By creating the Honorable Order
of Anya, we recognize the brave contribution both the Oracle
Scribe and the Oracle's Daughter have made to our Kingdom."

My father took a slight step back. "Honored Defenders of
E'veria," he said, "with the knowledge that you will forever
have the ear of your grateful King, arise!"

A cheer filled the hall, and as people rushed forward to con-
gratulate our friends, Julien took my hand and we slipped away.

In silence we walked through halls deserted but for
guards and the occasional serving maid, continuing upward
to the chambers we would share in our very own wing of the
castle.

Although I had desperately longed to be alone with
Julien for weeks, by the time we reached the guarded door
of our shared chambers my face was so hot that had someone
thrown water on me, it might have steamed.

Eyes to the floor, I refused to meet the guard's gaze as he
opened the doors for us to enter. Once we were within, the
guard closed the door behind us. Julien left my side for just a
moment to lock it.

I pressed my suddenly icy hands to my cheeks in the hope
of cooling them, but when Julien stepped behind me and
wrapped his arms around my waist the familiar gesture put
me at ease.

"I thought the ball would never end," he sighed. "Everyone got to hold you but me. It was torture."

I laughed, having felt the same frustration for the last several hours. Turning within his arms, I looked up into the deep green of my prince's eyes and my sudden shyness dissolved. I reached my hands around his neck. "I'm all yours now, Julien."

And I kissed him to prove it.

A shiver of heat surprised me as his lips moved to the space just in front of my ear. When he spoke, the feeling of his warm breath at my ear nearly took mine away.

"As I am yours."

Julien scooped me into his arms and his kiss took possession of what had been his forever. Our colors melded and a new thread, one of pure, white light, joined the dance as love and desire entwined to complete the perfect union of our souls.

J awoke to the tender gaze of emerald eyes, easing me from slumber. Beside me, Julien was propped upon one elbow, wearing a smile that said he was completely content to simply watch me sleep.

I caressed his cheek. "Good morning, Bear-prince."

His smile widened. "Good morning, my very own princess."

We stayed like that for a long moment, allowing the joy of love, and the sweetness, the *rightness*, of our bond to wash over and through us.

"I am amazed to love you more than I did even a moment ago," Julien whispered. "Thank you, Rynnaia. Thank you for becoming my bride. Every moment in my life has led to the wonder of our bond. I am so very grateful. And overcome. And . . . humbled by it all."

I thought of the scar on his arm, the scar he earned from the dagger I had thrown with intent to kill. *"Every* moment?" I teased.

He chuckled. "I am grateful, even for that," he said and pressed a kiss upon my forehead. "It was The First who made you slip on the ice that night, you know," he said. "He's been with us all along."

"Indeed." I nodded. "But it took me a long enough time to notice."

Julien shook his head and reached to brush a curl from my cheek. "No, it took exactly the right amount of time. His time."

It was true. Had I not suffered the burden of deception, I might not have recognized truth when it called. Had I not felt pain, I would not have appreciated comfort. The thorns of my past had served their purpose. Now each painful fragment of my life had bloomed into an unfading flower of hope.

I am Rynnaia E'veri, I thought as I reached up to caress Julien's face. *I am known and I am loved.*

"Yes," Julien whispered, "you are."

Though I would not have entertained the notion a few months ago, I had no doubt that all of Rynloeft smiled over us now. Still, we both gasped when suddenly, from that sacred space deep within our union, the tender voice of The First spoke our names.

Still, Rynnaia. Still, Julien. I will be with you.

Embral e' Veria whispered truth into our souls and sealed our bond with his own.

You are Mine.

THE END

Want more?
Set sail with Cazien de Pollis and Erielle de Gladiel
in Eyes of E'veria, book three
The Seahorse Legacy

e-book available now – coming soon to paperback

About the Author

Serena Chase lives in Iowa with her husband, two daughters, and a giant teddy bear of a dog named Albus. A frequent contributor to *USA Today*'s Happy Ever After blog, she also writes for Edgy Inspirational Romance, coaches her local high school's Color Guard, and puts very little effort into battling her coffee addiction. She loves to connect with readers! Find Serena on Facebook, Twitter (@Serena_Chase), Pinterest, and her website www.serenachase.com

ACKNOWLEDGEMENTS

*A*nd so, we reach the end of Rynnaia and Julien's journey. But is it the end? Not exactly. For, although the Eyes of E'veria tales-to-come do not feature the Prince and Princess in starring roles, Julien and Rynnaia will make an appearance from time to time, offering help—and possibly hindrance—to the next friends who step out of this tale to bring us into their own.

I am deeply honored that you would read this book—especially if you made the investment of time to read its predecessor, *The Ryn*, as well. My prayer is that through this fairy tale you will come to more clearly see the beautiful adventure life can be when you entrust your heart and hope to the One Who Woos.

This book would not be what it is without the valued input of my editorial team. For developmental advice, for coaching me through the first (official) rewrite, and for her never-failing encouragement and friendship, Sandra Byrd, I bow to you. An additional curtsey (curtsy?) goes to Jenny Quinlan of Historical Editorial for her amazing developmental advice once that first (45th?) rewrite was completed. She challenged me to go deeper with both Rynnaia and Julien—and they are better, "rounder" characters for her having pointed out their

515

defects. Thank you, Jenny, as well, for the careful attention you gave the line-by-line copyedit, knowing full well I would likely rewrite a scene or two after and screw up something that you had already fixed. *bites lip and hopes for the best* I am so blessed. Also, a giant hug goes out to my "final" proof-reading team: Tamara Leigh, Mom, Heather, Delaney . . . (did I forget anyone?) . . . what would I do without your eyes? And to Lori Twichell for your enthusiasm and advice: THANK YOU so very much.

To Joy Tamsin David, my blogging partner and the dear one who stepped in and handled the myriad details of the Eyes of E'veria blog tour when I was burning the midnight oil and—let's face it—freaking out a lot, YOU ARE AMAZING! Many thanks also to the blogging community members who have so enthusiastically embraced Julien—I mean, *The Ryn*—and now *The Remedy*: people like Rel, Amber, Lydia, Juju, Lori, Embassie, Christy, Tina, Jenny . . . and to Joyce Lamb, curator of *USA Today*'s Happy Ever After blog: I could go on and on, suffice it to say: Ladies, I love you. Thanks.

Beyond all of these, however, I must thank my husband, Dave, and our daughters, Delaney and Ellerie, who continue to love me even when I spend exceedingly long hours in another realm.

Reader, I do hope you will come back to E'veria again with me in 2014 when Eyes of E'veria book 3: *The Seahorse Legacy* begins the retelling of a new tale within the world built in these first two books of the series. As you may have guessed from hints layered throughout this tale, there is a certain pirate—and a certain newly knighted young woman—whose stories will soon intersect. I very much look forward to sharing this adventure upon the sands and seas—as well as quite a bit more snarky humor than found in the first two volumes of this series!—and a fresh—and not-entirely-welcome—romance, with you in *The Seahorse Legacy* (Eyes of E'veria, book 3.) Until then, you can keep abreast of all Eyes of E'veria news, and my other writing projects by liking my official author page on Facebook or by visiting my website, serenachase.com. You can also follow me on Twitter: @Serena_Chase and view my ever-expanding inspiration board on Pinterest.

Finally, to the One who knew and called my real name, who reached out to me through a book, wooed my heart, and promised beauty, adventure, and romance far beyond anything I could ever dream: *I am yours.*

Affectionately,
Serena

Made in the USA
Columbia, SC
02 June 2018